A Lady's Rules for Ruin

A Lady's Rules for Ruin

USA TODAY BESTSELLING AUTHOR
Jennifer Haymore

This book is a work of fiction. Names, characters, places, and incidents are the product of the author's imagination or are used fictitiously. Any resemblance to actual events, locales, or persons, living or dead, is coincidental.

Copyright © 2023 by Jennifer Haymore. All rights reserved, including the right to reproduce, distribute, or transmit in any form or by any means. For information regarding subsidiary rights, please contact the Publisher.

Entangled Publishing, LLC
644 Shrewsbury Commons Ave., STE 181
Shrewsbury, PA 17361
Visit our website at www.entangledpublishing.com.

Amara is an imprint of Entangled Publishing, LLC.

Edited by Heather Howland
Cover design by Bree Archer
Author font design by Elizabeth Turner Stokes
Cover images by VJ Dunraven/PeriodImages and FairytaleDesign/depositphotos
Interior formatting by Britt Marczak

Manufactured in the United States of America

First Edition December 2023

AMARA

ALSO BY JENNIFER HAYMORE

The Lions and Lilies series

The Duke's Rules of Engagement
A Lady's Rules for Ruin

Secrets of the Ton series

Earls Rush In

At Entangled, we want our readers to be well-informed. If you would like to know if this book contains any elements that might be of concern for you, please check the back of the book for details.

Chapter One

Spring 1820

Frances Cherrington barely managed to curtsy at her partner before spinning around and hurrying off the dance floor. The warm air of the ballroom pressed in on her as she weaved through the dense crowd, passing people dressed in every manner of attire from simple dominoes to the full regalia of the King of Prussia.

The Worthington Masquerade was always the most scandalous party of the Season. Though it was early in the evening, with most people still greeting one another, Frances hadn't heard of any wicked behavior yet. But after the "grand reveal" at midnight when everyone would tear off their masks, the dancing and carousing would extend into morning. Between then and now, the hundreds of attendees, all members of London's elite, would have several hours of opportunity to seek out scandal…and she knew they would.

Frances's stomach churned. The court jester she'd just been dancing with—or Mr. Bramble, as she would address him under ordinary circumstances—had such a terrible body odor, she'd felt like retching throughout the country dance. Now, dodging sheikhs, servants, and sorcerers, she struggled toward the doors leading outside.

Oh, to be anywhere but here, wearing this awful costume and pretending to want the same thing as all the other unattached ladies here. She was quite certain she was the only unmarried woman in England whose sole ambition was to hold on to her spinsterhood with both hands and never let go.

She adjusted the uncomfortable mask. Simply ripping it off would be ideal, but then her brother and sisters would be even more annoyed with her for not waiting until the grand reveal.

Her twin sister, Martha, had browbeaten Frances into wearing this inaccurate and disrespectful representation of Queen Cleopatra of Egypt. The costume consisted of a white linen dress edged with an ostentatious gold fringe studded with paste gems meant to resemble lapis lazuli. A thick gold-and-blue belt cinched her waist and a heavy, scratchy black wig covered her hair. The itchy mask covered her face from her nose up. It was painted gold and featured thick stripes of black around the eye holes and a large diamond shape at the top meant to resemble the flared head of a cobra with two ruby eyes.

Frances could only be grateful that no one had been able to discern the identity of the miserable woman beneath the mask. Not yet, at least.

"There you are!"

Frances reeled to a halt as thick fingers wrapped around her arm. Pursing her lips at his proprietary grasp, she looked up at her brother, Charles.

"Where are you running off to?" he demanded.

"I was going outside for some air. It is stifling in here."

"Why aren't you lining up for the quadrille like everyone else?" His eyes narrowed beneath his domino mask. "Have you given your dance partner the slip?"

"That happened only once," she muttered. Her actions that long-ago night had caused her brother years of embarrassment and consternation, which was why she'd never done it again. "I assure you, I've given no one 'the slip.'"

Truthfully, she was thankful no one had asked her for the quadrille. Or for the following dance, the Scotch reel, either.

Instead of releasing her, Charles sighed. "Fine. Come with me. We want to discuss something with you."

"Outside, I hope?" she asked.

"Yes. Come along."

Charles could be so infuriatingly overbearing. Still, she didn't want to make a scene, so she gritted her teeth and let him lead her outside. When they exited the ballroom through the open French doors, Frances was finally able to take a clean breath.

Well, it wasn't particularly *clean*. Hints of coal smoke and sewage laced the air, but that was the familiar stench of London, far preferable to Mr. Bramble's noxious odor.

They skirted a group of masked people flirtatiously guessing at one another's identities and descended the stairs to the garden path. The gardens were lush, lit with gas sconces that cast glowing golden streaks across the well-manicured paths. People laughed and chatted loudly, enjoying the cool night air after being enclosed in the humid heat of the densely packed ballroom.

Charles pulled Frances along until they reached a tall sycamore tree standing sentry at the garden's far edge. Seated on the bench below the tree were Frances's twin, Martha, and their youngest sister, Esther, who had been a belle of society before her marriage and was now a popular young matron of the *ton*. Like Charles, both of her sisters were dressed in plain dominoes, "So as not to draw attention from your magnificence, Frances," her twin had said as she'd helped Frances into her gaudy dress.

Her sisters rose as she and Charles approached, both of them frowning. This was a coordinated attack, then, Frances thought with an inward sigh.

Esther launched right in. "You didn't smile once during that last dance with the court jester," she said accusingly. "Why do you always have to look so exceedingly *dour*, Frances?"

Of course Frances hadn't smiled. She'd spent the entire dance on the verge of gagging.

"Did you know he was Mr. Bramble?" Esther continued. "That he's the heir to not only a respectable fortune, but also a significant estate near Birmingham?"

"I knew it was Mr. Bramble," she told Esther. "But you must forgive me for not being up-to-date on his future financial standing. Though, I guarantee you that it would have made no difference whatsoever in my treatment of him. The man smelled awful."

Esther gasped at her blunt description. *"Frances!"*

"Esther," she replied, rolling her eyes. Honestly, they should be impressed at her ability to hold on to her composure.

It had taken all her willpower to hide her reaction to his stench. But no. Instead, here they were, reminding her of her failures. *Again.*

Her status as the sole unmarried Cherrington sibling was a daily topic of conversation in their household. Her five siblings were obsessed with this ridiculous notion that she must attend every event of the Season with the singular intent of finding a husband. Even tonight, the very night before her twin was due to depart for Egypt.

Her family was deaf to Frances's proclamations that she had no desire to marry. Over and over, she'd tried to explain to them how she didn't want to be shackled in a prison of her husband's making. She didn't want to be owned. She didn't want a man decreeing how she should dress or behave, what she should be interested in, where she should be or when she should be there.

"You should be dancing the quadrille right now," Charles insisted. "Yet you don't make any attempt to present yourself as friendly or approachable, even after all the work your sisters put into creating that wonderful costume for you."

She looked at the three of them standing before her in a unified front. She'd been on the opposite side of this show of family unity more than once. Separate from the rest of the Cherringtons, set aside, apart. The black sheep. Usually on the receiving end of their scolding, disappointment, badgering, and disapproval, just like she was right now.

"You have been sending me to balls, parties, soirees, musicales—all manner of social events—all season long," Frances said to her brother. "I am exhausted. I am *finished.*"

Though, at the moment, she'd happily dance with anyone if it meant she'd be free of this intervention. As long as he didn't smell bad.

Charles spun to address her sisters. "You two manage this, please. I need a drink."

With that, he swiveled and stalked away.

"*Why* are you being like this?" Esther demanded after they'd watched him go. "Charles wants—we *all* want—to see you properly settled." Then she added in an ominous tone, "Time is running out for you, Frances."

"You are well aware I have no interest in being properly settled," she shot back. "And I am only five-and-twenty. Do you believe that any day now I will magically transform into a wrinkled crone?"

Esther sniffed. "Of course not, but you know as well as I do that eventually you will be on the shelf, and then no one will want you."

Frances huffed. No one wanted her *now*. She wasn't unattractive, but Esther was right in that she *was* somewhat elderly for the marriage mart. She would bring no impressive dowry to a marriage—in fact, she'd bring no dowry at all. Also, and perhaps most important, at these events, she was not in possession of a "come hither" attitude when it came to luring the opposite sex. In fact, her attitude tended to border on "leave me alone!"

All men sensed it, and most had the sense to stay away.

Martha took the short silence as her opportunity to break in. "I am sure Mr. Salt would love the opportunity to dance with you before we all leave in the morning."

Frances cast her eyes heavenward. Her twin had been foisting poor Mr. Salt upon her for months.

Martha had discovered her passion in antiquities, specifically Egyptian antiquities, soon after the Cherrington sisters had moved to London when the twins were seventeen. She had sought company among those with similar interests, leaving Frances alone at home, feeling unmoored and lonely. Then, when they were two-and-twenty, Martha married Oscar de Havilland, and they'd left for Egypt a few months later.

Like Martha and her husband, Mr. Salt was an antiquarian, and he was traveling back to Egypt tomorrow with them. Insisting Frances come tonight was a final, desperate—and *futile*—effort on Martha's part to bring him and Frances together.

"There is nothing between Mr. Salt and me, Martha. And do you really believe, even if I wanted to, that I'd be able to secure a proposal from Mr. Salt tonight? The night before he's departing to another continent?"

"Maybe?" Martha said hopefully.

Frances threw up her hands in frustration.

"Mr. Salt would be a perfectly acceptable solution for you," Esther said. "Nobody *actually* wants to be a spinster forever." She said the word "spinster" like each syllable was covered in mold. "Not even you. So please, Frances, do stop pretending you are content with it."

Frances crossed her arms tightly, knowing she looked angry and stubborn, but she didn't care. She wanted to roar in frustration. Why didn't they listen? Why didn't they understand? They'd never even *tried* to understand.

"I don't want to marry," she pushed out, knowing her words were falling on deaf ears. "I am happy on my own. I am *free*."

Esther scowled. "How in heaven's name are you free? It is the opposite. You are trapped. Caged in our brother's home, and as time goes on, you have less and less of a chance of escape."

Martha lowered herself onto the bench with a despairing sigh. "All I desired was that you'd find a husband while I was here."

Frances groaned. She loved her sister even if they didn't always see eye to eye. As they were twins, they shared a different bond than she felt with her other sisters or even with Charles, who had once been Frances's favorite playmate. She and Martha had always quibbled and quarreled about matters both significant and paltry. They had different interests and different goals. Nevertheless, they knew each other in some intrinsic way that connected them deeply, in good times and in bad. Which was why Frances felt like a piece of her was ripped away whenever Martha left.

Frances and her sister had already argued before the masquerade—she hadn't wanted to come to begin with, and she certainly hadn't wanted to wear this abominable costume—so she didn't want to become embroiled in another argument with Martha right now. Not with less than twenty-four hours before her sister was to leave London.

Frances had no idea when she'd see her twin again, or even if she'd *ever* see her again.

She lowered herself beside Martha. "I'm sorry."

"It's entirely your fault that this is happening, Frances," Esther snapped. "You are so *stubborn*."

Someone appeared on the path behind Esther, partially cloaked by shadow. It definitely wasn't Charles. This man was dressed in gold, not black, and his hair was lighter than her brother's. Frances widened her eyes at Esther, trying to communicate to her to stop talking before the entire ton learned of this conversation.

As usual, Esther ignored her. "You push potential suitors away, just like you do everyone else. That's so selfish of you, and—"

"Good evening, ladies."

Esther spun around as the man stepped fully into the light cast by the nearby gas lamp.

The Earl of Winthrop flashed his charming smile. One of the rare masquerade attendees to forego a mask this evening, Winthrop was dressed as the Greek god Apollo, with golden robes and a cape with an emblem of the sun embroidered on the shoulder. A laurel wreath adorned his light-brown hair. The godly garb only enhanced his broad, muscular chest and narrow waist. No doubt his masculine appeal had drawn the attention of every lady in attendance. But it was his confidence and amicable demeanor that garnered him the reputation of being the most charismatic lord of the ton.

Frances despised him.

She tried to keep the scowl off her face as Martha and Esther rose to greet him. The man even carried a lyre. How fitting, she thought with a huff. His costume was perfect. His behavior was perfect. His smile, smug as she found it, was perfect.

No one was *that* perfect.

She was alone in her assessment of the man, of course. The disappointment and frustration on her sisters' faces melted away as they smiled and batted their lashes at him. It didn't matter that they were both married. Lord Winthrop had this effect on everyone—even her brother. His title alone could bend people to his will, but with his charming smile, they seemed enthusiastic to be bent.

Not Frances, though. She refused to fall for the façade he portrayed to the world. The more time they spent in the same circles, the more the man annoyed her.

"Good evening, Lord Winthrop," her sisters said, nearly in unison.

He nodded and turned his smile on Frances. "You look quite regal this evening, Miss Cherrington," he said to her. "Or should I say, Queen Cleopatra?" His amber eyes twinkled with mischief.

She scrambled to bury her surprise. Until now, no one she'd come across tonight had recognized her, or even mistaken her for Martha. But Lord Winthrop knew who she was, and specifically that she was Frances. She lifted her chin. "Miss Cherrington will do."

"Lord Winthrop!" Charles must have been hovering somewhere nearby because he hustled right over, glass of punch in hand. "Good evening."

Winthrop nodded genially. "Cherrington." He turned to Frances again. "I was just preparing to ask your lovely sister if she'd join me for the next dance."

She groaned inwardly. Of all the people at the masquerade, it *would* be the Earl of Winthrop who had come to rescue her.

Charles blinked, his jaw dropping in shock. "Really?"

Her brother was anything but circumspect. People could read him easier than an alphabet primer. He might as well have shouted it to the world: "You want to dance with my difficult and stubborn little sister? You? An earl of the realm? You must be addled, man, but good God, yes, yes! Go, sir! Dance with the girl, marry her, and impregnate her with a dozen children while you're at it! Huzzah!"

She really didn't want to dance with the smug, sunny

earl when a dark cloud dogged her every step, but with Charles about to make this unbearable moment even more unbearable, she saw no other choice for escape.

"I would love to dance with you, my lord," she lied, pouring far too much syrup into her voice. She shot a pointed look at her siblings and took the earl's proffered arm. "Shall we?"

His lips broke into another broad, *perfect* smile.

"Excellent. Come, Miss Cherrington," he said in his smooth, aristocratic drawl. "Let's dance."

Chapter Two

As he walked along the well-lit garden path with an irritated Frances Cherrington on his arm, Evan felt lighter. God only knew why. He was well aware that she didn't like him—or many people, for that matter—and she certainly didn't want to dance with him.

Before he'd stumbled across her, Evan had been wandering through the grounds alone, debating with himself whether to stay at the masquerade. The truth was, he was having a difficult time distracting himself from thoughts of the letter that lay on his desk. From thoughts of what that letter meant.

But then, in the far corner of the garden, he'd come upon the three Cherrington sisters, two of whom seemed to be berating the third. When he realized they were berating Frances, some undefinable emotion had surged within him, and without thinking, he'd stepped in. Then, to remove her from a situation that was clearly making her miserable, he'd asked her to dance.

Miss Cherrington looked delectable tonight. The white dress she wore hugged her deliciously curvy body, and the belt she wore cinched her small waist. Her lips were pressed into their usual flat, tight line, making Evan fantasize about using his own lips to soften hers until they were parted and gasping with pleasure.

He only wished he could remove the wig that covered her thick, brown hair and the mask that hid half her expression. He liked seeing all those prickly reactions of hers travel over her heart-shaped face.

Watching her from across the ballroom earlier, he'd observed that she hardly met anyone's gaze. That was Frances's usual way of operating—she did not easily welcome others into her space; in fact, she seemed to deliberately will people away. Like a true queen with that aura of mystery, she was aloof and disinterested in the nonsense the masses were up to, but at the same time, regal and beautiful.

He leaned toward her and spoke quietly, as if they were sharing a secret. "As much as you tried to pretend you were thrilled for the opportunity to dance with me, your demeanor informs me otherwise."

She slanted a glance in his direction. "You are correct. I have no desire whatsoever to dance with you."

He released a surprised laugh. Frances was who she was—forthright and open. No pretense. So damned refreshing. She stood apart from all the other unmarried ladies, especially those of her age whose desperation to marry, and marry well, was so thick, it was like a layer of hopeful pudding that he found impossible to spoon through to find the essence of the woman underneath.

"Then we don't have to dance," he told her.

"Good."

He hesitated, certain that if he asked what she'd like to do instead, she'd tell him to go away.

He didn't want to go away.

So instead, he said, "If you aren't enjoying this rout, you should leave. I, myself, am considering going home early."

"You, sir, are an earl and can do whatever you please. You are not bound by the dictates of your family."

"And your family has dictated you stay?"

"They have," she grumbled. "Quite vehemently."

"I'm sorry. That sounds…unpleasant."

"I assure you it is." She stopped walking suddenly and pulled her arm from his. "Perhaps you should find someone else to dance with."

Clearly, she expected him to excuse her from dancing with him, then run away with his tail between his legs. Drawing to a halt, he gave her a pointed look. "I'd rather keep talking to you." Behind them, a group of people erupted in loud laughter. "I find you interesting."

Her jaw dropped. "You find *me* interesting?"

His heartbeat quickened—surprising her gave him a thrill he didn't want to read into too deeply. "I do," he told her. "I'd say with no margin of doubt that you are the most interesting woman here tonight. I needed a diversion, and you are a perfect one."

She blinked, then began walking again. He kept stride alongside her. After a moment, she asked, "Why do you need a diversion?"

That goddamned letter.

Trying like hell not to show his discomfiture, he gave her

an easy smile. "Nothing for you to be concerned with."

"Oh dear." She put her hand over her chest in mock horror. "Don't tell me you're hiding from some marriage-minded mama."

He scoffed. "No. I have managed to hold them off so far this Season."

She gave him another skewering look. "Why *aren't* you married, my lord? How old are you? Thirty-three? Thirty-four? You are years older than my brother, and Charles has already been married for three years."

He considered her for a moment, then decided there was no harm in speaking the truth. "I am not against the institution of marriage, per se. It is just that I have never found a suitable potential bride."

She rolled her eyes heavenward. "You are an earl. I am certain every single debutante in London has been paraded before you and all your…perfection"—she waved a hand in his direction—"at one point or another."

She thought him perfect? He hid a smile, knowing better than to call attention to her words. "I have courted a few ladies, but in the end…" He held out his hands as if to say, "What can one do?"

What *could* one do? He didn't know. He had never found anyone to seriously pursue, because unlike most of his peers, he'd never marry for anything but love, and he'd never met anyone he believed could really love him.

He shoved that dark thought deep back into the well from whence it had come.

She blew out a little puff of air. "Then if it is not a matter of a matrimonial pursuit, why did you say you wanted a diversion?"

"*You* are not a lady who can be diverted, are you?"

"No," Frances agreed proudly. "I am quite impossible to divert, actually."

Unfortunate, considering he had no intention of sharing anything about that letter. "As I said," he said mildly, "it is really none of your concern."

"Ah, is it a *private* matter, then?" Her voice lowered and there was a little taunt in it as she asked, "Dare I say…a secret one?"

She was goading him, and maybe even starting to enjoy it a little, judging by the slight gleam in her dark eyes. "You may dare."

"The debonair earl has secrets," she mused.

"Doesn't everyone?" As they reached the terrace, he leaned the lyre against the railing and then turned back to her, the corners of his lips cocked upward. "What are yours, Miss Cherrington?"

She pursed her lips, clearly thinking it over. She must have many secrets. But would she share any with him?

He doubted it.

She looked down at her gloved hands, the fingers gripping the rail, then glanced up at him from beneath her lashes. "Perhaps we should agree to allow our secrets to remain just that, my lord."

His eyebrows shot up. She'd sounded demure. Flirtatious. Entirely *unlike* the Frances Cherrington he'd come to know.

She seemed to notice how sensual her voice sounded at the same time he did, and she immediately straightened her spine, her expression turning grim as she turned back to the garden.

He studied her as the truth of it struck him. She didn't

want to flirt.

"I think I'm beginning to understand," he said. "You are here to be offered on display for the marriage market. But you are not enjoying it."

"Of course, I am not enjoying it." Frances's dark eyes snapped to him, and she was fully herself again. "Who would enjoy being put on display like a slab of meat at the butcher's?"

"I'd never compare you to a slab of meat, Miss Cherrington."

She held his gaze for a long moment and then abruptly broke the eye contact. "Well, that's what it feels like," she groused.

He propped a hip against the rail and casually scanned the crowd. "Most of the unmarried ladies here seem to enjoy being on display." The noise from the ballroom spilled out from the house, and people were raising their voices to be heard over it. "That party, for example, appears as if they are enjoying it immensely."

He gestured to a nearby group of young women who were whispering and giggling over a young man dressed as a peacock, who preened before them, long green feathers fluttering. A lady dressed as Red Riding Hood stepped boldly forward from the group. "Dance with me, Sir Pea*cock*!"

At the Worthington Masquerade, a lady didn't need to wait for a gentleman to ask her to dance. The usual rules of society meant absolutely nothing here.

"Oh, my darling, there's nothing pea-like about this cock," the man drawled. Slipping his arm under Red's cape, he drew her tightly against him, and they walked away, peals of laughter from the rest of the group following them as they headed toward the ballroom.

Frances blew out a sharp breath. "*They*," she muttered, "are not me."

They certainly were not. "So, *have* you met any potential suitors this evening?" Evan asked her.

She snorted. "No."

"Why is that?" He leaned in close, his shoulder brushing hers. "We are surrounded by unmarried men. Surely all of them cannot be unsuitable for a beauty such as yourself."

He watched her take in his comment about her beauty before seeming to dismiss it outright. "Perhaps all of them are suitable; perhaps none. I don't care."

"Don't you?"

"Not in the least," she said flatly.

"Why not?"

"I have no intention of pursuing—or being pursued by—any of them."

"Despite your family's wishes?"

Stepping back from him a little, she scowled at him. "You keep asking me questions. Have I not yet frightened you off? I frighten all the dashing men off within moments. Why are you so persistent?"

"I believe you just called me dashing," he said with a grin, unable to resist this latest slip.

She frowned. "No, I did not. I said I frighten dashing men off. I did not necessarily include you in that group."

"I see," he said lightly.

"*Why* are you smiling?" She sounded utterly frustrated.

"Because I am enjoying our conversation, Miss Cherrington."

Her frown deepened even as her eyes went wide, which only made his smile grow. He'd surprised her again. God, how he loved how she reacted to him.

"Now tell me why you have no intention of being pursued by a suitor despite your family's wishes," he said.

She lifted her chin. "Because I have no intention of marrying."

"But isn't that the goal of every young lady?" In his experience, it was. He thought about the young women of his class and how they could be separated into two groups: the unmarried and the married. Those who were unmarried generally were doing everything they could possibly do to join the second group.

"It is not one of *my* goals," she said primly.

"What are your goals, then?" He was truly curious.

"There are many. Yet I am prevented from pursuing them." She waved her hand in the direction of the ballroom. "My family believes that husband-hunting should occupy my every moment of every day."

"Can't you simply tell them that you'd prefer to occupy yourself with other pursuits?"

"I've tried," she said. "Trust me, I have *tried*. I believe you witnessed such an attempt when you snuck up on us in the garden."

He had done no such thing, but he wasn't willing to risk falling into an argument with her. Not when she'd just begun to open up. Her brother and her four sisters had been married off in the last three years, so she was the last single Cherrington standing. He could only imagine what kind of pressure they were piling on her to tie the proverbial knot. "Then what will you do? Continue to be forced to attend social events and pretend to hunt for a husband for the rest of your life?"

"Until I am on the shelf, as they say."

"When will that be?" He was totally ignorant about these kinds of things.

"A few years from now, I imagine. Evidently, I have several more Seasons of this to look forward to." She gave a hollow laugh, then rolled her eyes in his direction. "Thanks for reminding me, my lord."

"If you despise it that much, there must be a way out." Evan hated thinking of her having to endure parties that made her miserable again and again only to be berated by her family for not behaving like the perfect debutante. "It seems to me that the easiest solution would be just to marry someone and be done with it."

She barked out a laugh. "That is *exactly* what I am trying to avoid!"

"What else is there?" he asked. "In our society, if you're a young lady who's eligible to marry, then marriage is what you are expected to pursue."

She stared over his shoulder at the ballroom where guests were tumbling out, clutching their sides in laughter. "Hmm," she mused. "Then perhaps I should ensure that I'm *in*eligible."

He shifted on his feet, not liking the direction this was going. "But you will only become ineligible when society determines your age to be too advanced. I don't see how you can speed that along."

She stared at him, her eyes narrowing, then resumed watching the merry crowd.

Frowning, he stepped closer to her. "Are you all right, Miss Cherrington?"

She turned to him again, a tight smile curling her lips.

"I am quite all right, my lord." Her voice was crisp and sure. "Thank you ever so much for this enlightening conversation."

Enlightening? It certainly had been for him—he now felt like he might partly understand Miss Frances Cherrington—but he couldn't imagine what *she'd* felt was enlightening about it.

"Now, if you'll excuse me," she said, "I'm off to find my destiny."

"Your—?" But she'd already swiveled and disappeared into the crowd.

He blinked at her abrupt departure. He had been enjoying their conversation so much, and then...

Well, he had no idea what had happened.

Her destiny?

What the hell was Frances Cherrington about to do?

Chapter Three

Frances strode away from Lord Winthrop, her heart beating hard and heavy against her ribs. She had to push Winthrop from her mind.

And she had to find Mr. Salt.

When Frances had been talking to the earl, they'd painted a picture of her life looming ahead of her, a long line of men who either politely snubbed her or gazed upon her like some kind of prey, with her sisters and brother on the periphery, pushing her toward each and every one of them.

And all of a sudden, it had struck her.

There *was* a way out of this.

Her family would continue to force her to parade through the marriage mart, but only as long as she was marriageable.

What if she was no longer marriageable?

There were only three things that would prevent her from being a suitable potential bride in the eyes of society. The first was being already married—Winthrop had unhelpfully offered that one up. That was *not* an option. The second was being too old to marry, but could she continue living like this for several more years?

But while speaking to Winthrop it dawned on her that there was a *third* way to become ineligible for marriage.

She could be ruined.

Not only that, but she could stage her *own* ruination. *Tonight.*

The thought made her heartbeat race with excitement. If she were ruined, the pressure from her family would stop. They'd no longer expect her to mingle with society or be incessantly polite and gracious. She would be free to live her own life on her own terms.

She'd need to do it *safely*, of course. She'd need to make a careful plan with rigid guidelines and then follow it with precision.

Rule number one: Select a safe man to compromise you.

She thought of Winthrop's handsome face beneath the laurel wreath. Being ruined by him, having him wrap his arms around her and tease her mouth with his arrogant, masculine lips…*ooh*. A delicious spark had rolled down her spine.

No. *Absolutely not.* Winthrop was the *opposite* of safe.

While they were speaking, she'd caught a glimpse of Mr. Salt's thin blond hair in the crowd, then his black domino cape, swirling slightly as he turned away.

The man was utterly benign. She'd never felt any semblance of danger in his presence. He was the opposite of Winthrop, who'd used his wiles on her tonight. She couldn't believe how much she'd opened up to him and told him about her true feelings. The dratted man was an annoying sorcerer of charm.

She shuddered. If she ever encountered Winthrop again,

she'd have to fend off his trickery. Be tightlipped and circumspect.

Actually, it'd be better to just avoid the man altogether. Which should be easy, considering what she was about to do.

Rule number two: Choose someone who won't bother you in the future.

If a man ruined her, the condemnation would fall upon her shoulders as the wicked wanton, not on the man's. Unlike women, men were expected—and even encouraged—to indulge in such behaviors. She wouldn't have to worry about his reputation being damaged alongside her own. However, she couldn't risk them being forced into marriage, which was yet another point in Mr. Salt's favor. He was leaving for Africa tomorrow morning. If *he* ruined her, by the time the news of her ruination came out, he'd be long gone and completely safe from any repercussions.

A few moments later, she saw Salt excusing himself from a group before heading in the general direction of the refreshments room, his plain black domino trailing after him.

Nerves jumped under Frances's skin as he drew nearer.

Rule number three: Endeavor to meet the gentleman covertly, yet in a place frequented by gossips.

Well, here they were. The Worthington Masquerade, the one night of the year filled with scandalous liaisons and people whose sole purpose was to gossip about them.

Mid-step, she hesitated. Her plan was *truly* scandalous. She'd never been forward with a man before, and now—

Well, that was the point of this exercise, wasn't it?

Firming her jaw even as heat slid up her chest, she avoided three Elizabethan noblemen sidling up to a group of tittering dairymaids and serving wenches and finally intercepted Salt's path. She looked up at him and smiled. "Good evening."

He jumped—literally *jumped*—backward. But then his eyes lit with delight. "Oh!" He bowed formally. "Your Majesty. What a wonderful costume! Thoroughly enchanting!"

"Why, thank you," she said demurely. Well, as demurely as she could. She *was* Frances Cherrington, after all.

"I am utterly charmed," he gushed. "You appear as though a specter from my dreams has emerged directly from a royal palace, a most exquisite place of far more culture and refinement than those from antiquity."

Her brows popped upward at that. Fortunately, he couldn't see them behind her mask. Did he really think she looked *more* refined than the actual Cleopatra? That was absurd. She felt like the most horrendous fraud in this costume.

"Would you do me the honor of dancing the next set with me, Your Majesty?"

"Oh, I would love to!" Frances exclaimed, then winced. She had sounded almost theatrically overexcited.

The quadrille had just ended so her timing had been perfect. She and Mr. Salt took their positions in the line, and when the first chords of the reel began to play, they bowed to each other. He was staring at her in a way she'd never seen before. He generally treated Frances with polite but not quite sincere interest, but he eyed "Cleopatra" as if she were a confection he couldn't wait to devour.

She weaved in and out of the line of the ladies and gentlemen. By now, Frances had danced the Scotch reel so many times, she could execute the steps in her sleep, so she went through them mechanically as she continued to think.

Did she have the courage to do this?

That boiled down to one question: did she want her life to remain the same, or did she want to be free?

The answer was easy. *Freedom.*

So, yes, she had the courage.

Salt took her hand in his limp one as they stepped toward each other for the few counts they'd be together. "Your regalia continues to draw my most tender eye," he murmured, panting slightly as they moved in a circle.

"Why, thank you, sir." She studied him, even as they moved apart again. He hadn't identified her—hadn't made any indication whatsoever that he might think she was Frances Cherrington, and he'd certainly never spoken to Frances with such passionate admiration before—which confirmed her suspicions about him. He'd paid attention to her over the past months, but he'd never truly *looked* at her.

Arm in arm, she and Salt shuffled to the side, weaving around other couples.

"I am so very fascinated by the magnificence of ancient Egypt," she purred, trying not to cringe at how ridiculous she sounded, "so representing its most famous queen is simply *exhilarating.*"

His eyes widened behind his mask. "I am utterly fascinated by it as well. In fact—"

Oh no. She shouldn't have gone there. Or...maybe she should.

His face alight with enthusiasm, Salt began talking about a remarkable new discovery near the "second cataract," whatever that was.

She pasted on a smile and pretended to listen to his animated chatter about Egypt for the remainder of the dance as she completed forming her plan.

When it was over, she and Mr. Salt stood in their line again and bowed to each other.

Rule number four: Give yourself (and him) a reason to relocate somewhere more private.

She sidled closer to him and spoke in the most charming voice she could muster. "I hear the gardens are just lovely this time of year. Would you like to join me outside? I am *so* eager to hear more about your exciting travels to Egypt." She twisted her face into a—hopefully—inviting expression.

His eyes widened in surprise and, dare she say, excitement. "Why yes, I'd love to join you."

They ventured onto the terrace and then descended the steps to the garden as Frances studied her surroundings. Since the last time she'd been outside, it had grown louder. Crowds of people were scattered everywhere, laughing, drinking, and stealing covert and not-so-covert touches. Martha, Esther, and Charles were nowhere to be seen. Everything was perfect for Frances's plan.

Rule number five: Pretend that every word out of his mouth is the most important morsel of English you've ever heard.

Arm in arm, Frances and Salt strolled along. As he discussed the objects he'd pilfered from various Egyptian tombs, she made exclamations of wonder and amazement, all the while scanning the path in search of people she knew.

Rule number six: Locate the witness—the person who will share "your secret" with the world.

There was Mr. Hargreaves with a group of gentlemen she didn't recognize in the dimness—no. Hargreaves wasn't one to gossip, so his friends probably weren't, either. Miss Fitzwilliam and her sisters were huddled together whispering—no again. They were squeakily innocent and probably wouldn't believe their own eyes if they saw Frances do anything untoward.

And then Frances's gaze snagged on the perfect tangle of women. Five of them stood clustered near a tree, giggling together as if they were debutantes. They had been debutantes at one time, but they were all married now. Years ago, they had been the belles of the ton, diamonds of the first water, etcetera, but Frances knew them in her mind as The Backbiting Biddies, which was exactly what they were. They were led by Henrietta Grassley, who stood taller than the others and whose aquiline nose was unmistakable. She was dressed as a priest, which was the most ironically hilarious thing Frances had seen all night.

It was more perfect than she could have hoped for.

As they neared the group of women, she drew Salt to a stop. He turned to her, his brows drawn together quizzically.

Rule number seven: Behave as if you are overcome by his words, his handsomeness, his virility...

"Oh, sir. All this talk of Egypt has made me"—she hesitated, moving infinitesimally closer to him—"admire you so," she finished with a breathy sigh.

Frances had always been terrible at pretending to be anything other than her plain, honest self. Her fumbling attempts at flirtation tonight had been as fake and as gaudy and as uncomfortable as her Cleopatra costume.

Surprisingly, though, Salt appeared enamored. He stared at her with an expression that she could only interpret as sheer adoration. "Miss..." He gulped. "May I inquire as to your name?"

She shook her head. "Oh, good sir, I just hope you remember me. Remember this night."

"I shall!" he declared fervently. "It is a night I will never forget." He pressed even closer to her. She held her ground as he stared into her eyes. "My queen…" His throat moved as he swallowed. "I depart for the great continent of Africa tomorrow, but may I give you a small token to remember me by? Perhaps…a kiss?"

A strange combination of victory, nerves, and repulsion flooded through her. She'd done it! She'd been sufficiently alluring and now he would fulfill his role in her plan. The thought equally terrified and thrilled her. She took a shaky breath.

"Yes," she breathed.

He wrapped his arms around her and drew her so close, their noses, made larger by their masks, bumped awkwardly. His breath was hot on her mouth as he murmured, "Oh my queen…"

Every part of her demanded she pull away.

Rule number eight: Make it believable. This is essential.

Firming his grip on her, he turned his head slightly so their masks—and noses—didn't get in the way and pressed a kiss to her mouth.

Anxiety roared in her ears as she battled her instinct to jerk back and run as far away as she possibly could. *No. Stay. Let him do this. Allow him to do what he wants for another second. And another…*

God. This was disgusting. *Why* did people insist kissing was enjoyable? His lips were wet and hot and mushy, and his breath smelled of vinegar.

Another second…

She had to give it more time. Enough so that all the Backbiting Biddies would witness it without any question as to what was happening.

Another second…

She couldn't bear this much longer. Truly, she couldn't. Now he was smashing his mouth against hers. Esther had once told her that kissing was "lovely." Her other sisters had all agreed. This was yet another way she differed from them. How could anyone enjoy such a thing as this? This wasn't lovely in the least.

Another second…

This was enough. Surely it had to be. Was it enough? Please, God, let it be enough.

Another second…

Enough. She pulled back, her hands dropping to his forearms where she forced herself to push him off gently rather than shove him unceremoniously away, which was what her body was telling her to do.

Rule number nine: Walk away.

She forced herself to smile up at him, though she was certain it appeared more of a ghoulish grimace. But, no matter. Salt's powers of observation were clearly underdeveloped, as he *still* hadn't recognized her.

"Good evening, kind sir," she murmured, then dodged around him, ignoring his faint, "But, Your Majesty…" and walked briskly toward the group of women.

…and ensure your witness has seen everything.

As she rounded the corner, she tore off her mask, her wig coming along with it, leaving her face and her bound chestnut-brown hair exposed. She passed the Backbiting Biddies who all stared at her, mouths agape.

There. It was done.

Rule ten: Suffer the consequences with your head held high. Your new life is about to begin.

Finally, she'd be free.

Chapter Four

Evan was glad he'd gone to last night's masquerade. Miss Cherrington had been just the diversion he'd needed.

This morning, he had awakened with his body hard all over, erotic images of Frances Cherrington underneath him swirling through his dreams. He'd relieved his lust with his hand, fantasies of her running through his mind as he'd done so. That wry twist of her lips, those brown eyes that seemed to miss nothing, her clean lilac scent, the luscious curves of her body that Cleopatra's dress had done little to hide.

But during breakfast, as he'd read the *Times*, drank coffee, and eaten a piece of buttered toast, other thoughts began to intrude.

Thoughts of the letter.

He needed to do something about it. So, with a deep breath, he'd gone to his study and faced it.

He sat behind his desk and looked down at the sheet of paper lying flat on the polished surface. His butler had handed it to him yesterday morning. After he'd opened it and read through its contents, he'd locked himself in his study until it was time to dress for the masquerade. Now, the letter lay surrounded by piles of open ledgers from April for the past ten years.

The letter itself was blunt, short, and written with a feathery hand, which made it difficult to decipher. Nevertheless, it had taken Evan's breath away. Now, he read it for the fifth—or forty-fifth—time. He'd lost count.

> *21st of April 1820*
> *My lord,*
> *Thank you for your faithful remittance of the funds required for our discretion and the continued maintenance of Mstr S. Dickens. Unfortunately, due to steeply rising expenses, we must increase the annual amount to £200.*
> *Please remit the additional funds at your earliest convenience.*
> *Yr obt svt,*
> *Thos. Thomason*
> *Harlowe's Home for Boys*

When he'd read it yesterday, Evan's first thought was, "Who the hell is Mstr S. Dickens?"

His second was, "Who the hell is Thos. Thomason?"

His mind in a swirl, he'd gone over the ledgers, and there it was, remitted every April for six years straight. A hundred and sixty pounds. After his father passed away, and thinking it was a generous and worthy charitable donation to a London orphanage, Evan himself had approved for the sum to be sent for the last four years.

He hadn't known he'd been sending the funds to support a *particular* child.

And why had his father sent the funds to support the boy to begin with?

There was only one clear answer to that question.

Evan had known from the time he was a small boy that his father had kept a mistress. Several of them, in fact. But he didn't just keep mistresses—he made good use of whorehouses and brothels across the country. After the old earl had died, Evan had come across a well-worn copy of the 1795 printing of *Harris's Guide to Covent Garden Ladies*. The book had been dog-eared, with ladies' names circled and notes written in the margins, describing the previous earl's personal experiences with a variety of them.

When he'd found it, Evan's stomach had churned, thinking of his mother, who rarely ventured to London. Perhaps this was the reason she was so bitter and unhappy. With a sick feeling in his gut, he'd thrown the little book into the fire and watched it burn.

Now, Evan stared down at the letter. Knowing what he did about his father's proclivities, him having a by-blow shouldn't come as too much of a surprise. But it still made anxiety swirl through him.

He might have a *brother.*

Evan was the only son of Mark Bennington Locke, the Earl of Winthrop, and his countess. When he was a lad, Evan had asked his mother why he had no brothers and sisters. She'd shushed him and ordered him to be satisfied with the family he had.

He'd always wanted a brother. Now, it was a little late. He was four-and-thirty, after all, and this boy was clearly still a child. Evan didn't even know how old he was.

On the other hand, the letter might be some kind of

perverse attempt at blackmail for two hundred pounds per year. The previous earl may have been known for his libertine ways, but that was no proof Mstr S. Dickens was the result of one of his liaisons.

Two hundred pounds was an exorbitant amount for the keeping of one child. Evan would take this Thos. Thomason to task for that ridiculous demand, and the implied threat of exposure beneath it, whether the boy was his brother or not.

But first, he had to get to the bottom of Mstr S. Dickens's true identity.

His mother resided at the dower house at Pleasant Hill, the family estate in Hertfordshire. He'd ride out there tomorrow to ferret out what she knew, if anything. It wouldn't be a pleasant conversation—conversations with the dowager rarely were.

But it needed to happen.

...

As planned, Martha had left with her husband and Mr. Salt early the morning after the masquerade.

When her twin had said goodbye, Frances had returned her hug stiffly, forcing her expression into blandness, though her heart was begging, "Please don't go!"

But Martha had gone. Frances had managed to hold in her emotions until she was alone in her room that night. She'd sobbed, muffling the sounds with her pillow. She was determined to never, ever reveal exactly how much her twin leaving gutted her.

The following morning, she slipped out of bed and washed the salty tracks of tears from her face before going down to breakfast, which she ate quickly before returning to her room. Now that she was destined to be a spinster for the remainder of her days, she was determined to focus on finding her true passion. Frances had spent the past few years thinking that if she could only discover some occupation that would make her time more meaningful, then her life wouldn't feel so aimless.

Frances was a list-maker. She'd started with the habit as a young child, listing all the people in her family when she was first starting to write. This progressed to lists of colors, clothing, toys owned by each of her siblings, the lists becoming more complex as she grew older. Now she wanted to make a new list of the things she might enjoy doing with her life. All the things she could be.

Before they'd married, each of her sisters had found their own passions. Frances had even written them in a list once, including her own name with a sadly blank space next to it. Martha had her ancient civilizations. Mary, the eldest, was a devotee of the Bible and of her charity work. Harriet, the second youngest, was talented in and fascinated by all pursuits considered feminine and ladylike. The baby of the family, Esther, was consumed by the fashion and goings-on in the beau monde.

Sitting at the little desk under the window of the bedroom she'd once shared with her twin, Frances drew out a sheet of paper and dipped her pen into the ink.

1) *Artist (Paint? Watercolor? Pencil or charcoal drawing? Shall I draw people, places, or <u>something</u> else? Must acquire a drawing master.)*

Tapping her pen on her chin, she considered something that would entail being among children. She truly enjoyed children, and her nephews adored her. Perhaps a governess? But no one would hire a governess who'd been the subject of a scandal. Her ruination would also ruin that prospect—something she hadn't considered when she'd plotted it. But perhaps there were other ways she could work with children.

She began to write again.

2) *Charity Worker (In a charity involving children? Must ask Mary.)*

3) *Musician (What instrument? <u>NOT the pianoforte</u>—too ordinary. Something interesting and unique—perhaps the cello?)*

4) *Scholar (But a scholar of what? <u>NOT EGYPT!</u> Talk to Lilly. Perhaps...astronomy? Physiology?)*

5) *Sewing/Embroidery (Writing this makes me cringe. But perhaps I have a hidden genius for sewing and will create beautiful work while finding it fulfilling? Must practice sewing more interesting/artistic items—not stockings!)*

6) *Traveler (I could travel the world and write about it. This might be interesting. Where to begin?)*

7) *Shopkeeper (But what would I sell?)*

8) *Novelist (I will write a book about—*

The door to her room burst open so hard, it banged on the back of the wall. Frances leapt to her feet and planted herself in a wide stance, fists raised.

It was Charles, his face as crimson as a boiled lobster's, waving a broadsheet in his hand and bellowing, "What is this, Frances? What the hell is this?"

Frances clasped her fists to her chest and bit back a grin.

It had happened. She was ruined.

Chapter Five

It was almost noon when the dowager countess deigned to see Evan, though he'd arrived hours earlier. Her butler announced him at the door to her private sitting room.

"Come in, Winthrop," she said in a brusque voice.

He stepped into the elegant space. She was sitting in her favorite chair, back straight, hands clasped in her lap. His mother was a narrow, tall woman, blonde and stern. Once a great beauty, she was still a stunning figure, though age had bestowed deep brackets around her mouth and eyes, and rows of parallel grooves were carved in her forehead. "Good morning, Mother."

The dowager scanned him up and down. Never an affectionate sort, she nodded curtly. "You look well, as usual. Please." She gestured to a sumptuous-looking red velvet chair. "Sit."

He sat on the edge of the chair.

She gazed at him evenly, her blue eyes narrowed. "You

appear to be under some strain. Do you bring bad news from town?"

"Not exactly."

"Then why have you come to see me?"

His mother wasn't interested in small talk today. That was perfectly acceptable to him. "I have a question for you."

"What is it?"

Nerves suddenly clogged his throat, making him hesitate. He'd never spoken to his mother about such a private matter.

Seeing his hesitance, her stiff, narrow shoulders stiffened even further, and her lips turned down. "*What is it*, Winthrop?"

It had always been odd—and he'd found it rather cold—that she never called him Evan. Since he was a child, she'd addressed him by his title.

He swallowed hard. "I have some questions about my father's...proclivities."

Her gaze sharpened. "What proclivities?"

"I know about his mistresses."

She pursed her lips. "You and the rest of Britain. What of it?"

"I am interested in learning more about one of them."

Her mouth twisted and her thin brows rose haughtily. "And you've come to *me* about this matter?"

"Yes. I know you were aware of his many liaisons." He cleared his throat. "But I thought there might be one in particular that you might have some information about."

"Why would I have information on any of my husband's doxies? Believe me, I stayed as far out of that man's business as my carriage could carry me. I know nothing—"

"I am led to believe that one of them bore him a son."

She jerked back as if he'd slapped her but quickly

composed herself and offered him a tight shrug. "Ah. I see."

"Do you know anything about *that* mistress?"

"That woman wasn't his mistress," she bit out. She rose from her chair jerkily and walked to the window. Drawing the curtain aside, she gazed out over the manicured lawn beyond.

Clenching the arms of his chair tighter, Evan leaned forward. "Who was she then?"

His mother didn't look at him. "Just a whore."

Evan cringed at her caustic tone.

She let out a long-suffering sigh, and her shoulders seemed to deflate a little before she seemed to straighten and grow taller. Dropping the curtain, she turned to him again, her face a blank mask. "Well. I always assumed you'd learn about your real mother eventually."

His *real* mother?

What was she talking about?

"But of course you know it changes nothing," she continued. "You are the earl and I am your mother in everyone's eyes but our own."

He blinked at her, stunned.

What just happened?

In his mind he scrolled back through the conversation. His father… Mistresses… A *particular* mistress who bore him a son.

Him? He, *Evan,* was the son of one of his father's mistresses?

The woman standing before him was not his mother?

Oh God.

He swayed a little, clutching the velvet armrests to hold himself upright.

He'd come to learn about S. Dickens's mother, not to learn about…

His own real mother?

Evan felt like he'd been thrust into a completely different reality.

"You...you are not my mother." It was a question, but it emerged as a statement, flat and hoarse.

The dowager was cool and quick to answer, her eyes utterly devoid of emotion. But that was nothing new. She'd always displayed the emotion of a brick. "I assumed you had already confirmed that fact."

"Right." He swallowed again, but it hurt. His mouth was so dry. "I...need a drink."

"You know I do not keep spirits in this house."

"Tea, then. Lemonade. Milk. Water. Sludge. *Anything*," he croaked.

She heaved a sigh but moved to the bell. As she rang for tea, Evan tried to compose himself, though he could not stop his heart from galloping like a horse trying to escape imminent death.

It made sense. So much sense. The dowager had never offered him an iota of love or affection. She had called him son and allowed him to call her mother, but their relationship had never gone further than that. Nursemaids and governesses had raised him until he was sent to Eton at the youngest possible age. He'd found his real family, his true and long-standing support, in his three friends there—the Duke of Crestmont, Oliver Jameson, and Viscount Coleton.

His mother—ex-mother?—no, what was she? *The dowager* resumed her seat across from him. "I suppose you have questions."

"I...yes."

She made an impatient "proceed" gesture with her hand. He simply stared at her for a moment. He had always wondered at their opposite personalities—where she was cold and aloof, he had always been warm and friendly. He had always ached for her to hug him—he was the affectionate sort—but she'd always pushed him away when he'd come too close.

And why had he never noticed that she looked nothing like him?

"Why did you allow it?" he finally pushed out.

Her frown deepened. "Allow what?"

"Me to call you mother?" His voice sounded weak, as far away as if it were coming from a different planet.

Her nose wrinkled with distaste. "I weighed my options carefully and decided it was better to be the proud mother of a son than a barren woman who couldn't produce an heir for her husband."

He flinched at that, then asked, "How did you accomplish such a deception?"

She shrugged. "It was simple. Winthrop sent the whore and me to my father's country estate in Northumberland."

The "whore" she spoke of was Evan's real mother. Where was she? *Who* was she?

"We were far from society or even any village of note," the dowager continued. "My father was part of the scheme, of course. He wanted me to bear Winthrop an heir as much as the earl himself did. No one outside of my father, my maid, and the midwife laid eyes upon us for several long months." She shuddered lightly. "It was insufferable."

"What happened to her?" he asked.

"Your mother?"

Swallowing hard, he nodded.

"Winthrop paid her handsomely for the child then sent her on her merry way."

"What was her name?" he asked. It came out as a whisper because his windpipe had closed so tight he could hardly breathe.

"Eliza MacPherson."

"Eliza MacPherson," he repeated slowly, opening and closing his fists over the armrests. "I'm...Scottish?"

She scoffed. "Hardly. She was born, raised, and had been working in a Covent Garden whorehouse. I couldn't get the stink of it off her, even after five months in the country."

"Where is she now?"

"How should I know?" she answered crossly. "She eagerly took the small fortune in coin and ran, as people of her class are wont to do. For all I know, she is living like a maharajah on the other side of the world."

He jerked to standing, unable to be in this awful woman's presence a moment longer, even as a small part of him, that child he once was, was still hoping to see her face soften, love glow in her eyes, her arms reach out to him.

Now he knew for certain that none of that would ever happen. "I must go."

She arched an imperious brow. "Your tea hasn't arrived."

"I'll take it in the main house." He bowed succinctly. "Good evening, Mo—Lady Winthrop."

"Just call me Mother, as you always have done." She sighed, appearing bored. "After four-and-thirty long years, we wouldn't want anyone to think anything was amiss *now*, would we?"

Evan turned on his heel and strode out of the dower house and across the lawn to the main house. He entered and went straight up to his room, where he lay on top of the counterpane and stared up at the ceiling, dry-eyed, for the rest of the day.

Chapter Six

"You are ruined!" Esther exclaimed. "Good Lord, Frances. What have you done?"

"Oh, Frances!" Harriet, who was a year younger than Frances, dabbed at tears with her lace handkerchief. "Oh, dearest Frances…"

Frances sighed, got up from her chair, and went to her sisters, who'd just entered the drawing room where she'd been banished after her brother had blustered at her for what felt like an eternity. It had actually been five minutes. She'd checked.

Charles had finally worn himself out, had ordered her to go to the drawing room, forbade her to leave it, and had summoned all her sisters except her twin, whose ship was now somewhere off the coast of England. Esther and Harriet had arrived together, but Mary was in church and could not be interrupted.

While Esther scowled at her, Frances wrapped her arms

around Harriet. "It's all right, Harriet. Everything will be fine."

"How can it be fine?" Esther snapped. Then, her already narrow eyes narrowed even more. "Do you know what happened? Did Charles show you?"

"He did not, but I have a feeling I know what they are saying."

Esther's jaw dropped. "Which means you're *guilty*! That's why you demanded to leave the masquerade early, isn't it? Not because you had a headache from the weight of your wig. Because you knew you'd caused the scandal of the century!"

"Esther." Frances sighed. "Please stop being dramatic."

Esther held up a hand. "Don't move. I'll be back." With a *whoosh* of her skirts, she turned and left the room, closing the door with a sharp *snick* behind her.

Frances led the distraught Harriet to the sofa. Harriet had always had the softest heart of them all though she rarely showed it, so determined was she to be the perfect young lady, and now to be the perfect wife. Frances begrudged her none of these things.

"Truly," she told Harriet now. "I'll be all right."

Harriet shuddered. "I cannot fathom what those horrible wretches are saying about you."

"Never mind them. They can't hurt me."

"But they can!" Harriet exclaimed, blinking damp lashes. "And they will. I have no doubt about it."

"Then I must stay away from society altogether until this dies down." *Oh, drat*, she added in her head.

"It might be a very, very long time until this dies down," Harriet said. "Oh, dear Frances, I fear you shall never be accepted in society circles again!"

Double drat.

Esther burst into the room waving the broadsheet. "Here it is." She thrust the paper into Frances's hands. "Read it and weep."

Frances scrolled down. A list of who was seen dancing with whom at the masquerade, a couple of engagement predictions resulting from the dancing at the masquerade, a story about a certain Lady M— who hadn't attended the masquerade, but whose sheets were found quite tumbled the morning after due to her assignation with an intimate friend of Lord M—.

Then she found it.

It wasn't written text…well, it mostly wasn't. It was a caricature—Cleopatra decked out in gold and a mysterious man in a black domino, his cape winding around both their bodies, their protruding lips locked together, her eyes wide in shock, and his hand creeping around to her over-generous backside while a group of onlookers watched, their eyes bugging from their heads.

"Well, that's not very flattering," Frances muttered. Then she read the caption.

"A clear lesson to refrain from believing a simple disguise will conceal one's indiscretion: Miss Ch—ton and Mr. S—t, a traveler from afar, observed in flagrante delicto at the Worthington Masquerade."

Dash it all. She'd hoped the Backbiting Biddies hadn't identified Mr. Salt, but they clearly had. She was doubly grateful he was long gone.

"Mr. S—t," Harriet murmured. "A traveler… Oh Lord"—she gasped—"is that…that must be Mr. Salt!" She burst into renewed sobs. Frances put an arm around her while Esther sank down on her other side. After a few minutes, Harriet mostly controlled her tears. "How could Mr. Salt do this? We all thought he was such an honorable man."

Esther's scowl deepened. "Charles, Martha, and I left you alone after you danced with the Earl of Winthrop hoping that you would encounter Mr. Salt or another potential suitor—and engage in *polite conversation*. We never suspected *this* would happen." Sinking into an armchair across from Harriet and Frances, she groaned softly and pressed her palms to her eyes. "What a dreadful mistake that was. Now I understand why one must never leave an unattached female to her own devices. It can lead to only one thing: *disaster*."

Harriet turned her watery gaze to Frances. "Oh, Frances. Did he…did he *assault* you?"

Frances raised her hand. "No, no, not at all. I was…" She gulped, every bit of her rebelling against saying it, but she *must* say it. "A willing participant." When both of her sisters stared at her blankly, she added, "*Very* willing."

"But that very evening, you told Martha and me that you had no interest in him," Esther said suspiciously.

"That's true. However, I was…curious."

"Curious?" Harriet asked with a frown.

"Yes." She nodded, maybe too vigorously. "You told me kisses were lovely," she said to Esther. "I wanted to experience one for myself."

Esther gasped. "Frances! Of all the reckless, stupid, foolish—"

"We must write to Mr. Salt right away," Harriet said. "He will marry you, Frances. He *must* marry you!"

"No!" Frances exclaimed. She lowered her voice. "Mr. Salt isn't for me, Harriet. All he cares about is Egypt." Then she said what she'd rehearsed in her mind. "He kissed me only because I was Cleopatra. He didn't even recognize me. I would be miserable with a man like that, you know I would. It was just one silly little kiss. Honestly, it was nothing."

"It was *not* nothing!" Esther shrieked.

Harriet covered her face with her hands, and Frances patted her shoulder. "It's all right. Mr. Salt must stay right where he is."

"But—" Esther began.

"In any case, he is completely unreachable. Did you know he's heading for a year-long dig at the second cataract?" She still had no idea what that meant or where the second cataract even was, but she did know it was far, far, *far* away. "Even if someone attempted to contact him, he's nowhere that he could be found for the next year, at least." She shrugged. "It's hopeless. I shall simply have to face this scandal head-on. *Alone.* And that's the way I prefer it, honestly."

"Do you realize what this means?" Esther breathed.

"What do *you* think it means?" Frances asked, interested in her society-obsessed sister's opinion.

"You shall be shunned. The ton will never acknowledge you as one of their own ever again." Esther's eyes went almost as wide as those of the onlookers in the caricature. "And, worst of all, no man will have you now."

・・・

Evan was generally a cheerful person. He always attempted to find the positive aspects of every situation. But this revelation had caught him off guard, and he found himself unable to eat or leave his room.

He remained in his room at Pleasant Hill for three days. Then, before dawn on the fourth day, he roused himself. Needing to do *something* to pull himself out of this melancholy, he rode south through London, straight to the Thames waterfront and the comfort of the boathouse.

All he wanted to do was to take down one of the shells and row until his arms felt like jelly. Maybe that would wipe this feeling away and clear his mind so he could make a decision about his future.

The land and the boathouse building technically belonged to the Duke of Crestmont, but Crestmont, Evan, Jameson, and Cole shared every aspect of the place—from building and designing to the use of the boathouse and the boats that occupied it.

But the boathouse wasn't empty as Evan had expected. In fact, all three of his friends were there, pulling down the boats for a morning row.

After securing his horse, he entered through the open barn-like doors, and they looked up from the shells in surprise.

Jameson pushed a callused hand through his longish brown hair. "There you are!"

"Where have you been?" Cole asked. "We heard you'd left town."

"I did."

Crestmont eyed him. "Pleasant Hill?"

"How did you guess?"

The duke shrugged. "You often have that expression on your face after a visit with your mother."

Evan was taken aback. Did he? Maybe a part of him had known all along that there was something not quite right with his relationship with the dowager.

Jameson frowned. "Are you all right, man?"

Cole put a reassuring hand on his shoulder. "Want to talk about it?"

He shook his head. He couldn't discuss what had happened with anyone. Not yet. "Let's just get out there."

Cole suggested a race, and Evan agreed. They took down the fast new boats that Jameson had designed last year, *Evie* and *Gray*, named after Crestmont's two children, and carried them out to the dock they'd built at the river's edge.

Energy thrummed under Evan's skin. He knew his boat would win no matter who he partnered with. He ended up teaming up with Cole in *Gray*, their most usual pairing, and when Jameson called it, he began to row.

Quickly, he slipped into the familiar cadence. Sitting with his back to Cole, he didn't have to focus as much as Cole did to keep them synchronized. He just rowed like hell against the steady current of the Thames, keeping Jameson and Crestmont's shell in sight, even as they steadily inched ahead of the two other men.

Soon he was deep into the rhythm, loving the way his chest and arms burned and sweat broke out over his body only to be cooled by the wind as they skimmed over the surface of the water.

His mind cleared. His body was on fire. He felt like he was flying. Like nothing could bother him now, nothing could muddle his mind.

Evan understood why he'd hardly been able to leave his bed at Pleasant Hill. He had been in mourning. He had been grieving for his lost childhood with a mother he didn't know and for the mother he'd loved throughout his life despite her coldness. Now he knew that his and the dowager's familial relationship—as flimsy as it was—was over, once and for all.

He was illegitimate. Which meant that he wasn't the Earl of Winthrop, not really. He was plain Evan Locke...or... no, that wasn't right. Locke was his father's surname, but he was illegitimate, so he should use his mother's name. He was Evan MacPherson, bastard son of Mark Locke, the Earl of Winthrop.

His whole life had been a lie. In the space of an instant, his identity had been obliterated.

So what was he to do now? Walk away from the titles he'd held and the legacy he'd been raised to honor for thirty-four years? Begin anew, as someone he didn't even know?

Would that be the right thing to do? Probably. How could he be so selfish as to hold on to something that had never truly been his?

"Oy!" Cole called behind him. "We won, man. You can slow down now."

Evan blinked out of his reverie. Had they really already gone five miles? He looked overhead, and sure enough, he saw they were indeed in the shadow of one of the arches of the Kew Bridge.

Crestmont and Jameson pulled up beside them and immediately stopped rowing, leaning forward, their chests heaving with exertion. Evan barely felt winded.

"I think we should race back," he said. "What do you say?"

Crestmont shot him a baleful look. Jameson's expression was more irritable. Evan sighed. "Fine, then. A leisurely row back to the boathouse."

They did just that, their rowing slow and casual though

the boats traveled at a good clip now that they weren't fighting the current. The four of them took in all the new construction on the banks of the Thames but hardly spoke. They had rowed together for so long and had developed such an understanding of the way one another operated on the water, there really was no need to speak. Conversations could wait. Now was the time for enjoying their favorite pastime.

When they reached the boathouse dock, they gathered the shells and carried them back into the boathouse where they used clean cloths to wipe away the sheen of grime left on the boats by the fetid river water.

"So," Jameson said to Evan as they worked, "no gloating today, eh? No comments about how elderly Crest and I are?"

It was a joke between the four of them—at two years older than Evan and Cole, Jameson and Crestmont were the old men of the group.

"Haven't felt much like joking in the past few days."

"You do seem a fair bit grimmer than usual," Cole said.

Jameson frowned. "Usually, you're not grim at all."

Crestmont took Evan's soiled piece of toweling and handed him a fresh one. "What happened with your mother?"

Evan kept his eyes on the line of scum he was rubbing off. "It didn't go well."

"Why did you go to see your mother anyhow?" Cole asked. "You usually avoid such encounters unless necessary."

He wasn't ready to tell his friends about his mother's revelation. But he could tell them the reason he'd gone to begin with.

"Apparently"—he took a deep, fortifying breath—"I have a brother."

He told them about the letter that had led to his visit to

Pleasant Hill. When he finished, the boat cleaning had been forgotten, and they were staring at him.

"Jesus Christ," Jameson muttered under his breath.

Cole whistled. "That would be a damned uncomfortable topic to broach with one's mother under any circumstance."

"It was uncomfortable. Very." Even though the dowager and Evan hadn't ended up talking about that letter at all. He hadn't ended up asking her about S. Dickens because it seemed like such a small thing in light of the other news he was suddenly, unexpectedly contending with.

But he couldn't tell his friends any of that. He just wasn't ready. As much as they'd shared over the years, as much as he trusted them, the fact was, he wasn't who he'd claimed to be throughout the entire length of their acquaintance. He needed to come to terms with it in his own mind before sharing it with them.

"What did your mother say?" Crestmont asked. "Did she confirm or deny?"

"She wouldn't speak of it." It wasn't quite a lie.

Jameson crossed his arms, his scowl drawing his brows together. "Two hundred pounds a year for 'maintenance?' Sounds more like blackmail—you give this Thomason fellow the funds, and he'll keep quiet about the previous earl's illegitimate son."

"That's exactly what I thought."

Cole scratched his head, frowning. "Given your father's reputation, anyone would believe he fathered a bastard. It would be no surprise if Thomason invented the boy just to extort money from the earl."

"There might be a way to find out for certain," Jameson said. "Thomason might have proof, but if he doesn't, there could be a record somewhere."

"At the church where the lad was christened, perhaps," Cole said.

Evan rubbed his temple. "I suppose my next step is to visit Harlowe's Home for Boys and see what this is all about."

"I'll go with you," Jameson said.

"So will I," Cole and Crestmont said in unison.

Evan held up his hand. "Thank you, but no. This is something I must do on my own."

Chapter Seven

Rule ten: Suffer the consequences with your head held high.

Rule ten, Frances thought, might be the most difficult of them all.

She had tried to be patient, but she had been confined to the house for a week and a half. Her brother possessed a temper that burned and then sputtered and disappeared. The scandal, though, had flared for days, keeping Charles in a state of agitation for a longer period than Frances had ever seen. According to Esther, Frances's ruination was the talk of the ton, with ladies chattering about it in their drawing rooms and men gossiping over their card games at their clubs.

Frances spent the time developing her plan. She was going to try out each of her potential vocations in a deeper sense. She'd hired music and drawing masters, and Charles's wife, Lilly, had brought her academic texts on botany, astronomy, geology, and physiology. She'd started writing a novel about a young woman trapped for years in a prison of a house and planning a daring escape. Finally, she had contacted two large children's charities in London to see if they were interested in obtaining a genteel patron, not to give them money—of which she had none—but to help in a more active sense.

As for travel, she'd begun to dream up her first trip: to the Lake District, where she'd spent the happy days of childhood with her brother and sisters on the banks of Lake Windermere. It was far too early to ask Charles about such a journey when he wouldn't even let her leave the house, but she would do so as soon as he calmed down.

She'd begun a list of items she might sell as a shopkeeper, but none had really piqued her imagination:

Hats (but who would make them?)
Sweets (but who would bake them?)
Clocks (would need a connection to a clockmaker)
Perfumes (would need a connection to a perfume-maker)
Dry goods (…no)

It seemed like most of her ideas would require some kind of partnership with an expert in the good provided, and she had no such connections. She decided to return to this later.

She spent some time considering taking up sewing and embroidery, but the more she did so, the more she thought about seamstresses becoming blind, their fingers swollen and arthritic after years and years of sewing in dim light.

As she sat at her desk after breakfast, her pen poised above the paper, where she'd written exactly one and a half pages of her novel, *Trapped at Westerly Manor*, there was a tap on her door.

"Come in."

It was Barker, one of the footmen. "You've received a letter, miss." He held it out to her.

A few years ago, Charles hadn't been able to afford the footmen, and he'd had to let them all go. Now, however, after the influx of coin from his wife's architectural designs, their household had as much staff as they'd ever need.

Lilly was an architecture genius, the buildings she created modern and striking, but as far as Frances knew, she had never once received credit for any of her designs. Instead, the acclaim had gone to the men who'd hired her.

Lilly didn't seem to care much about her lack of fame. Instead, she was content to see her visions developing into reality. That was how much she loved what she did.

If only Frances could find something like that.

"Thank you, Barker." Happy to take her attention away from the novel that already seemed resistant to being written, Frances took the proffered note. As Barker left, she slipped her finger under the seal and unfolded it.

4th of May, 1820
Miss Cherrington,
We were delighted to receive your offer to volunteer at our home. In fact, we have found ourselves in great need of someone in possession of a genteel upbringing to assist some of the boys in learning proper manners and deportment.

If you would do us the honor of calling upon us today, at one o'clock in the afternoon, we would be pleased to receive you.

Yrs Sincerely,
Thos. Thomason
Harlowe's Home for Boys

She folded the letter and laid it on her desk. Fortunately, Charles was gone for the day, and if Frances had a chance of anyone in this household being sympathetic to her position, it was Lilly.

She found her sister-in-law in the nursery, where she sat on the floor rolling a ball to her eighteen-month-old son, Arthur. Frances lowered herself behind her nephew and pulled him onto her lap so she could help him to pass the ball back to his mama. He giggled when she tickled his sides and pressed a kiss to his cherubic round cheek.

Speaking over Arthur's downy hair, she got right to the point, a habit of hers that put off so many. Fortunately, by now, Lilly was used to it.

"Lilly, I have decided to pursue a charitable endeavor, and I was wondering if you would like to join me."

"What charitable endeavor is that?" Lilly asked.

"I have decided to become a patron of an orphanage."

"In Lambeth with Mary and the reverend?"

Mary and her husband, the reverend Robinson, had recently opened their own home for orphans—The Lambeth Home for Waifs and Strays.

"No, the place I plan to go to has no affiliation with theirs. It is a boys' home and, since I am not in a position to support their endeavors financially, they have asked me to assist in teaching the boys."

Seeing the look of disbelief on her sister-in-law's face, she asked, "What is it? I am quite good with children, you know."

She had three nephews—besides Arthur, Mary had two sons, Joseph and Timothy. All three adored their Aunt Frances.

"You possess a rare skill with children, Frances." Lilly

rolled the ball back to them. Frances caught it and gave it to Arthur. "I've witnessed it firsthand. But I daresay you haven't had much experience with the types of boys you might encounter at a London orphanage."

Frances shrugged. Boys were boys, weren't they?

"Not only will many of them be somewhat older than this one"—Lilly smiled at her son then continued—"but they have, most probably, been exposed to the harshest and roughest conditions possible."

"Oh, I know that," Frances said breezily. She wasn't so sheltered that she'd never laid eyes upon the urchins who prowled London's streets day and night. She wasn't concerned about young rapscallions—she was actually looking forward to engaging with them. "I'll be perfectly fine. And"—she gave the ball, which had rolled to the side, back to Arthur—"what a boon it will be for the poor lads to learn manners from someone who has been rebelling against manners for the past five-and-twenty years."

Lilly's uncertain expression made a kernel of doubt sneak in. Was she being too confident? Perhaps she was. Children didn't frighten her but, judging from Lilly's skepticism, perhaps they should.

Well, she'd find out soon enough. Hopefully. "Anyhow, I was wondering if you'd like to join me. I am scheduled to arrive at one o'clock."

After a long pause, Lilly responded in a quiet voice. "Frances. You know Charles has forbidden you from leaving the house."

Drat.

Frances shrugged lightly. "That is only because he doesn't want me to show my face in society right now. I will be at Harlowe's Home for Boys, as far from society as one can venture without leaving London altogether."

Still, Lilly hesitated, a frown marring her brow. "I wouldn't be surprised if the gossip about you has reached all corners of London, including that one."

Frances straightened. "Then I will stand tall and endure their stares. Please, Lilly. I won't get into any trouble. I swear, if I am stuck here another day thinking about my disgrace, my head will explode. Don't you think this silly penance has lasted long enough?"

Lilly pressed her lips together. Frances had a feeling she agreed, but Lilly was not the type of woman to openly contradict a decree her husband had made.

This was yet another reason Frances had no desire to marry. What kind of life was it when one felt inhibited from expressing their true opinion? She shuddered. She could never live that way. The repression of being a married woman would probably kill her.

It was a good thing she'd escaped it.

Finally, Lilly looked away. "I'm sorry, but I cannot join you this afternoon. I have a meeting with Mr. Nash at half past one."

Mr. Nash was the much-lauded architect of the king... and one of the men who took credit for Lilly's brilliance.

Frances had to admit, however, that Mr. Nash was also the reason they lived in the comfortable style they did. She did appreciate him for what he'd done for their family. At the same time, she despised him for not openly celebrating Lilly as she deserved.

"But," Lilly continued slowly, "you could take Peggy with you, perhaps."

Frances's heart jumped into her throat. Lilly had given her permission to take her maid, which meant she wasn't going to stop her from going!

Frances made a silly face at Arthur, who chortled, before she said, "I'm sorry you cannot come. Perhaps next time I go you won't be busy."

"Perhaps not." Lilly smiled. "Be safe, Frances. I want to hear all about it."

Chapter Eight

At one o'clock precisely, Frances and Peggy were beckoned into the office of Mr. Thomas Thomason.

Located in the heart of St. Giles, Harlowe's Home for Boys was a sprawling building that encompassed half the block, its coal-blackened brick façade making the place appear somber and serious, even with the spring sun brightening the sky to a peony blue overhead. Inside, the long corridor smelled dank as they passed rows of closed doors, and all Frances could hear were the distant sounds of harsh adult tones doling out commands, and below that, something that sounded like weeping.

She had regretted coming the moment she set foot in this bleak place, yet she forced herself forward, one foot in front of the other. From the odor to the sounds to the filthy walls and dark corners to the way her shoes seemed to stick to the layer of grime on the floor, all her senses screamed at her that something was wrong here. It was nothing like the orphanage

Mary and the reverend had founded, which was clean, bright, and airy, and while Mary and her husband were somewhat sterner than Frances might have been, the children were well-fed, well-dressed, and happy.

Thomason's office was cluttered and dark, a small window behind his desk letting in the only light. The man himself, thin with wisps of graying hair and a yellow-tinted complexion, rose when they entered.

He looked her over, and Frances could tell from his expression alone that he'd read the caricature in the broadsheet. A slight smile curled his lips. An *inviting* smile.

Did this man really think that because she'd kissed one man there was a chance she'd want to kiss him, too?

Disgusting.

She straightened her spine and stared back at him as *un*invitingly as she could.

"Miss Cherrington." His voice dripped syrup. "Thank you *so much* for coming."

Firm. Businesslike. Let him know what you're here for and be clear that it's for nothing else.

Frances didn't want to be alone with this man. Ever. She was grateful Peggy was here with her and even more grateful that her maid had sidled up to her until their arms were pressed together. Peggy was only eighteen years old. Slight, short, and timid, she had mousy brown hair and small eyes set close together in her round face. All in all, she was far less intimidating than a footman would be standing at Frances's side. Still, Frances hoped she'd be a deterrent against this man attempting anything untoward.

"Good afternoon, Mr. Thomason," she said in a clipped voice. "My companion and I are eager to assist *the boys* who reside here."

Only the boys. She wanted nothing to do with him. She kept her stern gaze on him, and he met her eyes for a moment, then looked away, clearing his throat.

"Wonderful. That is just wonderful." He riffled through a pile of papers on his desk before looking up at her again. "I had quite a specific task in mind for you today…"

She narrowed her eyes at him, and he finished quickly. "Involving one of the children." He walked around his desk. "I'll take you to him directly. It's a simple matter, really, but this particular boy can be…well, somewhat obstinate at times."

Frances raised a brow. Obstinate. She was quite familiar with the descriptor as it had been lobbed toward her several times in the past.

"Please follow me." He led her out into the corridor, Peggy trailing behind them, lifting her skirts and hurrying to keep up with their longer strides. "The child's name is Robert Dickens, and he has resided at Harlowe's Home for the past six years. He is seven years of age."

Frances nodded. Seven. Older than she was accustomed to, but if she could manage a toddler, a seven-year-old would be far easier, she was sure.

Thomason continued, "Most happily and fortuitously, he has acquired a particular patron from the highest level of society."

"Oh?" Now, this was interesting. She wondered if it was someone she knew.

"Indeed. What we require today is for young Robert to receive a brief education on the proper ways of addressing a lord. We wish for him to adequately represent Harlowe's

Home for Boys when he meets his patron face-to-face later this afternoon."

"I understand," she said, already scrolling through the etiquette in her mind. Bowing, showing proper deference, speaking only when spoken to, the use of "my lord," and "sir," etcetera, etcetera.

"Excellent," Mr. Thomason said. "I have instructed him to be brought to a private room, so you will be able to focus on his study."

With that, Mr. Thomason paused at one of the closed doors. He knocked lightly, then, when there was no answer, pulled it open.

The room was utterly bare except for a small, dirt-encrusted window letting in a bit of dim light, and two rickety wooden chairs facing each other in its center.

Mr. Thomason sighed loudly. "It seems he has not arrived yet. Most of the boys are in the play yard now, but I imagine Robert must still be in the dormitory."

The play yard? Frances had heard that many orphanages put children to work at young ages. Perhaps Harlowe's Home for Boys wasn't so bad after all.

"Please wait here, Miss Cherrington. I'll go fetch him myself." Mr. Thomason stepped around Frances and Peggy and strode briskly away, Frances watching from the doorway.

Turning the corner and heading toward Mr. Thomason, a threesome appeared—a young, burly man and an older, tired-looking woman bracketing a small boy. Dressed in a costume of rags so filthy and tattered Frances wondered how they remained on his body, the child squirmed against the firm grip of the man who held his upper arm so tightly Frances was certain his grip would leave bruises in the shapes of his meaty fingers. The woman carried a bundle of clothes.

Mr. Thomason slowed. "What is this?"

The woman looked worried. "I'm sorry, sir, but I couldn't get 'im into these."

Mr. Thomason frowned down at the boy. "Why not?"

"He said they cause him pain."

Mr. Thomason made an ugly noise. "What say you, boy? Do you not wish to wear these lovely new clothes Mrs. Vestry has offered you?"

The child glowered at the man. Even from several doors down, Frances could see the most intriguing eyes peering out from his horrendously dirty face. They were not quite orange and not quite brown. They reminded her of the lion Frances had seen at an exhibition once, its eyes fierce and angry. The child's thick, curly mane of dirty blond hair only enhanced the impression.

"No!" he exclaimed, still trying—and failing—to wrench his skinny body away from the man. "I don't want 'em!"

Thomason's fists clenched at his sides, and Frances wondered if the reason he contained his ire was because he felt her watching from behind. What would he do if she wasn't there?

Honestly, she didn't want to think about it, but she imagined it would be something that wasn't very nice.

"Put him in the room," Thomason gritted out to the burly man.

"Aye, sir." The man hoisted the boy by the waist and trudged toward Frances, forcing her to step out of the way. The child fought like a little demon, clawing and punching—but his efforts were mainly directed at air.

Thomason held out his hands to the woman. "Give me

the clothes."

She gave him the bundle and Thomason dismissed her and followed the man and the boy into the room. Frances and Peggy exchanged a glance then hurried back inside as it dawned on Frances that this was *the* boy. Robert Dickens, seven years old.

The burly man literally tossed the flailing child away from him. Frances gasped, but it seemed that the boy was accustomed to being thrown about. He stumbled, rolled, then crouched on all fours, looking up at the adults, wild-eyed. He was quite small. He looked much younger than seven.

Thomason dropped the bundle of clothes onto one of the chairs. He loomed over the boy and looked down at him, his expression pinched with a cross between disgust and dislike before gesturing behind him in Frances's general direction. "This is Miss Cherrington. I expect you will treat her with courtesy and respect. If I hear otherwise—" Making a strange motion, sweeping his hand through the air as if he wielded a sword, he glared at the child, letting the threat hang until the little rascal gulped and nodded.

Mr. Thomason and the burly man strode out of the room. The child jumped up and sprinted after them, but the door was slammed shut in his face as he reached it. Frances heard a lock being turned on the other side.

Excellent. She'd left the prison of her home for a new kind of prison. She wondered how long she'd be locked in here with this untamed creature who'd turned and was glaring at her, rubbing his abused arm. Wisely, Peggy, face wrinkled in consternation, had retreated to a corner. Frances took a breath and gazed steadily at the boy.

"All right, Robert," she said, after they'd stared at each

other for about a minute—which felt like forever. "I am here to teach you proper—"

"I ain't Robert!" the child declared.

Frances raised her brows. "Oh?"

"I'm Bobby, not Robert. Robert's a *stupid* name."

"Oh, I see." She sat in the chair opposite the one holding the clothes, smoothing her skirts. "My Christian name is Frances. When I was a child, I insisted everyone call me Francesca, because it was a far more exotic and beautiful name than dull old Frances. So I understand completely. If you wish to be called Bobby, then Bobby you shall be. But I would request that you call me Miss Cherrington."

The child stared at her, and in a businesslike manner, she removed her bonnet and set it aside. As she began to remove a glove, finger by finger, she saw from the corner of her eye that he was inching closer.

"I expect you'd rather be in the play yard than here," she said. "I can't say I blame you."

"Play yard?" He frowned. "What's that?"

"Where the children are outside playing right now."

He looked at her as if he deemed her of very low intelligence. "There ain't no children playing."

"No? But Mr. Thomason said—"

"We don't *play*."

So Thomason had been lying. She was less surprised than she ought to be. "What do you do, then? When you are outside?"

"We work."

"What kind of work?"

"We all do different things, but I deliver the coal and such, mostly."

Frances frowned. The child was *seven*. "Who do you deliver coal to?"

He blinked at her. "Everyone."

"Everyone?" How could that be? "Do you mean everyone in London?"

He nodded proudly. "That's right. Everyone in all of London."

Obviously, one small child was not delivering coal to every single inhabitant of London. But the fact that he thought he did said a great deal.

"Well, then. I suppose it is good I am here. Because it means you do not need to deliver coal today. You have the afternoon off."

He gnawed on his lip, gazing at her warily with those bright, orange-tinted eyes as if he didn't quite understand the meaning of "afternoon off."

"Now, as I see it," Frances went on, "we have a few critical tasks to accomplish. The first is getting you out of that filthy shirt."

He took a big step back, glowering. "It's *my* shirt."

"Be that as it may, it is torn, and furthermore, it stinks. Would you like to go about life scaring people off because you reek of rotten fruit?"

Honestly, the smell was ghastly. Had this child been rolling in the pigsty?

She leaned forward, picking the whitish garment from the pile of clothes and shaking it out. It was a linen shirt, scratchy with starch. "Oh, yes. I see how this could be uncomfortable for you. I can't blame you for not wanting to wear it." She tossed it over her shoulder and retrieved the second item from the pile. "And these breeches"—she shuddered—"equally scratchy."

She tossed them away, too. "It appears we have run out of options." She shrugged. "I'm sorry, Bobby. You must continue to stink. It's quite unfortunate. I can hardly bear to be in the same room with you, ripe as you are."

Bobby scowled. "Ripe? Like…a lemon?"

"Like a lemon that's too old and brown and soft and covered in mold," she clarified.

He scrunched his nose. It was an adorable little nose, Frances decided, but it would be even more adorable if it wasn't so crusty. The child was in dire need of a bath.

"Well, hopefully, I will be able to bear you for a few moments longer. Do you know why I have come to visit you today?"

Bobby shook his head warily.

"It is because you are going to meet someone soon. He is a great lord, and you must learn how to behave properly in his presence."

"I don't want to."

"Well, that doesn't matter in the least. Sometimes, as much as we dislike it, we are forced to do things we don't wish to do." Like delivering coal to all of London, she thought. Surely that activity couldn't be high on the list of a seven-year-old's desires. "Do you know what I had to do last week?" she asked confidentially, leaning slightly in his direction.

He shook his head again.

"I had to go to a *ball*. And I was forced to dance with a gentleman I didn't like." She scrunched up her nose just like Bobby had a moment ago. "I didn't want to. But I had to." She sighed heavily. "It was terribly dull, and I had to hold his hand for a very long time, and his hand was quite…*fleshy*. But

I endured it." She smiled. "And now, because I did that, I am able to be here with you."

And, Lord, was she grateful to be here with this little urchin instead of on a ship bound for Egypt standing in the shadow of Mr. Salt.

She continued. "I know you don't want to, Bobby, but this man you are to meet—he is very important. And he might be able to give you things you wouldn't have otherwise."

"Like…chocolate?"

"Do you like chocolate?"

He nodded vigorously.

"So do I! Next time I see you, I shall be certain to bring you some."

"Really?"

"Really. And maybe, just maybe, the great lord might give you chocolate, as well."

His eyes widened, and he chewed on his lip. "Is it very hard to learn?"

"To greet a lord? Not at all," she promised. "I daresay this will be the simplest lesson you've ever learned." She had the notion, knowing what she did so far about this child, that he'd endured some harsh lessons she couldn't even imagine.

He glanced back at the door. "What about Mr. Thomason?"

"What about him?"

"Is he comin' back?"

"Eventually. But no matter what happens, I intend to tell him how good you've been and recommend that you be given an extra serving of your supper tonight." She had no idea if he'd find that appealing, but she couldn't think of much else to offer him.

He studied her for another long moment, then slowly nodded, his thin shoulders straightening under his filthy shirt. "Teach me, then."

...

Evan was irritated. He'd gone to Harlowe's Home for Boys yesterday morning and had been turned away with the excuse that the boys were busy with their lessons and couldn't be interrupted. From what he'd been able to observe of Harlowe's Home for Boys, he was more certain than ever that the two hundred pounds Thomason had demanded was a bribe, and that the man intended to pocket the money. None of it was intended for the "maintenance" of S. Dickens, or any of the residents of that unfortunate place.

Anger lashed through him at the thought that a boy who might or might not be his brother had been living in these conditions without Evan's knowledge.

Thomason had bade him return at five o'clock the following day, and, as much as he wanted to barge through the place and find the child, Evan had managed to wait until a quarter to four.

So when Mr. Thomason said he'd arrived too early and came up with yet another excuse as to why he couldn't see the child—apparently, he was occupied with his daily prayers in the chapel—it was all Evan could do not to string the man up by his toes then tear the place down, brick by brick.

Instead, he gave the man his most winning smile. "Alas, that is unacceptable. I pay for the maintenance of this child—"

Thomason raised a brow. "*This*...child?"

What was this man playing at? Evan's temper flared,

but he held himself in check. "Yes, *this* child. S. Dickens. Therefore, I have the right to interview him at any time I please."

"Well—"

Evan held up his hand. "I will see the boy now. Thank you."

Thomason looked furtively this way and that, then rose. "I shall personally fetch him from chapel, my lord. Wait here, if you please. I will bring him to you."

Evan sat for several minutes, shifting in the hard chair provided to him, then standing and pacing the little office. Finally, the door opened.

It took a moment for him to register what he was seeing. His gaze skimmed over the jaundiced appearance of Thomason, then locked on the two women who stood just behind him, one of them holding the hand of a young boy.

Frances Cherrington.

What the hell was she doing here?

She seemed equally surprised to see him. Her lips parted, and her eyes widened with shock. "Lord Winthrop?"

"My lord." Thomason's voice sounded like it came from far away. "This is Robert Dickens and one of his excellent tutors who volunteers here at Harlowe's Home, Miss Cherrington."

Of all the people in London, why did *she* have to be here? There was no way Frances Cherrington would let meeting under these circumstances go unexamined. She was going to ask questions that he couldn't—and wouldn't—answer.

Evan forced himself to focus on the child who gripped Frances's hand. The boy looked up at her as if wanting her to reassure him that he was safe. *Robert.* He turned the name over in his mind. *Robert* Dickens, not S. Dickens. Where had the "S" come from?

Then he and the boy locked eyes.

There was no doubt about it. Robert Dickens was his brother.

Chapter Nine

Of all the places she'd expect to run into the Earl of Winthrop, an orphanage was at the bottom of her list. What was *he* doing there?

The man in question gaped at the boy beside her in shock.

Frowning, she glanced between the earl and little Bobby Dickens, and her breath caught in her throat. The link between them was clear as day. Bobby was slight and small, his face rounded with youth, whereas Winthrop was tall and broad, his face chiseled and masculine.

But the eyes?

There was no denying it. Where Bobby's eyes were bright and striking like a lion cub's, Winthrop's were more muted, the eyes of a caged beast rather than a wild one. But the same unique amber hue lay under the outward color.

The earl had a son. And, judging by his horrified expression, the existence of the child had only very recently been revealed to him.

She pursed her lips. *Well, well, well. The perfect lord isn't perfect, after all.*

The silence extended until, from the corner of her eye, Frances saw Mr. Thomason squirming.

She cleared her throat. Then, extremely belatedly, she curtsied, squeezing Bobby's hand so he would notice and hopefully, follow it up with a bow of his own. "Good afternoon, my lord."

Bobby—quick learner that he was—gave a little bow.

"May I present Bobby Dickens. Bobby," she said formally, "this is the Earl of Winthrop."

"It is. A pleasure. To meet you. My lord," Bobby said mechanically, an exact quote of what she'd taught him. *Good lad*, she thought with satisfaction. She beamed at him.

Winthrop visibly gathered himself. "Miss Cherrington." He looked Bobby up and down, then turned to Mr. Thomason. "I should like to speak to the boy in private."

"Of course, sir. We have a room set aside for just that purpose. Please follow me."

Frances wasn't surprised when the man stopped at the door to the sparsely furnished room she, Bobby, and Peggy had just vacated. "Here you are, my lord."

"Thank you." Winthrop stepped inside, and when Frances attempted to release Bobby's hand, he gripped it harder, looking at her with imploring eyes she could easily translate. *"Please,"* they told her. *"Don't leave me alone with this strange man."*

She'd only known the boy a few hours but, apparently, *she* no longer qualified as a stranger. She nodded. "I will be present for the interview," she informed the men.

Both of them looked at her in surprise.

"Miss Cherrington," Thomason began rudely, "Lord Winthrop expressly requested a *private* interview."

Frances gazed at the earl evenly, giving Bobby's hand a reassuring squeeze.

The earl's face was paler than she'd ever seen it. He looked from Frances to Bobby to their tightly clasped hands. His throat bobbed as he swallowed.

Clearly, Winthrop didn't know whether to trust her. He'd implied as much at the masquerade. In this instance, she couldn't really blame him. If she were one of the Backbiting Biddies, she'd rush straight to the gossip columnists with this juicy tidbit. But she wasn't like them. She might not like the man, but the Earl of Winthrop's secret—illicit as it might be—was safe with her.

He shifted from foot to foot, finally asking, "May I trust in your discretion, Miss Cherrington?"

She raised her brows at him. "You may."

He gave another nervous swallow, then nodded tightly. "Very well. But *only* you, Miss Cherrington. Everyone else must remain outside the room."

Frances glanced at Peggy, whose gaze flickered between her and Winthrop. Finally, she relented and nodded. After having spent time with Bobby Dickens, Peggy must know as well as Frances that nothing untoward would be happening in any room where the seven-year-old was present.

"I'll be just outside, miss," she promised.

Thomason stepped out after Peggy, closing the door firmly behind them, this time refraining from locking them inside. Of course, he wouldn't dare lock the earl anywhere, while it had clearly been a simple decision to lock the door when it had been just her and Bobby.

It was another example of a man's careless attitude toward a woman's freedom.

Winthrop stood at the center of the room near one of the chairs, his hands clasped behind his back as he studied them. Bobby still gripped her hand firmly.

The earl addressed her first, his voice as congenial as always. "Have you been volunteering here for long, Miss Cherrington?"

"Today is my first day, my lord." And, if Bobby wasn't here, it would be her last. Everything about this place made her shudder, and the scars she'd seen on Bobby's back—well, those had been enough to make her want to burn this place down and see Mr. Thomason and every adult here prosecuted for treating innocent children like this.

"I see." The earl looked down at the boy. She looked at Bobby, too. He had finally submitted to being dressed in his new clothes—clearly, Thomason had wanted him to dress in these garments to impress the earl.

She'd experienced a fast-growing fondness for Bobby. He was wary and frightened, and she understood why—she'd feel the same way in his situation. But as their time together stretched on, they'd both relaxed, and now he felt comfortable enough with her not only to agree to wear the scratchy new clothes but to want her at his side as he faced the earl.

Winthrop turned to Bobby. "So, Miss Cherrington is your new friend, is she?"

The boy lifted his stubborn little chin. "She's going to give me chocolate."

"Chocolate?" Winthrop turned to Frances. "How generous of you."

"Bobby likes chocolate and so do I," Frances said lightly.

"Next time I visit, we will share some, won't we, Bobby?"

He nodded vigorously.

"Well," the earl said, "as it happens, I am also quite fond of chocolate. Perhaps we should share it between the three of us."

Bobby scowled. "No. Just me and Miss Cherrington."

Frances fought a smile at the earl's surprised look. Like her, this boy wasn't going to bow to Winthrop's every whim like the rest of the world did. "Sorry, my lord. It will be just enough for the two of us."

"Well, then. What if I brought double the amount next time? Then, would you be inclined to share?"

Frances reluctantly admitted that she liked him asking Bobby rather than her. The boy pondered for a second and then said, "Maybe."

She watched the earl's smile slowly slip away while he studied Bobby, who still maintained his grip on her hand.

"Robert—" Winthrop began gravely.

"Bobby!" the boy exclaimed, stomping his foot impatiently. "I'm *Bobby*!"

Frances braced for Winthrop's scowl and stern correction. He surprised her by nodding. "My apologies, Bobby. I have something to tell you, lad. I'm not certain what you will think of it, but I wish to be honest about why I have come to see you."

Bobby frowned at him.

Good Lord. Was he about to tell Bobby that he was his father? Just like that? And in her presence, no less?

The earl's eyes flicked to her, then he took a deep breath and lowered himself to one knee before them. "Lad. I am..." The earl sucked in another breath. Then, staring straight into the boy's lion eyes, he said solemnly, "I am your brother."

Frances gasped.

His *brother*? Not his father? She quickly reshaped the relationship between them in her mind. It made sense, really. The previous Earl of Winthrop had been a notorious philanderer. Could it be that the current earl only recently discovered Bobby's existence and he'd come to meet the boy?

Most men, upon learning of such a relationship, would ignore it or even bury it. But Winthrop was here, lowering himself to Bobby's level and sharing the truth with a vulnerability in his expression she'd never seen before. It was unexpected and a bit overwhelming to take in.

"We don't have the same mother," he continued, "but our father was the Earl of Winthrop."

"No, *you're* the Earl of Winthrop," Bobby said.

"You are correct. I am the *new* earl because our father has died, and…" He trailed off. "The point is, we have the same father, and that makes us brothers."

Bobby stared at him, then shook his head vigorously, curls bouncing. "No."

Winthrop's brows rose. "It is true—"

"No, it ain't. 'Cause you're too old to be my brother. And I already have a brother, anyhow."

Winthrop jerked back in surprise, which was a good thing because it distracted him from the indelicate way Frances's mouth fell open. "You do?" he asked.

Bobby nodded once, dropping her hand to fold his thin arms across his chest.

The earl appeared dazed. He'd lost all trace of his usual cheerful confidence. She felt sorry for him, which was entirely unacceptable, given her general opinion of the man.

A long silence ensued, the boy staring at the man with a mutinous expression, a seemingly speechless Winthrop gazing back, his eyes shining, lips parted but no words emerging.

She couldn't imagine the level of shock he must be experiencing.

To break the extended quiet, Frances asked, "What is your brother's name, Bobby?"

"Jasper."

"Jasper," the earl murmured.

"Aye. *He's* my brother. *Not* you."

Winthrop stood and abruptly turned away.

Oh dear.

Frances cleared her throat. "Is Jasper here? At Harlowe's Home?"

Bobby shook his head. "No. He left last year 'cause he became a big boy. You can't stay here when you're a big boy. You've got to fend for yourself."

"Oh? How old is he?"

"Twelve, I think."

Her mouth fell open again. "Boys are sent away at *twelve*?"

"*Eleven*," Bobby corrected, a proud tinge to his voice. "You're a big boy when you're *eleven*. Jasper—he's twelve now, and he's a good hard worker."

Winthrop turned back to the boy, blinking away an edge of panic in his eyes. "Is his name Dickens, like yours?"

"Aye," Bobby said. "And we look exactly the same! So everyone knows we're brothers soon as they set eyes on us."

This final shock seemed too much for the earl. He sank down into one of the chairs, head in hands.

Frances squeezed Bobby's shoulder gently. "Do you know where he is?"

"At the docks." Bobby puffed his little chest out. "He sees lots of big ships, and he says we might sail away on one, one day. He comes to see me sometimes. He brought me chocolate once."

"Does he come to visit you often?" Frances asked.

"Every Sunday," Bobby said. "Jasper'll take me from this place soon. He promised. And then, when he goes on the big ship, I can go with him."

"Do you wish to leave Harlowe's Home?" Frances asked him.

Bobby shrugged.

At that non-answer, Winthrop lifted his head abruptly, seeming to snap out of his shock. "Are they cruel here?"

Frances thought of how the burly man had literally tossed Bobby into this room as if he were a sack of grain. Then she thought of the scars on his back. They were *definitely* cruel here.

"Sometimes they beat us. If we're very bad. I'm bad a *lot*. And…" Bobby grimaced. "Sometimes they make us take baths."

"Well, baths aren't so terrible, now, are they?" Frances said.

The boy gave her a baleful look.

Winthrop's jaw tightened and his lips firmed. "We're leaving," he said. "You're coming home with me, Bobby. Right now."

"Now?" Bobby took a big step back, his eyes round as saucers.

"Now."

"But Jasper won't know where I've gone off to."

"I'll send word to him."

This didn't convince Bobby. He reached for Frances's hand and gripped it even tighter.

Winthrop came to them and knelt to bring himself eye to eye with the little boy again, and Frances blinked at the unguarded tenderness in his expression. "Have you ever ridden in a carriage?"

"No," Bobby said doubtfully.

"Well, would you like to ride in mine?"

Bobby hesitated, then glanced at Frances, who gave him what she hoped was an encouraging look, then back at the earl. "Only if Miss Cherrington comes."

Winthrop's eyes went to her again.

Frances had no wish to spend more time than necessary in the earl's presence. She turned to Bobby. "It's all right. You'll be—"

"Miss Cherrington will come, too," Winthrop declared. "And her maid, as well."

Frances snapped her mouth shut and glared at Winthrop. How like him to just assume she'd follow his every command. Surely he knew by now she wasn't one of those sycophants who dogged his heels, eager to bask in his charm.

The earl seemed impervious to her irritation. "Are you ready, lad?" he asked.

Bobby hesitated.

Frances crouched down between man and boy. As annoyed as she was at the earl's audacity, his home couldn't be as bad as this place. Darkness leaked from the walls here. "Lord Winthrop has as much chocolate as you'd ever want," she told Bobby. "And he will never, ever beat you." She narrowed her eyes at Winthrop. "Isn't that right, my lord?"

"Never, ever," he agreed, his voice solemn.

"There. You see?"

"But…what if Jasper doesn't find me?" Bobby asked, his eyes roving from Frances to Winthrop and back again.

"I will make certain he does," Winthrop said.

"Promise?"

"I promise."

"And if he cannot find Jasper, then I shall," Frances said.

Bobby looked at Frances. "Will you come, too?"

Frances pursed her lips. She'd do this for Bobby, *not* the earl. "Yes. I'll come."

Bobby hesitated, but something in their countenances must have told him it would be all right because he finally nodded.

"Let's go." Winthrop rose and took Bobby's free hand in his own.

Hand in hand, the three of them left the room, Peggy following as they walked down the corridor toward the exit. As they neared the door, though, someone behind them exclaimed, "Oy! Where're you goin'?"

Frances glanced back to see Thomason's henchman at the far end of the corridor. The three of them walked faster, Bobby at a jog to keep up the pace.

Moments later, they burst into the sunlight of the street, Peggy right behind them.

"This way," Winthrop said, leading them around the corner.

There, a coach and four awaited them, Winthrop's crest on the door. Before the coachman had a chance to get off the box, Winthrop yanked open the door and held out his hand to Frances. With a pointed look—had they been in any other circumstance, she'd have found a way to avoid his touch—she allowed him to hand her in. Bobby and Peggy scrambled in after her. To the coachman, Winthrop commanded, "Home. Now."

Since Bobby and Peggy had sat on the opposite bench, Winthrop took the seat beside her, his body pressing against her in an intimate way she refused to think about. She also refused to think about the way his strong, firm grip as he'd helped her into the carriage made something inside her flutter. That didn't mean her body didn't think about it, though.

She felt alert, on fire.

Traitorous, foolish body. Falling for his charms like every other simpering miss when she knew better. She scoffed out loud, and when Winthrop sent her a questioning look, she raised her brows at him in challenge. They both looked away, and within seconds, they were off at a gallop, leaving Harlowe's Home for Boys like a bad memory behind them.

Chapter Ten

The boy was positively feral. After three days with his brother, Evan was about to pull out his hair with frustration.

He refused to bathe.

He refused to sit down at a table and eat with a knife and fork.

He refused to change his clothes.

He refused to allow anyone to comb his wild blond curls.

He seemed to have no appreciation for the fact that Evan had saved him from a life of filth, poor nutrition, and ill treatment. Instead, he glared at Evan as if he were the enemy.

"Where's Miss Cherrington?" he demanded for the hundredth time in three days. The nurse Evan had hired gazed at him, her face blanched, while the two maids Evan had asked to remain with Bobby this morning looked on with interest. "I want Miss Cherrington!"

"Miss Cherrington," Evan said, trying to keep his voice even, "does not live here."

"I don't care!" the boy yelled. "You said you'd find Jasper. Where's my brother?"

He rushed for the bedchamber door, but Evan blocked it with his body. Guarding the door handle, Evan took a steadying breath. He needed help, but for God's sake, Frances Cherrington already knew far too much about his private life. As soon as they'd parted after bringing Bobby home, Evan had vowed to keep his distance from her from now on, no matter how entertaining he'd previously found her prickliness to be. If she pointed those barbs at him now, he was simply too overwhelmed to handle it.

Still, she'd been perfect with Bobby. Patient. Truthful. Supportive. Forthcoming. Evan had tried to emulate her, but Bobby wasn't having it.

The truth was, his brother didn't trust him. He didn't even *like* him.

"Bobby, I need to go now. You stay with Miss…er—" Damn. This was the third woman he'd hired to help him with the boy.

"Hastings," the woman supplied.

"Miss Hastings."

Bobby sent her a withering glance.

"I'll send up some chocolate," Evan promised. "And Miss Hastings will take you up to the nursery. You might find some of my old toys up there."

Bobby hesitated. "Are they good toys?"

"Quite good," Evan promised.

Finally, Bobby grumbled an assent.

Someone knocked on the door. "My lord?"

It was Franklin, Evan's butler. "What is it?" Evan asked over his shoulder.

"You have a caller, my lord."

Thank God. It had to be the elusive Jasper Dickens he'd been hunting for the past few days. Yesterday, his agent had found the youth at a workhouse near the docks. The boy hadn't been able to leave his post—breaking stones in the back of the enormous building—but, since today was Sunday, he'd be given the morning off and had been promised a guinea should he show up at Evan's door this morning. If he didn't show, Evan planned to go fetch the lad himself.

Was this twelve-year-old another brother? It seemed likely, but Evan didn't want to jump to conclusions.

"I'll see you later, Bobby," Evan said, and slipped out.

"It's Miss Frances Cherrington," his aged butler said, his voice wavering as Evan closed the door behind him.

Evan released a breath. Not Jasper, then. Miss Cherrington, whom he really did not want to see right now. Probably coming to check on Bobby.

He would offer her his most pleasant smile and a short update—*Bobby is doing well, thank you*—and then send her on her merry way. "Very well. Show her to my study."

"Yes, my lord."

A few moments later, Franklin knocked on his study door, and Frances Cherrington stepped inside. Evan rose to greet her, looking past her for one of her sisters, or at least a maid. There was no one. Miss Cherrington was unchaperoned.

Instead of his usual polite greeting, he asked, "Where is your maid?" a little more sharply than he intended. He'd really rather not risk a lady's reputation on top of everything else he was managing right now.

Still, she didn't deserve his irritation. He took a steadying breath. This entire situation—his ornery brother, or possible *brothers*. His parentage. Frances Cherrington's presence. It was throwing him off-balance. His life was spiraling out of control.

He needed to hold onto his equanimity.

"I escaped," she replied before he could apologize.

He jerked back, all thoughts of equanimity abandoning him. At his expression of alarm, she scoffed. "Are you concerned about a scandal, my lord?"

"Well, yes, actually. I am."

"My reputation is no longer a concern."

"Of course it is," he shot back. A lady's reputation was *always* a concern.

She waved a dismissive hand. "And *your* reputation is perfectly safe. No one knows I am here, and no one saw me at the door, as I came in the back way. I generally don't leave my bedchamber until well after noon on Sundays, and everyone knows better than to interrupt my rest before then."

Goddamn. Frances Cherrington was in his house, alone, and talking openly about being unconcerned about her reputation. And about her bedchamber. Where she slept, scantily dressed, at night. Where her *bed* was located. Heat crawled up his neck, and he shifted uncomfortably. His butler was still hovering at the doorway, and he met the man's unflinching gaze. "That will be all, Franklin. Thank you."

When the door closed, he turned his focus back to Frances. "Isn't your brother-in-law a clergyman?" he asked suspiciously. "Don't you go to church on Sundays?"

"Not very often lately. Mind you, it is not that I have anything against church. It is just that my eldest sister used to drag me from bed before dawn every Sunday morning, and now that she is married, I am enjoying the opportunity for more sleep."

Evan narrowed his eyes. "Didn't she marry three years ago?"

"Has it been that long?" Frances shrugged. "It feels like yesterday. In any case, do not worry. Even if my presence here were discovered—and it won't be—my reputation is already damaged beyond repair. This indiscretion doesn't hold a candle to what I have already done."

He frowned. "What are you talking about?"

She eyed him. "You don't know?"

"I've been busy." Chasing after previously unknown members of his family, obviously.

"Ah." She nodded. "Still, I daresay you're the only person in society who hasn't heard of my embarrassing episode."

Frances Cherrington had an embarrassing episode? How could that be? He'd just seen her a few days ago. "What embarrassing episode?"

"You'll hear about it soon enough, I'm sure," she said.

He stared at her in confusion. Frances had just reprimanded him for thinking she'd rashly sacrifice her standing in society. Now she was saying her standing had already been compromised, and yet she didn't seem upset in the least. "Well, it can't be that bad."

"Oh, but it can."

"Now you're making me curious. Are you going to tell me what happened?"

"I'd rather not."

She had put on a proud mask, but was that a bit of a flush creeping across her cheeks? "I'd rather hear the truth from the source."

She met his gaze, her expression dry. "I am sorry to

disappoint you, my lord, by not submitting to your every whim. I request that you refrain from discussing this topic any further. I'm merely here to ensure you haven't harmed Bobby."

He ground his teeth.

Be polite, an inner voice warned. *Smile and brush it off, like you always do.*

Forget it. His usual cheerfulness had fled sometime between learning he was illegitimate, the visit to Harlowe's Home for Boys, and Frances Cherrington's arrival today. "My brother's wellbeing is no concern of yours."

Her eyes narrowed. "I am here because I have no confidence in your ability to care for a child. You are a charming bachelor, *not* a father."

"Did you just call me charming?" Irritated as he was, he couldn't let that slip go.

She threw up her hands, then crossed her arms tightly. "I'm serious, Winthrop. I need to see Bobby. I need to ensure he is all right."

She must be serious, since she hadn't added a "Lord" before his title.

He sank into his desk chair, the energy draining from him. She'd likely take that as a great insult—men never sat in a lady's presence unless the lady herself was seated. But he was damned exhausted. He rubbed his forearm over his brow. "That child is…" He swallowed hard. "A *monster*."

Instant righteous anger darkened her face. "He is not! How dare you call him such!"

"Because he is," he said. "In your presence he was… well, he behaved like a human. Likely overwhelmed by your hypnotic beauty." Her mouth opened to interrupt him, but he continued. "However, the instant I tore him out of your arms, he transformed into a little terror. I've had to employ servants to watch him day and night for fear he'll escape. They have reported back to me that his behavior is quite beyond their control."

"He is frightened." She gave him a hard look. "Have you, or has anyone in this house, been cruel to him?"

"Absolutely not." And he could say that with absolute certainty. He'd forbidden his staff to lose their temper with the boy and had kept two of his most conscientious servants with Bobby at all times.

"And what of his brother Jasper?"

"I found him just yesterday and he is supposed to arrive today. If he doesn't, I'm going to the docks to fetch him myself."

"I'll go with you."

Like hell she would. He didn't want her within a five-mile radius of the place where that workhouse was located.

"You will not," he said. She was poking her nose into business that she had nothing to do with, and he couldn't risk any more of it. He needed to reel this conversation back. "As I said, my brother is not your concern, Miss Cherrington. None of this is."

"Of course it's my concern!"

Frustration burned through him. Frances had met Bobby only a short time before he had. It didn't matter that the boy had been quick to trust her while he was still wary of Evan. *She* wasn't his brother.

He took a deep breath and tried again. "I am sorry you have become involved in this, but it is a family matter, and your continued concern is unnecessary."

She pursed her lips and studied him for a long moment. "There is something I don't understand," she finally said.

"What's that?"

"Why didn't you retrieve him from that horrid place earlier?"

Evan sighed, but she went on. "Did you learn of his existence only recently? The night of the masquerade, perhaps? Was that why you said you needed a diversion?"

He stood abruptly, went to the sidebar, and poured himself a brandy. He had already brought Frances Cherrington far enough into his confidence—he hadn't been offered a choice in the matter. Now, she wanted to know even more.

Could he let her in further?

Did he want to?

He tilted a glass to her in offering.

She raised her brows, then, pressing her lips together, she nodded. "Yes, please."

He hadn't expected that answer. Frances was one of a kind, that was for certain. So damned pretty, with her heart-shaped face, big brown eyes, and chestnut hair that looked velvety soft—yet she didn't seem to notice his attraction to her. It seemed to be the least of her concerns. Instead, she possessed enough pluck to come here on her own today to check up on the boy she hardly knew. He couldn't deny that beneath his irritation surrounding the situation, his respect for the woman was growing.

She deserved an answer to her question, he decided. She already knew about Bobby's relationship to him, so giving her a little more information wouldn't make a difference.

He poured another brandy and brought it back to her, watching as she took a sip and tried to hide her reaction to the potency of the drink.

"You are correct," Evan told her. "Evidently, my father sent an annual sum to the home for his upkeep, and then when he died, I continued to approve the payment, thinking it was a charitable donation. Until the morning of the masquerade, when I received this." Returning to his chair, he opened a drawer, retrieved Thomason's letter, and pushed it across the desk to her.

Setting her glass down on his desk, Frances took the note and read quickly, her jaw dropping. "Two hundred pounds? The impudence of that man! The child was dressed in filthy rags when I first encountered him."

Evan took a hearty swallow of brandy. "Unsurprising."

She studied the note again. "The man's writing is a terrible scrawl. Look." She turned the paper so he could see the writing and pointed at the name. "It looks like he wrote Master S. Dickens, but perhaps he meant Master*s* Dickens. Both Dickens brothers."

"You could be correct. I was wondering why he gave Bobby the initial S."

"Which means he is even more of a villain," she said darkly. "He demanded money for the upkeep of both brothers when he'd already sent Jasper away to fend for himself."

She was right. Thomason was a menace who shouldn't be anywhere near children. Evan needed to do something about that.

Frances sank into the chair on the opposite side of his desk. "So…you've spent your entire life unaware that you had a brother? Possibly *two* brothers?"

That, and so much more. Evan thought of his own parentage. His own dirty little secret. His own "embarrassing episode."

He took another deep gulp of his drink. "That's right."

She studied him, her eyes taking him in, reading all the raw parts of him he couldn't find the energy to hide right now. "Did you decide to bring him home with you the moment you read this?"

"Not at all. I assumed… Well, I don't know what I assumed." That Harlowe's Home was doing a superior job raising his brother? If he'd given it a second thought, he would have realized that was unlikely.

"I don't know what I assumed about the place, either," Frances admitted. She stared at her glass of brandy, turning it slowly on the desk. "I went there intending to volunteer my services, but I thought it would be more like a school. Where the boys were educated and treated kindly." She closed her eyes. "I had no idea."

"How could you? I certainly didn't. I simply wanted to meet him. To confirm…" He shook his head. "Well, one look at him established that he is indeed my brother. My father had distinctive eyes, and he seemed to have passed down a bit of them to both of us."

Frances nodded. "The similarity is unmistakable."

"But when I saw that place…" Evan took another deep drink, finishing what was left in his glass. "I knew I had to bring him home with me."

Frances sipped her brandy and waited the requisite moment to get it down before she responded. "I am relieved you brought him home," she told him. "If you hadn't, I think I might have never forgiven you."

He smiled grimly. "Well, that makes two of us."

The question was, and had been for the past few days,

what to do with the boy now? He wasn't prepared to be a father—she was correct there. But what else could he do? Send him away to school? He had been sent away at Bobby's age, and it had taken years for him to find his way. And then only thanks to the friends he'd made. He'd been lucky in that regard. Few people had a Crestmont, a Jameson, and a Cole in their lives.

Evan wasn't going to send the boy away. Which meant he needed to keep him.

That decision gave him a deep sense of rightness. It didn't mean it wasn't terrifying.

Of course, there was the added complication of this other boy, Jasper. It was possible that he and Bobby were half brothers through their mother and Jasper was no relation to Evan whatsoever.

But it was also possible that the previous Earl of Winthrop had had a long-standing affair with Bobby's mother, producing not one but two sons.

There was a soft knock on the door. "Come in," Evan said.

Franklin opened the door. "Sir, Jasper Dickens has arrived."

Evan glanced at Frances. She had a stubborn look on her face, and he knew, without a doubt, that she wasn't leaving unless Franklin bodily removed her. And in a battle between Frances and Franklin, he really wasn't sure who'd win.

He didn't know how this meeting would go or what, if anything, would be revealed.

And Frances Cherrington would be here, yet again, to witness how it unfolded.

He sighed.

"Show him up," Evan said.

Chapter Eleven

Frances tried to remember to breathe in the few moments it took for Jasper to arrive. There were a dozen different variations on how the next several minutes could go, and she had no idea what to expect.

There was one thing she could say for certain—she'd been wildly curious about Jasper Dickens, and it seemed she'd come at the perfect time to meet him.

And not only did her nerves thrum in anticipation of what was to come with this mystery youth, but they also thrummed from her conversation with the earl.

She'd been completely alone for the first time in her life with a man who was not her relative. Surprisingly, it had not been awful. Well, no more awful than their usual encounters. They'd argued, but he had not tried to compromise her, which was what she had been incessantly warned would happen if she let a man be alone with her.

Instead, they'd…*communicated*. And all the while she

had appreciated his finer features. How straight his nose was, and how strong his jaw. How his amber eyes sparked fire when seen at different angles. How his broad shoulders stretched the fine wool of his coat. How long and masculine his fingers were, with their bluntly cut nails. How a smile teased at the corner of his lips when she amused him.

She had always found the Earl of Winthrop attractive — her and every other person in London.

Her attraction to him was frustrating. She knew better. But even so, being here with him, alone, the sole source of his attention, had fanned that attraction into a flame.

It was a flame she must ignore. Winthrop was still who he was, and now he had other things on his mind. Those other things had eclipsed his usual practiced charm today. A line was carved between his brows, and he seemed far more likely to frown than to flash his magnetic smile. She had never seen him like this before and wondered how many people had witnessed this side of the affable earl.

He was under a great deal of stress, so she really couldn't blame him. He'd taken in an unexpected brother, a young boy whom he had quickly taken full responsibility for. And now he was about to meet another who might also be his brother.

A gentle knock on the door preceded its opening. "Jasper Dickens, my lord," the butler said.

Frances and the earl rose as the youth stepped around the butler, and Frances stopped breathing.

There they were. The amber eyes. Even more like Winthrop's than Bobby's. His hair was blond, like Bobby's, but straight, and his stature was small and thin just like his younger brother's, though there was a wiry strength about him.

She glanced at the earl, who was holding himself remarkably still. "Thank you, Franklin. You may go." He moved his gaze to the boy. "Come in, Jasper."

The butler disappeared, but Jasper didn't come in. He stood at the threshold, those eyes he shared with his brothers narrowed in suspicion. "Where's Bobby?" he demanded. Like Bobby's, his voice was tinged with the rough accents of the Rookery. "Harlowe's says he's been snatched. Did you steal my brother?"

"He is here," Winthrop said flatly. "I brought him home."

The furrow deepened between the boy's brows. "This ain't his home."

"It is now."

Jasper's jaw firmed in a way that reminded her of the earl. "Where is he? I'll take him with me, and we'll be gone from this place. And you'd best give me that guinea you promised me, too."

Winthrop raised a brow. "You intend to return to the workhouse? Will they accept a child without his mother?"

Frances gasped. The workhouse? Bobby hadn't said Jasper was living in a workhouse. For God's sake, he was just a child himself.

"We won't be going back there," Jasper declared.

"Where will you take him, then?"

"We'll make our own way."

Winthrop took a measured breath and gazed evenly at the boy. "Jasper. Do you know who I am?"

Jasper looked away. "Aye," he muttered.

"I am not only the Earl of Winthrop," Winthrop said, "but I am also your brother."

Silence.

"You knew that, didn't you?" Winthrop asked softly.

Jasper shifted uncomfortably, clutching the doorframe. She could see the whites of his knuckles.

"You knew our father, didn't you? When you were younger?"

Jasper looked up at that, his expression defiant. "His *lordship*," he spat derisively. "He'd come by our flat and give me a copper to go away till he was gone. Before Bobby was born, he'd take my mum away for days and days. Then, she got sick and we never saw him again. Curse him to the devil, I say. I'm *glad* he's dead."

Frances stood very still, but her mouth was dry, and nausea curdled in her gut.

"I agree," Winthrop said darkly, then added, his voice very low, "Curse the bastard." He spared her an apologetic glance. "Forgive me, Miss Cherrington. And forgive me for not introducing you sooner. Jasper, this is Miss Cherrington."

Jasper looked her up and down, suspicion still radiating from him. "Who're you?" What he really meant was, "What do you have to do with all this?"

"I am a friend of Bobby's."

"He never told me nothing about you," Jasper said accusingly.

Winthrop raised a hand. "Bobby is here with me now. He is safe, he is cared for, and I want nothing more than his happiness. Would you take that away from him?"

"Aye," Jasper grumbled. "To get him away from the likes of *you*."

"That's hardly fair," Frances cut in. "You don't even know Lord Winthrop."

"I knowed his father, and I say that's plenty."

"Well, I didn't know your father," Frances said. "But he and the current Lord Winthrop are very different."

Jasper snickered, no doubt realizing she had no basis for that statement. In truth, she did have very little. But after seeing the interaction between Winthrop and Bobby at Harlowe's Home, then speaking to the earl today, she was certain of it.

Winthrop released what sounded like a long-suffering breath. He seemed exhausted...and worried. She felt a renewed burst of sympathy for him.

"Jasper," he said quietly. "You are my brother. My blood. So is Bobby. I can't make up for anything our father has done. All I want is to do right by you. Will you let me try?"

Jasper crossed his arms and gave his older brother a mulish look. "Maybe."

Well. It was a start.

...

Frances ended up staying at Lord Winthrop's house for most of the day. She'd eventually sent two notes home. The first was to summon Peggy because God forbid someone might discover she was at Lord Winthrop's house without an escort. *Oh, the horror!* She wouldn't want her brother to find out and need to make use of his smelling salts.

The second was to inform her brother and Lilly that she would be home before dinner but was spending the day "working with some children from Harlowe's Home for Boys," which was definitely not a lie.

Not at all.

For heaven's sake. She was a ruined spinster of five-and-twenty years old. It was ridiculous that her family insisted on knowing her whereabouts at all times.

Still, that was the way of things. She could only hope that as she aged into her spinsterhood, she'd be given more freedoms. Though she knew she'd never have as much as even Jasper Dickens, a youth of twelve years, did. He was granted those freedoms because he was from a different class, and he was a boy.

She instantly felt terrible for thinking those thoughts. She had many freedoms Jasper did not, thanks to the position in society she'd been born into. Perhaps she should feel thankful for what she did have rather than resentful for what she didn't.

Still, the part of her that craved her freedom, even though she had escaped once and for all from the shackles of the dreaded marriage mart, was struggling for more.

Perhaps she would never be satisfied. What if she was the kind of person who, no matter how much they were given, always wanted more? She didn't want to be that person. But she didn't know how much was enough, either.

Her mind roiled with these thoughts as she and Peggy walked home from Lord Winthrop's grand house in Berkeley Square.

"What did you think?" she mused to Peggy as they turned down Davies Street toward home. "Will they stay?"

"The lads?" Peggy asked. "Oh, yes. I think so, miss."

"I think so, too." A feeling of accomplishment settled over Frances. Bobby had been relatively easy to win over—he'd been almost as happy to see her this morning as he had Jasper. Then, he'd jumped up and down with excitement when she'd handed him the piece of chocolate she'd had in her reticule, exclaiming that, since he'd had chocolate twice today and then seen Jasper and her, it was definitely the very, very best day of his life.

Jasper was older, though. He was more suspicious, and he had a tough shell that was more difficult to crack. After his initial meeting with Winthrop, he'd become calm and watchful where Bobby was wild, quiet where Bobby was loud. All day, she'd used Bobby's rapport with her to her advantage, speaking to Jasper through his younger brother, ever so gradually coaxing him to lower his guard.

She had felt a smug self-satisfaction when Winthrop's charm hadn't worked on the boys. Whenever he reverted to it, they shied away from him because, like Frances, they didn't trust it. But then he had been so determined to do right by them that she softened to him and his plight. He didn't know these boys, but it was clear he already saw them as family. She had no doubt he'd leap into flames for either of them. His honesty and loyalty had shined through, and despite herself, her heart stood up and took notice.

A few days ago, she'd considered him a smallminded buck about town who relied on his charm to bend others to his will. Now, she was beginning to see the strong, loyal man underneath. If he continued being wonderful in her presence, she feared she'd be half in love with the man by month's end.

She rolled her eyes at the thought.

By the time they'd left, Jasper had grudgingly agreed to spend the night. And only because the earl had promised to buy them ices of the flavor of their choosing—Frances had recommended pineapple—from Gunter's Tea Shop, which was just down the street from Winthrop's townhouse.

Jasper had been suitably seduced by the idea. Bobby had been in raptures.

Today, bribery, Frances thought. *Tomorrow, true brotherly love.*

It would be a process. They were three brothers wading through the shock of their changed circumstances.

But now she needed to put them out of her mind and focus on her own matters. Matters that didn't include what the earl was doing at that very moment, and whether he wished she was there to distract him from his troubles or ride beside him in his carriage or sip whatever that awful drink was in his study together, alone.

Her mind offered no relief, though. She mentally replayed images of Winthrop throughout her dinner with Lilly and Charles, so deep in thought they'd asked her if she were ill. Afterward, she couldn't focus on the book she was reading—*Emma*—which she'd thought delightful when she'd first begun it last week. And, when she went to sleep that night, she dreamed of traveling to distant lands and watching lions in their natural habitats. The man in her dream who stood beside her, enjoying the exotic exploration right along with her?

It was Lord Winthrop, of course.

Chapter Twelve

Evan was nervous about the social repercussions of taking Jasper and Bobby into society, but he couldn't keep two growing boys locked up in his home, and the truth that he intended to raise his two illegitimate younger brothers would inevitably come out. Might as well get it over with.

So, a few days later, Evan decided they'd make their first appearance in public. At Cole's club the previous evening, Evan had told him, Crestmont, and Jameson about how he'd met the boys and taken them in. Somehow, Frances Cherrington, despite not being present for once, had insinuated herself into the conversation, and he'd ended up describing how she'd been an uninvited witness to his first encounters with Bobby and Jasper.

His friends had wanted to meet the boys, and Cole and Jameson agreed to come along on today's outing. Crestmont couldn't join them—he had an appointment on the river with his wife this morning. The duchess's matchmaking business was thriving these days, and it was the only time all week she had a moment in her busy schedule to row with her husband.

The news of Evan's brothers would ripple through the ton after this, and Evan was happy Jameson and Cole would be there to help him control the wagging tongues. People would whisper about Jasper and Bobby's origins, and he intended to forestall lies and exaggerations. He would be open and honest and insist on the facts: He had discovered he had two half brothers. He'd taken them into his home. He planned to raise them.

For the rest of their lives, his brothers would have to live with society's judgment for the circumstances under which they'd been born, something they'd never had a choice in. Yet, in history, many natural sons and daughters of peers had grown to become important, happy, successful people. That was what he wanted for Jasper and Bobby.

For himself, though? He'd thrust those thoughts away. He'd deal with his own situation later. Right now, Jasper and Bobby were most important. He didn't have the time to worry about the dowager's revelations or the lie he was living.

In his few spare moments, he had, however, begun to research his mother, Eliza MacPherson. The dowager had said she'd come from a Covent Garden whorehouse. He'd sent inquiries about her to various brothels in that area. He'd received no response yet.

This afternoon, though, he, Cole, and Jameson were taking the boys to Hyde Park at the fashionable hour. Evan expected that three grown men would be able to control two smallish boys. Furthermore, he'd determined that if he kept a firm grip on Bobby's hand, Jasper wouldn't go anywhere. The boy wouldn't leave his younger brother—he had a fierce, vaguely familiar protective streak.

They took the fifteen-minute walk from Berkeley Square to Hyde Park Corner and started the promenade on the footpath adjacent to Rotten Row. Both were busy at this hour, the footpath packed with pedestrians while people on horseback and driving carriages paraded up and down Rotten Row. Evan's neck prickled as he felt curious eyes taking in their group, observing how he held an unfamiliar little boy's hand.

Evan had expected Jasper and Bobby to like Jameson instantly given that Jameson was a commoner who'd spent his early childhood, while not in squalor like these boys had, in some degree of poverty, giving them something in common. But Jameson remained stoic, and the boys seemed a bit afraid of him. Instead, it was Viscount Coleton who had them giggling.

"Where did it go?" Cole asked as they progressed along the path running parallel to the Serpentine River. He weaved around their small group, searching all around for the penny that had just disappeared from his hand. "Do you have it, Jameson? Jasper, you took it, didn't you?"

Jasper shook his head, a smile playing at the edges of his lips.

"Deuce it, Winthrop!" Cole exclaimed. "It was you, wasn't it? You rapscallion! You knave! Give it back, at once!"

"Don't have it," Evan said. "I have no idea where it went. I think you dropped it."

"Balderdash!" Cole said. Then he turned to Bobby. "It was you, wasn't it, lad? Nipped it straight from my hand, didn't you? I've heard of pickpocketing, but I think you might have invented pick*hand*ing."

"I didn't take it!" Bobby exclaimed, bubbling with laughter. Something tightened in Evan's chest at the sound. It was the first time he'd heard it.

"Wait...I see it!" Cole stopped in front of them, forcing Evan and Bobby to reel to a halt. Cole's eyes narrowed at the side of Bobby's head. "A bit of a glimmer, a little shine..." He reached forward and swiped his hand behind Bobby's ear. He came out holding a shiny penny between his thumb and forefinger. "Well, look at that! It was hiding behind your ear all along. How could it have ended up there?"

Bobby giggled. "I dunno!"

"Are you sure?"

Bobby nodded, and Cole handed the penny to him. "After that magical feat, this belongs to you. Well done, lad."

With big eyes, Bobby took the coin and held it fisted in his little hand. It made Evan wonder whether the boy had ever handled coin.

Two hundred pounds a year. Thinking of Thomas Thomason's ridiculous demand, Evan ground his teeth and tightened his hand on Bobby's. He would very much like to throttle Thomason right about now.

"Lord Winthrop!"

Evan jerked his head up. John Turlington, an old acquaintance from school, grinned at him from across the path. Turlington wasn't a bad chap, but he'd had no interest in rowing so hadn't been in their group of close friends.

Polite greetings were exchanged among the four men, followed by everyone's agreement that it was a fine day. Then, Turlington's gaze dipped to the boy clutching Evan's hand.

"And who is this young fellow?"

"This is my brother, Bobby. And this"—Evan gestured

to Jasper, who stood at his other side—"is our other brother, Jasper."

"Why, I didn't know you had brothers, Winthrop."

"Neither did I," Evan said easily.

"I didn't know he was *my* brother neither," Bobby told Turlington.

Evan smiled and shrugged. "We discovered one another a week ago."

"Oh. Well…that's…er…" Turlington clearly didn't know how to respond.

"I'm sure you'll see more of them, as they will be residing with me," Evan said.

The conversation continued for a few moments longer, and Evan was happy Cole and Jameson took over. After a short while, they were on their way again, and Evan released a long breath.

Within a few days, everyone would know about Jasper and Bobby. And between Evan and his friends, they'd ensure the rumors didn't wander off track. People might speculate that Evan was the boys' father, but that would be shot down as soon as those people were reminded of the previous earl's proclivities. Gossip might recede, but it was never forgotten, and salacious gossip had run rampant about the previous Earl of Winthrop during his lifetime.

Without warning, Bobby yelled, "Miss Cherrington!" and rushed toward Frances, who was sitting by herself on a blanket on the nearby lawn, holding a piece of charcoal and hunched over a drawing in her lap, her expression hidden by the pale blue brim of her bonnet. At Bobby's greeting, she straightened and looked up, her expression lighting with joy. Evan had never seen Frances Cherrington's face so radiant before, and it made warmth burst through him.

Not just warmth. *Heat.*

"And, lo and behold, the lady materializes in your life yet again," Jameson said under his breath.

A lesser woman would have toppled over when Bobby collided with her, but Frances held her ground, laughing and squeezing the boy in return. "What are you doing here?"

She raised her smile to Evan. For a moment, he just gazed into those intelligent brown eyes. God, she was pretty. Her smile stole his breath.

Bobby tugged her to her feet, her blue muslin skirt falling to her ankles. "Evan brought us! Did you see all the horses? There's so many! Oooh! Look at those birds!" Bobby ran over to Jasper who was standing at the water's edge watching a pair of swans.

"Good afternoon, Miss Cherrington," Evan said. Frances had been there when he'd met Bobby, then Jasper, and now she was present for their first outing in public. The woman had an uncanny knack for being present during the most important events of his life.

And, surprisingly, it no longer bothered him. He glanced at Cole to see him raising a questioning brow. From their conversation about her odd intrusiveness into his affairs last night, Cole and Jameson would expect him to want to be free of her presence as quickly as possible.

Yet, he found himself inexplicably happy to see her.

"My lords. Mr. Jameson." Smile gone and her usual serious expression firmly back in place, she dipped into a curtsy, and they all bowed.

Her maid hovered nearby. At least Frances hadn't left her house unattended this time.

"I am glad to see the boys out," she said.

"It was time," Evan told her. "I couldn't keep them in the house forever."

"Well one would hope you wouldn't keep them locked up in a house *forever*," she said with a visible shudder. "That would be horrid."

"It would indeed." Evan gestured to the paper she held. "What's this?"

She pursed her lips. "My drawing master gave me the assignment to draw a creature from the wild."

"Which animal did you decide to draw?" Jameson asked. He and Cole leaned closer, trying to get a look.

She stared at the drawing for a moment, then grimaced. "I believe I should abandon this pursuit." She turned the paper so they could see her attempt. "What do you gentlemen think I've drawn?"

Evan studied the blob of gray and black. Damned if he knew what that was supposed to be.

"A turtle?" Jameson guessed.

"No, it's bigger," Cole said. "Rounder."

Jameson raised a brow. "Turtles are round."

Cole frowned. "Yes…but, no. I meant fatter."

"What do *you* think it is, my lord?" she asked Evan. There was a hint of challenge in her voice, as if daring him to guess correctly.

"Um…" he said. "Er…" What could he say that wouldn't hurt her feelings?

She huffed out a breath. "Oh, I'll put you out of your misery. It's that swan." She gestured toward where the swans were both ducking their heads underwater. "A hopeless, inept rendition of a lovely creature, I know."

"No, not at—" Evan began, just as Cole said, "It's really—" but she raised her hand to stop them.

"Don't worry, my lords. My feelings are made of stronger stuff than that. I have created a list of possible occupations for myself and thought I might prove to be an excellent artist— my sister Harriet is one—but it seemed she hoarded all the family talent in that regard."

A list of possible occupations? Evan found his interest piqued, but she balled up the drawing of the swan before he could pose the question.

"There will be no training my lack of talent out of me, as much as Monsieur Beaufoy says it can be done," she said. "Art is not for me. Anyhow, I believe I'd prefer to view others' works of art than create my own."

"I feel the same way," Evan said. Actually, *she* was the work of art he'd prefer to view. He could study her all day— every detail of her, like the dark curl that brushed over her cheek, the tiny freckle at her temple, or the way her long, dark lashes framed her eyes.

They stared at each other, the moment drawing on until Jameson cleared his throat and Frances jerked her attention to Bobby and Jasper, who were still watching the swans. "The boys seem well."

Evan frowned—did that surprise her?—but Jameson spoke before he could. "I expected a pair of rascals, but they've been shockingly well-behaved."

That was because Evan had bribed them not only with chocolate, but with another ice from Gunter's—and he'd promised this time they could eat their ices in the square instead of the dining room.

Frances turned appraising eyes on him. "It appears they

are growing more comfortable with you."

Bobby was more comfortable with him now, but Jasper was still reserved. He was just twelve years of age, but he'd been living as a man full grown, with all the accompanying responsibilities. This was an enormous change in his circumstances, and the lad still wasn't certain about it.

He watched the boys move on to a nearby bush, where some sort of insect had captured their attention.

"They'll be fine." Cole grinned. "Now that they have an older, wiser brother to look up to."

"I hope you're right," Evan said. "There are no instructional treatises on how to raise newly discovered orphan brothers." Evan hadn't the faintest idea how to raise boys. Just thinking about the future made panic bubble in his gut. He supposed they'd muddle along until they figured it out.

"Bobby's a little young, but you could send Jasper to school," Cole suggested.

Evan shook his head. "He's not ready for school."

He would keep both boys with him, at least for now. Not only to help them get caught up on their education, but he also wanted them to get to know him, and vice versa.

"They need…someone, though," he told Frances, Cole, and Jameson. They needed *him*, he realized, and he intended to be there for them. But he couldn't do it alone. "Someone besides me. A permanent nursemaid?"

"I believe they're too old for a nurse," Cole said.

"A governess then?"

"Do you know if they can read and write?" Jameson asked.

"Jasper can read." No thanks to Harlowe's Home for

Boys. He'd told Evan that his mother had taught him a little before she died, and once he and Bobby had been sent to the home, he'd struggled to find things to read. For the most part, he was self-taught. But while his reading was rather brilliant given how little instruction he'd received, he was lacking education in all the other disciplines that any proper school would expect from a youth his age. "He's taught Bobby his letters, but that's all. Their other skills are lacking."

"You will require a highly skilled governess," Frances said. "One who can not only bring them up to snuff in the schoolroom, but who can manage their not-quite-gentlemanly upbringing."

"There is no rush," Evan said. "I still need to get to know them. We will go from there."

They all watched the boys. Bobby was holding a large leaf and trying to scoop something up from within the bush.

Evan glanced at Frances. "So…no more drawing?"

"Not today," she confirmed. "Or ever. I suppose I should go home and send a note to Monsieur Beaufoy to tell him his services are no longer required."

Frances was less prickly today, more subdued than usual. He wondered why. Perhaps it was because he was in Cole's and Jameson's company. He resisted the sudden urge to ask her to join them, to spend the day with them. He wanted to talk to her, to learn more about her list of pursuits and why she found it necessary to create one to begin with. He wanted to coax her to tell him more about her "embarrassing episode." And he wanted to watch her interact with the boys—she was so easy with them, so natural. He wanted her to teach him to be like that.

But he held himself back. They were in public, with his

friends. As much as he wanted to learn more about Frances Cherrington, this wasn't the time or the place.

Instead, he bade her good afternoon and then reminded the boys to do the same.

"But when will we see you again?" Bobby asked, frowning.

"I hope it will be very soon." Frances glanced at Evan, then looked quickly away. "Well, goodbye, then."

She curtsied, and the gentlemen bowed. Bobby threw his arms around her and she knelt down and whispered something in his ear that made him grin. Then, he and Jasper scampered down the path, Evan hurrying to follow them, casting one last look back at Frances as she watched them go.

Cole whistled out a breath after they were out of hearing range and Jasper and Bobby had moved ahead to the water's edge again, where they watched a group of children sailing newspaper boats. Cole glanced back to where Frances and her maid were folding up their blanket. "Well, that was awkward."

Evan frowned. "What was awkward?"

"You didn't see that?" Jameson asked.

Cole sighed. "His attention was divided by his brothers and Miss Cherrington. Once he saw her, it was impossible for him to notice anyone else."

Evan scowled at Cole, not liking the implication his friend was making. "What the hell are you talking about?"

"Your inability to take your eyes off Miss Cherrington," Cole replied easily.

"That's ridiculous," Evan said.

"And yet you didn't see Mrs. Van Horn and her two daughters approach on the path behind us," Jameson said.

"And how, when they saw Miss Cherrington, the lady turned around, grabbed her daughters' hands, and dragged them back the way they'd come."

Evan knew Mrs. Van Horn, of course. Everyone did. She was a society matron, and her daughters had been foisted as dancing partners on Evan more times than he could count.

This must have something to do with her "embarrassing episode." Was it bad enough that three ladies of society would cut her in public? "What happened?"

"You haven't heard?" Jameson asked under his breath. "Hell, man. Even *I* know."

"Just tell me," Evan snapped, his voice sounding more impatient than he intended.

Cole gave him a pointed look, then glanced around them once again, and finding the other pedestrians more involved in their own conversations than listening to them, he leaned back in. Evan glanced at the boys, still fascinated by the paper boats.

"Frances Cherrington," Cole said quietly, "was seen embracing a man in the gardens at the Worthington Masquerade."

Evan's jaw went iron hard. "What is his name?" He would go straight to that man and demand he do right by Frances. He'd throw down his damned glove, if necessary.

"Something...Salt, I believe? I don't think any of us are acquainted with him. Are you?"

"No," Evan said flatly. "Where is he now?" And why the hell hadn't he already proposed?

Cole shrugged. "There's the rub. The day after the masquerade, he left England for some godforsaken, never explored place deep in Africa. He is inaccessible. She's beyond redemption, they're saying. She's been cut from society like the fat off a beefsteak." Cole made a snipping motion with his fingers.

Evan had spent time with Frances at the Worthington Masquerade, and he'd fantasized about kissing her in the gardens that night. But, knowing the risk to her, he never would have actually done it.

Someone else did, though. Uncaring of her delicate position in the world, of how deeply the claws of society would rake her.

A memory of their conversation bubbled to the surface. Frances had said she was seeking her destiny. Surely she hadn't meant a destiny of being ruined in the eyes of the ton. Perhaps she'd planned to trap this Salt person into marriage? That didn't seem like the woman Evan thought he knew.

Why, then, had she done it?

His mind kept circling back to Frances Cherrington in a passionate embrace with a man. In the gardens. At the masquerade.

He couldn't fathom her kissing anyone.

Anyone but him, that was.

Chapter Thirteen

The following week, Evan summoned his solicitor to instruct him on the revisions he intended to make to his will to include Bobby and Jasper. After the man left, Evan stood and stretched, then went to his study window overlooking the square. It had been drizzling outside earlier, so it wasn't as crowded as it would usually be on a spring day, though there were a few people venturing outside hunched under their coats.

During the hours he and his solicitor had discussed the distribution of his assets upon his death, Evan had come to a conclusion.

He would continue keeping his secret. He would not tell the world that he was a bastard, and he wouldn't relinquish the earldom to his uncle. But not for his benefit. Instead, he would use the title and all the privileges that came with it to offer his younger brothers the opportunities that were their due. He wanted to make up for the years that had been so difficult for them. He wanted to set them up in the world as gentlemen who could spend their adulthoods pursuing whatever vocation they desired. He intended to use his position as the Earl of Winthrop to support them each step of the way.

But when he was gone, it was right and proper that his uncle or one of his cousins, the true blood heirs to the earldom, should inherit.

That meant he could never marry. Could never allow himself to fall in love. He couldn't spend his life alongside someone who didn't know his deepest secret. And what woman would have him if she knew the truth? If he managed to find a woman who would love him, even once she knew he wasn't the true earl and therefore she would never be a real countess, he wouldn't ask anyone to carry that burden.

Also, he couldn't risk having children. He would not leave behind illegitimate children born to mistresses as his father had, and a son born to him and a wife would either mean continuing the cycle of deception—and he couldn't fathom doing that—or raising a child whose very existence would be enshrouded in scandal. That was equally awful.

He, Jasper, and Bobby were learning how to be a family. The three of them could be happy. They didn't need anyone else.

A knock sounded on his door. "My lord?"

"Yes, Franklin?"

"Miss Cherrington is at the door."

Despite himself, a smile tugged at the corner of his mouth.

They'd seen Miss Cherrington twice over the past week. First, they'd encountered her when he'd taken the boys to the tailor to start working on their wardrobes. She'd been on the street examining the shops' exteriors, her maid beside her looking bored. When Evan had asked her what she was doing, she'd said, "Studying London commerce."

Why she'd wish to study London commerce, he had no idea.

After that, Bobby and Jasper had started chattering with her, and she'd gone into the hatmaker's with them to shop for some new hats for the boys, and then into a grocer's, where he'd bought them all some sugar candy.

All the while, Evan observed how people looked at her, how ladies swerved on the street to avoid coming too close to her, and even though she had tried to appear immune, he had wanted to put his arms around her and protect her from the cruelty. He desperately wanted to ask what, exactly, had happened at the masquerade, but her request that he not bring up the topic echoed in his mind. Respecting her wishes when she received no respect elsewhere was the least he could do.

They'd encountered Frances two days later at the park again where she'd been writing in a notebook. She'd set the book aside and tossed a ball with Evan, Jasper, and Bobby on the grass while her maid had fretted about her being in the sunlight for so long. They'd sat together on the grass afterward, and it was there that Jasper had finally opened up and revealed his passion for the game of cricket.

Evan had been trying to convince himself he wanted to see Frances Cherrington less, but the truth was, he'd been wanting to find reasons to see her more. Hoping to run into her. Waiting for her to knock on his door. Not only was she excellent with his brothers—he loved watching her with them—but her direct speech and straightforward demeanor made him feel settled and calm.

He couldn't help but wonder what surprise she had in

store for him today.

"Also, this letter just arrived for you." Franklin held out a folded sheet.

Evan took it and said, "Send Miss Cherrington up, Franklin. Thank you."

The butler bowed and left, and Evan turned over the note, broke the seal, and unfolded the piece of paper. Every available inch of the sheet was covered in handwriting.

17th of May, 1820
My lord Winthrop,
Your letter was forwarded to me by Mrs. Phillips. I knew Eliza MacPherson when she left that lady's establishment in the year of our Lord, 1785.

Evan had been born in early 1786.

I corresponded with her after she left London for a time. I remember her as a child, then a very comely young lady, always friendly and cheerful, and full of dreams. As she grew older, she became a favorite of—

"Good afternoon, my lord," came the familiar, crisp voice from the doorway.

Reeling from what he'd just learned, Evan snapped his gaze up to where Frances Cherrington stood, instinctively flattening his hand over the page so she couldn't read it.

But Frances was looking from him to the letter and back to him again. He felt the insane urge to hide it from her, but that would be far too obvious. Instead, he pasted a nonchalant expression on his face. "Miss Cherrington."

God. What else did the letter say?

Oh, damn. He hadn't stood. Gentlemen always stood when a lady entered the room. Quickly, he did so, his chair scraping back over the hardwood.

She quirked a dark brow as she watched him. "I believe I have interrupted something."

"Not at all."

She glanced down at the letter again. "I also believe you just told me a lie, my lord."

This woman was truly like no other. Accusing him of being a liar. Imposing on him yet again during a significant moment in his life. *He'd found someone who knew his mother!*

But also, she looked lovely in her white dress.

No, that wasn't quite right. The dress had nothing to do with it. Frances always looked lovely to him. It was the honesty in her brown eyes, the openness in her expression, the candor of her speech.

She was right, after all. He *had* been lying to her.

He, too, glanced down at the letter on his desk. He saw words, numbers...

protector

adored

18

Manchester

Manchester? Was his mother in Manchester? He swept up the letter, then, remembering his guest, forced his hand down to his side.

"It appears that letter"—Frances gestured in the general direction of the letter—"contains information of great importance."

He cleared his throat. "How can I help you today, Miss Cherrington? I assume you are here to visit my brothers?

If so, they are upstairs awaiting a new parcel of books and toys—"

"I am here to see Jasper and Bobby, of course, but I wished to speak with you about something first."

He took a slow breath. "Of course. Please sit down."

She sat in the chair across from his desk, and he resumed his seat, keeping the letter clenched in his hand.

She noticed and raised her brows, giving his hand a pointed look. But she said, "I'll arrive straight to the point then leave you alone. I've been interviewing governesses for Jasper and Bobby."

"Er...*what*?"

"Your brothers require a governess, as we discussed at the park last week. I know you have been quite busy, so I have made a list of possibilities for your consideration and have further listed my opinions on each one." She opened the reticule hanging from a loop around her wrist and drew out a folded sheet of paper. "My favorite is Miss Renshaw, the last on the list. She is experienced with young boys of different dispositions, intelligent, soft-spoken, nonjudgmental, and seemingly possesses the patience of a saint."

She slid the paper across his desk.

This was highly irregular. "Miss Cherrington—"

Frances raised her hand. "I know you're about to tell me something along the lines of this wasn't my responsibility, or that you didn't want or need my involvement in this process. I am sorry if you feel this is intrusive. However, you cannot deny that I know your brothers, that they like me, and that I am fully capable of understanding what sort of governess would be most beneficial for their successful growth and education."

He leaned back in his chair, his argument dying on his lips. Because there was no argument. Today was the first afternoon he'd been away from his brothers; otherwise his time had been consumed by them and he hadn't had a moment to give a thought to the governess issue.

"I cannot deny any of those assertions," he admitted. "I will interview these ladies."

"Thank you, my lord." Her smile reached her eyes but not her lips in that way Frances had of not smiling while he knew it was lurking beneath her skin, ready to come out if she'd let it. She rarely did.

Now she will leave, he thought. He was still holding the paper under his desk. He'd laid it across his thigh, pinning it there gently so as not to wrinkle or smudge it.

"What is the matter?" Her gaze moved to his desktop, as if she could see through the mahogany to where he balanced the letter on his leg. "You are making attempts to appear relaxed, but you are not doing a very good job of it. I sense something is upsetting you. What on earth is in that letter? Is it something to do with Jasper and Bobby?"

Evan gritted his teeth, then pried them apart and tried to loosen the muscles that had gone tight across his shoulders. His misplaced eagerness to see her a few short moments ago had waned with the arrival of the letter and vanished completely now. The woman was so damned *nosy*. "Miss Cherrington—"

She waved her hand. "I know, I know. Again, it is none of my business. However, if it is anything to do with Bobby and Jasper—"

"It has nothing to do with Bobby or Jasper."

Her brow crinkled. "And yet you are highly distracted by

it. Is it something else I might be able to help with?"

"I assure you, it is not."

"But—" She bit her lip as if deliberately cutting off the rest of what she'd been about to say, then seemed to come to a decision. She nodded once. "Forgive me. I'll leave you to it."

She rose and turned toward the door. This time, he remembered to rise with her.

"Miss Cherrington?"

"Yes?"

He held her gaze for a moment. She didn't deserve to take the brunt of his frustration. After all, she had no idea she'd arrived at precisely the wrong moment.

"Thank you," he said. "For the list. And…for stopping by."

She raised her brows in surprise, then nodded briskly. "You're welcome, my lord."

With that, she left, closing the door behind her. Evan breathed out slowly, then lifted the letter, flattened it on his desk, and continued to read.

As she grew older, she became a favorite of some of our most esteemed patrons, and one of them eventually set her up in her own apartment. She kept the identity of her protector a secret, but we were all so happy that she'd found someone who adored her.

Evan shook his head at that. If it was his father the lady was referring to, he was no protector. He wondered if the man had ever truly adored anyone.

The last time I saw her, she was about to leave London to journey north on her protector's behest. It was perhaps half a year before I heard from her again. She was living in a house at 18 Queen Street in Manchester. I remember it because when we were girls, she always wished to be queen someday, and she'd wear a crown of flowers and dance with me. And she was eighteen years of age when she left London.

That meant his mother had been eighteen or nineteen years of age when she'd given birth to him. That made her only in her early fifties now.

We wrote to each other a few more times, but after that, we lost touch. It is my fault, probably, as I was busy with my own life. I do not know if she is still at 18 Queen Street, but perhaps you might try searching for her there.

I wish you the best of luck, and if you discover anything, please let me know. I would love to renew a correspondence with my dear friend.

Mary Ann Smith

He would find her. He'd ride up to Manchester himself if necessary. But he couldn't leave Jasper and Bobby, not right now.

Evan withdrew a new sheet of paper and wrote a letter to 18 Queen Street, Manchester, inquiring after Eliza MacPherson.

...

The next five days might as well have been five years. Evan had told Franklin to bring him any correspondence the moment it arrived, but there was nothing. For the first two days he knew there wouldn't be, as the post took thirty hours to deliver letters from London to Manchester. Something arriving on the third day was highly unlikely. But on the fourth day, he couldn't sit still. And on the fifth day, he felt like he was losing his mind.

He knew, logically, that the letter might not come today. It might arrive in a week, or several weeks. He might never receive a letter at all.

He started to plan his trip to Manchester. He'd take the boys with him. They could hire a carriage. They could rent rooms in a hotel. It would be an adventure.

How long should he wait for a letter before they left?

A week, he decided. No more. He couldn't wait longer than that to find out where his mother was. And then to meet her face to face...

Would she be more like him than the dowager had been? Would they be able to forge that connection Evan had never been able to with the woman he always thought was his mother?

A sudden urge to see his brothers gripped him. Leaving the pile of paperwork he hadn't been able to focus on, he left the room—only to encounter Mrs. Norton, his housekeeper, bustling toward him in the corridor.

"Oh, sir, a letter has arrived for you. I decided to bring it up directly, since Franklin said you were awaiting one."

"Yes, Mrs. Norton. Thank you." He took the proffered letter, and as she walked away, he opened it, right there in the corridor.

20th May, 1820
My lord,
I regret to inform you…

Chapter Fourteen

When the butler opened the door of the Earl of Winthrop's house, Frances didn't miss his quick scan of the area to ensure Peggy was with her. Her maid was, indeed, just behind her, standing at the bottom of the steps.

"Good afternoon, Miss Cherrington," the butler said.

This place contained the few people in London who didn't look at her with their eyes full of some negative emotion. In the last few weeks, people's expressions upon recognizing her had ranged from disappointment to morbid curiosity to horror that they might be seen in the vicinity of a fallen woman.

Winthrop appeared to be the only person in town who didn't know of her fall from grace. Though it seemed impossible that he didn't know. *Everyone* seemed to know.

Perhaps he didn't care?

"Is Lord Winthrop in?" she asked the butler.

"Yes, Miss Cherrington. He is in his study, I believe."

"Thank you. I will see myself up." She'd been here enough times that the old man certainly needn't mount the stairs on her behalf any longer.

"Of course, miss."

He stepped aside, and Frances hurried into the house, smiling to herself. She had something in mind for this afternoon that she was certain Jasper and Bobby would enjoy.

At the top of the stairs, she turned to go down the corridor toward the office. But she stopped when she saw Lord Winthrop leaning against the wall, his head in his hands. It looked like he was holding a folded paper. Another letter?

She turned to Peggy. "Wait for me in the entry hall," she ordered quietly.

"But miss—"

"Peggy, do as I ask, please."

Peggy twisted her lips but kept them shut as she turned around and returned the way they had come.

Frances approached the earl cautiously. "Lord Winthrop?"

Dropping his hands, he looked up, eyes shining. Oh, no. Her heart leaped into her chest. "What's wrong?"

He rubbed his eyes, then dropped his hands to his sides, one of them still clutching the paper. Did this have something to do with the letter she'd seen him reading the last time she was here? "Miss Cherrington…I…" He shook his head. "It's nothing."

A lump formed in her throat, and she felt her own eyes getting watery. "Are Jasper and Bobby all right?"

"Yes, they are fine. It's…" His voice dwindled, and he looked away.

She watched him try to blink away the sheen in his eyes.

Goodness. Something awful had happened. Curiosity burned inside her—what could have upset him so deeply?

She put her hand on his shoulder and squeezed gently—his shoulder was incredibly hard. "Whatever it is, I am sorry. Is there anything I can do?"

She knew he'd say no.

He shook his head. "No."

She drew in a shaky breath. "All right." She hesitated, then added, "I came to ask your permission to take the boys out this afternoon. If you wish to be left alone, Peggy and I could take them. Perhaps we could take one of your maids as well."

"Out?"

"Yes. My twin sister and her husband have stolen some significant historical objects from Egypt and brought them to our country. I thought I'd take the boys to see them."

He cocked a brow. "Stolen?"

"Yes."

"What kinds of objects?" he asked her.

"Jewels. Scrolls. Statues. Ancient pieces of furniture and writings, canopic jars and sarcophagi. But if I know Jasper and Bobby—and I do, to some extent—they will be most impressed by the mummies. The items are currently located in private rooms at the British Museum."

"That's a good idea." Evan's eyes looked drier now, but he still leaned heavily against the wall. "As most of your ideas are when it comes to my brothers," he added quietly. "I want to show them that there is a vast world out there beyond the Rookery and the docks."

"Viewing these items will certainly be a start." She hesitated, then spoke in a softer voice. "I would like to help, my lord. But perhaps I can help best by leaving you in peace."

He nodded.

"I'll go fetch the boys," she said. "Are they in the nursery?"

"No. The workers are upstairs. My brothers are in the music room with Miss Hastings."

She hesitated, then squeezed his shoulder tighter. "It is going to be all right."

He gazed at her with hollow eyes. "What is?"

"Everything. Jasper and Bobby might not know what has affected you so deeply, but even so, they will help you through it."

"How do you know?" he asked her.

She thought of those moments during her life when her family had come together. When their mother and father had died. During all the drama that had surrounded Harriet's and Charles's marriages.

"Jasper and Bobby were an unexpected change to your life, but sometimes the unexpected can be a blessing. The three of you are family." She shook her head. "It's difficult to explain. I just know."

He pushed off the wall, standing a little taller and shoving the paper into his pocket. Her hand slipped from his shoulder, but he took it and squeezed for just a second before letting her go.

"I don't want to be alone," he told her. "I want to be with my brothers today. And…"

He raised his hand and touched her cheek softly.

She held her breath.

And what?

The moment stretched on for an eternity as he seemed to

search her eyes for…something. Heat bloomed from the point of contact and spread to every corner of her body. When he traced her cheekbone with his thumb, she nearly melted to the floor. She might have even whimpered.

His fingers fell away, and he cleared his throat. "And I'd like to see the Egyptian artifacts, as well."

...

They gathered the boys, and, along with Peggy, they headed out.

During the half-hour walk through London's busy streets, Winthrop and Frances told the boys about the great civilization that had flourished for thousands of years on the banks of the Nile. Frances liked how Winthrop, who was clearly no Egyptophile like her sister, spoke of the place and its people as a civilization the British people could learn from, rather than one that was obviously inferior. Frances had heard her own brother-in-law, one of the foremost scholars of Egypt, describe the Egyptians as lazy, barbaric, and submissive. His self-righteous attitude made her skin crawl.

When they arrived at the British Museum, Frances was immediately recognized—she supposed there were a few benefits to looking exactly like Martha—and given access to the rooms that housed the artifacts Martha and her husband had brought back from Egypt.

The first room contained a series of sculptures and figurines taken from tombs found near the ancient city of Memphis, now known as Cairo. They watched as the boys ran their hands over the stone figures, some as small as a fingernail while others loomed over them, dwarfing the room.

"What's this?" Bobby asked, pausing over a figurine about the size of his palm.

"That's a sphinx," Frances told him. "It has different parts. Can you tell what they are?"

"The head looks like a man with one of those funny Egypt-man hats."

"Right, it's a man," Frances said, sharing a quick smile with Winthrop.

"And the rest of it…" Bobby frowned.

Jasper tilted his head. "Is it a cat?"

"It is a large cat." Frances stroked its smooth back. "Specifically, a lion. Sometimes sphinxes had eagle wings, but this one is just a lion with a human head."

"Why did they do that?" Bobby asked with a scowl. "I don't like it."

"The sphinx was a sacred creature in Egyptian mythology. It was a guardian of sorts, and if you were in ancient Egypt, you might see sphinxes as enormous as the grandest palaces of England guarding important places."

Frances stepped back as the boys continued to study the statues. Winthrop moved to stand beside her. "For someone who feigns no interest in Egypt, you certainly know a lot about it."

"My sister has been obsessed with the place for almost ten years. During all that time, I haven't been able to help but absorb a few bits of knowledge."

"Why do you sound so contrite about that?" he asked, brow furrowed.

Frances's jaw felt stiff. "I do not support what Martha and Oscar do."

"Why not?"

She sighed. "I know this may sound absurd, and I understand the lure of learning about long-lost cultures, but I feel that in their morbid fascination, they are essentially grave-robbing."

"I see," he said slowly.

"People bury their dead as they do for a reason," she continued, her voice taut. "The ancients didn't expect my sister to go digging through their carefully laid-out tombs. And you can be certain they wouldn't like it if they knew some foreign entity came in and pillaged their treasures and brought them to some faraway place for people to gawk at." She shivered. "It just feels so...*wrong*."

"Have you told your sister this?"

"I have." Frances ground her teeth. "She laughs at me. She believes I am a fool."

"I don't think you're a fool."

Frances glanced at him. He seemed sincere. Feeling a smile creeping over her lips, she looked away quickly. "Thank you."

They went into the next room, which contained a variety of mummies and sarcophagi, and Frances raised her brows at Winthrop. *You see? Grave-robbing.*

He nodded and stood behind the boys as they touched the mummies' wrappings with tentative fingers and wondered aloud about the people's fates, especially the two that were child-sized. Frances wrapped her arms around herself and watched. She had to admit, even she got a little thrill from seeing the mummies, wondering about their lives in that faraway place so long ago.

That didn't take away from the fact that Oscar and Martha were thieves.

They spent over an hour viewing the artifacts, and as she'd predicted, the boys were enthralled. But as she watched the earl patiently managing his brothers, her mind kept wandering.

She couldn't stop thinking about how sad Lord Winthrop had been earlier. What had happened? She hated that he'd been so affected and that she had no idea how to help him.

But how he'd touched her when he'd decided to go with them to the museum, and then what he'd said—

I want to be with my brothers today. And...

And...you, Frances.

She'd been convinced he'd been about to say it.

Did he want to spend more time with her? Because, more and more, she realized that it wasn't just the boys who were drawing her back to the Earl of Winthrop's house.

It was the earl himself.

...

Later that night, Frances stood from her desk where she'd been trying to focus on the dullest book she'd ever tried to read. It was one of the science texts Lilly had brought for her, a geological treatise entitled *Essay on the Theory of Earth, With Mineralogical Notes.*

She stretched, pushed away her confusion about stalactites, lithophytes, and incrustations, and gazed out her bedroom window into the dark mews beyond. Behind her, her list of potential occupations lay on her desk. While she'd given up on her drawing lessons that day at the park and her cello lessons soon afterward—she had been unable to learn anything about music besides the fact that she had no ear for it—there were still several things on her list of occupations she wanted to try. She'd certainly pursue science more, but geology definitely wasn't speaking to her.

When she turned back to her desk, number six on her list caught her eye:

6) Traveler (I could travel the world and write about it. This might be interesting. Where to begin?)

After imagining the lives of the ancient Egyptians with the boys, Frances found herself thinking about traveling. Not to Egypt to rob graves, though. She planned to start with a far shorter journey and go from there.

A large part of her didn't want to go. She didn't want to leave Bobby and Jasper right now.

And she really didn't want to leave the earl.

Logic told her that was the exact reason she *should* go. The truth was, she was growing too attached to the boys and far too attached to their handsome older brother.

It was time to talk to Charles.

She went downstairs where Lilly and Charles spent quiet evenings in the drawing room after their son was asleep. When she entered, her brother looked up from the book he was reading and Lilly looked up from where she was drawing architectural plans on the large table Charles had placed there for that purpose.

"Is everything all right, Frances?" Lilly asked. The question wasn't unfounded; Frances rarely disturbed them at this hour.

Frances swallowed hard. Now was not the time to allow nerves to get to her. "Yes, everything's fine," she told Lilly.

She sat on the sofa across from Charles. "I wanted to ask you something."

"Very well." Her brother set his book aside then focused on a point beyond her shoulder. Lately, he seemed unable to look directly at her. "What is it?"

Poor Charles. He'd taken her ruination more to heart than the rest of them put together. Lilly had assured her he wasn't angry anymore; he was just confused about how such a thing had happened, and he worried about her future. He hated thinking that no man would want her, not when, in his mind, she had always been the most marriageable of his sisters.

"Charles thought that I was *marriageable*?" Frances had asked, shocked. Her? The untalented, morose Cherrington sister? She'd always thought Charles had believed her to be the most *hopeless* of his sisters.

"Why, he's always thought that, Frances, dear," Lilly had said.

Charles was, evidently, also distraught at how people were treating her. He'd heard gossip about her at his club that had forced him to leave, feeling angry and useless. He was upset that there was nothing he could do to repair the situation.

"But that's men for you," Lilly had said. "Always trying to fix things. Frustrated to no end when the problem they are trying to solve is truly unsolvable."

Now Frances willed him to look at her, but he resolutely refused to meet her eyes. She gave up with a sigh. "I was hoping you'd give your permission for me to leave London for a while."

Charles frowned. "Where would you go?"

"I've been feeling homesick for the lake," she told him.

As much as she and Charles failed to see eye to eye lately, she knew he'd understand that. She knew *he* felt homesick for the lake sometimes, too.

Things had been so different when they were children. Even though Frances was younger than Charles by almost four years, he'd always allowed her to join him in his play. They'd both loved being outside and playing along the lakeshore.

She'd missed him dearly after he'd gone away to school when Frances was ten. When their father died seven years later, Charles had summoned his sisters to join him in London and then sold the lake house to pay their father's debts.

Frances had arrived in London to find her beloved brother completely changed. He wasn't interested in spending time with her anymore. Instead, he had become the stern, upright "man of the family" and expected her to behave like a sedate, proper young debutante and immediately begin the hunt for an acceptable husband.

At the time, it had been so confusing to her. Thrust into this new life, watching her sisters change like her brother had, she'd felt left behind. Lonely. She'd tried to change with them, but altering her nature, as much as she'd tried, had proven impossible.

Her siblings had attempted, in their way, to guide her, but instead, piece by piece, they had stripped away that free spirit she'd had back at the lake until she'd felt like there was nothing left. Now, she was widely known as the dour, cheerless, and sullen Cherrington sister.

Charles nodded. Was that understanding in his expression? "You wish to visit the lake," he said slowly, as if trying the idea out on his tongue.

"Yes. I know Shorewood has been unoccupied since our uncle the earl has been in London for the Season. With his permission, I might stay there."

Charles glanced at his wife. "What do you think, Lil?"

Lilly came to stand beside her husband's chair. "I think it's a brilliant plan. I've heard the Lake District is lovely this time of year."

Charles released a gusty sigh. "It might be best for the family if you were to leave London for a spell."

"That's probably true," she agreed. For more reasons than he knew.

"But," Charles continued, "you must travel with a full retinue of servants."

"Oh," she said, waving her hand dismissively, "Peggy will be enough."

"Absolutely not. You will take two maids, a footman, and William as well."

William was their stalwart coachman who'd stayed with their family even during their years of poverty. "No, I wouldn't take William from you, Charles."

"I insist," he said.

"That seems an excessive number of people to accompany just one person." And far more supervision than she'd like. This was meant to be an escape, after all.

"I. Insist."

She sighed, knowing this was Charles's attempt at propriety, though God knew it was too late for that when it came to her reputation. "Very well."

"How long do you wish to stay?" he asked.

"A month, perhaps?" When she'd first thought about

returning to the Lake District, she intended to stay for as long as possible, but now...

Now she had attachments. Three in particular—a man and two young boys—if she were being honest with herself.

And that was a problem.

He nodded once. "I will request permission from our uncle for you to stay at Shorewood. But I don't want you gone for too long. Through the first of July, at the latest. Hopefully by the time you return, London will have moved on from this devastating scandal, and we will be able to begin the reconstruction of our family's good name."

Frances winced. If that was what he needed to believe to let her go, she'd accept it. Pushing the embarrassment away, she forced a smile. "Let us hope. Thank you, Charles."

Before he changed his mind, she hurried back up the stairs.

...

On the last day of May, Frances knocked on the back door of Lord Winthrop's house. She'd promised Bobby she'd visit this week, and she needed to tell him and Jasper that she wouldn't be able to return for a while.

She would miss the occupants of this house dearly. Jasper, who was so thoughtful and wise for his age. Bobby, whose face lit up every time he saw her. And the earl...

It was *definitely* for the best she was leaving the earl. She liked him a little more every time she saw him. That gave her a small thrill, but it was also dangerous.

She couldn't resist her attraction to him anymore. When she looked at him, so broad and strong...well, his looks had always appealed to her. But now she knew there was so much more to him than she'd originally thought. That his kindness was genuine and not the façade she'd thought it was. When she watched the way he treated his brothers, the tenderness in his amber eyes, her heart melted into something no more substantial than pudding.

And being in his presence made her *yearn*.

She didn't know what for, exactly. She'd already established that she didn't like kissing.

"Miss Cherrington?"

She jerked back to herself. "Good afternoon, Mrs. Norton," she said to the housekeeper. "I've come to call upon Jasper and Bobby. Are they at home?"

As she was alone, Frances had gone to the back door today. Although her reputation was ruined, there was no need to have Winthrop's name attached to any gossip about her. The ton had already seen them out and about together, but it was common knowledge that the earl and her family were friendly. Furthermore, when they were in public, they had always been in a group, so there had been nothing scandalous for the mongers to gossip about.

Her knocking on his front door, though, unchaperoned? Well, if anyone saw her, there would be talk.

"Master Bobby and Master Jasper are upstairs with Miss Renshaw, their new governess," the housekeeper said. "Please come in."

Winthrop had hired Miss Renshaw, then. A warm feeling spread through her. Smiling to herself, Frances ascended the two flights of stairs to the newly remodeled attic nursery. It smelled of clean sawdust and fresh paint and contained two new desks, a bookshelf filled with the gleaming spines of new books, and piles of shiny new toys.

"Good afternoon," she said to Miss Renshaw. The older woman greeted her from where she sat next to Bobby. She did look a bit tired around the eyes—something Frances hadn't seen when she'd first met her. She couldn't blame the woman—these boys were a force of nature.

Bobby jumped up and ran toward her.

"Goodness!" she exclaimed as he threw his skinny arms around her. "What a change in just a few days. Look at all this. It's a wonderland."

Jasper, who had been sitting on the floor with a book in his lap, looked around as if seeing the place for the first time. His blond hair was combed and clean. He was dressed smartly in a pair of trousers and a new-looking dark waistcoat buttoned over a fresh white linen shirt.

"The best part is the bat and ball Evan got us so we can play cricket together," Jasper said. "But they're downstairs."

Evan. Winthrop's Christian name. Frances had never heard it before, and something about it coming from Jasper's mouth—the familiarity of it—made a kernel of happiness bloom inside her.

"Evan and us went rowing with Lord Coleton yesterday," Bobby said, "and 'twas even more fun than cricket."

That's right—she remembered that Winthrop and his friends were passionate competitive rowers and had a boathouse on the Thames.

"But Jasper still likes cricket best," Bobby informed her.

"Evan says I can play every day if I like," Jasper said.

"He only needs someone to play with." Miss Renshaw's voice was as calm and soothing as Frances remembered. "Unfortunately, I am not much of a cricket player."

"I'm sure Lord Winthrop will be happy to play with you when he is able." Frances wished she could play a game with Jasper right now. She enjoyed cricket—she had been the only one of Charles's sisters who was willing to play with him when they were children. Charles had told her she had a "good arm" for bowling.

She knelt so she was eye to eye with Bobby. "I came with some news for you both. I am leaving for a while."

"No!" Bobby exclaimed. Jasper frowned.

"I'm sorry. I must leave town. I'll be back soon, though."

"How soon?" Bobby demanded.

Frances took a measured breath. "In about a month."

"A month?" Bobby was utterly appalled. "That's forever!"

"I'll write to you both," she said.

They both looked at her with doubtful expressions. "I can't read," Bobby complained.

"That's not quite true," Miss Renshaw said patiently. "You know your letters, don't you? And you're learning a few words every day. We will keep practicing until you are able to read Miss Cherrington's letters all by yourself."

Frances wholeheartedly approved of this woman as the boys' governess. She was sweet, encouraging, and steady. Frances gave her a grateful smile.

Bobby chewed his lip. "I don't *want* you to go."

"I must go," she told him. "But I'll come to see you as soon as I return to London." She looked at Jasper. "And we will have a picnic and play at cricket."

An hour later, she left the nursery, her steps heavy. She was going to miss those boys. Watching Jasper and Bobby open up into bright, sweet lads in the past few weeks had been such a pleasure. And now she wouldn't see the next steps in their progression.

At least she was confident that the earl was taking excellent care of them. Jasper and Bobby were so lucky that he, out of all the lords in London, was their brother. She couldn't imagine anyone in this entire city who would have done a better job of caring for them.

"Miss Cherrington."

She stopped, one foot hovering over the next stair, and turned. At the top of the staircase stood the earl himself. She felt that blasted warmth welling inside her again. She forced her voice to remain steady. "Good afternoon, my lord."

"I heard you'd come to see the boys."

He seemed better than he had that day they'd gone to the museum. While he'd kept a smile on his face and had seemed to enjoy his brothers' excitement about the Egyptian artifacts, he'd been quieter than usual. Now, it seemed his disposition had begun to return to normal.

"Yes." She hesitated, then decided he'd learn about her departure soon enough. "I came to tell them goodbye."

A shadow passed over his face before it cleared. "Goodbye? Are you going somewhere?"

"Yes. I will be leaving for the country the day after tomorrow."

He stepped down the stairs until he was two stairs above her, gazing down at her. She wished she could read the expression in his eyes.

Then, he murmured, "May I speak with you? Privately?"

Privately? Her mouth went dry, but then she shook herself free of those blasted nerves—and the thoughts of kissing him, which she'd been thinking about more and more over the past few days. Finding a private place, pulling him to her, and kissing him on those perfectly shaped, soft-looking lips.

Ugh. She was being ridiculous. She was turning into the exact kind of silly, lovelorn fool who usually made her roll her eyes in disgust. She despised kissing, she reminded herself. She'd tried it once, and it had been no fun at all.

"Of course, my lord," she said tightly.

He led her the rest of the way down the stairs and into a drawing room that could easily hold fifty people. It was vast, with high, elaborately plastered ceilings and wall paintings that looked like they were drawn by an Italian master. The room made her feel small and inconsequential.

He closed the door behind them, and they were alone in the echoing space. "Would you like something to drink? Another brandy?"

Brandy. That's what that awful drink had been. Still, awful or not, she felt the need to hold onto something. "Yes," she said. "Thank you."

Moving across the room, he busied himself for a few moments uncorking a bottle and then pouring amber liquid into two glasses. She looked around at the gilded furniture, the potted palms, the scarlet velvet-upholstered furniture, and for the first time, really considered this man's true status. Like her uncle, the Earl of Wydwick, Winthrop was an earl of the realm, but his earldom was richer and more ancient than her uncle's. He was a man of enormous wealth, an aristocrat to his marrow, but he was so friendly and unimposing with everyone, sometimes his lofty status was easy to forget.

For years, she'd thought him a phony, but his affability wasn't an act. He truly *was* warm and friendly. He honestly cared.

Frances could no longer conjure the irritation she used to feel in his presence.

Walking back to her, he handed her the glass, and she took a sip, this time expecting the fire as the liquid coursed down her throat.

His smile was light and his manner casual as he asked, "How long will you be gone?"

"A month, I think."

His smile fell away. "A month? That's a long time."

"If you'd asked me before, I would have said it was not long enough."

"And now?"

The way he looked at her... Frances shifted on her feet. "I must confess, it feels too long."

He studied her. "Is that so."

She took a quick sip of her drink to hide her grimace. Her answer had been bolder than she'd intended.

He studied her for a long while, his expression sliding into an intensity that made sparks erupt throughout her body. She drew in a shaky breath as he stepped forward, so close that she could smell his fresh scent. Cut grass and fresh air.

"Frances?" he murmured.

She blinked up at him. He'd never called her Frances before.

"Yes?" she managed, truly breathless now. He was so close, his essence blanketed her.

"Thank you for taking Jasper and Bobby to the museum. They loved it. So did I."

"I'm glad," she said, trying for a casual tone.

"At first, I worried about your presence when I met Bobby,

then Jasper, and then when we encountered you on our first outing. And then..." His voice drifted off as he reached up to touch a lock of her hair. "You have been nothing but..." He shook his head. "Well, you have been perfect. Kind and thoughtful, when my brothers and I needed it the most."

Kind and thoughtful? She quirked a brow. "I don't think anyone has ever called me either of those things before."

His chuckle was low and delicious. "You are both. Thank you for caring about us. About my brothers."

"They are..." She shook her head, unable to continue. It was difficult to put her fondness for the boys—inappropriate fondness, given her lack of familial relationship with them—into words.

He licked his lips—Lord, what wonderful lips—and nodded. "I know. I feel the same way about them. I never thought—" His breath caught, and she tilted her head in question.

He pulled in a deep breath that made his broad chest expand. "I never thought I'd feel...*family*. But you were right. They are my family. And I feel it with them."

"I understand," she said. In the past, she had often felt that comforting sensation of being surrounded by family. She longed for those days.

He gazed down at her. "I will miss you when you're gone."

"I'll miss you, too," she whispered, his words pulling the truth out of her.

"Frances..." He leaned closer, his breath a warm brush over her cheek. "May I kiss you goodbye?"

Chapter Fifteen

Oh Lord. Oh *yes*.

But she didn't like kissing.

But his lips…

Maybe kissing *his* lips wouldn't be so bad. Thinking of those perfect lips on hers made a shudder course through her. And suddenly she wanted him to kiss her more than anything she'd ever wanted in her life.

"Yes," she breathed.

He took her brandy from her clenched hand and set it, along with his glass, on a nearby table. Then he slid his fingers behind her neck, their tips sinking into her hair, and drew her close. He brushed his lips gently across hers, and they were so warm and soft, hers parted slightly.

He sipped at her mouth, a leisurely perusal, like he was exploring something delicate and delicious, taking his time.

All her previous knowledge of what kissing was crumbled to dust and blew away under the soft, erotic feel of the Earl of

Winthrop's lips over hers.

This was nothing like what she'd experienced with Salt. Not at all. This didn't make her want to push him away. Instead, it made her want to pull him closer, closer, until he was touching her like this everywhere. She let out a small, needy whimper, and he laughed softly against her mouth.

"You are just as delicious as I imagined you'd be."

Then, he kissed her again, his arms wrapping around her and tugging her closer until she was pressed against his hard chest. She trembled so hard he surely must feel it, and his arms tightened around her as if to hold her safely in his embrace. As she slipped her arms around him and pushed her palms to his back, a deep ache began to bloom in her core, and all she could think was, *More. I need more of this. More, more, more.*

They kissed for long moments. She didn't know exactly how long, and she didn't care. All she cared about was this man and how he was touching her. How he was making her *feel*. Her nerve endings were on fire, her heart pounding. He tasted like the country, fresh and clean, as he coaxed her lips open with his tongue to deepen their connection.

"Mmm," she said against him, and she mimicked his movements, pressing against him, fisting her hands in his coat as she pulled him even tighter to her.

Finally, he drew back. They stared at each other, their chests heaving with their breaths. He smiled, his eyes flashing with something akin to victory. "You're flushed."

She touched her lips with her fingertips. "I'm..." She dropped her hand and stared at him. "Hot."

"So am I," he said with a small wince. "You have no idea."

There was no way he could feel like she did. She was

overheated all over—even her big toe was buzzing—and he looked perfectly composed.

"I...I don't like kissing," she said in a tremulous voice.

He frowned. "You didn't—"

"I mean before," she said before he got the wrong idea. "I considered kissing quite an unpleasant endeavor. And in that, I was the anomaly among my sisters. As usual."

But it turned out her sisters had been right. Kissing was wonderful, but only when you were engaged in the act with the right person.

Her knees felt wobbly. Lord, she needed to sit down before she melted into the carpeted floor. In this room, however, that particular problem was easy to solve. Chairs and sofas were scattered everywhere. She selected the closest chair and sank into it.

He was studying her carefully. "And now?"

"Now..." she mused. She touched her tingling lips again. "Well, now I understand. Kissing is"—a tremor ran through her body—"a pleasure I could never have imagined until today."

"So that means you liked it."

She nodded.

His smile bordered on cocky. "You like kissing me better than you liked kissing Salt."

So he *did* know about her ruination. She blinked at him, feigning innocence. "Salt? Salt who?"

He laughed but then sobered quickly, a quizzical expression forming on his face. "Why, then?"

"Why what?"

"Why did you kiss him?"

Frances stiffened. "To be perfectly honest, my lord, I'd

rather return to the subject of kissing *you*. I have no interest in discussing Mr. Salt in any capacity."

"So you are not in love with him."

She snorted.

He shook his head. "It makes no sense, Frances. I've been thinking it over, and I cannot understand why you'd do it. And then, on top of that, to get *caught* doing it—" His brows drew together. "You told me yourself, you're too intelligent to get caught in such a fashion."

All the soft warmth that had been pulsing through her moments before was quickly dissipating. She straightened in the chair—which actually wasn't a very comfortable chair at all. It was like this room, beautiful and glittering and cold. She met Winthrop's questioning gaze. "I don't wish to talk about this, my lord."

Sighing, he sat across from her in a chair exactly like the one she was on. He dropped his elbows onto his knees and rested his chin on his clasped hands as he studied her. Finally, he spoke. "Call me Evan."

She just looked at him.

"You have been present at some of the most significant events in my life," he explained. "And after what just happened between us, I think we've earned the right to address each other by our proper names."

She gave him a small nod, thinking of how Jasper and Bobby had called him Evan earlier. Now, she could address him the same way. The thought set off a flutter in her belly, and she tried it out loud. "Evan."

He gave her a crooked smile. "That's better. Now explain why you kissed Salt after our encounter at the Worthington Masquerade. You said you were heading off to your destiny. But you were not behaving like an innocent, besotted miss."

She narrowed her eyes, wondering if he thought her besotted *now*. Because she was worried her besotted-ness was written all over her face. "How do you believe an innocent, besotted miss behaves?"

"Wistful. Dreamy. Hopeful. You were none of those things at the masquerade. Instead, you were determined. Serious. Like a soldier who had been given a very specific order. You mentioned finding your destiny. But, from the way you were saying it, it seemed to me you weren't searching for a destiny of love and marriage. So what was it, Frances? What *were* you searching for?"

She gazed at him, considering. She'd never planned to tell anyone the truth about what she'd done at the masquerade, but Winthrop—*Evan*—had seen through her actions even when her family had not. He hadn't made the conclusion her family had made about her encounter with Mr. Salt—that she had been a reckless fool.

Somehow, Evan understood her better than her own family did. Furthermore, he had known about her disgrace for some time, yet it hadn't changed his behavior toward her in the least. He hadn't cut her, nor seemed disappointed in her, nor treated her like an outcast. And unlike her brother, he could still look her in the eye.

Maybe she could tell him. But first, she needed his assurance that he'd keep the information to himself.

"I have kept secrets for you," she said.

He frowned at her sudden change in topic. "You have."

"Though they are not secrets anymore and everyone knows about your brothers, I didn't tell a soul about them.

Can I depend on the same discretion from you?"

"Of course," he said.

"If I tell you about what happened at the masquerade and *why* it happened," she continued, "I would ask you to never again mention Mr. Salt in my company."

He seemed to consider. "I will agree to those terms." He grimaced. "More than happy to agree to them, actually. The thought of you kissing another man is repulsive to me."

She frowned at him. "Why?"

He met her eyes, staring into them before answering. "Because I prefer to think of you kissing only me."

His words stole the breath from her lungs. She bit her lip and looked down. Another woman might have said something coy or flirtatious, but she didn't know how to be either. Finally, she looked up at him and told him the truth. "The thought of kissing anyone but you is repulsive to me, as well."

"Hm." Another slow, cocky smile spread over his lips. "I like that."

She scowled at him, a familiar annoyance sparking through her. "Don't like it too well, my lord. You may never receive another kiss from me."

"We'll see about that," he murmured.

She gritted her teeth. "I did not want to touch Mr. Salt. And the act of doing so..." She shivered. "Yes, it was repulsive. But it achieved the desired result."

A deep line appeared between his brows. "Which was?"

"I was ruined."

He was silent for a long moment. Then, "You *wished* to be ruined?"

"Yes."

"Why?"

"So I could be removed from the marriage mart. You saw firsthand how it upset me. And it was you who gave me the solution."

His jaw dropped. "I told you that you could be either married or aged out of the marriage mart. I did *not* tell you to go off and ruin yourself!"

"That's true. You conveniently ignored that option. But when you told me that marrying or growing old were my only choices, it occurred to me that you were quite wrong. I realized ruination was the best solution. It would free me from any obligation to the marriage mart or to marriage itself."

His brow furrowed as he worked out her motivations. "And you chose Salt...because you knew he wouldn't be in a position to offer for you afterward. He would be long gone into the far reaches of the world."

"Exactly."

"But there's still one thing I don't understand."

"What's that?"

"You said at the masquerade that you didn't wish to be married, but you never told me why."

She took a breath and then tried to explain once more what she'd tried to explain to her family for years. "Becoming proper wives is the only goal my sisters and I were expected to strive for. My sisters have all achieved that goal, and brilliantly, but they have also accomplished even more. Beyond their brilliant marriages, they have found their individual passions. Mary has her religion and her charity work. Harriet and Esther are popular young matrons in the community. Harriet is a talented artist and singer. Esther is a tour de force in our social sphere. And Martha..." She groaned softly. "My twin sister is pursuing her passion for ancient civilizations and alongside her husband has already made several noteworthy discoveries. But me? I haven't done anything of significance. I have no passions. I've felt like I've been trapped in a cage, all alone."

"You aren't alone, Frances," he said.

She realized he was right. Right now, she truly didn't feel alone. She felt connected...not only to the man sitting in front of her, but to the two amazing children upstairs. It was a surprising feeling, and she loved it more than she should.

Still, she continued, trying to make him understand. "I feel like being married would be an entirely different sort of prison, but one that will be even smaller than the one I live in now. At least as a single woman, I have some autonomy. If I married, I would have none.

"I have always lagged behind Charles and my sisters, not knowing my passions, not understanding my own desires. All I want is the opportunity to explore myself, but I haven't had it. Instead, I've been yanked from one ball, one soiree, one party, one masquerade to another, constantly being told how to be more ladylike, how to be more appealing to men, but how I have failed so terribly at doing that. Over and over, they tell me that I am not trying hard enough. They say I'm unfriendly. That I repel people."

"You don't repel *me*," he said tightly.

She didn't know how to respond to that statement, so she looked away again, heat creeping over her cheeks. "I just wanted to be free from all that. I couldn't bear it anymore. I really couldn't."

"But *ruined*?" Concern carved an even deeper line between

his brows. "There is no return from ruination. It's permanent. That kind of dark cloud will hover over you forever."

"I know." She shrugged. "I can endure a cloud. I was at the point where I was quite sure I wouldn't be able to endure one more pointless parade through the marriage mart."

"So, your goal was to cement your status as a ruined spinster."

"Yes. So I could have my life back for myself and never have to worry again about being brought before potential suitors like I'm a horse at auction."

He made a noise that sounded like a cross between a growl and a sputter. "At the masquerade you compared yourself to a slab of meat, and now you're comparing yourself to a horse. You've never been meat. You're certainly not a horse. At auction or anywhere else."

"Well, I'll take that as a compliment, I think," Frances said, fighting a smile. "But that's how it made me feel. And now I *am* free. Everyone knows I'm off the marriage mart once and for all. My brother has loosened his tight rein over me—back to the horse metaphor, I know." She did smile then. "My sisters have started to speak to me about things other than potential marriage partners. My life has improved."

"Despite being ruined?"

"*Because* of being ruined," she said emphatically.

"Despite being shunned and cut in public?"

Her chest clenched a little as it did every time she saw someone turning away from her. It had happened several times over the past week alone. She lifted her chin. "Well, that is not ideal, I must admit. But I still think it's an improvement over how I was living before. And that will certainly diminish as time goes on."

"I hope so," he muttered. "For your sake."

"That's kind of you to say," she said, then something softened inside her. "But do you know what those people have shown me?"

"What?"

"That they weren't worthy of being my friends to begin with. The people who matter, whom I actually like and respect…well, none of them have shunned me." Like Evan. He had known about her ruination all along and it hadn't changed his behavior toward her in the least. *He* was the kind of person who deserved her friendship.

"I see."

"And now I am leaving town, able to travel the English countryside completely on my own without restriction for the first time in my life. Well, on my own with four servants. But before being ruined, I would have never been allowed to go anywhere by myself."

Evan's expression darkened. "You've returned to this talk of you leaving."

She tilted her head. "You don't like the idea of me traveling alone, or you don't like the idea of me leaving London?"

"I don't like the idea of you leaving *me*," he said. "And the boys, of course. They are never going to stop asking me when you'll be back."

Her chest experienced that fluttering sensation again. He didn't want her to leave. For the first time in recent memory, she felt appreciated. *Wanted*. Those were rare feelings for her to experience, and she took a few seconds to savor them. Then, she smiled at him. "The time will fly with your brothers, and I will be back before you know it," she said. "And you, Jasper, and Bobby will be the first people I visit as soon as I return."

Chapter Sixteen

It had been a fortnight since Evan had received the letter telling him his real mother was gone. When he'd first read it, he'd felt abandoned, like he was singlehandedly navigating a life through a dangerous storm. But then Frances had come. Her presence had taken some of the weight off his shoulders, and throughout the day at the British Museum, she had quietly checked on him, making sure he was all right.

Evan's mother had died of consumption. With the money Evan's father had given her, she had bought the house in Manchester and let rooms in it to support herself. A year before her death, she'd married, and her husband had been the one who'd responded to Evan. He'd said in the letter that she was gone and had been for nearly thirty years. They'd had no children, but he'd written that she had been a kind and loving wife.

Evan rubbed his temples. Every time he thought of his mother and started to feel that sense of abandonment well up, he remembered Frances. Thoughts of her made him feel less alone, even though she had left London a week ago.

He missed watching her interact with the boys, seeing how they hung on her every word and how she made them feel important—even loved. He missed her barely there smile that reached her eyes quicker than it reached her lips. He missed her caramel-colored hair and sweetly curved body, and the soft, tentative touch of her kiss—

He hadn't nearly had his fill of either her hair or her body on that last day in his drawing room. Why the hell had he refrained from kissing her again? God knew, he'd wanted to.

The way the creamy skin of her breasts had swelled above the neckline of her light-blue dress when she'd taken in a deep lungful of air…

He sucked in a breath and adjusted himself in his chair. Thinking of her like that was making him hard. Thinking of her being far away, though, made something strange and painful twist in his chest.

A light knock on the door had him looking up. "Come in."

It was Franklin. "Another letter for you, sir."

"Thank you, Franklin."

When the door closed behind the older man, Evan turned the letter over. The folded sheet of paper had traveled some distance, if the charge mark on the front indicating the postage of one shilling was any indication. He sat down at his desk, opened it, and read.

My Lord Winthrop,

The Parish of Windermere has recently taken in an abandoned child. He arrived into our care with a letter pinned to his coat. The letter, written by the previous Lord Winthrop, promised financial assistance for the care of the child. The child's mother is nowhere to be found, the unfortunate evidence suggesting she has departed the country.

Therefore, the child is being kept as a ward of the Parish, and we will be providing for his care. We humbly request that you send either a portion, or all, of the funds promised by the previous earl for his keeping.

Yr hmbl & obt svt,
Rev. Wm. Barton

As he read, Evan's mouth dropped open.

How many more of Evan's brothers had his father left scattered around England?

...

On a particularly beautiful mid-June day, Frances decided to row one of the boats to the village of Bowness. She had been enjoying her uncle's house, Shorewood, on the banks of Lake Windermere, for over two weeks. She had read five books and skimmed over two scientific tomes, had gone on long, exploratory walks, and had written another page in her novel.

The novel was four pages long so far and already consisted of three lists of events that didn't seem very novel-like. She was beginning to think she was more of a list-writer than a novelist.

Her uncle didn't plan to return to the district until later in the summer when she would be long gone, so she had the run of his country house and its lush grounds that were such a bright green this time of year, she felt like she'd passed through the veil into the land of faeries.

Almost three hundred miles away from the constant buzz of disapproval that surrounded her in London, Frances's mind had cleared, and she felt like she could take a deep breath for the first time in months. And as she did so, she realized something.

She couldn't get Evan off her mind.

Something had shifted inside her that afternoon in his drawing room when he'd held her in his arms and kissed her. Something essential to whom she'd always thought she was. Evan's kiss had *changed* her.

Shaking that disturbing thought from her mind, she paused halfway down the slope that led to the water's edge and turned back to her maid. "Are you coming, Peggy?"

"My heels are sinking into the grass, miss," Peggy groused.

"I know," Frances said. "So are mine. Isn't it glorious?"

Peggy scowled. Poor girl. Dragged from coal-dirtied, putrid London to this idyllic place that smelled of clean hay and fresh water, dirtied her heels, and made her constantly sneeze.

"Do you need help?" Frances asked her.

"No, no. I'm coming," Peggy grumbled, primly lifting her skirts and taking mincing steps down the grassy slope.

Frances turned and, gripping her journal to her chest, strode the rest of the way down the hill, loving the feel of the heels of her half-boots sinking into the soft grass. There had been a terrific rainstorm last night that had left the area shiny and clean and gave Frances the sensation of being in a land made of jewels. The grass sparkled like emeralds. Just ahead, the lake glittered blue sapphire, a perfect reflection of the sky, dotted with a few pearly white clouds drifting past.

A minute later, she was at the shore. After setting her journal onto one of the bench seats, she began to drag the boat toward the water.

"You'll ruin your shoes, miss!" Peggy called, a note of panic in her voice.

Ah, such a city girl. "Never fear. I spent my childhood beside this lake. I know how to launch a boat without getting my feet wet."

"Well, I don't!" Peggy's voice was a near screech.

When the boat was half floating, Frances helped her maid climb in. Peggy fell into it in a jumble of skirts and limbs. Sorting herself on the rear bench, she muttered about how unladylike the whole process was. With a great push, Frances launched the boat into the lake and hopped inside neatly before a drop of water touched her.

Peggy gaped at her. "How on earth did you do that?"

"Skill, Peggy," Frances told her. "Pure skill."

It had been a good eight years since she'd last rowed a boat. She'd had a little flash of nerves, imagining falling face-first into the lake for a second before she'd pushed hard and simply allowed her body to do what it knew how to do. And she'd succeeded.

She picked up the oars. "Off to Bowness," she said cheerfully. She glanced at her journal. "Then on the way back, I should like to pause for a while on the water to record my observations of the area."

"Very well, miss. You must remain ducked well beneath your bonnet, though, or you will turn quite brown from this scorching sun."

Frances shook her head. Peggy had already forced her to wear the largest-brimmed straw bonnet she'd brought. She'd be fine.

She started rowing, feeling the comfortable pull on arm muscles that hadn't been used in years and watching Peggy, who gripped the edge of the seat in terror and looked right and left as if she feared capsizing. "Peggy, this might be the largest lake in England, but it's not large enough to contain waves, nor sea monsters, nor anything that will topple us. We are quite safe."

"We're *rocking*," Peggy said tightly, her face pinched into a grimace.

After a while, they neared Bowness. Set back a short walk from the water, the village's rooftops and church spire were hardly visible above the thick greenery. A few minutes later, Frances beached the boat. She jumped out onto dry land and reached a hand to Peggy, who stood up shakily. The boat gave a little groan and a warning rock as Peggy reached for Frances, and Peggy screeched as if she feared for her very life.

"It's all right," Frances said, keeping her voice calm. "Just take my hand and climb out. Easy." She could hear the rapid footsteps behind her—some gentleman likely, lured by the cries of a female in distress.

"Allow me to help, miss," a low voice said.

She recognized that voice. Dropping her hand, she whipped around and met the equally shocked gaze of the Earl of Winthrop.

It was then that Peggy fell overboard.

• • •

A dozen things happened at once. There was a splash, then

a sudden cacophony of screams—Frances's maid, Miss Renshaw, Bobby, Mark, perhaps even Jasper.

Jasper and Bobby sprinted toward Frances. Miss Renshaw called for them to stay back, managing to pluck up Mark who'd been hurrying after them. Frances ran to her maid, who appeared to be drowning in water that was a foot deep, her thrashing about painfully exaggerated. Evan lunged after Frances, grabbed her by the waist, and set her neatly back down behind him, the boys crowding around her, before going up to his ankles in water and plucking the maid out.

She was soaked and muddy, screaming and shaking and distraught. Frances detached herself from Bobby and Jasper and squeezed the maid's hands into her own. "You're all right, Peggy. Everything is all right."

Eventually, she succeeded in getting the girl to settle down. When the air was no longer rent with screams and shouts and sobs, Evan asked Frances the question that had been competing with the din of the maid in his mind.

"Why on earth are *you* here?"

"Why are *you* here?" she retorted, glancing back at him. "And with Bobby and Jasper and Miss Renshaw?" Then her eyes wandered behind him to the three boys standing in a row, Jasper in the middle holding both the younger boys' hands, and Miss Renshaw standing behind them. "And who…"

Her voice dropped off, and he knew she was seeing what he had the first moment he'd laid eyes on Mark.

Yes. It was the eyes. That amber tint all four brothers had inherited from their father.

"Miss Cherrington, I'd like you to meet my brother, Mark Smith." He always felt a little breathless when he uttered the boy's Christian name. It had been their father's name, as well.

"Good morning, Mark. It is nice to meet you," Frances said.

Mark forestalled any conversation by inserting his thumb into his mouth.

Frances blinked at him, then turned back to Evan. "How old is he?"

"Five."

"My goodness, my lord," she said under her breath. "I'm starting to harbor concerns that you might have brothers scattered across the entirety of England."

"As am I," Evan said, his own breath gusting out in a sigh. Then he frowned. "Why are *you* here, Frances?" Could it be a coincidence that they both found themselves three hundred miles away from London in the same village?

"I spent my childhood not far from here. Our beloved family home, Windermere Cottage, was sold years ago, but my uncle's estate, Shorewood, is nearby. I am residing there for the time being."

Her uncle…the Earl of Wydwick. Bosom friend of none other than the late Earl of Winthrop. That would explain why Evan's father had been carousing in this area—he had come to visit the earl.

Frances turned back to the maid. "Peggy, we need to return to Shorewood to clean you up. Do you think you can get into the boat?"

Peggy looked as horrified as if Frances had just suggested she saw off her own leg. "No!" she declared hoarsely. "No boats! Never! *Never* again!"

Frances pushed out a breath. "Peggy, we need—"

Knowing exactly how to remedy this situation, Evan

broke in. "I am certain Mr. Barton at the rectory"—he gestured to the one house in the village situated near the water's edge—"will be happy to supply his fire for you to dry off while I row back to Shorewood to fetch a carriage for you to return in."

"Oh, thank you, sir," Peggy breathed, shuddering as a light wind gusted past. "I shall never venture near a boat again—those contraptions are far too dangerous for the likes of me."

They helped the sodden maid to the rectory, where Mr. Barton and his wife fussed over her. It was agreed that Miss Renshaw and the boys would stay while Evan and Frances rowed back to Shorewood to fetch the carriage.

Side by side, Evan and Frances walked to the boat. God*damn*, he was happy to see her. He couldn't seem to wipe the smile from his lips.

The way he was starting to feel about this woman...

This *stubborn* woman, he amended when they arrived at the boat. She wouldn't allow him to hand her into the boat like a gentleman, instead insisting on helping him launch it from the beach.

As a team, they pushed the boat into the water and hopped in. Evan was impressed at how she managed it—there was no way he would be able to maneuver so gracefully if he were towing around all those skirts and petticoats.

Regardless of her apparent skill, Evan took up the oars before she could get to them.

She shot him a pretty scowl. "I can row, you know."

"I do not doubt it." He grinned at her.

She didn't grin back. "I *should* be the one to row. I know how to get there, and you don't."

"Even if I couldn't see the grand house on the rise above the bank over there"—he gestured to the elegant house in the distance he was sure must be Shorewood—"you could instruct me on which direction to take."

Her scowl deepened. "I could get us there more efficiently."

He laughed. "Frances, I haven't rowed for a few weeks. I miss it. Will you allow me this? Please?"

"Well, before today, I hadn't rowed in eight *years*. I missed it, too." She crossed her arms. "But very well. I wouldn't want those lovely muscles to shrink, now, would I?"

He watched as she recognized her inadvertent flirtation. Her face went stony, and she turned away, even as his smile widened. God, he'd missed her.

Never, ever had he thought he'd be in a boat with a lady arguing about who should do the rowing. It was *magical*. As he started to row, his cheeks began to hurt from how hard he was smiling.

"What are you grinning about?" she asked crossly.

"You. You're entertaining."

She cocked a brow at him. *"Entertaining?"*

"You are one of a kind, Frances."

She lapsed into silence before she shrugged. "I am rather different from most females of my acquaintance." She met his gaze. "I am told—repetitively—that that is a terrible thing."

"On the contrary." He thought it was a wonderful thing. "I didn't know you liked rowing."

"I do like it. I suppose it's a product of having grown up near a large body of water and having been the 'boyish' one of my sisters, always forced to do the rowing whenever we girls found ourselves in a boat together."

"I'll take you out in one of our shells sometime when we're back in London."

She tilted her head. "Shells are not like boats, though, are they? I've heard they are tippy."

"Tippy?" He shrugged. "I've only tipped a shell over... oh, perhaps a hundred times."

Her brows popped up. "A *hundred* times?"

"It's not a problem if you know how to swim. And something tells me that you are one of those rare ladies who does indeed know how to swim."

"You would be correct. I do. However, tipping over into the sewage-filled waters of the Thames sounds disgusting."

"We'll be careful. We won't capsize." He locked eyes with her. "Do you trust me?"

She stared at him, considering. Then she said something that made delight course through him. "I'm beginning to."

A bird call trumpeted in the distance, and they both looked up as a pair of cranes soared low over the surface of the water, their black-and-white necks arched forward, their wings long and elegant.

"Now that's a sight rarely seen in London," Evan murmured.

"Aren't they lovely? They mate for life, you know."

"Is that so? Just like humans."

"Well..." She paused. "Some of them, anyhow. Your father was not one of them."

He burst out laughing. He loved her directness. "True."

"So, tell me about little Mark. He seems timid, but sweet."

"He is quite shy. The opposite of Bobby and Jasper, who have lived in London their whole lives and have much more world experience." He sighed. "Mark misses his mother, but the woman abandoned him last month seemingly without a care." He could only be thankful she'd left that note pinned to the lad. Otherwise, Evan would never have known about him.

A frown creased Frances's brow. "That's awful. I cannot imagine why anyone would leave their child like that. What that woman must have gone through."

He nodded. That was a new way to look at it. Since he'd arrived in the area, he'd heard nothing but vitriol and scorn toward Mark's mother.

"So, you have found three brothers," she mused. "Do you think there might be more? A sister or three, perhaps?"

He shook his head. "I don't know, although I have spent several days scouring my father's accounts for any further payments that are out of the ordinary. I found none."

"Well, there's that, at least. But I imagine you still must be on your guard."

"I am. And I will continue to be." Pausing rowing, he combed his hand through his hair.

"And you intend to keep all three of them with you now?" she asked.

"Yes," he responded, feeling a surge of protectiveness for his three little brothers. "They are my blood, and it's my duty to care for them." He picked up the oars again and gave a strong, satisfying pull. "More than that, I *want* to."

"They are so lucky you found them," she said.

It came upon him as he rowed and watched her gaze at him with her eyes warm and her lips twisting up in that almost smile of hers—a jolt of awareness. He'd known the first time he'd laid eyes on her that he was attracted to her. But now he knew that he wanted her. He wanted her not only in his bed, but also in his life.

He wanted to make her his.

Chapter Seventeen

Frances could not stop staring at the Earl of Winthrop's lips. Those *appealing* lips she'd dreamed about so many times since she'd left London.

She was smitten. She knew this before she left town, but she'd been fighting it then. And now, watching him rowing, his arms and chest flexing under the fabric of his coat, she didn't want to fight it anymore.

She'd never been smitten before. The sensation was altogether new. And rather exciting, now that she wasn't rejecting it anymore.

And miraculously, he was *here*. Sitting across from her on a boat on Lake Windermere, *her* lake.

"I'm glad you're here," she said. A warm flush broke out on her chest as he gazed at her with those steady amber eyes.

The oars stilled, skimming the surface of the water.

"Frances."

No one had ever said her name like that before. With a

low, sensual growl that whispered across her skin and left gooseflesh in its wake.

"Yes?"

He pulled one oar into the boat, then the other. He removed his hat and leaned forward on the seat facing her, his fingertips lightly touching her knee. She stared at his long fingers, felt the heat of them through the layers of her skirts.

He scooted closer to the edge of his seat, and so did she, moving until their knees bumped. Keeping one hand on her leg, he touched her cheek gently with the other, stroking downward until his fingers moved under her chin. With a firm tug, he loosened the bow of her bonnet and then removed it from her head and set it beside her.

Exposing her to the scorching sun. Peggy would have the vapors.

"I cannot stop thinking about kissing you," he murmured.

All thoughts of Peggy vanished.

She licked her lips automatically. "I can't either."

A smile flickered across his face. "Ah. You threatened me last we met that I might never have the pleasure of another of your kisses. I'm starting to hope you might have changed your mind."

She laughed gruffly. "I think I changed my mind the moment after I said it."

His smile widened, and he squeezed her knee.

And then he was kissing her. This time, it wasn't tentative or exploring. It wasn't a quest of sweet discovery like the last one had been.

This was an explosion of passion. She wrapped her arms around his neck, thrust her fingers into his thick, soft hair, and pulled him closer. He kissed deeply, his lips parting, his tongue probing between her lips until she opened them. Their tongues touched, and a shudder ran down her all the way to her toes.

His hand skimmed up her side and, very gently, passed over her breast. And even though his touch was light, she gasped into his mouth. He tightened his fingers over her, and even through her dress and petticoat and stays and shift, she could feel his fingers brushing over the sensitive peak of her nipple. She curled her hands in his hair, and he kissed her even deeper, pulling her to the very edge of the bench seat with one arm while his other hand explored the curves of her breasts until she was shaking, her whole body an aching nerve.

Something splashed nearby, and they jerked apart. Both of them gasping, they looked around, seeing nothing but ripples radiating outward from where a fish had jumped out of the water.

Frances turned back to Evan, whose hair was delectably rumpled, his cheeks flushed, his amber eyes dark as he met her gaze with his own.

He managed a shaky laugh. "It's good these seats are positioned so far apart."

"Why is that?"

"Because if I were any closer to you, I might have taken liberties."

Her breath caught. "What kind of liberties?"

His smile grew wicked, his eyes flaring with heat. "The kind where I remove your dress and everything beneath it and explore your body everywhere."

She gasped softly at how the erotic words felt like gentle fingers caressing her skin, but she didn't break the eye contact.

"I'd like that."

He groaned. "Don't say that."

"Why not?"

"Don't tempt me. I'm already too tempted. I don't want to ruin you."

"I'm already ruined," she reminded him.

"No. I'm not speaking of mere kisses."

Her skin prickled. "I know."

He groaned and tugged her toward him to kiss her again, this time softly. He pulled back far too soon. "I'm going to row to Shorewood now," he said, reaching up to loosen his cravat and unbutton his coat.

Then, in his shirt and waistcoat, he took up the oars and swung them over the lip of the hull and back into the water.

Her jaw nearly dropped as she watched muscles strain against the confines of his shirt as he rowed in long, deep strokes, each pull making the boat leap forward eagerly.

This man was truly exquisite.

He rowed in silence for a while, and she watched him. He worked with his jaw clenched, with singular determination, not meeting her eyes, looking over his shoulder every once in a while to ensure they were still headed in the correct direction. Sweat began to bead on his chest revealed by the vee of his shirt. Frances ached to see the rest of that chest. She ached for another one of his kisses.

All of a sudden, he stopped rowing. The oars went into the boat with a soft *thunk*, though the boat continued to glide forward for several yards before it began to slow.

He moved to the seat beside her, the boat rocking as she adjusted so they were balanced. He pressed up against her side, and she could feel the heat of him on her skin, despite the layers of fabric separating them.

She slipped her arms around him because there was nowhere else her arms wanted to be.

"I thought if I rowed hard enough, I could row the desire out of me," he said. "But it's not working."

"Kiss me again then," she said.

"I thought you'd never ask." And then he kissed her even harder, with a sharp edge of desire that had every nerve in her body thrumming. One of his arms wrapped behind her back. His fingers dug into her hair at the base of her scalp, dragging her toward him. His tongue glided into her mouth for a lick, a small taste, and she was lost.

She shifted and moved over him so she straddled his lap and plunged her hands under his waistcoat at his lower back so she could feel his solid muscles. He trailed his fingertips down her waist to her thigh, where he rucked up her skirts and gripped her stockinged leg beneath the knee, pulling her even closer. His lips moved from her mouth to her jaw and then down her neck until he was nipping along the top edge of her bodice.

"God," he muttered. "I want this off you."

She gave a husky laugh. She felt the same about his waistcoat and shirt. Instead, she teased, "You want me naked in the middle of Lake Windermere? I don't think so, my lord."

He gave a little growl and his hand traveled up her leg, over her garter and the back of her thigh. "You're so damned soft."

"And you're so damned….muscly," she breathed, digging his shirt out of the waistband of his trousers and pressing her palms against the rippling muscles of his bare back. His skin was taut, hot, and purely, delightfully male.

Finally, skin against skin, they both shuddered, him touching the back of her thigh, her fingers moving over his shoulder blades.

"I want you," he said, his lips brushing against her ear.

The amazing thing was...she wanted him, too. Her whole body *ached* for him. For his touch, the pleasure she innately knew he could give her. "Yes."

He pulled back just a little, far enough so his eyes could search hers. She saw the hesitation in his expression, and she couldn't be sure, but there seemed to be a bit of vulnerability there, too. His hand still held her leg, his grip firm, as if he couldn't bear to release her just yet.

He laughed softly, his fingers making brushstrokes under her thigh. "I want you more than I've ever wanted anything."

Her chest felt tight. "Is that true?"

"It is."

And she'd never wanted anything like she wanted him. It buzzed under her skin, this ache for him. This desire. This *demand*.

Then he glanced up and, with a slight frown, looked toward the shore, where the immaculately maintained, modern house sat on the rise overlooking the beach.

They were already nearly at her uncle's house. She shifted off him. Even though people probably couldn't see exactly what they were doing out here, they were getting a little too close to be certain. Evan was too good a rower.

She pulled in a shaky breath. "We should get back to Peggy."

He nodded, and with a sigh he returned to his seat and took up the oars once more. He was quiet the rest of the way to the beach. She was perfectly content to watch him, for now.

She didn't think she'd ever seen any picture more appealing than that of the Earl of Winthrop rowing, his powerful shoulders flexing with every pull.

Still, as much as she willed it to, the constant thrum of need under her skin refused to dissipate.

He beached the boat, and she allowed him to properly help her out, only because she knew he desired to play the gentleman. He lifted her out of the boat and set her gently on the ground. She smiled up at him. "Thank you, Evan."

"My pleasure," he said, his rumbling voice a pleasure of its own.

Side by side, they began to walk up the grassy incline. Just as they reached the front door, she leaned toward him, allowing her lips to barely brush his jaw.

"I want to see you again," she whispered. "Meet me at the beach tonight at eleven o'clock."

Chapter Eighteen

By half ten, Evan finally got Mark to go down. As he had every other night for the past several nights, the boy had cried himself to sleep, whimpering for his mama. It was damned heartbreaking.

Tonight, though, he hadn't turned away from Evan as he had for the past several nights. Instead, he'd wrapped his arms around Evan's neck and had wept into his shoulder.

Poor sweet boy. Walking into the room he'd rented for his brothers, Miss Renshaw, and the maid they'd brought up north with them—with Evan's valet, the group of them had made quite the convoy traveling up here—Evan laid him down gently. His eyes flickered open, and Evan brushed a soothing hand over his forehead. "Sleep now, lad."

Mark's long eyelashes finally fluttered as his eyes closed, and his little chest rose and fell in sleep. Evan watched him for another couple of minutes before rising and quietly stepping out of the room, closing the door softly behind him.

There. Everyone was abed. It had been a long afternoon and evening—by the time he and Frances had returned to the rectory, Jasper had thrown a ball through one of the reverend's windows, Bobby had climbed onto the roof, and Mark had been curled in a corner sucking his thumb. Frances had helped him get the boys under control, but her maid was still wet and shivering, and all too soon, she'd had to leave.

He'd taken the boys back to the inn, ordered them a trio of much-needed baths—which had resulted in quite the battle from Bobby—and had finally gathered everyone to a dinner in the common room before reading them a bit of *Robinson Crusoe* before their bedtime.

By the door in the sitting room, he grabbed his coat and slipped out into the corridor. He hadn't informed anyone but his valet that he was going out tonight, and had told Johnson so he could find him—"Only in the event of an emergency."

The Sun Inn was a fine establishment, filled with tourists from all walks of life come to explore the wonders of the lake. For Evan, who'd never visited the area before, its beauty was a pleasant side effect of his real purpose for being here.

Throughout dinner with his brothers earlier tonight, he'd thought of how he was creating this new family—the four of them all unwanted boys who he hoped could one day find comfort and family in one another. But during the pleasant meal of fresh fish from the lake, he kept thinking of the thing that would make their family complete.

Frances Cherrington.

Not only was that a selfish thought, but he'd been willfully ignoring his biggest secret of all. The fact that he wasn't really the Earl of Winthrop.

He hadn't even told his closest friends—those men who'd

been more his family than his own family ever had—about his true parentage. How would he ever be able to bring himself to tell Frances, the woman he most wanted to see him as someone to be admired?

The truth was, he was ashamed of his true parentage. And, worse than that, he was ashamed of the title he'd stolen and the position he pretended to hold, when, as a bastard son who couldn't legally hold such a title, he didn't deserve it.

He couldn't have Frances forever, because she didn't want to be married. And she especially wouldn't want to marry a liar or a pretender. He was both of those things.

But maybe he could have her for a short time. A short time would be better than nothing.

He hurried out of the inn and descended to the dock situated in front of the establishment. He could have walked to the Earl of Wydwick's house tonight, but he loved being on the water and would choose to traverse over water rather than over land any day.

He'd already arranged for the use of the boat tonight, and he found it just as he'd requested, with a basket of food and wine as well as a pair of sturdy blankets tucked under one of the seats.

He stepped in, readied the oars, and cast off.

Twenty minutes later, the hull scraped over the rocky beach, and he jumped out, secured the boat, then, his nerves buzzing with the anticipation of seeing Frances soon, he found a grassy spot invisible from the house but with a prospect of the lake, its surface reflecting silver from the waxing moon. He laid out one of the blankets and the food, then lowered himself onto it and waited.

She arrived not long afterward, and, checking his pocket

watch, Evan saw that she was early. He wondered if she was strung as tightly with anticipation as he was. He rose from the blanket and walked to the beach to greet her.

"Frances?"

She spun around to face him. Her hair was down in long waves framing her face, and she was wearing only a thin night rail under her cloak. He swallowed hard, feeling like a green boy.

He'd had women before, but none like Frances Cherrington. None who'd initiated their liaison as she had. None who had fire racing through his blood or made him want to kneel in worship at their feet.

"My lord," she breathed, her gaze sweeping over him, and he could see color rising in her cheeks even in the dim moonlight.

He reached out to her. "I've found a place where we can be comfortable."

She slipped her hand into his, and he led her to the blanket. When she was seated, he lowered himself beside her and offered her a bit of wine. She took it gratefully, her hands trembling.

"Are you nervous?" he asked quietly.

"Yes."

His Frances. Direct, as always. He loved that about her.

"I'm not going to ravish you, Frances. We can sit here and enjoy the moonlight and talk all night long if you wish it."

She looked at him, a little frown turning down the corners of her lips. "I was always warned if I ever found myself alone with a man who wasn't my direct relative that he would waste no time in ravishing me."

He laughed. "I imagine most women are told such things."

"To keep us in line. To ensure we remain docile and

obedient." She took a sip of the wine.

"Probably," he agreed. "But they're not completely wrong. Some men are disgusting pigs who will take what they want without any regard for a lady's desires. Though the responsibility to behave should be placed squarely upon the shoulders of those men, not on the ladies they impose themselves upon."

"You are not one of those men," she said confidently.

"No. I am not."

"But what do you want?" she asked softly. "Do you want what I want?"

"What do you want?" he asked

"To be with you," she said simply.

"Then, yes. I want that, too."

They stared at each other for a moment. It was inevitable. They surged together. As soon as he touched her, his cock stiffened to a nearly unbearable degree, thrusting against the falls of his trousers, demanding satisfaction.

He pushed the cloak off her shoulders, and it puddled around her in velvety folds. He kissed her until she was breathless, panting, and clutching at his lapels.

Finally, he drew back to shrug out of his coat and grab his shirt behind his neck, pulling it over his head. Then he spread out her cloak across the blanket and laid her down upon it before moving to pull off her damp shoes one by one, revealing bare, stockingless feet. She gazed up at him, her chest heaving like she'd run a mile, her eyes glittering in the moonlight as she took in the bare flesh of his torso.

She reached for him. "Let me touch you."

He leaned over her, caging her body with his arms and holding himself above her as she explored him, running curious fingers over his biceps and forearms, then up, over his chest. His cock throbbed, and it was almost all he could do not to rock against her. When he sucked in a breath as her fingertips passed over his nipples, she hesitated.

"Are you sensitive there?"

"Yes," he gritted out.

"So am I."

He smiled, then reached to untie the neck of her night rail. He pulled it down over her shoulder until one pale, pert breast was exposed. Then he knelt and licked the tip. She jerked under him.

"Sensitive?" he asked.

"Yes." She gave a little moan. "Do it again."

Her wish was his command. He dove into the task, cupping her breast in a perfect handful, kissing, licking, and dragging his teeth over her flesh until she squirmed. All the while, her hands continued to roam over him, swirling around his nipples again and again, driving him mad with desire. He switched to her other breast, covering that one and then pulling off the other shoulder for access. But he wanted both of them.

He reared up onto his knees. "Sorry, Frances. The nightgown must go."

Her eyes widened, but before she could say anything, he had gripped the hem of the garment and was tugging it up her body. He tapped her hip. "Up," he commanded.

She lifted her bottom, and he passed the night rail over her body inch by inch, revealing pale, creamy skin. She smelled like clean muslin and lilac soap. She was a confection of delight, and he wanted to taste it all.

He *was* going to taste it all. She was his, for this moment, offering herself to him, and he would take full advantage of every second of it.

He pulled the garment over her head, leaving her fully naked. He allowed his eyes to peruse her slowly, his fingertips trailing in a caress that followed his gaze.

Her hair cascaded around her heart-shaped, flushed face, and her pert breasts were tipped with rosy nipples that rose and fell as she breathed. Her waist was small but flared into generous hips that revealed the dark triangle of hair between her legs.

Not yet, he told himself.

Her thighs were plump and pale, and her feet were half the size of his, small and delicate. She was so feminine, a beautiful, sensual woman on full display. Revealing herself to him completely, without a qualm. His throat grew thick with emotion. He was all too cognizant of the gift that she was offering him. He'd never make her regret it.

Starting at her little feet, he scattered kisses up her warm, soft skin until he reached her hip bone. Then he moved up, kissed her on her lips again, and said, "Frances, I want to kiss you everywhere."

"All—all right," she breathed.

"Everywhere."

Something in the way he said it made her breath catch. "Oh," she said, wide-eyed. "Will that be…enjoyable?"

"Yes," he said confidently. "For us both."

He waited while she considered this. Then she said, "Yes, please."

With a self-satisfied grin, he traveled back down her body once more, stopping to lavish attention on her breasts until her hands were tangled in his hair and she was pushing him closer.

He slid his hand between her legs, seeking out her center.

His fingertips collided with a scorching wetness that made him growl.

It was perfect. He was so hungry for her. Without any further delay, he moved down her body and pressed her legs open, baring her to him.

Even in the dim light, he could see the pink wetness that showed how ready she was for him. He kissed a spot high on the inside of her thigh then pressed his lips to her glistening folds.

"Oh!" she cried out, her body twitching.

He kissed her. She tasted hot and clean and perfect, and when she began to squirm, he clamped his palms down on her thighs, holding her in place. He circled the taut little bud above her opening over and over, flicked his tongue over it, then teased her without touching it. When she was begging, "Please, please, please," punctuated with sweet little whimpers, he returned his attention to that sensitive nub, sucking it, kissing it, teasing it.

Under his hands, her thighs grew tense, and all of a sudden, she cried out, her body going rigid, then, despite the pressure he kept on her thighs, she jerked and spasmed as she tumbled over her peak.

He gentled his torment as the contractions slowly lessened and her body grew limp. He pressed one last kiss to her heated center as he kicked off his shoes and removed his trousers. Then he crawled over her until he looked down at her pretty face. She stared at him with glazed eyes.

"Kiss me," he commanded. "Taste yourself."

She kissed him and kissed him, and soon, her arms were tight around him and her tongue was darting hungrily into his mouth again.

She was a vixen. He smiled into the kiss, even as his cock felt like it was going to burst if he didn't feel her tight walls clenching around him soon.

"I need to be inside you," he whispered gruffly.

She canted her hips. "Yes," she whispered back. "Yes, yes, yes. Please. *Now*."

Nearly blinded by the lust that had been accumulating in him all afternoon, he thrust into her with one long, hard push, feeling her tight resistance, the sensation so blissful it made his eyes slam shut.

She cried out and went stiff. For a whole different reason this time.

He froze. He'd hurt her. "Oh God," he choked out. "I'm—"

"No," she said, her voice shaking. "It's all right. I'm all right."

She wasn't all right—he could tell by her grimace—but he'd do what it took, whatever it took, for her expression to become glazed over by desire once more. He pressed a gentle kiss to her lips, his own thighs trembling with restraint. His body was telling him to move *more, faster, harder*, but he wouldn't listen to it. The only thing he would listen to was Frances—her words, her expression, her needs. Because nothing was more important.

He kissed her softly and thoroughly, stroking his thumb over her cheekbone, painfully slowly, starting to move in small and then longer strokes. He turned them both to the side so he could reach down and press his hand between them, stroking that sensitive bud above where they were joined.

He took his time, ignoring the calls of his base instinct to drive into her. Instead, he tried to soak in all the sensations of her. Her soft, sweet lips, the wet heat between her legs, the tight clasp of her body over his.

"God," he whispered, "you're so beautiful. This...this is beautiful."

Soon she was gasping into his mouth, arching into him, driving him deeper with her movements, her pain either diminished completely or driven to the background. Her need overtook her, and she was craning up toward him, murmuring, "Please, Evan. More. Please."

She was ready for all of him now. But first, her pleasure. He pressed his fingertips over her sex and drove in at an angle that made her whimper in pleasure rather than pain. Yes. That. He knew he could do it. Bring this woman over the edge into ecstasy a second time. He focused on it, a singular goal driving through him and into her. *Bring her to the brink, then push her over it. Feel her release.*

And soon enough, she cried out, her body going stiff, then spasming around him. Oh God. Fire crackled in the base of his spine, but no. He couldn't come, not yet. First, he had to see her through. Gritting his teeth so hard he was surprised they didn't break, he stroked her until she relaxed under him, her shuddering body limp with gratification.

Then, he really let go, loosening the reins and allowing his body to roar to life. He thrust into her like a man possessed. Never had he been so in the moment, so consumed by lust, by pleasure.

But then, it was too much. He was going to come. A gut-wrenching groan lurched from him as he pulled out of her. Then, with his weight on one forearm, he worked his cock until his release spattered over her lower belly and he moaned her name.

Chapter Nineteen

Evan gathered Frances close and pulled the blanket over them. There, in the cozy comfort of his arms, Frances felt boneless and light as air. After a while, he shifted his weight.

"Mmm," she said, her eyes fluttering open.

He was sitting up and gazing down at her, his expression full of soft warmth, a genuine affection that made her insides melt. "Are you all right?" he asked her.

"I am," she replied. "More than all right." She felt languid, relaxed. Comfortable, like she didn't want to move ever again.

He reached over to the basket and brought out a napkin, which he used to gently clean her. She smiled, studying the divot between his brows as he focused on the job. He was so thoughtful.

He glanced at her, his own smile playing at the edge of his lips. "Are you laughing at me?"

"No," she said. "Not at all."

He dropped a kiss on her lips and continued his ministrations to her body. When he finished, he refilled her cup of wine. "Do you want to eat?"

"Honestly, I don't want to move."

He looked back down at her. "Moving is completely unnecessary." He pulled the basket closer and withdrew three wrapped packages.

Telling her she needed her strength after all that exertion, he fed her a bite of roast chicken.

"Mm." Her stomach growled in agreement, and he fed her more chicken and bits of cheese and bread. Then he helped her sit up to drink wine. She leaned against him, his arm wrapped around her. He tucked the blanket over both their shoulders. Frances looked out over the moonlit water and sighed happily. She wondered when she'd ever felt so content in body and spirit.

Never, that's when.

"I never thought it would be that good," she murmured, laying her head against his shoulder.

"Why not?" he asked, his fingers playing in the wavy ends of her hair.

"Mary calls it a 'wifely duty.' Throughout my life, Mary has made me understand that if it is a duty, it is something to be endured, not enjoyed."

"Poor Mary," Evan said.

She laughed. "Yes. Poor Mary." She gave him a critical look. "Honestly, before these last few weeks, not only did I never believe I'd enjoy the act, but I was certain I'd never want to try it."

"And what happened in the last few weeks?"

She pushed against his shoulder with her own. "You

happened."

"I'm glad I happened," he said with a grin.

She sighed. "So am I." She tucked herself to him again. "So...what now?"

He didn't respond for a moment. Then he said, "What do you want, Frances? Because right now, I'm willing for this to go however you want it. And I hope to God it's not something that entails us never seeing each other again."

"Oh no," she said quickly. "Not that."

"What would you like, then?" Pulling away from her a little, he pushed his knuckles gently under her chin, forcing her to look him in the eyes. "What do *you* want?"

Frances would be a fool if she didn't understand this for what it was. It was the first time in her life that a man—or anyone, for that matter—was willing to put her desires over their own. And she was new when it came to lovemaking, but she knew he'd put her needs over his when they'd been joined. She would never forget his trembling restraint as he held himself over her, the gentle way he worked her passion until her pain had all but disappeared.

This man was a wonder.

She gazed at him, the earnestness in his eyes lending her strength. "I would like to be with you whenever it is possible for both of us."

One side of his lips twisted into a smile. "That could be arranged."

"I would like to keep it a secret. I don't want anyone to know but the two of us."

"Easily done," he said.

"When were you planning to return to London?"

"The day after tomorrow." He brushed a kiss over her

nose. "When are you planning to return?"

"In a week."

He looked thoughtful for a moment, then hummed. "I think I'd better keep the boys up here for an extra few days. The country air is doing them good. And the extra time will help Mark get to know his three brothers in an environment he's already familiar with."

Spending more time with him and the boys? Frances couldn't think of a single thing that sounded better. "I can't wait to show you all my secret places."

"Secret places, hm?" He waggled his eyebrows, then dropped his gaze suggestively down over her body, which was half covered by the blanket, half on full display.

And she was half inclined to take the blanket off and show him every bit of her.

Oddly, though everything about this night was new to her and shocking in its utter delightfulness, she didn't feel shy in his presence. She felt alluring. She loved his appreciative expression when he looked at her, those little flares of heat in his eyes.

She nudged his shoulder playfully. It was a rock-hard shoulder, covered with muscle from all the rowing he did, and he didn't move an inch. "I didn't mean *those* secret places."

He locked eyes with hers, the moonlight sparking fire in his amber depths. "I want to discover all your secret places, Frances. *All* of them."

"That's not very fair," she said. When he looked at her with brows raised, she added, "Unless I can discover yours as well."

Something flashed through his eyes, but it disappeared before she could interpret it, and his expression relaxed. "We will discover each other, then."

"Good."

"Is it a deal?" He raised his hand to shake hers to seal their agreement, but when she did so, he pulled her flush to him, then bent down and kissed her.

Gripping the edge of the blanket, she kissed him back, wiggling and gasping as the tips of her breasts rubbed over his chest. He felt so good. Everything about him felt *so* good.

They kissed for a long while, their lips and tongues melded together, tasting and exploring. After long minutes, Evan pulled away, his breaths coming out in sharp rasps. He rested his forehead against hers, his fingers pushing into her hair at the sides of her face.

"Pretty Frances." He kissed her nose. "Sweet Frances."

She huffed out a laugh. "I'm not sweet."

"Oh, you are. Do you know what's especially sweet?"

"What?" she asked.

"The little snorting sound you make every time you give one of those disbelieving laughs."

"*That's* sweet? It drives my family mad."

"I *love* it," he announced. "I love…" He hesitated before continuing, "…so much about you, sweet Frances."

She shook her head but only slightly, given that he still held the sides of it. "There's that word again. I must inform you, the words 'sweet' and 'Frances' do not belong in the same sentence. They do not belong in the same *room*."

"We're not in a room."

"The same country, then."

"I beg to differ, my sweet."

She blew out a breath in mock annoyance. "You are the most exasperating man I've ever known."

He pulled back slightly, a mischievous smile quirking his lips. "Oh? And how many men have you *known*, sweet Frances?"

By the emphasis he put on "known," he was referring to the word in the biblical sense.

She gave him a calculating look. "What would you say if I said I'd known many men? Perhaps…ten?"

He laughed. "I wouldn't love it. But it wouldn't change how I felt about you. Most of all, I'd be surprised as hell."

"Why? Did I play the part of the innocent virgin so perfectly?"

He seemed to consider this. "Well, you did not protest, nor hide, nor act overly modest, nor behave as if the act shocked you or felt unnatural to you."

She shrugged. "I have never been one to hide my true feelings. And I felt none of those things tonight."

"I'm glad."

"Is that how virgins typically behave?" she asked, truly curious.

"To be honest, I haven't bedded many virgins."

She raised her hand. "Never mind. That's already too much information about the women you've bedded. I don't want to know any more."

"That's excellent, as I have no interest in any other women."

"Is that so?" she asked, noting the flirtatious tone of her voice yet again. It seemed to come to her naturally when she was with this man. But this time, she didn't fight it.

"Why would I want to think about any other woman when the most alluring woman in the world is sitting next to me?"

"Ah...I understand. A pretty lord with pretty words dripping from his tongue. You are quite skilled at making a woman feel desired, my lord."

He pulled back a few inches more, frowning slightly. "There is no reason to waste pretty words on you. I'm not trying to make you feel desired due to some ulterior motive. The truth is, I desire you. More than I've ever desired anyone." His voice grew rough. "It's simple fact. And I wouldn't lie about that. Not to you."

Emotion tightened her chest, and she raised her hand to touch his cheek with her fingertips. "No one has ever made me feel desired before, Evan. So someone saying it out of the blue...like this...you must understand my cynicism."

"People are either blind, or they are fools. You're desirable. Ridiculously so."

"Ridiculously?" she asked with a raised brow.

"So desirable, that sometimes I...*grow*...into quite an uncomfortable state when you are near."

Her brows rose further. "Really?"

"It's true. I have nearly embarrassed myself multiple times in your presence."

"Like when, for example?"

He grinned. "At the Worthington Masquerade."

"Really?"

"Yes," he said.

"Where else?" she asked breathlessly.

"In the park."

She gasped. "What? *No!*"

"It's true."

"Where else?"

"In my study. In my drawing room."

She stared at him for a long moment, then glanced down at his lap, then back up. "Do you desire me now?" she asked, almost shyly.

"Mmm. I think you should check."

Tentatively, she reached down under the folds of the blanket that hid his lap, feeling his muscled thigh, then moving her fingers upward to the patch of hair between his legs. He held very still as she reached the smooth flesh of him, the part of him that had been inside her not so long ago, and trailed her fingers over his long length.

The skin was soft, but beneath, he was all steel.

Proof that he desired her.

She gazed into his eyes as she explored further, wrapping her hand around his length and gliding it up over the taut ridge to the flared head, then passing over the tip. He hissed out a breath, his eyes fluttering closed as she encountered a drop of wetness that she smoothed out with her thumb.

"How extraordinary," she breathed.

"I actually believe it is somewhat ordinary," he managed tightly. "But I'm happy you think otherwise."

"I do," she confirmed. There was truly *nothing* ordinary about this moment.

She explored some more, stroking back down him, taking in the velvety skin over his hardness, all the way to the base of him, where she let her fingers drop farther down until she cupped the warmth of his ballocks in her hand. She rolled them gently between her fingers, knowing she must be gentle because she'd seen Charles hit there once with a cricket ball. That hadn't been a pretty sight.

"Jesus Christ, Frances," Evan hissed out. "Are you sure you've never done this before?"

"Quite. Do you think if I had I'd be so curious?"

"I…maybe…don't know."

He seemed to have lost his powers of speech. She rolled him in her palm once more. "Do you like that?"

"Y-yes," he managed. "But I need you."

She trailed her fingers back up over his steely length. Her own body was growing needier by the second, more desperate to feel him over her, inside her again, despite the dull residual ache from losing her virginity.

He groaned. "It feels so damn good when you move your hand like that."

She gripped him in her fist. "Like this?"

"Yes. Exactly."

She glided her hand up toward the tip.

"Yes. All the way. Squeeze."

"I won't hurt you?" she breathed.

"No." He threw his head back. "God, what I wouldn't give to have your mouth on me right now."

She blinked in surprise, but then it made sense. He'd kissed her deeply between her legs earlier, and the pleasure had been so intense she'd had to bite her cheek to keep from screaming so loud they'd hear her in Bowness.

People must do these things to bring each other pleasure. How had she never known?

"I want to put my mouth on you," she told him. "I want to bring you pleasure that way."

Slowly, his head lowered so that he was staring at her, his eyes narrowed with what she was beginning to recognize as arousal.

"But I have never done anything like that before. So, forgive me, but you'll have to teach me how."

Chapter Twenty

Frances watched Evan's Adam's apple move as he swallowed. "I want that," he rasped. "I want to explore everything with you. Show you. Teach you. But…" He hesitated, then closed his eyes. "Not now."

"Why not?"

"Because I am not sure I'd survive it."

"Why not?"

He laughed huskily. "Demanding little vixen, aren't you?"

"Perhaps a little demanding," she agreed, "but mostly just curious."

"One touch of your lips on my cock…" He swallowed again, shaking his head. "And I might explode."

"And that's bad? I *want* to taste you."

She felt a shudder run through him. "And I want to taste you again." He leaned forward so his breath was hot against her lips. "You were so"—he kissed her—"damned"—another kiss, this one deeper—"sweet."

Need bloomed deep within her, so intense, her thighs pressed together instinctually, as if to contain it.

"I want you again," she said, pulling him closer. "Is it terrible of me to say it?"

"No. It is the opposite of terrible." Firmly, he removed her hand from him, then laid her gently back down onto the blanket before situating himself over her. "But you are new to this, and I cannot use you too hard tonight."

"Why not?"

"I want you to be able to walk tomorrow."

She blinked at him, then scoffed and straightened her spine. "I'm not made of glass, Evan. I'm a flesh and blood woman. A strong one, at that. And I want to feel you inside me again. My body *aches* for you."

He groaned softly. "Stop tempting me."

"Are you rejecting me?" How could he? It was clear that he wanted her. Not only from the arousal written all over his face, but she could also feel the heavy weight of his erection on her thigh.

"No," he said, gazing into her eyes. "Never."

"Then give me what I want, my lord," she demanded, the needy throb in her body so deep and strong that she couldn't remain still. She pressed up against him while pushing down with her hands cupping his backside, pressing her pelvis against his. "Now."

Keeping his eyes locked on hers, he reached between them, taking himself in hand and moving to her sex, rubbing up and down along her slickness. She gasped.

And then he found her opening and held there. She gazed up at him, her breathing stopped, her body tensed in anticipation.

"Are you sure you're ready for me again?"

She ran her hands up his back and gripped his rigid upper arms. "Yes."

Not breaking eye contact, he pushed in ever so slowly, and she arched, welcoming him in as every nerve in her body flared to life with pleasure. "Ohhh," she breathed. "Yes, Evan. Yes."

Finally, he was fully seated inside her, her body full with him, her walls clenching tightly around him.

"Are you all right?" he asked, his voice holding a slight tremor.

"More than all right."

He began a tender glide of movement within her, pulling out almost to the tip and then back in, each time so deep, she exhaled in a little gasp. Lowering himself onto his forearms, he kissed her deeply as he moved inside her, his fingers tangled in her hair.

Sensation gripped her, overwhelming and consuming. She could think of nothing but the feel of him, the power of him, his heat, and his possession. Soon, her body was moving in a rhythm that matched his. They were joined together in a timeless dance, their bodies perfectly synchronized.

Her aching desire didn't ebb, but it grew until she was moaning, thrashing underneath him. He took one of her hands and moved it between them. "Touch yourself," he rumbled in her ear. "Take yourself over."

She touched her finger to the place above where they were joined, then rubbed it with just a little more pressure, and almost instantly, her body erupted in pleasure. She cried out, her body thrashing with deep pulses of bliss.

"Yes, Frances," Evan groaned into her hair, moving even deeper, even harder, into her. "Come for me, sweet. Just like that."

Her body finally stilled, and she withdrew her hand from her center, now far too sensitive to touch. Evan moved inside her, his muscles straining, and she wrapped her arms around him, loving the sensation of every deep thrust.

He seemed to grow inside her, touching all the sensitized places deep within her, and she whimpered.

Suddenly, with a low curse, he pulled out of her. She watched his face as he pumped himself furiously, and he spilled his seed on her thigh this time, his expression twisted in pleasure as he groaned out his release.

Afterward, he sank over her, rolling them to their sides and tucking her body tightly against his, their heaving chests slowly settling as the minutes passed.

Wrapped in Evan's strong arms, Frances fell into the most comfortable and deepest sleep she'd ever had.

• • •

It was chilly tonight.

Evan burrowed deeper into his blankets.

Wait.

Something was…off. There was a weight on his shoulder and…was that hair blowing across his lips?

Pushing away the hair with his free hand, he opened his eyes and waited for them to adjust in the dark. Pinpricks of lights started to appear in his vision. He blinked, and there they were, in better focus now.

No, not lights. Stars.

He was suddenly wide awake, realizing a few things at once. Frances was sweetly nestled against him, her head in the crook of his arm. *Her* hair was what had been brushing over his lips.

They'd fallen asleep. A heavy slumber that only the coolness of an approaching dawn could wake.

Holy hell, what time was it? He scrambled around with his hand, miraculously finding his waistcoat in the pile of clothes beside him, and his pocket watch. He squinted at it in the darkness to no avail. The moon had been shining brightly last he'd had his eyes open, but it was nowhere to be found now. Now, the stars provided the only light.

He wrapped his free arm around Frances and turned toward her.

"Frances? We need to get up. We need to get you home."

She jolted awake with a little yelp, and he tightened his arms around her. "Shh. It's me. Evan. We fell asleep."

She looked up at him, eyes blinking sleepily. "What time is it?"

"I don't know. But…it's later. Perhaps near dawn."

"Oh dear," she murmured, stretching her body against him. Instantly, his cock roared to life.

Not now, he thought, gritting his teeth. But he couldn't really blame it. A warm, naked Frances Cherrington stretching like a cat along the full length of his body? *Yes, please.*

Studiously ignoring his arousal, he rooted around for her clothes before locating her night rail and helping her into it. Then he found her cloak and set it on her shoulders before donning his trousers and shirt. Quietly, they cleaned up their picnic and the blankets. When they finished, he caught her hand in his own.

"The boys would like to see you tomorrow." He glanced up at the sky. "Or...later today."

"Can I show them one of my favorite places?"

"We'd love that."

Holding her hand, he walked her to the back door of the house, watching carefully for anyone who might be about. But the place—typical of the country—was silent, all the servants abed.

At the door, he stopped her with a little tug on her hand. She turned around. God, he hated to leave her. He wanted to go upstairs with her, climb into bed beside her, and wake to bright sunlight, holding her in his arms.

But that scenario was most likely never to be. That could happen only if they were husband and wife, and both had their reasons for avoiding marriage.

He tugged her into his arms and kissed her deeply, passionately, moving his mouth over hers in a kiss of longing and desire and heat and lust that she wouldn't soon forget.

When he pulled back, they were both breathing hard.

"Good night," he managed, forcing his arms to fall away from her when they wanted nothing more than to draw her closer.

"Or...good morning, I suppose."

He nodded. "Right. Good morning. I will see you soon." As soon as he possibly could.

With a small smile, she opened the door and slipped inside.

Chapter Twenty-One

Frances woke at noon feeling like she'd just had the most wonderful, most erotic dream of her life. She might have seriously entertained the idea that it was, indeed, a dream if her body hadn't been so deliciously sore.

It was true, then. It had happened. And she was, most decidedly, no longer a virgin. She laughed out loud at that. For a woman determined to be a spinster for life, who had professed no interest in a man's touch, who had tried kissing once and despised it, she had turned into quite the wanton.

She couldn't *wait* to do it again.

And, she was going to see him later today. They likely wouldn't have time to explore each other in the carnal sense, but she would have a chance to show him—and the boys—some of her favorite sites in the area. She'd missed Bobby and Jasper, was curious about little Mark with his amber eyes and long, dark lashes, and she always enjoyed watching Evan with his brothers. How he treated each of them like they were important and loved, like they *mattered*, made her heart butter-soft.

And they were growing to love and respect him, too. She saw it in the way they listened to him, the way they responded to what he said, the way the younger two hugged him and the way Jasper had begun to imitate him.

The brothers' burgeoning relationship was a beautiful sight to behold, and she felt honored to have witnessed it. Indeed, Evan reminded her of Apollo, the Greek god he'd dressed as at the masquerade. Only the good traits of Apollo, of course. How he was protective and dedicated to his brothers, as Apollo was to his children. How he was solid, logical, and responsible, like Apollo, who ensured the sun rose and set every single day. How handsome he was.

Giddiness bubbled through her as she leaped out of bed and called on Peggy to help her dress.

Downstairs, there was a note waiting for her.

Miss Cherrington,
We will fetch you at two o'clock for our scenic adventure, which the four of us are looking forward to with great anticipation.
Winthrop

She glanced at the clock and realized it was already almost two, which was more good news. She wouldn't have to wait long. She drank a cup of tea and ate a biscuit, and by the time she took the last bite, a footman informed her that Lord Winthrop had arrived.

Calling for Peggy, she jumped up, grabbed her journal, and went outside, where two carriages stood in the drive.

Evan was standing at the door of one, looking impossibly handsome in striped trousers with Wellington boots that hugged his calves. His tailcoat was a deep forest green, a sharp contrast to his crisp white cravat. He wore a tall hat and carried a walking stick to complete the look.

"My lord. Excellent thinking to bring a walking stick," she said, "as I intend for us to walk today."

He raised a brow. "Are we to be hiking over the English countryside, then?"

"We are."

"You do realize I have with me a very young boy?"

"I do indeed. But don't worry—we're just going to climb one of those hills." She gestured to the peaks looming behind Shorewood. "And if Mark becomes winded, I will carry him upon my shoulders."

"I see," Evan said. Then his gaze moved beyond her, to where Peggy was standing. Frances glanced back over her shoulder to see that her maid was utterly pale, her eyes wide as she gaped at the hill.

"Peggy?" she said.

"I cannot do it, miss," Peggy breathed. "I'm already nigh bedridden from yesterday. I cannot face a climb up a mountain."

"That's quite all right, Peggy," Evan said kindly. "Miss Renshaw, my brothers' governess, is here, so Miss Cherrington will have adequate female companionship."

Peggy's gaze slid in Frances's direction.

Frances looked at Evan, whose lips twitched in a semblance of a smile. "Well, then. Thank you, my lord. Miss Renshaw will be a lovely companion for the day. Peggy, you may have the day off."

Peggy perked right up. "Truly, miss? Oh, thank you!"

"You're quite welcome."

Her maid scampered off, and Frances turned back to Evan. "Well done, you," she said in a low voice.

He laughed. "The poor girl was terrified."

The door to the second carriage opened and little legs dangled from the doorway before Bobby leaped out.

"Miss Cherrington!" the boy squealed, running toward them and throwing his spindly arms around Frances. Kneeling, she hugged him back. When he pulled away he said, "Evan says we are to spend the day with you today and that we must be perfect gentlemen."

"Ooh," she said. "And what do you think about that?"

"I'm glad you will be with us, but"—he scrunched up his face—"I don't know nothing about being a gentleman."

"I doubt that," she told him. "In fact, you are the most gentlemanly seven-year-old gentleman I've ever known."

"No I ain't!" he said with a cheeky grin.

"Oh, but you are." She leaned toward him. "The last seven-year-old boy I knew was my brother. He pulled the pins out of my hair all the time. It was extremely rude and ungentlemanly." She smiled at him, then gestured to her hair. "*You* have not pulled one pin from my hair in our entire acquaintance. Therefore, you must be a true gentleman."

He giggled, then held a secret—but not so secret—hand toward her hair. She rose to her feet to evade him and turned to Evan. "We can drive to the base of the hill, my lord, then walk the remainder of the way. Does that sound acceptable?"

"Certainly."

She took the hand that Bobby had been reaching out. "Thank you, kind sir, for offering to help me into the carriage.

What a *gentleman* you are."

She threw a saucy look Evan's way before walking to the carriage with Bobby, where she showed the boy how to hand her inside as a true gentleman would. When she was settled in, she said, "Well done!" and he leaped up beside her, pressing his small body against hers. He pulled a handful of "treasures" out of his pocket and chattered in great detail about each seed and rock he had found on their travels, including the shiny penny Lord Coleton had given him that he carried with him always in case he saw something he wanted to buy.

Outside, Evan went to speak to the coachmen, then came to the door a moment later with one of them, who asked Frances where they were going.

Frances gave him instructions as Evan climbed in beside Bobby.

When the coachman nodded and closed the door, Evan looked down fondly at the boy. "Did I not say that Miss Cherrington and I would ride in this carriage and you three boys were to ride with Miss Renshaw in the other?"

Bobby made a small noncommittal sound as the carriage jerked into motion, then turned back to Frances. "And this is the best one." He pointed to a little rock with reddish-orange veins. "It's jasper! Just like my brother."

"It is very beautiful," she murmured, glancing over his head at Evan. He'd clearly had wicked intentions in his plan for them to be in this carriage alone together. Bobby had thwarted them, but Evan's return smile made it evident he wasn't angry.

"What's that you have?" Evan gestured to the small book in her lap.

"I thought I'd try my hand at travel journaling. So far, the journal consists only of lists of sights along the road from London to the Lake District. I brought it to Bowness yesterday in hopes of writing about boating on the Windermere Water, but alas...we had a man overboard situation and I was distracted from it. I must attempt to jot something down today."

Ten minutes later, the carriage rumbled to a halt, and the three of them poured out of it as the second carriage rolled to a stop behind them, and Jasper, Mark, and Miss Renshaw emerged. Jasper approached them brandishing a grin, a cricket bat, and a ball. He was dressed in his own fashionable trousers and coat, and smaller versions of Evan's Wellington boots, looking like a young, sporting gentleman.

What a change from when he'd first appeared in worn wool trousers, a dirty linen shirt, and that wary frown on his face. He'd taken to his change in circumstance like a fish to water.

"You'll be playing with me, Miss Cherrington, won't you? You promised."

She smiled. His accent still needed a bit of work to complete the role of the "young gentleman." "And I shall," she told him. "Fortunately, there is a good clearing at the top of the hill, and no windows for you to break."

Jasper winced, then glanced at Evan. "I didn't mean to do that. Truly."

Frances felt a pang in her chest. Jasper looked so forlorn about what he'd done. She shouldn't have brought it up. He had felt truly awful about breaking that window.

He was a sweet boy, as rough as his young life had been, with a good, open heart. Affection for him surged within her.

Evan spoke softly. "I know, lad. I've already sent for a new window for Reverend Barton. He'll have his window better than new in no time at all."

Looking down at the tips of his boots, Jasper nodded. Evan put a hand on his shoulder and squeezed.

"Well, Miss Cherrington," Evan said, turning to her. "Where are we off to?"

"We will walk that way." She pointed up the hill, then noticed the coachmen pulling baskets and whatnot from the boots of the carriages. "What's all that?"

"Evan brought us a picnic!" Bobby exclaimed.

"'Cause we've got bottomless pits for stomachs," Jasper added. "Especially me. I'm always hungry."

"I like beefsteak," Mark said in his high-pitched little voice.

"So do I," Frances agreed, sharing a small smile with Evan at the little boy's non sequitur. "Beefsteak is *delicious*, isn't it?"

Mark nodded.

All three boys were too skinny, in Frances's opinion, so she fully approved of the picnic plan. "Excellent. Let's go." She took Bobby's and Mark's hands and began to walk, with Evan holding the cricket bat over his shoulder, Jasper tossing the ball in his hands, and Miss Renshaw following. The coachmen, laden with blankets and baskets, lagged behind.

It wasn't long before Mark whimpered that his feet hurt.

"Climb up on my back then," she told the boy, kneeling beside him. When he approached her shyly, she hefted him up, her forearms tucked under his knees, and then stood to come face-to-face with Evan scowling at her.

"What is the matter with you?" she asked him.

"I can carry him."

Frances snorted. "As can I, thank you."

"No," Evan insisted. "Hand him over."

Frances gave him a dry look. "Are you afraid I will drop him?"

"I am not afraid of that in the least. It is more my responsibility, as the gentleman, to carry the burden."

"Oh, he's no burden at all." She looked back at him. "Are you, Mark?"

He shook his head and wrapped his arms tighter around her neck. He was strangling her a little, but Frances would die before showing it.

"See?" she told Evan brightly.

"Come to me, lad," Evan said, reaching for the boy.

She cocked a brow at him and took a step backwards. "And tear that coat that I'm certain your valet sewed over your shoulders this morning? I think not. Unlike you, I have dressed appropriately for a walk up a mountain." She gestured to her simple, high-waisted white muslin dress, its only decoration a trim of pink ribbon around the hem, sleeves, neckline, and over her ribs, tying in a large bow at her mid-back. She'd brought a shawl but had left it in the carriage, knowing the day's physical activity would keep her warm.

Evan gave her a once-over, his eyes flaring. Then he gestured to himself. "This is a perfectly adequate costume for a promenade."

"On the flat and even pathways of Hyde Park, perhaps," she said, trying to hide a grin. "Where all the gossipmongers would see you and comment about how fashionable you are."

He rolled his eyes and held his hands out for Mark, who willingly went into his arms. With an impressive move, he adjusted Mark so he was sitting atop his shoulders.

"Well, I am shocked I didn't hear any evidence of a rip or a tear," Frances said. "Your valet must be very good at his job."

"He is." Evan flashed her a smile that made her knees feel soft. He was so sinfully, devastatingly handsome. Then he glanced up at his littlest brother. "There, lad. Now you have the best view of any of us. You can be our lookout. Let us know if you see anything, all right?"

"All right," Mark agreed.

As they walked the rest of the way up the hill, Jasper prattled on about how Evan was going to take him to Lord's Fields to watch the Gentlemen Versus Players cricket match, and how he'd one day be a part of the players team, and maybe he'd be as good a bowler as Mr. Howard, but maybe he'd also get to play on the gentlemen's side as a given man like Mr. Howard would this year, and surely the gentlemen would win with Mr. Howard on their side, wouldn't they?

Bobby ran ahead, then up a mound off the trail so he could be taller than Mark for a minute, then wound through a stand of trees. He saw a rabbit and chased after it like an eager puppy, returning a few minutes later—empty-handed, of course—with a pink-faced Miss Renshaw in tow.

Taking his position as lookout seriously, Mark called out various sights from his high perch on Evan's shoulders. "There's a green tree!" he yelled with great authority. "There's a yellow flower! There's a blue lake!"

They reached the top of the hill after about half an hour. Frances stepped ahead, taking in the view of the valley below. From this distance, Lake Windermere expanded from what appeared to be a river to a wide lake with islands dotting its center, then narrowing once again. Across the water, verdant rolling hills rose from the banks, bright green in contrast with the dark blue lake and light blue sky.

She wondered if she'd ever felt so free. When she saw Evan kneeling on the grass where he'd deposited Mark, looking up at her with a smile, she smiled back.

Was this what happiness felt like?

Frances sat on the blanket the coachman spread over the grass. She clasped her knees to her chest, listening to the chatter of the boys. For the past several years, she'd always felt best being alone. People stifled her, made her feel inadequate, made her believe that her desires weren't worthy.

Oddly, though, Evan and his brothers had the opposite effect. From the first time she'd been in their company, they'd made her feel appreciated. Cherished, even. Admired for who she was.

She gazed at them all, from the perfectly handsome man to the twelve-year-old youth who was already doing an excellent job of emulating him, to the two little boys, very different from each other, but each precious in his own way. At that moment, she adored them all.

...

Evan could watch Frances Cherrington play at cricket all day. He didn't think he'd ever seen a more stimulating sight than her swinging the bat then whooping with joy as she lifted her skirts, giving erotic flashes of her ankles, and tallied up runs, or her squeal of victory when she bowled him out.

They ate and played and talked and laughed for hours, until the sun hung low over the hills on the other side of the lake. After a vigorous game of tag with the boys, a glowing Frances plopped down on the blanket beside him. He handed her a cup of lemonade, and she drank deeply. "Mmm."

"Who won?" Evan asked.

"I did, of course."

"No, you didn't!" Bobby looked down at them from a low-hanging branch of the twentieth tree he'd scrambled up today. The child climbed better than a monkey. "*I* won."

"Please do come down from there, Master Bobby," Miss Renshaw pleaded from the blanket she shared with the coachmen, a sentiment she'd repeated often throughout the day. "It's dangerous."

"Oh, very well," Frances said grudgingly, setting down her lemonade. "I suppose Bobby won. That child is quicksilver fast. Did you know that, my lord?"

"I have experienced his speed from time to time," Evan said, thinking about how he'd had to chase after the boy and his bad record at having caught the scamp.

Rubbing his eyes, an exhausted Mark wandered over and leaned against Frances, who put her arm around him and drew him close. She'd won him over quickly today, first with her offer to carry him, then with how she included him in every activity she and the older boys did, including playing cricket. He had handled the ball with natural dexterity, at one point catching one of Jasper's hits in both hands, then looking down at it with wide eyes as if it had appeared there magically. Frances had cheered as if they'd just won the most important match in history.

Evan gestured to the book lying beside Frances. "You didn't even open your travel diary today."

She blew out a breath, making the loose wisps of brown

hair whip around her face. "I decided I enjoy spending time with you and the boys far more than writing." She shrugged. "I fear it is another pastime at which I am not destined to succeed."

"What other activities remain on your list?"

"I still have several books to read on the different sciences, but I haven't found any of them engaging yet. Sewing and embroidering is another one." She shuddered. "Though when I imagine my fingers swollen and callused, and my eyes going blind after sewing a million stitches late into the night, my stomach twists. I think I must eliminate that choice before I even try it. Same goes for shopkeeping."

"Why not shopkeeping?"

"What kind of a shop would I keep?"

He shrugged. "What do you like, Miss Cherrington?" he prompted. He knew what *he* liked. Her.

"I like..." She glanced around, her gaze finally resting on Jasper. "Well, I like reading."

Jasper looked up from his book on the opposite end of the blanket. "*I* like reading." Then, his expression brightened. "I know! You could have a bookshop, then I will keep you flush, 'cause Evan's given me leave to buy all the books I want." He leveled a look at her. "That will be *many* books, you know."

"Now that is an intriguing idea," Frances said. "What is the book you're reading now, Jasper?"

"Gulliver's Travels."

"I've read that!" Frances exclaimed.

She and Jasper fell into a conversation about Gulliver and his travels. Evan leaned back on his forearms and gazed around him. In the distance, the sun drooped low over the green hills, the blue water of Windermere glistening below.

Birds chirped in the trees, and crickets had begun their evening calls.

Evan looked at his littlest brother. Mark cuddled up against Frances, his eyes now closed as her arm tucked him against her body and her pleasant voice rocked him to sleep. Across from Evan, Jasper was indignant as he talked about the Lilliputians turning against Gulliver for saving their capitol—"Who cares if 'twas his piss!" Jasper exclaimed. "He saved them!"—while Frances nodded, her attention rapt on the boy, not blinking an eye when the boy said the word "piss."

Evan would educate him about words to refrain from speaking in a lady's presence later on.

Right above them, Bobby had climbed to a wide branch and was relaxing on his stomach, hands dangling as he grinned down at Evan. Evan grinned back, then stretched and rose.

"Well, everyone, I think it's time to start back. The sun will be going down soon."

Jasper and Bobby groaned.

"Don't worry," Frances said. "Going down the hill is *much* easier than going up."

Evan picked up Mark, who wrapped his arms around his neck and promptly fell back to sleep against his shoulder. As Frances helped the coachmen and Miss Renshaw pack up the picnic, Evan realized that today had been one of those rare perfect days, one that he'd remember for a long time to come.

It didn't escape his notice that Frances Cherrington had been a part of it.

A very big part.

Chapter Twenty-Two

Evan and Frances strode hand in hand along the beach near Shorewood. The moon was full and bright, and it sent a shimmering glow across the placid surface of the lake.

The past few days had been, without a doubt, the best of Evan's life. During the daytime, he, Frances, and the boys had explored the waters and the shores of Lake Windermere, him wanting to touch her but somehow controlling himself.

Thankfully, the nights had been spent with him buried inside her.

A week had gone by too fast, and he'd spent too much of it worrying about it ending, the deadline bearing down on them. He knew she'd felt it as well.

Earlier tonight, she'd shown him her childhood home, Windermere Cottage, a small, picturesque house built down the shore from the rectory. He could feel her melancholy as she talked about her happy childhood there. The house was dark and quiet now, the new owner not in residence. Even the caretaker's cottage had been dark, though it was late at night and the caretaker might have been abed.

As they'd walked back toward Shorewood, she'd told him about her family's abrupt move to London when her father died, how things had changed from her carefree childhood days. How her brother had changed. How her family had seemed to turn against her.

Then she spoke of her twin—the one person who should never have turned against her—and how far apart they were in distance and priorities, but how close in soul.

"Why didn't you go to Egypt with her?" he asked Frances now.

"Martha wanted me to, but I would just be an outsider, and a cynical one, at that."

They strode along, allowing the fresh air to wash over them as they walked. "It's going to be more difficult in London, you know," she said. "For us to be together."

"I know," Evan said. "We will find a way."

"I will visit the boys as much as I can," she said. "But I will spend that time with the boys."

"As well as with me."

"Yes, when you're there. But I cannot think of a time we will be able to be alone together." She looked up at him, her eyes glassy in the moonlight.

"You've proven you're adept at 'escape,'" he said. Though most of the time she'd encountered him and the boys in London, her maid had been there.

"Yes. But my ability to escape comes only sporadically. It is not a long-term solution."

He drew her to a stop at the water's edge. They stood in silence, the only sound the soft laps of the tiny waves against the shore. He gripped her hand like he never wanted to let go. And he *didn't* want to let go.

She'd told him outright that she had no desire to marry. And even if she did, he couldn't bring her into his deception.

Now that he had three boys who needed him, he could never reveal the secret of his birth. Jasper, Bobby, and Mark were fighting a steep uphill battle against society as it stood. The considerable influence and power of the Earl of Winthrop was necessary to ensure his brothers grew up to be respected and admired. After all the years their father had neglected them and caused them to suffer, they deserved no less. And no one would be the wiser—only Evan and the dowager knew his secret. The dowager would take it to her grave. So would he.

None of that took away from how much Evan wanted Frances Cherrington. If circumstances were different, he'd have offered for her before either of them had left London, and back then, he hadn't even known the extent of what he felt for her.

But circumstances were what they were. They couldn't marry.

"Like you, I have decided I will never marry," he said, and then he emphasized his commitment to this course. *"Ever."*

A frown pulled her brows together. "You told me that you might marry someday but you hadn't found anyone suitable."

"I've changed my mind. Now that I have the boys, I need to focus on them."

"But they cannot inherit the title," she said. "Who will inherit once you are gone?"

"My uncle is still alive. If he predeceases me, then he has two sons who are next in line."

"It seems to me that you would want to find a mother for the boys."

They could use a mother, that was true. Someone like Frances, who'd love them for who they were, and who they adored in return. If he was looking to find his brothers a mother, there was no one who'd do the job better than Frances Cherrington.

His chest hurt thinking about it.

He swallowed and couldn't meet her eyes. "That won't be necessary. But what about you? Have you changed your mind about marriage?"

She shook her head. "Not at all. The thought of being shackled to someone terrifies me. Usually it's the men who dread being shackled, and indeed, my siblings have called me too manlike—"

"There is nothing about you that is manlike," he interrupted, his gaze grazing with appreciation over her femininity.

She laughed. "In any case, I cannot imagine being caged like that. It would suck the life out of me."

Evan squeezed her hand, imagining her in some loveless marriage trying to behave like a good wife. No, Frances could not be caged. It would drain the light in her brown eyes, the liveliness, the curiosity. "I wouldn't want that for you."

She leaned against him.

"I'd offer you a…formal arrangement," he said quietly, tucking a thick lock of brown hair behind her ear, then stroking down over her back and wrapping his arm around her waist, drawing her closer. "One where we could be together openly but you'd have all the freedom you'd ever desire. But I wouldn't have you suffer the social repercussions of that."

"I'd agree to it without a second thought for my own reputation." She swallowed. "I'd be your mistress, Evan. Happily. I would have the best of both worlds. It would be perfect."

He inhaled sharply as thoughts of her becoming his filled his thoughts. He'd buy her a house. A carriage. Whatever she wanted. She could have all the space in the world to be her own woman—go where she wanted, do what she wanted. Anything.

"But I've already had second thoughts," she continued quietly, "and they are not about my reputation. They are about my family. Becoming your mistress would make them the laughingstock of the ton. I don't think they would ever recover from the shame. I love them too much to do that to them."

He reined in his wayward fantasy, reality crashing back in. "I know."

Side by side, they stared out over the water. Well, Frances stared out over the water. He stared at her. She wore her dark cape as she had every night, but tonight the hood was down and so was her hair, the silver moonlight playing over the dark strands. In profile, she looked like the determined heroine of a novel standing tall and proud, her chin up, her nose straight, her jaw tight, waves of brown hair cascading down her back.

She was so damned beautiful.

Desire swept through him, a powerful tide, and with it, a terrible truth crashed over him.

After tonight, he might never have her again.

"Come with me," he said tightly. Still gripping her hand, he led her to the boat he'd brought tonight. He'd pulled it just over halfway out of the lake, just enough so it wouldn't drift away, and water lapped at its hull.

"Get in," he said, lifting her into the boat.

"Where are we going?"

"Nowhere." He got in behind her, then knelt on the flat boat bottom in front of where she sat on the stern bench, moving the picnic basket and blankets that still rested there to the bench seat behind him.

She watched him, a crease between her brows. "What—"

He wrenched up her skirt, pushed her knees apart, and buried his face between her legs.

She let out a gasp of pleasure as his lips collided with her heated flesh, and he groaned out his appreciation. She was so hot. She tasted so good. He pressed a finger inside her, stroking her inner walls in a way he knew she loved.

"Oh," she sighed. "Yes."

He hummed against her, and hell if he didn't feel the trembling reverberations of it traveling through her thighs.

His cock pressed against his falls, wanting her, demanding her. But it could wait.

He added another finger, pumping into her relentlessly. His vixen liked it hard, which was good, because so did he. He thrust into her, pressing his fingers and lips and tongue against her, giving her a brutal onslaught of sensation. Quickly, she rose to the brink, and as they did every time she was close to coming, her legs began to shudder, her core tightened, and, above him, her body began to bow. She gripped the edge of the seat, her breaths coming in short pants.

Come, Frances, he thought. *Come for me.*

As if she'd heard him, she did, a rush of heat coating his tongue, her core contracting against his fingers. He worked her through it, loving how sweet she tasted, how responsive she was to his touch.

When she finally came down, he unbuttoned his falls in record time, fairly certain he tore off at least two of the buttons. He shoved his trousers down and lay back until he was half reclined—his upper back padded by the blanket on the bench behind him, hauling her over him and positioning his cock under her. Holding her hip, he pushed her down onto him. They both gasped at his sudden invasion. Her body clenched around him, shadow aftershocks of her release, and she looked down at him with a glazed expression, her huge pupils making her eyes appear black in the moonlight.

"Ride me," he commanded, his voice a lust-shredded husk of itself.

He lifted her nearly off him, then yanked her down, and they gasped again. "Evan," she groaned, the sound of his Christian name on her tongue so erotic, his cock twitched inside her.

He adjusted her so she leaned over him, gripping the edge of the seat behind him, and then returned his hands to the dip in her waist, her hipbones just below his fingers, guiding her to move, slowly at first, as she recovered from her release.

It didn't take long, though, for her strokes to grow faster, deeper, and harder. He moved one of his hands to her fabric-covered breast and growled, "Take this off before I tear it off you."

She paused, removing the offending garment and tossing it away before grinding down over him again.

Now he could see all of her. Touch all of her as she moved over him. He was certain he'd never again see anything as appealing as Frances Cherrington at this moment, her face a play of desire and need, her body silhouetted by the moon, her long hair framing her face and falling over her chest, her beautiful pink nipples poking through the curtain of brown waves.

Cupping her breasts, he flicked his fingers over the taut buds of her nipples and tilted his hips to meet her every time she came to him.

He watched her, letting the image of her riding him sear into his memory, into every bit of his being. If he could never have her again, maybe this image would sustain him.

He tightened his fingers over her as sensation gathered in the base of his spine. He didn't want to stop. He never wanted this to end.

"I'm…" she bit out. "I'm…"

Her legs gripping his hips began to shudder. He had to hold out, let her enjoy her release before he took his own. "Yes," he said. "Come. Come over me. Just like this."

Her movements grew frantic, her hips rolling over him in desperate jerks until her lips parted, her body arched beautifully, and he felt the clasping ripples of her release up and down his near-bursting cock. He gritted his teeth so hard, it felt like his jaw was going to snap. *Don't come yet. Don't risk her for this. Wait.*

He waited…just barely, the change in her tempo helping him to hold off. But he was still so close. One more squeeze…

She was coming down, her pulses slowing, the tension in her body melting away. She jerked her body, sliding over him, the friction nearly unbearable.

He was done for.

A low groan escaped him, and he lifted her off just as he exploded, arching his body into the air. He moved his hand to hold himself, but she was there first, her hot mouth covering him, her hot hands pumping him.

Oh *God*.

"Fran…" he moaned, but with his body caught tight in the grip of pleasure, he could do nothing more than give in to the most powerful release of his life. He came deep inside her mouth, each of her swallows coaxing more spasms from him. It went on and on, until he was spent. Drained.

What felt like hours later, her mouth slipped off his softening cock, and she straddled him once more, leaning down to kiss him full on the lips. He tasted himself on her lips and tongue, and muttered, "Vixen."

"Mmm," she said. "I like it when you call me that."

He laughed softly. She was always surprising him. And always in a good way. "Come here," he said, pulling her close. When his lips were buried in her hair, he whispered, "God, I'm going to miss this."

"So am I."

"I'm going to miss *you*," he said.

She pulled back a little and touched his lips with her fingertip. "I'm going to miss you, too. So much."

"Promise you'll come to me as soon as you can once we are both back in London."

"I promise," she whispered.

He knew she meant it.

Why, then, did part of him worry that she'd never come at all?

Chapter Twenty-Three

Frances gazed out her window. It was a rainy day in early July, offering a slight relief from the hot and polluted London summer. In the next several weeks, most of the aristocracy would retire to the country to escape.

Not the Cherringtons, though. Thanks to Frances's father having lost their family fortune, the only property Charles owned now was this London townhouse, though that was likely to change soon, given Lilly's success. She'd just received a share of another architectural commission—this one for a new, fashionable address in London near the king's royal residence at Buckingham House that was to be called Belgrave Square.

In any case, like the last several summers, the Cherringtons would spend the entire season in London. Frances didn't mind. She enjoyed watching society leave in droves, their judgmental eyes turning away from her for a change. It was a relief.

The best part was that Evan was due home today or tomorrow, though he planned to stop at Pleasant Hill on his way home. His estate was comparatively close to London, and he had decided to spend the summer traveling back and forth between the two residences.

She couldn't wait to see him again. To be back in his warm, strong embrace, risky as it was.

And it *was* risky, in more ways than one. There was not only the risk of the gossipmongers' wagging tongues if their liaison was discovered, but also the fact that their activities held a danger of their own. If Evan got her with child, she didn't know what they'd do.

She'd fretted a little about it as the days went by, then sighed with relief when her courses had arrived the day after she'd left the Lake District. There was no child—which surely meant that him withdrawing before he found his release had worked to keep her from conceiving.

She looked back down at the open diary on her desk. The list of potential passions she'd written in April stared back at her:

1) ~~Artist (Paint? Watercolor? Pencil or charcoal drawing? Shall I draw people, places, or something else? Who knows. Must acquire a drawing master.)~~ *No talent.*

2) *Charity Worker (Something to do with children? Must ask Mary.)*

3) ~~Musician (What instrument? NOT the pianoforte— too ordinary. Something interesting and unique— perhaps the cello?)~~ *No talent.*

4) *Scholar (But a scholar of what? <u>NOT ANCIENT EGYPT!</u> Talk to Lilly. Perhaps…astronomy? Physiology?)*

5) ~~Sewing/Embroidery (Writing this makes me cringe. But perhaps I have a hidden genius for sewing and will create beautiful work while finding it fulfilling? Must practice sewing more interesting/artistic items—not stockings!)~~ Just too dull to even begin to try.

6) *Traveler (I could travel the world and write about it. This might be interesting. Where to begin?)*

7) *Shopkeeper (But what would I sell?)*

8) ~~*Novelist (I shall write a book about a young woman trapped in her home, unable to escape.)*~~ *Evidently, it would take me a lifetime to write a complete novel.*

She stared at "Charity worker," certain that she couldn't go back to Harlowe's Home for Boys without wanting to steal every single child from that place and give them a better life. She definitely didn't want to help Mr. Thomason in his pitiful attempt to make the place look better to outsiders. Would all her other charitable experiences be similar to Harlowe's Home for Boys? Depressingly, she thought they might. She didn't cross it off yet, though. She needed to speak to Mary—maybe she would have some ideas on how Frances might really be able to help.

She tapped her pen on the paper as she moved down the list, then crossed out "Scholar."

She'd read most of the books Lilly had procured for her. More like she'd *tried* to read them. Each page of each tome had been so grueling and dull; her eyes had glazed over and her mind wandered. She'd thought astronomy would be fascinating, but it seemed to be no more than Latin terms interspersed with mathematics. Physiology—more Latin.

Botany—*So. Much. Latin.*

She'd never enjoyed Latin. And having to navigate through as much as she had just in her brief exploration made her hesitant to look into any of the other sciences.

She moved down to number six and paused with the tip of her pen on the "T" in *Traveler.* She had loved being up north, but that probably had more to do with the fact that she'd returned to her childhood home and the happy memories there—and then Evan and the boys' presence—rather than traveling itself. In fact, the actual traveling—the long carriage rides up and down nearly the whole length of England—had been insufferably lonely. The thought of traveling the world all by herself seemed like an isolated and solitary endeavor.

Not to mention the fact that she'd completed only six pages in her journal—all of them written in the carriage during the days of travel when she'd finished the book she was reading and had absolutely nothing else to do.

She put a line through number six. She didn't want to be a professional traveler.

Where did this leave her?

She gazed down at the paper, then mused aloud, "I suppose I will just have to be a shopkeeper, then."

She thought of that beautiful day atop the hill overlooking the lake, of how Jasper had told her she should be a bookseller and smiled to herself as an image flitted through her mind of Jasper leaving her little bookshop with a mountain of books in his arms, Evan in the distance smiling at his brother, then beyond him, at her.

Looking out the window once more, she wondered what Evan would think. He'd support her, she knew. He'd never once implied that she couldn't or shouldn't do anything.

Was he home yet? She chewed the inside of her cheek. Could she come up with an excuse to wander past his house to check? Even in this rain?

Yes, she certainly could. The torrent had turned into a mist, and even Peggy could withstand a mist. Grinning, she stood, stretched, then went downstairs to find her maid. They were going for a walk.

...

Evan was still at Pleasant Hill, though he'd been due back in London yesterday. Mark had come down with a cold, and he wasn't going anywhere and risking the boy growing more ill.

Their time here had been lonely after the week at the lakeshore. The weather had been incessantly rainy, and that compounded with Mark's illness made none of them feel much like exploring. Of course, the dowager countess, upon hearing of Evan and the boys' arrival, had holed herself up in the dower house, claiming she was beset by gout despite never having had gout a day in her life, and refused to see them. That was for the best, Evan supposed. He couldn't imagine his erstwhile mother being anything but unkind toward his brothers.

Evan sat beside Mark on a sofa, his arm around the boy. Bobby lay on his back on the carpet in a brief rest between a series of somersaults, while Jasper read from his book of fables to the three of them. Evan's mind wandered, his gaze going to the window.

God, he wished Frances were here. They all missed her so much. The boys had asked for her. In the depths of his fever, Mark had cried for her.

Perhaps he needed to reassess his feelings about marriage.

Maybe he could tell her the truth. The thought made his chest squeeze so tight he felt like he couldn't breathe.

But perhaps she'd understand. Perhaps she'd agree with his decision to continue his deception as the Earl of Winthrop for his brothers.

Mark coughed. It was a wet, ugly-sounding hack, and it scared the hell out of him. The doctor had said it was just a common childhood cold, but that didn't stop Evan from feeling helpless and afraid.

Children died of colds sometimes. Everyone knew it.

He wished Frances were here. She'd make everything all right. He closed his eyes, then realized the room had gone silent. He looked up at his oldest young brother.

"Are you finished?" he asked Jasper.

The boy shrugged. "You said read till the end of the chapter, and so I did."

"Well done," he said with a nod. "Now, I think we should write a letter to Miss Cherrington. What do you say?"

"Yes!" the boys chimed.

They went to the escritoire in the corner, where Evan drew out a quill and a sheet of paper. With much input from his brothers, he began to write.

Pleasant Hill
2nd July, 1820

Dear Miss Cherrington,

Jasper, Bobby, Mark, and I miss you very much. We are delayed in Hertfordshire due to Mark being ill. Just a little ill, he says. And Bobby says so little that he will surely be well enough to travel soon.

Jasper says to tell you he's finished Gulliver's Travels *as well as* Waverley, *and has decided to read all of Walter Scott's other works. He also says that he plays cricket here, but it has been raining too much, and he doesn't like to muddy his new clothes. Also, he says it is not as fun when you aren't bowling to him.*

Bobby has a new collection of treasures to show you. He has also gone through the old nursery here and has picked out all his favorite toys to take back to London with us. He says his favorite is the rocking horse, which he says we must strap to the top of the carriage so it can watch the techniques of real horses to learn them for himself.

Mark says the rocking horse is his favorite, too, and he is glad it doesn't run like a real horse or it would buck him off, and that would hurt. He says Pleasant Hill is the biggest house he ever saw, and its lawn is very green, but it has bees, and they are very scary.

Evan wanted to go on. To write a paragraph about himself. About how much he missed her, about how much he wished she were here to help him with Mark, about how quickly the boys were learning new things, and how it seemed his chest swelled with love for them a little more every day.

He wanted to tell her to come up and join them, because it felt like something was missing from his family without her.

He did none of that. It was too personal, too private. For all he knew, Charles Cherrington would open this letter and read it before giving it to her.

He needed to keep it light and impersonal, so he signed off with a crisp closing and "Winthrop."

Three days later, they received a response.

London, 4th July, 1820

Dear Lord Winthrop, Jasper, Bobby, and Mark,

I walked by your house a few days ago and was sorry to see you hadn't arrived home yet. I can report, however, that it is still standing and looking as stately as ever.

I am so sorry to hear that you have been ill, Mark, but I am glad you are on the mend. You must take your medicine so you can get well as fast as possible because I can't wait to see you.

Bobby, I am eager to learn if the rocking horse learns proper equestrian techniques. You shall have to update me when we see each other again. And I am excited to see your expanded collection of treasures.

I now feel encouraged to read Waverley, *Jasper, as well as the other works of Walter Scott. I look forward to our future discussions on his books. Did you know, I read the other day that, for all his achievement with the pen, Walter Scott was granted a baronetcy in Scotland? Extraordinary! So now we must call him* SIR *Walter Scott.*

I do enjoy books. Indeed, I have been thinking more and more about becoming a proprietress of a little bookshop in London—perhaps in Mayfair, along the row of shops near the Mayfair Matchmaker. The more I think of it, the more the idea appeals. Perhaps we can talk about it more when you are back in London. I shall look forward to it.

And I have good news—it stopped raining yesterday, so we might be able to find a dry field upon which to play cricket when you return.

Yours truly,
Frances Cherrington

The boys ate the letter up, and of course, wanted to respond right away, which they did, with more updates on the weather, the new Sir Walter Scott novel Jasper was reading, and all their activities. The best news was that Mark was improving rapidly now, and Evan thought they'd be able to make the trip to London in just a few more days.

Evan couldn't wait.

Chapter Twenty-Four

Frances missed Evan and the boys. So much, that it had been growing difficult to focus on her research on how to open a bookshop in London.

She had discovered that she'd need to lease a space for such a shop and that London was not cheap—especially those parts of London where a new bookshop might be successful. She had dreams of opening it in Mayfair near the Duchess of Crestmont's matchmaking offices, a place that attracted lovers and dreamers of all kinds. She'd be more than happy to provide those people with all the reading material they'd ever desire.

She was nervous about approaching Charles with the idea, but perhaps her brother would see that helping her with a lease would be an opportunity for Frances to become self-sufficient. That someday she might even be able to pay him back and afford her own lodgings.

If he argued that aristocratic ladies didn't sully themselves in trade, she'd counter with the example of the Duchess of Crestmont, Lilly's close friend. The duchess ran a successful matchmaking business, had married a duke who was madly in love with her, and had won the acceptance of the vast majority of the ton.

Squaring her shoulders with determination, she folded her latest missive to Evan and the boys. Mark was nearly as good as new, Evan had said, and in a few more days, they'd be home. She couldn't wait.

Raising the letter, she pressed it to her lips, then to her chest. Which was a silly, starry-eyed gesture, she knew.

She couldn't help herself, though. Closing her eyes, she allowed the image of Evan's arms wrapped around her to flit through her mind. His fresh, clean outdoor scent. His lips on her hair, his body naked and pressed against hers…

All right, enough of that!

She brought her breaths, which had grown short and airy, back under control.

She'd ensure the letter was sent, then she'd go see Charles. Her heart beat with anxiety at thoughts of how Charles might react to her plan. She could only hope that he wouldn't shoot the idea down the moment it left her lips.

Rising from the desk, letter in hand, she walked to her bedroom door. When she turned the knob and opened it, the butler stood there, hand raised as if he'd been about to knock.

"Oh! I'm sorry, Rutherford. Did you need something?"

"Mr. Cherrington requires your presence in the drawing room, Miss Cherrington."

"Now?"

"Yes, miss."

"Very well." Frances clenched the letter tightly in her

hand as she followed the butler down the corridor. Charles rarely summoned her, and to the drawing room? Never.

Once downstairs, they paused in front of the closed door. The butler hesitated, glancing back at her as if to ask, "Are you ready?"

Frances gave a slight nod. What was this about? Perhaps there had been a new rash of scandalous talk about her.

Rutherford knocked on the door. From the other side, she heard Charles call, the word sharpened by a sting of impatience. "Yes?"

The butler pushed open the door. "Miss Cherrington, sir."

Frances stepped inside.

Three people stood in the center of the room…one of them a stranger looking uncomfortable and out of place. Frances blinked at him.

No. Not a stranger.

Mr. Salt.

No.

No, no, no!

Before she could turn and run, Martha rushed forward and threw her arms around her. "Oh, Frances. My dear sister."

Frances closed her eyes and breathed Martha in, inhaling the dust of travel, but also something deep and familiar, like fresh lilacs. Beneath everything, Martha felt like home and comfort and safety.

Something she desperately needed right now.

How had they found out? How could they possibly have returned to England so quickly?

A masculine throat cleared behind them, and she and

Martha pulled back, Frances's eyes meeting the replica of her own before breaking away.

Her sister held out her hand. "Come. Sit by me."

Panic flashed through Frances, and she swallowed hard. The last thing she wanted was to be trapped with Mr. Salt and her brother. In desperation, she turned back to Martha. "Perhaps you and I could speak in my room? We could have tea brought up. I'm sure you're exhausted from your travels."

"Sit *down*, Frances," Charles said.

Dread threatening to choke her, she allowed Martha to lead her to the sofa. Each step deeper into the room plucked at Frances's overly tight nerves. "Why are you home?" she asked. "Has something happened? Where is Oscar?"

She knew what the responses to those questions would be, but there was always the infinitesimal hope that it was something else.

"Oscar is well. He has plenty of work to keep him occupied in Alexandria while he awaits my return."

Martha tugged her down onto the sofa and looked expectantly at Mr. Salt, who took a seat across from them. Charles remained standing.

Frances did not like the look on Salt's face. With his mouth pinched, his brow furrowed, and a thin sheen of sweat on his forehead, he looked like he had a stomachache. A very bad one.

He cleared his throat again, and then his Adam's apple jumped as he gulped in a swallow.

"Miss Cherrington," he said stiffly. "I am here to make amends."

Frances was shaking her head before he finished the statement. "Amends aren't necessary, Mr. Salt. Please don't—"

Charles broke in sharply. "Let the man speak, Frances."

"No, really," she insisted. "I cannot fathom…please do not tell me you traveled all the way back to London because of…" She broke off, unable to continue.

"Nevertheless, I must do right by you." Salt stood, and within two strides he loomed over her. "Miss Cherrington," he said, his voice emotionless, "will you do me the honor of becoming my bride?"

"What? No!" Frances exclaimed, jumping up to face him so abruptly that he took a stumbling step back. "That is entirely unnecessary!"

"You *will* marry," Charles declared. "As soon as possible."

There was a moment of stunned silence. Then Mr. Salt said, "I fear marriage is the only possible solution. I will not have you be the one to pay for my indiscretion."

"*My* indiscretion, you mean," Frances corrected.

Salt looked shocked. "Not at all. I took most grievous advantage of your person. Now I must make amends."

"By marrying me? Someone whom you do not love?"

Salt stiffened further, if that were possible. "It is my duty. Honor demands it. Decency requires it."

She looked directly into Salt's pale blue eyes, and even though they flickered nervously away from her, she spoke very calmly. "Mr. Salt. I thank you for traveling all this way in an attempt to do the honorable thing. But I assure you, it was for naught. Society might consider me disgraced, but I am perfectly content with my position and with my life. I have neither a desire nor a need to be married. You do me a great honor. However, I must decline your offer."

She turned to leave the room. She had nothing more to

say, after all.

But as she approached the door, her brother stepped in front of her. "Frances, be reasonable."

Looking up into his flushed face, she raised her brows. "I *am* being reasonable."

"But you're not, actually," Martha protested, hurrying over to them. "The reasonable thing to do would be to marry."

Frances gaped at her sister. Martha had married for love. She knew Frances didn't love Salt. "Reasonable" or not, how could Martha want a loveless marriage for her?

"No." Frances glanced back at Mr. Salt, trying to appear contrite. She didn't mean to be rude, truly. "My apologies."

Martha took her hands. "Frances. Mr. Salt is so generous and kind—"

If her twin had such high regard for the man, then maybe *she* should marry him.

"—and he is offering to make it all right. This is the only way you'll ever be able to reenter society."

"You are not listening to me," Frances pressed. "I have no wish to reenter society." How could none of them understand that?

"He is here to save you!" An edge of panic bled into Charles's eyes. "You would refuse a gentleman's offer and willingly live in disgrace? You would continue to allow your family to suffer the repercussions of your selfish actions?"

She didn't want her family to suffer any repercussions, but for years they had refused to listen to her, refused to accept her choices. Desperate times had called for drastic measures.

Frances glanced over her shoulder to look at Salt. Hands clasped behind his back, he gazed down at the floor, a lock of blond hair hiding his expression from view.

She couldn't marry him. *She couldn't.*

She was in love with someone else.

Evan Locke, the Earl of Winthrop.

Evan had mentioned her becoming his mistress, which would bring her family even more pain and suffering, but he'd never mentioned marriage. There was no evidence that he loved her in return. If so, wouldn't he have offered for her?

No. He had no interest in marriage, and she'd told him numerous times that she had no desire to marry. She'd gone so far as to ruin herself to avoid it.

None of that mattered to her foolish heart. She was in love with him anyway. Not this pale-haired stranger who wouldn't look her in the eyes. This man who was ashamed of kissing her.

She thought of all the things she'd done far beyond kissing with Lord Winthrop. Shame had been so far removed from every touch they'd shared, she hadn't even considered feeling it.

But should she be ashamed of her time with him? Her siblings would probably think so.

She opened her mouth. Closed it. Squeezed her eyes shut. "Forgive me, but… Please. Let me go."

"Where?" Charles demanded.

"I just need to be alone. Please," she begged. "I need to think."

Charles turned to Martha and ordered, "Stay with her."

From the corner of her eye, Frances saw Martha nod.

It was only when she walked into her bedchamber, Martha right behind her, that she noticed she was still clutching the letter to Evan.

Chapter Twenty-Five

"I can't marry him," Frances insisted. "I don't even *like* him."

"Well, there is no reason for that," Martha said. "I know him better than you. He is kind and thoughtful, and he will make you an excellent husband."

Frances stared up at her bedroom ceiling. It was nearly an hour later. The letter to Evan lay crumpled on her desk, and Martha lay on her back beside Frances, both of them fully dressed on top of the counterpane. They had shared this room and this bed until three years ago when Martha had left to go live with her husband.

"You know I never wanted to marry," Frances told Martha.

"You made that abundantly clear each and every time you were forced to attend a function. But it isn't fair of you to force Charles to care for you for the rest of your life."

Frances knew that, and it was part of the reason opening a bookshop held such appeal. If it was successful, then she could support herself.

"And if you didn't want to marry," Martha added pointedly, "I would have suggested you not embrace a man in the vicinity of the Backbiting Biddies. Really, Frances. I thought you were smarter than that."

"How did you find out?" Frances asked.

"The day we arrived in Alexandria, I received three letters. Despite having been written nearly a week after our departure, they somehow arrived before we did."

"From Mary, Harriet, and Esther?" Frances guessed.

"Yes. Esther said she saw Henrietta Grassley and her crowd of gossips at the masquerade that night and had a feeling they were the ones who exposed you." Martha wrinkled her nose. "The Backbiting Biddies. I remember them well."

"How could you forget?" Frances thought of all the times Henrietta had pretended to be their friend and then spread ugly rumors about them.

"In any case, the day after we arrived, Mr. Salt and I boarded the very ship that had deposited us in Alexandria to return us home." She groaned softly. "I have hardly stepped on dry land for *ages*."

Martha had upended her life to bring Salt back to London. As unwelcome as their return had been, Frances had to admit their motives were pure. Salt had come because he was honorable, and Martha had come out of sisterly love.

"But I don't *love* him, Martha," Frances repeated.

Martha took her hand. "I know. But we do know he is a good man. As soon as I relayed the situation to him, he said he would return to London immediately and marry you. He already cares enough to travel thousands of miles to make things right. That is a far better start than some marriages these days."

Her sister wasn't wrong about that.

"He didn't know it was me he kissed at the masquerade, did he?"

"He did not. But once I told him, he sincerely regretted compromising you in such a fashion."

Frances grimaced. She'd bet he did. She shut her eyes. Every bit of her was aching for Evan. Unlike Salt, Evan had recognized her immediately at the masquerade. She didn't even know if Salt *liked* her. Evan did, though. He liked talking to her, he liked touching her, and he liked simply *being* with her.

And she loved him.

She felt nothing for the man downstairs.

"You need to do this, Frances."

"I can't." The words emerged in a near whimper.

"You must." Martha turned on her side to face her, and Frances mirrored her movements, her eyes stinging. "This crisis is destroying our family. While you were off enjoying your travels in the Lake District as if you had no worries in the world, our sisters and brother have been struggling."

Frances sighed. "I know Charles took it badly, and he hated hearing the rumors, but the gossip will die down. It has already. Things will return to normal."

Martha's eyes widened. "Really? Is that what you think? What about Mary? Several patrons withdrew their support from The Lambeth Home for Waifs and Strays."

Frances's mouth dropped open. "Because of me?"

"Yes. And Harriet was turned away from Almack's Assembly Rooms. Esther's friend Lady Holland revoked Esther's invitation to her celebrated house party next month.

And poor Charles has not only fielded mockery in his club, but when you were at the lake, our uncle the earl summoned him to chastise him for mishandling his 'wayward sister.' He ordered him to get you under control before he was forced to intercede."

Regret squeezed Frances's lungs in a tight fist. "No one told me any of this."

"No one wanted you to feel worse than you already did." Martha frowned. "But if you are to be believed, evidently you weren't feeling bad at all."

Frances flinched.

"This has affected all of us, Frances. You could fix it so easily by just marrying the man. And if you turn him down now, the scandal will be ten times worse. Charles, Mary, Harriet, and Esther will be so embarrassed. They will be scorned and censured. They might never recover."

Anxiety twisted in her stomach. "There has to be another way."

"Tell me, then," Martha challenged. "What is it? I am open to other options."

Frances was silent.

Evan.

But he wasn't an option. How could he be? What could he do to help her out of this situation, besides marry her? But he would never marry. "*Ever*," he'd told her.

"Seriously, if there is some other way to mend your reputation and save our family, I am listening," Martha said. "I will send Mr. Salt back to Egypt in a trice."

Evan, Evan, Evan, Frances's mind screamed. Maybe he had fallen in love with her just as she had with him? Maybe he'd change his mind and decide he wanted to marry her?

No. She slammed the lid shut on that thought. It was her desperation talking. A fantasy created by the lovesick, naive part of her that she'd foolishly allowed to blossom in the Lake District. She needed to gather her rationality, bring back her steady practicality, and forget about him.

The Earl of Winthrop was not going to sweep in and save her from this disaster.

She was on her own.

...

During the few days after he received Frances's letter, Evan's mind was consumed with her.

He was beginning to grow more comfortable with the idea of revealing the truth about himself to her. He tried to imagine the conversation. He would tell her exactly how he'd discovered his own illegitimacy on the heels of finding out about Bobby. He'd explain how, at first, he hadn't been sure how to proceed. But then, he'd taken in Bobby, then Jasper, then Mark, and he'd realized that his title could benefit them. It could, possibly, make up for all they'd endured in their early lives. It would give them opportunity, wealth, and identity. After all, they might not be able to inherit titles, but they did possess the blood of their sire as well as their brother. The blood of the ancient line of the Earls of Winthrop ran in their veins. And, while that might be meaningless in reality, in society it still meant *something*.

He would tell Frances that he needed to hold on to the title for the remainder of his lifetime. But when he died without an heir, his brothers' futures secured, it could revert to his uncle or cousins—the true, legitimate bloodline.

And that brought up another point—he would have to tell her that he couldn't risk having children. Frances had never talked about having children, but she'd never planned to marry. If she were married, would she want children of her own? It seemed likely, since she enjoyed the company of his young brothers so much.

After he told her all this, Frances might respond in a few different ways. He was terrified that she would turn away from him in disgust. Call him a fraud and a liar, and never speak to him again.

But while he would expect such treatment from anyone else, Frances wasn't an ordinary woman. He really wasn't sure *how* she'd react.

He'd seen her with his brothers, and it was clear that she understood their plight. In the years he'd known her, she'd never mentioned his title as if it held significant meaning to her. She also lived among the aristocracy and understood its foibles.

Honestly, it wasn't so farfetched to think she might understand his position.

And if she understood... Well, then he would need to convince her to marry him. He'd promise he wouldn't limit her. He'd vow to give her the freedom she craved so much.

The next question was, how could he prove that he would keep those promises?

Frances considered marriage a cage because her husband would have ultimate authority over her. He would dictate how she spent her days and nights. He would have legal dominion over her—so much so that everything she owned belonged to him. He wouldn't allow her to pursue her passions, whatever she might discover them to be.

Evan could answer to all of that. He could simply say he wouldn't do any of those things. He would give her every single freedom she wanted.

All right, there were limits to that. For example, he would insist that she remain faithful, but he had a feeling those weren't the kinds of limits she meant.

If there was one thing he knew, though, it was this: actions spoke louder than words.

He had to think of something to prove to her that he wasn't the kind of man who would cage her.

Soon, he'd be back in London. They'd meet one night, and he'd hold her in his arms. He'd whisper his truths to her, and if she accepted him as he was, he'd prove once and for all that he would never trap her. And once that was accomplished, he'd ask her to become his wife.

As Mark recovered, more than enough time passed for Frances to send them another letter. As they waited, some ideas began to form in Evan's mind. He sent a letter of inquiry north to Bowness and two letters to London, one to his man of business and the second to a jeweler. He received responses to those letters quickly.

But no letter came from Frances.

It wasn't like Frances not to respond. So as the hours, then days, passed with no word from her, Evan started to worry.

Chapter Twenty-Six

Frances remained in her room for the next few days, unable to drag herself from under the haze of panic.

Eradicating her fanciful thoughts of Evan left her with a very short list of two options for her future, both of which made her want to dive under her covers and never emerge: 1) Marry Salt and live a life that would make her miserable. 2) Refuse Salt and cause her family more suffering.

How could she make such a decision when both choices were so awful?

Her sisters came to visit. Evidently trusting that she had enough common sense to make the "right" choice, they dismissed her mood as "your usual dour self, Frances, when you ought to be smiling from ear to ear!"

She hadn't been able to bring herself to make a final decision yet, so she kept her mouth shut when Mary spoke of how she'd prayed to God to give Frances His heavenly guidance on how to be a good wife to Mr. Salt. She didn't argue when Esther prattled a list of all the social events Frances would be re-welcomed to when she was a married woman no longer constrained by scandal. Harriet had cried happy tears and hugged her tight before pulling back, and with a joyful smile, revealing that she was with child. If Frances got pregnant quickly, she said, then the cousins would be close in age and the best of friends, and the two of them could share the delights of new motherhood.

"Hardly," Frances had wanted to say cynically, "since if I do actually decide to marry the man, I will be thousands of miles away in a strange land." But she hadn't been able to bring herself to say even that much.

The only one of her sisters who provided a semi-calming presence was Martha. Having her twin close filled that part of Frances that was left empty when Martha was gone. She and Martha had spent hours together in the past few days, and Frances had told her about the things she'd done since her sister had left London. She even told Martha a little about how the Earl of Winthrop had taken in Bobby and Jasper, and how her affection for them and Mark had grown when she'd encountered them up at the lake.

Frances was glad, too, that Martha had returned with Salt. If he had come alone, Frances probably wouldn't have given marrying him a second thought. Martha's presence was a steady reminder of how important her family was to her. How she couldn't simply sacrifice their happiness to try to avoid a situation that was entirely her fault.

Salt had called upon her every day at one o'clock, and while her brother and sister had seen him, Frances hadn't. He'd told Martha he would continue to call daily until Frances agreed to meet with him.

Today would be that day.

She still hadn't made a decision. She went back and forth, making endless lists of pros and cons in her mind and on paper, the cons of both options far outweighing the pros. But neither choice stood out as the right one. In fact, it was the opposite—both choices felt *so* wrong.

As Frances deliberated with herself, her family planned her future for her. Without consulting her, Charles and Salt had drawn up the marriage contracts and signed them. Mary had informed her yesterday afternoon that the banns had been read in their parish church. They would be read two more times over the next two Sundays, and then, the Monday following the last reading, Charles had—again without consulting Frances—managed to reserve a time at St. George's Hanover Square for Salt and Frances to be wed. It was a "happy" miracle, Mary told her, since scheduling a wedding at that particular church was nigh impossible, as it was the most fashionable church in London in which to be married. Fortunately, someone who'd reserved the time months ago had broken off their engagement, and there was an opening that morning.

Frances's future hung in a tenuous balance. Getting to know Salt a little better today would hopefully tip the scales strongly to one side and she'd finally be able to commit herself to a singular course of action. This state of limbo was torture, and it wasn't in her nature to meekly allow others to take control of her life.

She needed to make a decision, once and for all.

Peggy helped Frances dress in one of her prettier day dresses, a light green cambric with honeycomb embellishments at the bodice and hem. When her hair was swept up into a stylish chignon, she went across the hall to Esther and Harriet's old room where Martha had been staying and knocked on the door.

"Come in." Martha was sitting at the writing desk, the replica of the one in Frances's room, and turned when Frances opened the door.

"Oh, good!" she exclaimed. "You've come out of our—*your*—room. Finally."

"Yes, finally," Frances said. "I thought I'd speak with Mr. Salt today."

Martha stood from the desk, smoothing her skirt. "Are you ready to see him?"

No. Actually, I'd prefer he hopped on the next ship to Egypt, and I never saw him again in my life. Frances shrugged. "As ready as I'll ever be. Though, if you don't mind, I'd prefer to speak to him in private."

"You know that is impossible."

Frances huffed out a breath. "Martha, I promise you. He's not going to ravish me on the drawing room floor."

Martha's cheeks went pink. "Frances!"

Goodness. Her twin was married. How could such a comparatively benign comment make her blush? Frances thought of all the wicked things Evan had said to her during their nights together, while at the same time doing even wickeder things to her body.

Now, *that* was something to blush over. Indeed, she felt heat spreading over her chest just thinking about it.

"Well, it's true," she said mulishly. "Nothing is going to happen."

"That is of no import," Martha said primly. "I will stay to chaperone you."

"Will you at least do me the courtesy of sitting in the corner and pretending not to listen to our conversation?"

"Of course," her sister said.

As they entered the drawing room, they heard the knock on the front door. A moment later, as Frances was tugging one of the heavy chairs into the far corner of the room for Martha, the butler said, "Mr. Salt is here to see you, Miss Cherrington."

"Excellent," Martha said. "Send him in."

"Send up some tea, too, will you, Rutherford?" Frances asked.

"Yes, miss."

Between moving the chair and her riot of nerves, beads of sweat broke out at Frances's temple. She dashed them away as Salt entered, turning what looked like a forced smile first to Martha, who greeted him fondly, then to Frances.

"Miss Cherrington. I am so glad to see you."

Frances stared at him. Was he telling the truth? It was difficult to know. She had never been particularly skilled at reading people's true intent. She thought of Evan and how strongly she'd distrusted his innate kindness at first.

"I am glad to see you, too, Mr. Salt," she lied. She had no idea what his Christian name was. If she married him, she might be forced to call him "Mr. Salt" for the entirety of their lives together.

She studied him. He was of average height, an inch or two taller than her. He seemed soft where Evan was hard—in his stomach and in the breadth of his shoulders—

No. *No, no, no.* She mustn't compare him to Evan. Ever. Right then and there, she forbade herself to do so.

He had blond hair and pale blue eyes, which might be

considered handsome. But they were nothing like the enticing amber—

No. No. *NO!*

She cleared her throat. "Please"—she gestured to the sofa—"sit down."

"Thank you," Salt said, but he hesitated, not wanting to be seated until the ladies were.

She turned her gaze to Martha, who fluttered her hand at them. "Oh…you two, please sit. I've been working on something for Oscar…" She hurried over to the sewing basket beside the sofa and pulled out an embroidery hoop containing her latest creation. "A handkerchief embossed with a likeness of the pyramids." She showed Salt the half-finished piece. "What do you think, Mr. Salt?"

Salt's smile became natural and real. "Quite lovely, Mrs. de Havilland. I am certain your husband will be delighted."

"Why, thank you." Martha gestured to the chair. "I will go over there and work with the utmost attention on my embroidery. You won't even know I am in the room."

She scurried over to the chair, plopped down on it, took up the needle, and commenced to studiously regard her handiwork.

Frances lowered herself stiffly onto the sofa, her palms pressed to her knees. Salt sat beside her, also on the sofa's edge, seemingly as tense as she was.

Finally, Frances spoke. "Were you surprised it was me?"

"I…uh… I'm sorry, I—"

"When you found out it was me you…er…" She scrambled to find a non-offensive way to say it. "When you discovered I was the lady dressed as Cleopatra?"

"Oh!" he coughed out. "Right. Um…well"—he looked

away, pink creeping across his cheeks—"yes. I was quite surprised, actually."

"Because my queenly costume was such a brilliant disguise?" she asked.

"Oh no, that wasn't it at all." He shook his head. "I mean, it was an excellent costume, to be sure. But no…it was…well, perhaps it was the costume, in a way. Your behavior did not at all reflect the Miss Cherrington I knew. Er…*know*."

She thought back on that night, how determined she'd been. How brazen.

"You seemed especially fascinated by my field of study," Salt continued, "while prior to that, I was given to believe you possessed little interest in the subject of Egypt."

Guilt squeezed at her chest.

"Yes," she mused. "Perhaps it was the costume. Masquerades give people leave to be more forward than they would be otherwise. Perhaps that happened with me, as well."

His throat moved as he swallowed. "Did *you* recognize *me*, Miss Cherrington?"

She opened her mouth to answer yes, of course she did, but then she hesitated. He would think she'd pursued him because she wanted him. But she had never wanted him.

So which would be worse? To say, "Yes, of course I knew it was you," and have him think that she had been attracted to him when she hadn't been in the least? Or to say, "No, I had no idea it was you," and have him think she was the type of lady to wander around encouraging strange men to kiss her?

Both answers were deceptive.

She looked down. "I had no idea it was you," she said quietly. Heat rushed to her face at hearing the lie emerge.

After a moment, she looked up again. Salt had the look

of a man trying to fortify himself against doing the thing he most dreaded in the world.

"You don't have to do this, you know." When his brow wrinkled in confusion, she added, "Marry me."

He frowned. "On the contrary. I must. It is the honorable thing to do. The right thing. I compromised you, and I must now face the repercussions of that."

She fought a flinch. Marrying her would be an unpleasant duty for him. A punishment for the mistake he'd made.

"It was just a mistake. We both made a mistake." Especially Frances. She hated herself for thinking that starting a scandal and ruining herself would be a perfect solution to her frustration. She'd been a selfish fool. Thinking only of herself. Not of her family, and most of all, not Salt himself. She'd done him a grievous wrong.

"Which is why I must make it right," Salt said. "You are a well-bred lady, and I will not see you suffer for my misconduct any more than you already have done."

But wouldn't marrying each other cause them both to suffer?

"You don't love me, though," she said.

He coughed and shifted in his chair as if trying to hide how uncomfortable the forwardness of her question made him. "That is hardly a consideration."

"Shouldn't you marry someone you care for?"

"I care for you, Miss Cherrington." He said it like a formal announcement, with no emotion behind the words.

"Shouldn't you marry someone you respect and admire and…" She wanted to finish with the word "want." But that was too forthright for this man. He might swoon if she said it.

Evan was a carnal man. He loved touching and to be

touched, and he'd taught her to love it, too. To shiver when he ran his hands over her, to grow warm and damp between her legs when he ran his hot kisses over her skin. He was rough and demanding and blunt when they were together, a direct contrast to his charming public façade. He spoke plainly, never held back, and demanded that she be just as open as he was. He'd brought out the sensual part of her she hadn't known existed. She'd never realized it was such an important part of who she was, and she'd loved every second of him drawing it out of her.

Salt, however... His kiss had been wet and soft and lacking the intensity and sizzling heat of Evan's touch every time he so much as laid a fingertip on her.

"Do. Not. Compare. Them," she told herself sternly.

But, her stubborn mind contended, she had been able to say anything about desire to Evan and he'd listen and nod and then proceed to make her feel it to her marrow. She would never say such things to Salt. Ever.

If she married Salt, she'd need to lock her carnal nature away, stuff it back into the box Evan had opened. Repress it. She closed her eyes briefly. How could she endure such a loss?

"Respect and admiration will follow, I am certain," Salt said now.

The tea came, and Martha set her embroidery aside to serve them before taking a nearby chair. The discussion turned almost immediately to Martha's and Salt's favorite subject: Egypt.

Frances watched their animated conversation in silence.

Lord knew she didn't want to marry this man. She didn't love him and never would, but he didn't deserve to be in the middle of this. He was kind and soft-spoken and good. He was innocent, trying to do right by her. It wasn't his fault she'd manipulated him.

This was her own fault, from beginning to end.

She felt worn down and out of options. Salt and her siblings rejected everything she said to try to convince them she didn't need to marry him. And a part of her knew they were correct. She and Salt marrying was the proper thing to do according to the world they lived in.

How could she argue against an entire world?

It seemed to her that the scales of her future were slowly tipping to one side. The side where she and Salt became husband and wife.

Chapter Twenty-Seven

Mark was getting better. He'd hardly coughed at all last night, and his breathing wasn't nearly as labored as it had been just a few days ago.

Generally, Evan liked spending time at Pleasant Hill. It was a pleasant place, after all, and filled with pleasant memories of him and his friends and their various antics over the years. It was a modern house—his father had the place built only twenty years ago, but the old earl had always preferred to spend his time in London, occupying Pleasant Hill only a few weeks out of the year. The dowager countess had lived here until Evan's father's death, but she'd rarely interfered with Evan's life. So, from an early age, he had endeavored to make good memories here, inviting his friends over at every recess and holiday from school, and, after his father died, holding house parties that were always well-attended thanks to the house's proximity to London. Not too far to be a days-long journey, but far enough that it was truly in the country.

But this visit had not been one that would leave him with happy memories. It had been full of coughing and worry, with the bitter presence of the dowager countess looming not too far away. Evan was ready to get back to London and to Frances. He could hardly sit still with the anxiety about Frances occupying his every idle thought.

Why the hell hadn't she responded to their letter? What was going on? The more he thought about it, the more the uneasy feeling grew in his gut. He'd given her no reason to cut him. Her last letter had made it sound like she was eager to see him and the boys.

What could have happened?

He hoped to God her brother hadn't somehow found out about them. What would Charles Cherrington do with that information?

If that had happened, though, surely he would have heard from the man by now, insisting he do right by his sister, demanding he marry her. Evan would have done so, of course. Happily...if she was willing.

But there was nothing but silence from the Cherrington quarter.

He needed to get back to London. He'd call upon her the very same day. If she'd decided to end their association, he'd make her tell him to his face. This silence was going to kill him.

"Evan?"

He looked up from his desk, blinking. "Jasper, what is it?"

"May I come in?"

"Of course. You are always welcome in my study here or in London, no matter how busy I appear to be."

Jasper nodded, then came inside and sat in the armchair across from him.

"Is something on your mind?"

The lad gave him a little nod. "I was only going to tell you about something I used to do all the time when I lived at Harlowe's."

"What's that?" Evan asked, leaning forward. It wasn't often that Jasper talked about his years at Harlowe's Home for Boys.

Jasper squeezed his hands over his knees and took a deep breath. He was filling out a little—his coat already a bit tight at the shoulders. Good. Evan would happily buy him a new one, and another, and another if he kept growing. All three of his brothers were too skinny.

With his straight back and serious expression, along with his love for baths—Bobby and he were in direct opposition on the matter of baths—and his new clothes and haircut, Jasper looked like a young gentleman. With his blond hair and striking eyes, he was a handsome lad. Evan had already seen girls Jasper's age turn their heads when he walked by. He wondered if Jasper had noticed it.

Jasper looked down at his hands. "I used to miss my mum. Lots."

"Of course you did," Evan said quietly. Jasper and Bobby's mother had died when Jasper was six and Bobby hardly a year old. Bobby didn't remember her at all, but Jasper certainly did.

"I used to sneak out of Harlowe's sometimes at night and go visit her. Sometimes it made me feel better, to be near her like that. 'Cause she was my mum." He squeezed his knees harder. "And…well, I missed her."

"You mean…you visited her grave?" Evan asked carefully.

Jasper nodded. "She got a pauper's burial, but I know where she's at."

Evan frowned. A pauper's burial? What the hell? Their

father hadn't even bothered to bury his years-long mistress properly?

Evan wished his sire was standing in front of him right now, just for the joy he'd get from punching the man in the gut. Hard.

He'd buy the woman a proper headstone as soon as they were back in London.

"It made me feel better," Jasper continued. "Seeing her." He gave a wry smile. "'Course, it would've been even better if she were standing there in front of me and I wasn't just looking down at her grave."

"I imagine it would have been."

"But it was still nice to see her. Though I couldn't really talk to her."

Evan nodded.

"I'd stay with her a while, tidying up her grave and the like." Jasper shrugged. "Then I'd go back to Harlowe's and pretend I'd been sleeping the whole time."

"How did you manage to sneak out of that place?"

Jasper did smile at that. "An older lad—he taught me how to pick the locks. I got pretty good at it. I could come and go as I pleased and no one was the wiser. I was never caught, not once."

"Impressive," Evan said, and he meant it. He'd been in a few scrapes as a youth wherein he'd wished he knew how to pick a lock.

"I think…maybe, if you went to London, you'd feel better, too. Like I felt better when I was near my mum."

"Er…" Evan cocked his head, trying to figure out what the boy was getting at.

Jasper lifted his hands and held them out, palms flat as if he was relaying something completely obvious. "Because you won't feel right until you're near Miss Cherrington again. Because you miss her."

"Oh." Evan swallowed hard. "Jasper. I am all right. Of course I miss Miss Cherrington, and so do you boys, but I've just been a little worried about Mark, is all."

Jasper shook his head, a stubborn movement reminiscent of Bobby. "You'll feel better being close to her again."

Before Evan could answer, there was a knock at the door and the butler opened it slightly.

"Excuse me, my lord. You have received a letter."

Evan's heart jumped to his throat as he took the folded sheet from the man. But it retreated as soon as he saw the writing on the outside, and then flipped it over to see the seal. The letter was not from Frances. It was from the Duke of Crestmont.

"Thank you," he said, sighing. The butler left, and he unfolded the note.

Hill Street, Lon.
13th of July, 1820

Winthrop,

I understand that you have remained in Pleasant Hill to await your young brother's full recovery, but I must impress upon you the fact that it is not uncommon for children to have a bit of a cough following a cold. Last year, Evie couldn't shake off a cough for the entire winter, but she maintained a full schedule of activities, and if you look at her now, you'd never know she suffered a day of illness in her life. From your description of his improving symptoms you laid out in your last letter, it is clear that Mark will be fine.

Crestmont

He folded the note and looked at Jasper, who was watching him. "Come," he said. "Let's go speak with our brothers."

They went to the nursery, where Mark was at his desk finishing up his lessons for the day and Bobby was dangling from one of the rafters.

"Evan!" Bobby said from high above them. "Jasper! Look at me!"

"Will you ever stop climbing things?" Jasper groaned.

"Never!" Bobby declared happily.

Evan went to kneel beside Mark's chair. His little feet dangled a foot off the floor. "How are you feeling, Mark?"

"Good," Mark said. "Look, Evan. I wrote my name." He held up his slate, where he'd written *M-a-r-k* in shaky, uncertain letters.

Evan beamed at him and gave him a one-armed hug. "Well done!"

Mark threw his arms around him and pressed a kiss to his cheek. "I love you, Evan."

That sucked the air out of Evan's lungs. No one had ever said that to him before.

He closed his eyes and squeezed his little brother tight for a moment. Then, eyes burning, he glanced over at Miss Renshaw who, hands on hips, was staring up at Bobby in a stance that suggested she was prepared to leap to catch him should he fall. "How was Mark's cough today?" Evan asked her.

"He didn't cough once all afternoon, my lord," she told him, not breaking her gaze from Bobby.

Evan took a deep breath and then let it out. "Well, Bobby, best get down from there. It's time to pack our bags. We're going to London."

...

When Martha told her Evan and the boys had arrived in London late last night, Frances's heart had leapt into her throat and, ignited by Evan's physical nearness, something sparked deep within her. A tiny glimmer of hope.

Frances sat at her desk, running her fingers over the wrinkled page of the letter she'd written to Evan last week. There might be a chance—a small chance, to be sure, but it was still a chance—that Evan wasn't as committed to his stance on avoiding marriage as he'd made himself out to be. Despite her longtime insistence that she'd never be someone's wife, when she thought about Evan, marriage didn't sound so bad. In fact, it was the only thing that felt *right*.

Maybe the same would be true for him?

That could very well just be Frances's desperation talking. But if there was even a tiny possibility that Evan was open to taking a wife, Frances might be able to avoid attaching herself to Salt while at the same time saving her family from scandal.

Thinking about it sent a surge of joy through her. She closed her eyes, picturing being Evan's wife. Sharing his bed and having him and his brothers an essential part of every single one of her days for the rest of her life.

She could imagine nothing better.

She wanted it with everything she was.

Evan would never cage her. He would never demand she be someone she wasn't. He would never force her to give up her dreams. Her desires. Her *self*.

He and his brothers were the only people she'd ever

known who'd given her leave to be herself. Who'd admired her for who she was rather than what everyone wanted her to be. If she became Evan's countess, he wouldn't lock her up and throw away the key. No. She knew him. He would do the opposite. He'd open the world to her.

In return, she wouldn't be the kind of wife who would interfere with the raising of his brothers, and Lord knew she'd never resent him for his dedication to them as some women might. She'd help him raise them. She'd love them as her own. She was already more invested in those boys' wellbeing than was entirely proper.

Still, a flood of doubt threatened to snuff out the tenuous hope building inside her.

What if Evan didn't love her? What if he saw her only as a potential mistress, nothing more? He'd had other lovers, and there was a possibility that he'd used the same pretty words with them, made them feel as wonderful as he'd made her feel.

She wasn't a fool. Women were known for throwing their hearts and souls into liaisons that ended up being nothing more than carnal amusements for the men. How many times throughout her life had she been warned?

Frances chewed on her lip. No. That wasn't Evan. She couldn't bring herself to believe it. As she had been honest with him, so had he with her.

The way he'd looked at her. That adoration. That respect. It had grown exponentially during those days up at the lake.

That could have been love.

Whatever it was, she would never believe it had been fake. He cared about her.

She needed to see him.

She would go to his house today after Mr. Salt's

afternoon call. She would tell Evan all the things in her heart and hope and pray that he felt the same. And then she'd get down on one knee and propose.

She pulled out a new sheet of paper, dipped her pen into the ink, and poured her heart out in a list of all the things she needed to tell him.

1) I am supposed to marry someone else, but I want only you.

2) I love you.

3) My heart is yours.

4) So is my soul.

5) I think you are the only man I will ever desire. Ever. In my life.

6) You make me happy.

7) You allow me to be me in a way that no one ever has.

8) I love being with you.

9) I love your kisses.

10) And how you touch me, and how you hold me.

11) I love how caring and kind you are.

12) I love how—

A knock sounded on her door, interrupting her from writing "much you love Jasper, Bobby, and Mark" for number twelve.

She stuffed the page into her desk drawer and slammed it shut before jumping out of her chair and spinning around. The door had already opened, and Charles hovered at the threshold, his narrow gaze moving from her to the drawer.

"What was that?"

"Oh, um." She put a casual hand on her desktop and tried to smooth out her expression into something less *guilty panic* and more *careless composure*. "I was just writing a bit of my novel."

"Really? How interesting. May I see?" He held out a hand.

She managed a tight laugh. "You may read it when I finish, Charles, and not a moment before."

He dropped his hand and shrugged. "Very well. I came to tell you that your visitor has arrived."

"Oh. Mr. Salt is here?"

"It is one o'clock."

"Already. My goodness." She smoothed her skirts. "Thank you. I shall be down in a moment."

As soon as Charles left, she retrieved her desk key from the drawer, locked it, then slipped the key into her pocket.

Then, she hurried downstairs, hoping that this would be the last meeting with Salt she'd ever have to endure.

Chapter Twenty-Eight

Frances rushed up the stairs, the key to her desk feeling heavy in her pocket. She'd just spent the past hour listening to Salt drone on about hieroglyphs, but she had hardly heard a word he'd said. All she could do was think about the list that lay inside her desk, about all she planned to tell Evan this afternoon.

She was going to see him soon. She had missed him so much.

By the time she arrived at the top of the stairs, she was almost running.

She was going to bare her soul to the Earl of Winthrop. She was going to tell him she loved him. She was going to reveal all her secret desires.

Such raw declarations would, no doubt, frighten many men away. Honestly, she didn't know how Evan would react. He'd told her, flat-out, that he never wanted to marry. He hadn't made any declarations of love to her.

He might be appalled by her revelations. He might *laugh*.

She hesitated at her door, doubt and fear barreling through her. Telling Evan what was in her heart might only set her up for further heartbreak.

But her heart was already broken. What were a few more cracks in a piece of crystal that was already shattered? At this point, she was desperate enough to set aside her pride and take the biggest risk of her life.

She would not be a coward. She would don her bonnet and her pelisse. She'd walk to his house. And if Evan loved her even a fraction of the amount she loved him, there was a chance he could help her escape from this horrible situation.

Turning the handle, she pushed the door to her bedchamber open.

Everything came to a screeching halt. Her feet. Her breath. Her heartbeat.

Charles stood there, the list she'd written for Evan in hand, his face flaming red.

Ever so slowly, he swung his head to face her. He spoke from between his teeth. "Frances."

She grappled for her key, fumbling in her pocket. It was still there.

Somehow, Charles had broken into her desk drawer.

"What are you doing?" she gasped. "What have you..." Her voice dwindled. A key was still in the lock on the front drawer panel. Charles had another key. "When did you start looking in my drawers?" she demanded.

"I have never. But you behaved so guiltily this afternoon that I knew something was wrong."

She couldn't say anything more, couldn't speak beyond the enormous lump that was forming in her throat.

"You have finally proven just how far you will go to destroy our family," he said quietly.

"How dare you break into my desk. How dare you read my most private—"

He strode over to her, took hold of her wrist, and yanked her inside the room before slamming the door so hard, the floorboards rattled under her feet. Then he dropped her hand and loomed over her, vibrating with rage.

She took a step back from him as he shook the page in her face. "Who…the hell…is *this* person?"

She was certainly not going to tell him. Frances was vibrating with rage, too. "What is *wrong* with you?" She snatched the paper from his hand and ripped it into dozens of pieces, then threw them onto the floor before whipping her gaze back to her brother.

Charles's fists clenched at his sides. "Frances, I swear, if you do not tell me who this blackguard—"

She raised her chin defiantly. *"Never."*

"You took a lover under my nose. And it was not Mr. Salt, even though you were caught kissing him." He pushed both hands through his hair, leaving it standing on end, and his expression contorted as if he was about to weep. "Frances… You are engaged to be married, and yet you have been giving yourself to someone else."

"No!" she said. "That's not what—"

"You understand nothing of men," he said, straightening. "Even not knowing this fellow's identity, I can tell you with absolute certainty that his only purpose was to seduce you into his bed. To thoroughly ruin you for anyone else."

"Please, stop," she begged. "This is none of your business, Charles."

"What of your husband-to-be?" her brother snapped back. "Is it *his* business? Should I tell him you've strayed before you've even said your vows?" He ran a hand over his face, deflating once again. "I cannot begin to understand you. Any other woman in your position would be grateful that Herbert Salt returned from Egypt to rescue you from your disgrace."

Herbert, she thought dully. So that was his Christian name.

Charles kept going. "Any other woman would be grateful to be given the opportunities your family has given you. Why...*why* do you rebuff our counsel—our help—at every turn?"

That wasn't fair of him. Their "help" was saddling her with a man she didn't even like, much less love. "You made a love match, Charles. When you thought you wouldn't be able to marry Lilly, you were devastated. No other woman could move you but her. And you were lucky, because in the end, you were able to marry her, and now you are happy together. Yet you expect me to be happy to be bound to a stranger I don't love?"

"Then *why did you kiss him*?" Charles shouted.

She heaved in a breath and blurted out the truth. "Because I thought being ruined would be the most expedient way of being taken off the marriage mart. I believed Salt would be far away and safe from any repercussions. I thought everything would be fine. It was a stupid idea. A mistake."

Charles stared at her as if she'd grown two heads. "You did this—you put all of us through this—*on purpose*? To defy your family's hopes and dreams for your happiness?"

She looked away, a flush of guilt warming her chest. "The

point is," she said, lowering her voice, "I don't love him, and I never did. How can you expect me to be grateful to be forced to live in a foreign land trapped in a marriage I never asked for and certainly didn't want? How can you not understand that?"

A muscle jumped in her brother's jaw as he gestured roughly at the torn pieces of paper on the floor. "Salt will never know of this. Do you hear me?"

"Yes." Truthfully, she didn't care to tell Salt anything, much less about her relationship with Evan.

"You will never speak to, or of, that man again. You will marry Salt in less than two weeks."

Wait. "I—"

Charles interrupted her. "You will *not* renege. The banns have already been read once. You are marrying Herbert Salt, and you will put this family through no further suffering regarding this issue, *do you understand me?*"

"Charles, *no.*"

"Do you know how hard I have worked to make this family respectable? Since I was thirteen years old, I have shielded you—all of my sisters—not only from our father's drunken tempers, but from our entire family's suffering image. I have worked nonstop for almost fifteen years to rebuild that image. I have given you everything. London Seasons, when I had to forego my own entertainments to pay for them. All the finery you wear. Every opportunity a young lady could ever dream of having. I have thrown myself into the task of protecting you, of ensuring your future, and you repay me with *this?*" Again, he gestured to her torn-up list.

Frances squeezed her eyes shut. Charles was right. After their mother had died, their father had been awful. Charles had taken the brunt of it. He'd protected her and her sisters from his rages. "I'm—"

"Your lover—this other man—isn't here. Salt *is*, and he is willing to have you. If you do not marry him now, the scandal will ruin us. *All of us*."

Frances's skin hurt. Her bones hurt. Her heart hurt. She wanted Evan. She wanted to be surrounded by him and the boys, see their smiling faces, feel the comfort of their approval.

"You have finally pushed me to my limit." Charles's lips thinned and his eyes grew hard. "You will remain in this room until your wedding day. The door will be locked from the outside, you will neither receive nor send any correspondence, and you will not see anyone outside of the family."

She gasped. "You can't do that!"

"You leave me no choice." His hands fisted into tight balls at his sides. "I hope that someday you will understand that my actions are motivated solely by what is best for this family. What is best for *you*."

"You're wrong," she shot back. "You don't understand me. You never will."

"Perhaps not. But I *do* understand what's good and what's right."

With that, he knelt and swept up the pieces of the letter. Crumpling them in his hand, he left her room without another word. She could hear a key turning, the lock tumbling into place.

She was in a real prison now.

Chapter Twenty-Nine

It wasn't until late in the afternoon the day after they'd returned to London that Evan was finally able to leave the house. Mark, who'd never been in a city before, had clung to him all day, and it was four o'clock before Evan felt confident his little brother would be all right if he left for a while.

"Where are you going?" Jasper asked suspiciously when he told him to look after their brothers while he was out.

Evan opened his mouth, then closed it. He didn't want to lie to his brothers—ever.

"To see a friend I haven't seen in a while," he finally said.

Jasper stared at him hard for a good ten seconds. Then, he nodded and turned away. "Tell her Bobby misses her. Lots."

Evan raised his brows. "*Bobby* misses her? Just Bobby?"

"And me," Jasper added grudgingly.

"And me!" Mark piped up. Evan glanced at where he swayed on the rocking horse across the room—did Mark even know what they were talking about? The excited look in his eyes suggested he did.

"Very well. I'll be back by dinnertime. Make sure you mind Miss Renshaw while I'm gone."

Evan walked to the Cherrington townhouse, which was less than a mile from his own house. He arrived at half four, well within the usual calling hours. At the front door, he hesitated, then adjusted his cravat, feeling suddenly nervous.

Swallowing hard, he knocked on the door. A footman answered, and he handed over his card. "The Earl of Winthrop to see Miss Cherrington."

"I am afraid Miss Cherrington is not at home, sir."

Evan ground his teeth. "Please tell her I am here, regardless."

"Yes sir." The footman's expression was utterly flat.

"Now."

"As I said, she is not at home."

"When will she be at home, damn it?" Evan growled.

"I cannot say for certain."

Evan resisted the urge to shove him aside and go find her in the house. He *knew* she was there. "Tomorrow?"

"Unlikely."

"The day after tomorrow?"

"I cannot say. Good afternoon, sir."

He was growing desperate now. "Just—"

But the man shut the door in his face.

He stood there in stunned silence for several moments.

He didn't understand why he was so surprised. She hadn't written him, so it wasn't a stretch to think that she wouldn't want to see him, either.

Had he thought she'd open the door and fall straight into

his arms, begging his forgiveness for making him worry?

Well, he'd certainly hoped for that particular outcome.

He walked home on leaden feet, and when he got to his townhouse, he sent a message to Viscount Coleton, telling him he was back in London, and asking whether he was going to his club tonight. If he was, Evan said he'd join him late.

When Evan saw Jasper at dinner, the boy raised his brows in question, and Evan sighed. "She wasn't home."

It wasn't a lie. That was what he'd been told, after all.

But it wasn't *true*, either. Evan knew in his bones that she'd been home. He'd *felt* her there.

After the boys went to bed, he went to Cole's club. Cole was already there and greeted him with a smile and a slap on the back. "Winthrop! Feels like forever since I last saw you."

"Just returned to London today," he told his friend. "And fair warning—I'm going to get foxed tonight."

Cole raised a brow. "Want to tell me why?"

"No," Evan said shortly. Cole didn't press the issue. Instead, he nodded and said he'd ensure Evan got home in one piece.

At the club, Evan barely spoke to anyone. As hearty conversation flowed around him, he drank and drank.

Then, he drank some more.

Frances hadn't answered his letters.

She had changed her mind about continuing their liaison.

He felt like the little boy he'd once been. He remembered how his father had raged at him one night, saying that Evan was a common bastard who would never live up to his title.

Now, he knew exactly why his father had said that to him. He *was* a common bastard.

He probably hadn't lived up to the title, either.

After his father's outburst, Evan had wandered around the cavernous house, lonely, frightened, and hurting. His nurse had the night off. He could have gone down to the cook who'd have given him some mulled wine and patted his shoulder, but he didn't want the cook to feel sorry for him.

Instead, tears streaming down his face, he'd gathered his courage and gone to his mother.

She had been dressed in her nightclothes. All he remembered were many-layered flounces of pink and light blue and yellow silk. She was very beautiful, and she looked very soft. Having her hold him in her arms would be like being held by the silkiest, most comfortable cloud. He wanted that comfort more than anything.

"Mama?" he'd said, rubbing the back of his arm under his running nose.

She'd looked down at him. "What are *you* doing here?"

"Mama—I..." But he'd been crying too hard to tell her how sad he was feeling.

Her face, always cool and composed, flashed with emotion, but it was gone too quickly for Evan to decipher it, and her expression flattened once again as she looked away. "Your bodily fluids are dripping onto my Persian carpet. Leave at once, child. Never show yourself to me in such an unkempt state again, do you understand?"

He'd stood a moment, gaping at her until she sighed wearily. "I suppose I shall have to call someone to remove you, then." Rising, she rang the bell.

Before any of the servants could witness his mother's cold-blooded rejection, he'd run out of the room, gone to his bed in the empty nursery, and cried himself to sleep.

Before that, he'd known his mother was aloof, but until

that moment, he'd never understood that she didn't love him. After that, he knew. He hadn't understood why except to think there must be something intrinsically wrong with him.

A few weeks after the incident, he was sent to Eton. He'd met Crestmont, Jameson, and Cole there, and over the years, they'd made him feel whole and deserving again, at least of their friendship.

And his time with Frances had given him hope that he might be deserving of love.

But now, it was clear that she had changed her mind about him. She was "not at home" and she was not responding to his letters.

She didn't want him. Just like his mother.

He'd been stupid to think that Frances Cherrington might love him.

She'd left a gaping hole in his chest he'd never again be able to fill, even with all the drink he was imbibing tonight.

He rolled his eyes up to the mantel clock. It wasn't even midnight yet.

Hell.

He downed the rest of his drink.

Chapter Thirty

When her brother locked her in her room the previous day, Frances had been more stunned than anything. She'd waited for a few hours, expecting him to return any moment to apologize and say he'd overreacted. But he never came.

At dusk, Frances had tried to open the door. She'd yanked at it, then tried to break it down. She'd pounded on it, demanding to be let out. She'd cried. She'd *begged*.

No one had come. No one had responded. Not Charles, not Lilly, and not Martha. Not even a servant. They'd just let her shout until her voice was hoarse and tears were streaming down her face.

Now, dry-eyed, she sat on her bed staring at the locked door. There was no escape. Earlier, she'd studied the drop from her second-floor window, debating whether she should try to jump to the cobbles below. No. At the least, she'd break a leg if she tried. It was simply too far down.

Today was Sunday. It was early yet, just a little before

eight o'clock. Later this morning, the banns would be read for a second time and Frances would not be in church to voice her objections to her own match.

Someone knocked on the door. She didn't answer, but she heard a key turning the lock. It was Martha who entered, a towering pile of books in her arms.

"Oh, good, you're awake," Martha said by way of greeting, heaving the books onto Frances's desk. "I know novels are your reading preference, so these are all novels. You've probably already read some of them, so I brought as many as I could carry so you'd have something to entertain you."

Frances knew this was a peace offering of sorts, but it wasn't enough. Not nearly.

She glared at her sister, not saying a word, her hands clenched in her lap. If she allowed herself to say something, she knew it would be filled with rage and vitriol.

Martha sat beside her on the bed. Every part of Frances vibrated with emotion. Rage was certainly there, but there was also sadness and regret, all of it topped by a strong sense of betrayal. By the knowledge that every single person in her family had forsaken her.

Most of all, the woman sitting beside her. Her twin. The person she should be able to depend on more than anyone.

She pressed down her welling emotions. She would not crack in front of Martha, nor any other member of her godforsaken family. Never again.

Finally, her sister spoke. "I have a few things to say."

Frances stared straight ahead at the striped damask wallpaper.

"First of all," Martha said, "I don't know what, exactly,

Charles found, but he did say that you have a..." She hesitated, biting her lip in the way that Frances sometimes did. "Paramour."

Frances sighed. *Paramour* was not the word she'd use to describe her relationship with Evan. It sounded so frivolous. Charles hadn't bothered to learn the extent of her feelings. He'd made assumptions and condemned her based upon them.

"And," Martha continued, "the fact of it has driven Charles straight out of his mind. You must try to forgive him."

Unable to stop it, Frances gave a cynical snort. "Unlikely."

Martha huffed out a breath. "Honestly, I have never seen him in such a state. I believe it is only temporary, however."

"Until I am gone from his life."

"Well...perhaps. But, though the rest of us can see it, he truly does not understand how despicable it is to lock you in your bedchamber."

Frances turned to Martha, brows raised. "*You* think it's despicable?"

"Of course!" Martha exclaimed. "He has caged you in here like some kind of...some kind of *criminal*. That is absolutely repugnant. Mary, Harriet, and Esther all agree—"

Frances's voice rose above her sister's. "Then why didn't you open the door last night? Why haven't you stopped him?"

"Oh, Frances." Martha groaned. "We cannot stop him."

Frances's eyes narrowed. "Yes, you can. Just unlock the door. Let me out of here."

"No, Frances. Really. We have been trying to make Charles see reason, but he is being stubborn. Mary even looked into the law on such matters late last night, but as your sisters, we have no legal leg to stand upon. As your closest male relative, Charles has dominion over you and has every right to lock you up if he desires to."

Frances gaped at her sister. "What about Lilly?" Surely if anyone could make Charles see reason, it was his wife.

Martha closed her eyes. "When Lilly couldn't talk sense into him, she…"

Alarm rushed through Frances at the expression on her sister's face. "What? What did she do?"

"After she heard that he locked you in your room and then how upset you were, she was furious. She tried to convince him to unlock the door. They argued, and when he would not budge from his position, she left the house in the early hours of the morning and took Arthur with her. They went to stay with the Duke and Duchess of Crestmont."

Frances gasped, then took a moment to let this sink in. She'd never imagined that Lilly would dream of leaving Charles, no matter how badly he behaved. But perhaps Lilly was stronger than Frances had given her credit for.

"I am glad she left him," Martha suddenly said, scowling at the floor. "He deserved it."

Her sister's spiteful words surprised her. "He did," Frances agreed.

"Yet," Martha continued, "Lilly leaving has had an unintended effect, and it is not in your favor."

"What's that?"

"It has made Charles even more obstinate. Without her calming, rational, and reasonable influence, he has grown more stubborn than ever. More insistent that he is in the right. Mired in his belief that this is the best course of action for you and for the family."

"For me?" Frances asked. "His *very* last thoughts are of

me, I assure you."

Martha stared at her for a moment, then shook her head. "No, I don't think that's true. He truly believes that your life here has been an unhappy one, that your"—she cleared her throat delicately—"er...paramour had evil intentions, and this is the only course of action where you might find safety someday."

"Good Lord," Frances muttered.

"Charles believes—or at least he has convinced himself—that marrying Mr. Salt is the only way you will have a chance at contentment. I think, for that reason alone, you should consider forgiving him, once all this is over."

"There is no chance of that," Frances said. "I have told him again and again that his opinions regarding my happiness are wrong. He has never listened. Only clung harder to his sanctimonious belief that I have always been wrong about my own desires and needs and he has always been right. Just like the rest of you."

Martha's lips pursed, and she looked down at where her hands were squeezed in her lap. Her posture and hands mirrored Frances's.

"About that," Martha said. "I've been putting a great deal of thought into it, and I think I was wrong."

Frances gasped. The Cherringtons were not a family who admitted to being wrong, ever.

Martha winced. "It pains me to admit it, but this is something else I wish to discuss with you."

When she didn't continue, Frances prompted, "Go on."

"I know we are different, but we are also twins, and essentially, in our very core, the same. I truly did think that Mr. Salt would be a perfect match for you, as Oscar has been to me. I thought he would make you happy, and I refused to see it from your point of view."

Frances cocked a brow. "And now?"

Martha shifted uncomfortably. "A part of me has always believed that, since I am the elder twin by a few minutes, I must know better. Logic has, of course, informed me that is foolish, but it nevertheless persists. In this case, though, I also thought, since I had experience being a wife and you did not, that I *must* know better."

Frances snorted.

"Now, though," Martha continued, "I am not so certain of that. The only person who knows what's best for you is *you*, Frances. During the past few days, you have told me about your hopes and dreams, your experiences at the boys' home and learning to draw and play the cello, however badly they went, your travels, how you explored the various sciences, and your idea about opening a bookshop. When your family is not pressing you to be something you're not, you simply light up. We have accused you of being dull and lifeless, sullen and moody, but that is the Frances weighted down by all the stipulations and expectations Charles and the rest of us have placed upon you. When they are gone, you remind me of the Frances you used to be. The Frances you were when we were young, when we were at Windermere Cottage before Charles summoned us to live in London."

Frances sighed. "I have tried to explain all that over and over. But none of you ever—"

"We never listened. I know. I am sorry." She took one of Frances's hands, gripping it between two of her own. "Please forgive me. I am so sorry."

Frances studied her twin. Despite all their shared

animosity over the years, she knew Martha. In her way, Martha was as forthright as Frances. Her apologies were rare, but when they came, she meant them.

"I am going to try to make it up to you," Martha said. "By being at your side and supporting you as much as I can."

Frances closed her eyes and bowed her head. A part of her that had felt on edge, knowing she and her twin had not been in accord for so long, softened.

She had her sister back. Even imprisoned as she was, it meant the world to her.

"You kissed Mr. Salt purposely, didn't you?" Martha asked. "I was surprised when I received the letters about it from our sisters, because you had been so clear about your lack of interest in him, but after talking with you these past weeks, I think I understand. You wanted relief from the pressure to marry. You orchestrated that kiss so that you would be deemed unmarriageable and taken off the marriage mart once and for all."

"Did Charles tell you this?"

"No."

Frances was a little surprised her sister had come to the correct conclusion on her own, but perhaps she shouldn't be. She nodded. "With Mr. Salt so far away and inaccessible, I thought I would be safe from being forced to marry someone I didn't want and didn't love."

"But you didn't count on the letters arriving in Alexandria so quickly. You didn't expect that Oscar and I would still be with Mr. Salt or that I'd tell him about what I'd heard and ask him to make it right."

"I underestimated you," Frances admitted, then added wryly, "As well as the speed of the post."

"That you did." Martha chuckled, then sobered. She squeezed Frances's hand. "You must understand that I acted in what I believed was your best interest."

"I know," Frances said.

"I'm sorry," Martha said again.

Frances pushed the edges of her lips up a tiny bit. That was all the smile she could muster. "I forgive you."

"But what about Lord Winthrop?" Martha asked softly. "Are you in love with him?"

Frances jerked back, yanking her hand away from her sister's. "What do you mean?"

Martha shook her head. "Frances, we are twins. Did you really believe I wouldn't be able to think it through?"

"What? How?"

"Something has changed in you since I saw you last. You're more…" Martha shook her head. "I don't know how to explain it. Confident, perhaps? No, that's not quite right. But it was enough for me to understand that something significant must have happened since I left London. The way you spoke of Lord Winthrop and his brothers…" She shook her head. "It seemed to me there was something more between you than friendship. And now, with Charles discovering you have a paramour…well, I put two and two together."

"What are you going to do?" Frances choked out. "Are you going to tell Charles?"

"No!" Martha exclaimed. "And I believe the question is, what are *you* going to do?"

"I…" Frances clamped her mouth shut, then muttered, "Nothing."

"Why not?"

"Because what could I possibly do?" She gestured wildly

around the room. "I am a prisoner. I'm two weeks away from marrying someone else. If I don't marry him, our family will be ruined. I'm out of time, Martha."

"Frances," Martha said sharply, "Winthrop is an *earl*. If you married a peer, all would be forgiven. Your reputation would be repaired, and Charles would be thrilled. We all would. Just think"—she hummed dreamily—"a Cherrington sister marrying an earl. It would be beyond Charles's wildest expectations for any of us."

Frances stared down at her hands twisted in her lap.

"If he cares for you, he will marry you," Martha said confidently.

"Not necessarily." As much as she'd fantasized about Evan whisking her off on his white steed to live happily ever after, the reality of the situation was very different. "Even if he does care for me, I am not certain he'd marry me."

"Why not?"

"He has just discovered that he has three illegitimate young brothers and has vowed to raise them to manhood. He doesn't want to marry because he wishes to focus on the family he has rather than start a new one."

Martha's brow wrinkled. "One would think he would desire a wife to assist him in that endeavor. It will not be easy for a single man to raise three children."

Which had been the same thought Frances had. "Be that as it may," Frances said, "he *doesn't* desire a wife. He told me so."

Martha sighed. "Do you love him?"

Frances looked away. "That doesn't matter."

"Are you certain?"

"Yes, Martha, I am certain."

"If the earl cares for you," Martha said gently, "he might change his mind about marriage. If only to help you out of this situation."

Frances had been ready to go to Evan and express her love for him to his face, but she would never have been able to accept it if he agreed to marry her for anything other than love. She didn't want his charity. She cringed as she thought of Charles's words: *"I can tell you with absolute certainty that his only purpose was to seduce you into his bed."*

Perhaps she had been blinded by her feelings and hadn't seen what had happened at the lake for what it truly was.

"I would never want him to marry me if he didn't wish to."

"But what if he *did* wish to?"

Frances pulled in a steadying breath. "If he wanted me… if he truly loved me as I love him—"

"You *do* love him!"

Frances nodded and looked up at her sister. "—then I would marry him. In a heartbeat."

Martha chewed on her lower lip. "Perhaps I could deliver a letter for you."

Chapter Thirty-One

On the bed, Martha opened one of the books she'd brought and began to read it while Frances composed her letter to Evan, explaining everything that had happened since her arrival in London. When she was about halfway through, she looked over her shoulder at her sister.

"Are you going to read this?"

Martha snorted, the sound identical to the cynical sound Frances often made. "I am not our brother."

Frances cocked a brow. "That's not an answer."

Martha blew out a breath. "No, I am not going to read your letter. I promise. So go ahead. Tell him how your heart aches for him, how you miss him, how you are a mere shell of a human without him."

Frances stared at her for a moment. She would have protested, but what Martha had just said was oddly similar to what Frances had been about to write. "Thank you."

She turned back around and proceeded to tell Evan the

truth. Her heart did ache for him. She did miss him, and when they'd separated, he'd taken something of her with him. She told him how she was being compelled to marry Salt even as she ached for Evan. And while she didn't reach the point of begging him to come on his white steed to save her, she did tell him the date of her upcoming nuptials: the twenty-fourth of July. Eight days from now.

When she finished, she folded the sheet of paper and sealed it before handing it to Martha.

"I'll deliver this myself later," Martha said, "but right now, I need to go. Mary is expecting me at church this morning. I'm taking the carriage and collecting Esther and Harriet on the way. We are going to have tea together afterward to discuss your situation. May I have permission to tell them more about your plight?"

It had been a while since Frances had gone with her sisters to one of her brother-in-law's sermons at his parish in Lambeth, but this morning, she had a sudden surge of desire to be with all her sisters. Of course, she knew Charles wouldn't allow it. "Please don't tell them about Evan—Lord Winthrop. But the rest…" She shrugged.

"Very well." Martha shuddered. "I'm anxious to get out of this room. It's like a prison."

Frances gave her a baleful look, and Martha slipped her arms around her. "I'm sorry, Frances," she whispered. "So, *so* sorry."

She slipped out of the room, closing the door gently behind her. Instantly, Frances heard the click of the lock.

Then, she heard Charles's muffled voice. "What is that?"

Frances went stiff all over. Had her brother been hovering in the corridor? Likely. She moved closer to the door to listen.

"Nothing," Martha said lightly.

"Show it to me," Charles demanded.

"It is none of your concern, Charles. Wait...what are you doing? That is mine!" Martha's voice rose with every word.

"Have you...what are you... Is this a letter to her paramour?"

"You give that back, this instant!"

Hearing the distinctive sound of paper tearing, Frances turned her back to the door and slid down it until she was sitting on the floor.

Long after the footsteps disappeared down the corridor and the voices had receded, she sat on the floor, clutching her knees in her hands. She'd never felt so drained and defeated. Her brother had ignored her, bullied her, disrespected her, and locked her up. And now, he'd finally succeeded in breaking her.

It was over. There would be no more fighting.

She would probably never see Evan, Jasper, Bobby, or Mark again. The pieces of her shattered heart stabbed at her chest.

She was going to do it. Marry Herbert Salt. Move to Egypt.

Live the exact life she'd hoped to never have.

Chapter Thirty-Two

Evan had spent most of last night hunched over a chamber pot in the throes of misery and regret. Hence, his deep-seated desire to go to church this morning wasn't surprising. Perhaps spending an hour or two in reflection and prayer would feel cleansing. Or perhaps hearing about Jesus's trials and tribulations would make his own feel earthly and insignificant.

He looked at the three boys lined up in front of him, dressed in their new Sunday best. The eldest and youngest of his brothers, looking like fine young gentlemen in their new clothes, grinned at him. Bobby, however, his hair a curly golden shine, pulled at his collar, a scowl marring his face.

"Well done, boys," Evan said. "All three of you look like proper gentlemen ready for church."

Mark gazed up at him with round amber-brown eyes. The child lived to please, but he was also adept at charming the adults around him, and he knew it. His long, fluttering eyelashes and his innocent looks and sweet exclamations had Miss Renshaw completely under his control. Evan didn't mind. Mark had been abandoned, and at night, he still cried often, asking for his mother. Evan had been forced to tell him the gut-wrenching truth that he was unlikely to see the woman again.

Mark adored Miss Renshaw—thank God for the excellent, patient governess Frances had found for them—but she was a governess, not a mother. It was becoming apparent that a real maternal figure in his life was what Mark truly needed.

Jasper and Bobby could use a similar feminine influence in their lives. Both of them were jaded and wary from their experiences at Harlowe's Home for Boys. Evan felt ill whenever he thought of all the other boys growing up there. It was clear that the place thrived on the abuse and neglect of its young occupants.

In any case, while Evan once might have dreamed of Frances Cherrington's positive, motherly effect on his brothers, now it was apparent they would never have it. Much like himself, Evan thought bitterly. He could have benefited from a mother's love so many times in his childhood, but he'd never had it, either. Jasper, Bobby, and Mark would have to make do without it, just as he had.

He wished that wasn't the case. He wanted to give them everything.

Today would be the first time they'd attend a service at St. George's Hanover Square as a family. A part of him hoped that Frances would be there. Even if it was from across the pews, he longed to lay his eyes on her again. Would she look away when she saw him, overtly cut him? Probably. Still, he preferred to dream that she would give him one of those special Frances Cherrington almost-smiles that always made him go half hard.

But she probably wouldn't be there. Her brother's house was in the same parish, but something told Evan that when Frances attended services, it was at her brother-in-law's church, not St. George's.

Still, he was dying to see her. She was definitely avoiding him, and it was killing him. He missed her so much, and he still had no idea what might have happened to make her reject him so brutally.

Damn, it hurt. Like the pain after a punch, a dull ache in his gut that wouldn't go away.

Sunday wasn't the proper day to make calls, but he'd try to see her again tomorrow. He had to.

"I hate these clothes," Bobby groused. "They are tight and itchy, and my hair feels funny."

"You mean because it's clean, for once?" Jasper teased.

"Well, you might not be comfortable, but you look dapper," Evan told Bobby. "Like the son of an earl."

"I don't *want* to look like the son of an earl," Bobby whined.

"What do you want to look like, then?" Jasper asked.

"A lion!" Bobby roared in a fairly decent representation of the king of the jungle. "That's what Miss Cherrington says I look like, so that's what I want to be."

Evan ruffled his brother's soft blond hair. "How about this—when we get home, I'll have someone make you the costume of a lion. That way, when we don't need to dress properly, you can wear it and be a lion as much as you like."

And that costume would be even more uncomfortable

than the fine clothes he'd had made for the boy, Evan would make sure of it.

"Hurrah!" Bobby exclaimed happily.

They walked the few blocks to St. George's, where the bells were ringing and the congregation was filing into the church. Evan found them a seat in the very back pew, first Mark, then Evan, Bobby, and Jasper at the end. Evan had carefully gone over the rules of church, and they had all seemed to understand. Though Jasper and Mark said they'd been to church, Jasper said the last time he'd gone was when he was six or seven years old. Bobby couldn't remember having gone to church at all. Evidently, the boys' spiritual education was not a priority at Harlowe's Home, even though Thomas Thomason had claimed Bobby was "in chapel" and couldn't be disturbed. The lying blackguard.

Evan was most worried about Bobby sitting quietly for the duration of the service, but Jasper had agreed to take him outside if sitting still proved too difficult for their little brother.

As people filed in, they glanced back over their shoulders at Evan and his brothers, their eyes round as they laid eyes upon the man flanked by the boys on the back pew. Bobby and Jasper were known as his brothers by now, but Mark was a new addition. Evan would ensure society received the same information about Mark as they had about Bobby and Jasper. Meanwhile, he sat straight and smiled at the gossipmongers until they turned away.

The rector began. They stood to sing, then sat, then knelt and stood again. After the Second Lesson, the reverend closed his prayer book. He moved some papers around on the podium and then selected one. Taking it up, he cleared his throat and read, "I publish the banns of marriage between Mr. Herbert Salt of the Parish of Bloomsbury—"

Evan blinked.

"—and Miss Frances Cherrington of Mayfair."

Evan stopped breathing.

Bobby frowned. "Frances Cherrington?"

The reverend continued, "If any of you know just cause or impediment why these two persons should not be joined together in holy matrimony, ye are to declare it."

Evan opened his mouth, then closed it, the breath whooshing out of him. He glanced down at his brothers. Bobby had been playing with a smooth rock from his pocket, tossing it between his hands and rubbing it to a shine with his thumb. But now he held it curled in his fist as he stared up at Evan. Jasper's and Mark's amber eyes were wide.

Bobby asked, too loudly, "Isn't that Miss Cherrington?"

Dozens of faces turned to look at them.

The reverend stopped speaking, paused for a long moment, then finished, "This is the second time of asking."

Frances was engaged? To *Salt*?

"It *is* Miss Cherrington, ain't it?" Bobby demanded.

Evan's stomach churned. He felt like he was going to vomit.

More people were turning to stare at them.

"Evan?" Jasper whispered.

Bobby jumped up. "Miss Cherrington's name is Frances 'cause she told me so." He swung around to face Evan, his little face twisted in outrage. "You can't let Miss Cherrington marry a Salt man."

"Bobby—" Evan began, leaning forward to grasp his brother's hand, ignoring the murmurs of the congregation swelling around them.

"She can't marry no one else, Evan," Bobby declared, shaking his head, his blond curls swinging wildly in denial.

"That's right!" Mark's usually tiny voice rang with stentorian force through the chapel as he stood up on the pew at Evan's other side and pointed at him. "'Cause she's going to marry *you*."

Chapter Thirty-Three

There would be no doubt now that not only was the Earl of Winthrop caring for his three illegitimate brothers, but he also had a tendre—or at least his little brothers did—for the ruined and disgraced Cherrington sister.

After the church exploded in a flurry of exclamations at Bobby's and Mark's outbursts, Reverend Hodgson reined them in with a roar to "Settle down, at once!" Chagrined, the congregation complied, though several glances and titters continued to be thrown back in their direction.

Evan stood. "We're leaving," he announced, then, to the rector, "Forgive the interruption of your service, sir."

"My lord," Reverend Hodgson said. "Is this true? Do you intend to marry Miss Frances Cherrington?"

Evan stared at the man for a moment, all too aware of the dozens of eyes taking this in, then mutely shook his head.

The reverend continued. "Then do you have just cause or impediment why Mr. Salt and Miss Cherrington should not be joined in matrimony? Any at all?"

Silence.

"If so, you must declare it at once," Reverend Hodgson demanded.

Evan looked at the rector, who stood frowning at him from the other end of the church, over the dozens of faces watching with greedy interest. *Yes,* he wanted to say. *She can't marry Salt, because I love her. So please, don't let her do it!* He opened his mouth, but no words would emerge. Instead, his three brothers were speaking all at once, a jumble of exclamations that sounded like a roar in his ears. He snapped his mouth shut and shook his head again.

Then he ushered his brothers into the cool air of a London summer morning.

The four of them walked home, Evan in numb silence. His brothers picked up on his mood and didn't say a word during the entire walk back to Berkeley Square.

She had decided to marry Salt.

After all she'd told Evan, after all the time they'd spent together, after all they'd shared. She'd refused to see Evan and then agreed to become Salt's wife? It went against everything Evan thought he knew about Frances Cherrington.

Nevertheless, in a sick way, it made sense. She believed marrying Salt would be the only way for her to repair her reputation. It was the only way she'd ever be able to be welcomed back into the fold of London society.

Evan had thought she didn't care about any of that.

If she had decided to marry after all, why the hell hadn't she chosen Evan? Why hadn't she given him a chance?

By the time they arrived home, the boys had had enough of the silence.

"Go to her house!" Bobby demanded. "Tell her *you're* marrying her, not the Salt man."

"She won't see me," Evan said tiredly. Even if she would, what would he say? *I know you're planning to marry Salt in a few days, but I'd like to submit my name as a contender?*

Ridiculous.

She'd made her choice. He needed to move on. In the drawing room, he sank onto one of the sofas.

"Then you should knock her door down," Bobby said, making fists and throwing a couple of punches into the air. "Make her see you. So you can tell her to come live with us."

"Maybe she doesn't know that you love her," Jasper said, sitting next to Evan. "You *do* love her, don't you?"

Mark sidled up on his other side and pressed against him.

Evan had withheld the truth from Frances. He'd never told her he was falling in love with her.

He hadn't told the boys the truth, either.

Evan pulled his littlest brother onto his lap and held him close. It might be too late to tell Frances the truth, but he wouldn't let his brothers go another minute without hearing it.

"I love you, Mark," he whispered into the boy's dark hair. He held out his arm to Bobby and Jasper, who came close. He embraced his three brothers tightly. "I love you, too, Jasper and Bobby. I'm so glad we are all together now. We are a family."

• • •

Late Monday morning, Frances heard the locks clicking open, and Martha entered, her shoulders stiff with the bearing of someone who was about to impart important information.

As soon as she was inside, the clicking sounded again. It

was Barker, locking Martha in with her.

Her brother had informed her last night that after her attempt to mail a letter to her "lover," she needed more than just a lock to keep her contained before her wedding. So he'd ordered the footmen to take rotating shifts to guard her door so they could monitor what came into and out of her room. Since then, Charles hadn't deigned to make the two-door journey down the corridor to see her. Her sisters had reported that he moved between his study and his bedchamber, hardly visiting any other rooms of the house, much less actual human beings. He even refused to speak to any of his sisters unless absolutely necessary.

"I have news." Martha plopped onto the bed. "Lord Winthrop made his presence known—quite loudly and with much commotion—during the service at St. George's yesterday."

"What?"

"Right after the banns were read, according to Esther's information."

Had Evan spoken out against her marrying Salt? Frances gripped the back of her chair. "Don't tease me, Martha," she warned.

"Oh, I am not teasing you."

"What happened?"

"He was sitting in the back row with his three brothers. When your name was read as part of the banns, one of the younger boys stood up and started complaining about how you couldn't marry a 'Salt man' and that you had to marry Lord Winthrop instead."

Frances squeezed the chair tighter. "Oh, good Lord," she rasped. It must have been Bobby. Sweet, vivacious Bobby, who never held his opinions to himself and could never sit still for more than a minute or two at a time. How on earth had Evan managed to get him to sit quietly at church?

"According to the witnesses, the boys started going on about how it wasn't right that you and Salt should be married. The ton has made quite the fuss about their accents—the children were so vulgar, it's being said, it was like their own poor aristocratic souls had left the holy house of the Lord and entered the Rookery. In any case, Reverend Hodgson was finally able to rein the congregation back under control, and Lord Winthrop slipped out with his little flock of uncivilized scamps, creating no further disturbance."

Frances closed her eyes. She'd known Evan would eventually learn of her upcoming nuptials, but publicly, with his brothers beside him, was not the way she'd hoped.

But nothing had changed. The world carried on as it always had—Evan and the boys had carried on—and here she sat in her bedchamber prison, planning to marry Herbert Salt next week.

It was truly over. A piece of her had held out hope that Evan would try to stop it somehow. But he hadn't. That had just been a fantasy.

This was reality.

• • •

Evan took the boys to the boathouse the following Sunday. Not wanting to endure another week of the banns being read for Frances and Salt, he'd skipped church. He just wanted to see his friends. He hadn't rowed with them since before he'd left for the Lake District.

Racing the boats, cleaning them, working on the

boathouse or preparing the boats for the upcoming race with the club from Cambridge, being with Crestmont, Jameson, and Cole...those things were soothing to him.

And God knew, he needed some soothing. He felt like a porcupine had rolled all over him, leaving him covered in painful open wounds, some of the quills driving straight into his gut, others into his heart.

He had no intention of mentioning Frances Cherrington to his friends. They didn't need to know what happened—at least not yet. She was getting married tomorrow, and it was all too raw, too painful. Maybe someday, when she was off in Egypt or God knew where with her husband, Evan would be able to talk about what had happened.

He hoped like hell they hadn't heard about the uproar at St. George's last week.

It was Mark's first visit to the boathouse, and Bobby had been excited to return. "Lord Coleton said he and I could row against you and Jasper!" he'd told Evan.

"I think I'll be in a shell with Mark today, Bobby. It's his first time."

"Then Jasper can row with Mr. Jameson."

Jasper had agreed to come only after he'd extracted from Evan a promise to play cricket afterwards.

Cole and Jameson were inside the boathouse when Evan and the boys arrived. Crestmont was outside with his two-year-old daughter, Evie.

Crestmont looked up from where he was watching Evie pick flowers from a cluster of daisies near the door. "You look like hell, man," he said as Evan approached.

Evan didn't have time to answer before the boys tumbled out of the carriage behind him.

Ignoring the boys completely, Evie dropped her armful of daisies and toddled toward Evan, her chubby arms held out. "Lord Winfrop!"

Evan scooped her up and tossed her into the air as he always did. She released peals of laughter as he caught her and spun her round, then swung her onto his back as Jasper and Bobby tugged Mark inside. He heard Jasper's voice as he told Mark the boats' names. "That one's *Blue*, and just below, that's *Red*."

"That's 'cause they're painted red and blue," Bobby added with a tone of all-knowing importance.

Crestmont blew out a breath. "Well, look at us," he said. "Surrounded by children. Never thought I'd see the day."

Emerging from the open doorway with Jameson at his heels, Cole grinned at them. "I intend to add another half dozen or so to the group."

"Just need to find the right woman, eh?" Jameson teased as Bobby and Jasper continued giving Mark his tour of the boathouse. "Or perhaps you have a few unknown brothers lurking about, too?"

"Highly unlikely," Cole said. "My parents only had eyes for each other. So if I do have any brothers, they'd be from before my father met my mother, and they'd be a hell of a lot older than I am. No," he sighed, "it's ensnaring the right woman that might prove impossible."

"Why's that?" Crestmont asked him.

Cole shrugged and looked away.

"You could go to Jo, you know," Crestmont told Cole, referring to his matchmaking duchess. "She'd find someone perfect for you."

"Not necessary. Thanks, though."

"Well, Cole's half dozen will complete our horde."

Jameson crossed his arms over his broad chest. "*I* have no desire whatsoever to sire children."

The three other men stared at him.

Jameson shrugged. "You all seem to have forgotten our pact. We agreed women are tender, tedious creatures. We vowed never to marry. You"—he gestured to Crestmont—"flagrantly broke your promise, and you"—he turned to Cole—"would do so if the right woman agreed to marry you." He narrowed his eyes on Evan. "And you. I don't know exactly what it is, but you have been hiding something from us. I think you're on the hunt to find a mother for those boys."

Evie wiggled to be set free and Evan complied, lowering her to the ground. Keeping an eye on her as she toddled inside toward the boys, Evan glanced at Cole, whose brows rose expectantly.

"I agree," Crestmont said. "But perhaps he's already found a potential bride." He turned to Evan. "If you didn't already have someone in mind for the position, you would have spoken to Jo by now."

"I haven't been looking for a mother for the boys, nor a woman to marry," Evan mumbled, not meeting any of their gazes. It was true. He hadn't been looking.

"Something is definitely going on with you, man," Jameson said. "You have lost all trace of your usual cheer. I think you should tell us what it is."

Cole studied him. "While you might have not been specifically searching for a mother for your brothers, I think you might have found one anyhow. *And*, I believe I might have worked out who the woman is."

"Who?" asked Jameson and Crestmont at the same time.

"Frances Cherrington."

Chapter Thirty-Four

Tomorrow morning at ten o'clock, Frances was going to stand before the rector at St. George's Hanover Square. Herbert Salt would stand beside her, and they'd make vows binding themselves together for life.

Between all Frances's siblings, she'd attended several weddings over the past few years, and one thing she could say about them was the ceremonies were quite long and rather dull. She wondered if she'd feel any different knowing all the words and instructions were being spoken directly to her.

Frances's four sisters had been keeping her company today. They had helped her pack and now sat scattered around her bedchamber drinking tea. Her relationship with them had changed, somewhat, since Charles had locked her in. She would never forget how they'd rallied to her side during these dark days before her wedding. They still didn't exactly understand her, but at least they had supported her, even if they hadn't been able to convince Charles to change his mind about keeping her confined like a prisoner, and even if they couldn't quite contain their excitement about their last sister finally getting married.

"I do wish Charles would allow us to have a wedding breakfast," Esther said with a sigh.

A few days ago, Esther had managed access to Charles's study. She'd put forward her idea for a lovely wedding breakfast wherein Frances could be reestablished in society before she and Mr. Salt left for Egypt.

Esther had received a flat, "Absolutely not."

There would be no celebration whatsoever. Instead, after the ceremony, Mr. Salt and Frances would return to the hotel where he'd been staying for the past few weeks. The following day, they, along with Martha, would quietly travel to Southampton, where they'd depart on the long voyage to Alexandria.

"He would never have allowed it," Martha said.

"Not with Lilly gone," Mary added, looking up from where she was rearranging the books in one of Frances's trunks.

All Frances's possessions had fit easily into two trunks. The first was full of clothing—summer clothing, since Egypt did not have the cool winters of England—and her few pieces of jewelry. The second contained her other possessions. It wasn't even completely full.

She didn't have much. That had never bothered her. Esther was the sister who enjoyed possessing "things," which her wealthy husband was more than happy to provide. Mary had the second most since, being the oldest, she had inherited many of their mother's possessions when she died, and she loathed throwing anything away. Then came Harriet, who was a competent artist, musician, and seamstress, and she kept many of the tools needed for these pastimes, as well as the fruits of her labors. Martha was the only one like Frances in this regard—she'd never held onto possessions. It struck Frances that maybe it was because, as twins, they'd always had each other. They hadn't *needed* Bibles or dolls or toys or paintbrushes or sheet music or needles and thread to feel whole.

For the first time in her life, Frances wished she had more. She wished she could assign value to inanimate objects as Mary and Esther did. Then, maybe she wouldn't feel so empty and meaningless when she looked at her two under-packed trunks.

"I suppose you are right, Mary." Esther sighed. "I wonder if Lilly will ever go back to him."

"She must," Mary said decisively. "He is her husband, after all." She shrugged off her sisters' baleful looks. "The Lord would want a wife to return to her husband. I might agree with you if Charles had harmed or abused her in any way, but he did not. He adores her. He treats her like a princess."

"Hence why she couldn't countenance him treating Frances like anything less," Harriet shot back. Frances raised her brows at her least-assuming sister.

"Exactly," Martha agreed, setting down her teacup. "I wouldn't blame her if she never returned to him."

"He's a boor," Esther said, nodding. "Lilly was right to leave him."

Mary sighed. "That's true—he has been a boor. I hope he realizes it sooner rather than later. If he knows what's good for him, he will."

"Lilly is the best thing that ever happened to him," Martha declared.

"You know"—sitting on the edge of the bed beside Frances, Harriet took her hand and squeezed—"I feel there's something about our brother that never really…matured." She frowned. "Does that make sense? I think he might have been thrown into the role of being responsible for us at too young of an age. Before he had the proper tools, tools that would have come naturally with some maturity, to do so."

"You're right," Esther said. "I am seven years younger than he is, and sometimes I feel like I am the older sister."

"And I have always felt a decade older than him, though I am a year younger," Mary agreed.

Frances thought of their father, who'd died when Charles was twenty. Truthfully, though, Charles had been responsible for his sisters long before that, as their father had rapidly descended into years of debauchery and drunkenness after their mother had died seven years earlier. From the age of ten to his death when Frances was seventeen, Frances had seen her father only a handful of times. The majority of those times, he'd been three sheets to the wind. He had been a violent drunkard who, by the time he died, had squandered the family fortune on drink and at the gaming tables. He'd even lost the portion brought to his marriage by their mother that had been meant to be divided among the sisters for their dowries.

Their brother had taken care of all of them from the time he was thirteen. He'd done his best. And look at them now. He'd brought them all back into the fold of London society. Excepting Frances, they were educated, proper ladies, happily married to upstanding members of the ton.

Frances had never given him credit for any of it. Instead, she'd resented him. Resented being brought to London, resented all the pressures of society that they'd faced here. He'd pushed back, then she had pushed back until it had become an endless cycle of them being at odds. Frances had gone from being the sister Charles had been closest to in childhood to the one he found most troublesome.

And now, it had culminated with him locking her in her bedchamber with a footman guarding her door.

"He has done some foolish things from time to time," Harriet said.

"Like imprisoning our sister in her room until her wedding day?" Martha asked, one brow raised.

"Yes, *exactly* like that," Harriet said. "Remember when the Duke of Crestmont was courting me, and Charles was in his cups and told the duke he would save our family from financial ruin with his piles of wealth?" She shook her head. "Now *that* was truly awful."

"But," Esther pointed out, "that particular story had a happy ending, at least."

"It did indeed," Mary said. "The duke married the matchmaker, and you were able to marry the man God truly intended for you."

"I was," Harriet agreed with a small, secret smile, her free hand rubbing over her still-flat stomach. She squeezed Frances's hand tight. "I can only hope for a happy ending this time as well."

Frances closed her eyes, trying to imagine a "happy ending" for her with Herbert Salt in the Egyptian desert.

She couldn't do it.

At the boathouse, after Cole had thrown out Frances's name like a punch to Evan's sternum, the children had started screeching, and the men had been compelled to rescue *Blue*. Of course it had been Bobby who had been singlehandedly trying to retrieve the shell from its stand.

They'd gone out for a row, Crestmont with his daughter cuddled in the ingenious floating pouch Jameson had designed to prevent her from toppling overboard and would further keep her above water should the shell capsize. Jameson rowed with Jasper, Cole with Bobby, and Evan with Mark. They'd had a rousing competition, with Jameson and Jasper winning but with Cole and Bobby right on their heels.

"Next time we'll beat you!" Bobby had declared.

"Doubt it!" Jasper had responded, beaming through the sheen of sweat covering his face. Jasper might have begun to like rowing a little, Evan thought with satisfaction.

Crestmont had reached the finish line at quite a distance behind, given his daughter's hands were too small to hold a scull—though no doubt she'd be rowing as soon as she was old enough. As usual, by the time they'd returned to the boathouse, Evie had been sound asleep. Nothing calmed the little darling, her parents always said, like being out on the water.

Evan and Mark hadn't finished at all, as Evan had spent the time teaching Mark how to row. He was impressed at how well Mark had taken to it—like catching the ball at cricket, his five-year-old brother had been quick to learn how to handle the sculls, just as Bobby and Jasper had.

It must be in their blood, Evan thought proudly. He wished Frances had seen it.

No, he wished she'd been *a part* of it.

That would never happen now.

Afterward, Crestmont had asked—no, he'd practically *ordered*—the three men to come to his house after the children had all gone to bed that evening. They had important matters to discuss.

Evan didn't *have* to go. He knew his friends were going to force him to tell them what had happened between Frances and him.

He knew it was going to hurt. Frances was getting married the following day, and he was not in the mood for an interrogation on the night before her nuptials.

He could easily lock himself up, bury his head in the sand, and ignore his friend's summons. But he'd already buried himself in a mire of self-pity and misery, and he was having trouble keeping his despair hidden from the boys. Jasper, Bobby, and Mark were sad enough about not having seen her in so long. He had no intention of piling his melancholy onto his brothers' thin shoulders.

His friends might have some advice for him. Maybe they'd even offer some sort of solution that Evan, trapped in his heartbreak, hadn't been able to find.

The boys, however, seemed to have no intention of sleeping that night, even after a full day of rowing and cricket. Dressed in their matching nightclothes, they crowded around him.

"Bobby thinks Miss Cherrington is marrying Mr. Salt soon," Jasper told him.

"She is, isn't she?" Bobby asked.

Evan sighed, feeling the fissures on his heart spread as if Bobby had just thrown a pebble at its already cracked surface. "Yes," he told them. "She is."

All three of his brothers cried out in matching denials.

"It's all right, lads." He managed to make his voice sound soothing. "She's made her choice."

"Has she, though?" Jasper asked, frowning. "Did you propose to her?"

"No, but—"

"Then what did she have to choose from?" Bobby demanded.

"I think you need to propose to her now," Jasper said. "Before she marries him."

Bobby nodded. "'Cause otherwise, she'll be married, and then you'll have to marry her, and she will have two husbands, and you're only supposed to have one, really."

"You can *only* have one," Jasper told Bobby. "If Evan doesn't marry her first, she won't be able to marry him at all."

"So he'll need to stop it!" Bobby exclaimed. His eyes widened. "I know what to do! We can go to the church and push the Salt man out of the way, then you can marry her instead."

Jasper nodded, his brow furrowed as he thought it through. "It might work. The three of us could hold him back. Tie him up—"

"Then you'll have her all to yourself," Bobby said.

"And she can come live with us!" Mark said.

"I think she'd like that over being with Mr. Salt," Jasper said.

They continued in this fashion for a good hour, until Evan finally convinced them it wasn't going to happen.

"She's made her choice," he said again. "It is Mr. Salt, and we have to respect that."

They had no intention of respecting that, though. They were still grumbling as Evan tucked them into their respective beds. "We'll be all right," he told them again and again. "Everything will be all right."

He had to believe that. He might have a broken heart, but he and his brothers had one another. He'd persevere for them, if nothing else.

It was nearly eleven before he was able to comfortably leave them. Mark fell asleep first, then Jasper, and finally Bobby, who was still grumbling drowsily even as he slipped into slumber.

Evan walked the short distance to Crestmont's house in Hill Street, his way lit by the eerie glow of the moon shining through the thick layer of coal smoke that blanketed the city.

Hell, he was probably too late. Cole and Jameson had probably left hours ago, and Crestmont was probably in bed with his wife. He half expected the place to be dark when he arrived, but instead, lights blazed in the first-floor windows, and a footman answered the door when he knocked.

He found his three friends gathered in Crestmont's drawing room, half-empty glasses of brandy in their hands.

"*Finally*," Cole complained as the footman ushered Evan inside. "We thought you weren't coming."

"The boys were difficult to get settled."

Jameson raised a brow. "Don't you have a governess for that purpose?"

"Sometimes," Evan answered shortly. "Not tonight."

"Sit down, Winthrop." Crestmont handed him a glass of brandy, and Evan took a grateful sip before dropping into the armchair. Crestmont took his preferred seat in the opposite chair.

"It's late," Crestmont said, "so I think we need to get right to the point."

"Of your interrogation?"

"Not at all," Jameson said. "Of relaying some important information to you. Information that Crestmont was gracious enough to bring us up to date on prior to your arrival."

"Information you might have known much sooner," the duke said, sending a pointed scowl Evan's way, "if you had kept me better informed about the goings-on in your life."

Evan raised a brow. "I didn't know you were such a rumormonger, Crest."

"Not a rumormonger," Crestmont corrected. "A married man who doesn't get out much, unlike you lot."

Evan sighed. "Look, if you are intending to tell me Frances Cherrington is getting married tomorrow"—he took a deep gulp of brandy—"don't bother. I already know."

"Yes," Jameson said quietly, "she is getting married tomorrow. But...do you know the circumstances behind the marriage?"

"Of course I do."

The men looked at him expectantly, and Evan sighed. If this was their style of interrogation, it could use some refinement. "Salt was the man who ruined her at the Worthington Masquerade. He left for Egypt soon after. I'd wager that someone informed him of Frances's—Miss Cherrington's—ruined state, and, gentleman that he is"—he took another deep swallow of brandy to wash out the bitterness in his mouth—"he returned immediately to London to do right by her. He proposed, she said yes, the banns were read, and they are marrying on the morrow." He gulped down the rest of the brandy. "And that, as they say, is that." He set the empty glass on the side table with a *thunk*. "Can we move the conversation along now?"

Jameson looked at Cole with wide eyes. "I think you're right."

"Right about what?" Evan said crossly.

"You're in love with her."

Evan made a derisive sound, picked up his glass, remembered it was empty, and set it down again. Crestmont got up and took his glass before going over to the sidebar to refill it. He brought it back a second later, this time filled to the brim, and Evan took a grateful gulp.

"Slow down, man," Crestmont muttered, "or you'll be sotted before we've even started."

"That's the point."

Crestmont sighed and took his seat. "Mrs. Cherrington has left Charles Cherrington. She's living here with us, for now."

Evan blinked. "Mrs.... Hold on a moment—are you speaking of Lilly Cherrington?"

"I am."

"Why?" He shook his head. "That makes no sense. The Cherringtons are madly in love."

Jameson made a sardonic noise. "Not anymore, evidently."

"What does this have to do with Frances?"

"Just about everything," Cole said, almost cheerfully.

"Explain."

"Very well," Crestmont said mildly. "Just over a week ago, Frances Cherrington attempted to visit you. Evidently, she had written some…er…preparatory notes for the meeting. Charles found them."

Evan frowned. He'd never really liked Cherrington. He disliked him even more after he'd gleaned from Frances how her family, specifically her brother, had pressured her to pretend to be someone she was not.

His frown deepening, he asked, "What was in the 'notes,' exactly?" He knew Frances made lists for everything, but what could she have written to prepare for seeing him?

"That, I don't know."

"You said she attempted to visit me about a week ago? But the banns were read for three straight weeks. So, at that time, she already knew she was going to marry Salt."

"Exactly," Crestmont said.

Evan nodded slowly. "So she intended to explain why she was calling it off between us."

"*Not* exactly," Jameson said.

"What then? Was she…" He looked between the men. "Was she hoping…"

"According to Lilly, she was 'pouring her heart out to her lover,'" Crestmont added. "It wasn't until this morning in the boathouse when Cole mentioned her name that I worked out that by 'her lover' she must have meant you. Again"—he pursed his lips—"something I would have deduced much earlier if you'd talked to me."

"She wanted me to…" Evan shook his head. "To intercede?"

"I believe so," Crestmont said.

"But it doesn't make sense. If she felt that way, then why wouldn't she see me? Why wouldn't she send me a message?"

The three men hesitated, looking at one another warily.

Evan didn't like those looks. His heart started ramming against his chest.

"What?" he demanded. "What is it?"

Jameson let out a breath from between his teeth. "That goes to the reason Mrs. Cherrington left her husband."

"Oh God." Evan was breathing fast now. "What did he do?"

"He locked Miss Cherrington in her bedchamber," Crestmont said.

"What?" Evan bellowed, jumping to his feet.

"She's been locked up for eight days," Cole said.

"With a guard at the door," Jameson added.

"And no way to get a message out to you," Crestmont finished. "That is why Lilly is here. What her husband has done is inexcusable, and she'll have nothing to do with it. Lilly heard that Miss Cherrington attempted to send a letter through one of her sisters. Again, Charles intercepted it."

With that, an icy rage settled over Evan. Feeling cold, and very, very calm, he straightened. His hands, which had been clenched at his sides, opened, each finger pushing straight.

"Stay calm," Jameson warned, his hand up as if to stop an imminent attack.

"There's more," Crestmont said quietly. "She had no desire to marry Salt. She doesn't love him."

So, she hadn't lied to Evan, after all.

"She is agreeing to it only because her family has manipulated her to believe they will be ruined beyond repair should she renege."

Evan pressed his lips together. Frances was a strong woman who knew her own mind, but her family had been chipping away at that strength for years. It was inevitable that they'd finally break her down. That she'd finally give in to their badgering.

"Lilly says Frances is bereft. Heartbroken," Crestmont said. "She believes Frances Cherrington is in love with you."

Chapter Thirty-Five

Evan looked up at the three-story Cherrington townhouse with its tidy flower boxes lining the façade. Its windows were dark, which was not surprising, as it was near one o'clock in the morning.

He didn't know which window, if any of them, led to Frances's bedchamber. Even if he knew which one it was, he couldn't scale the wall, nor could he hail her from here like some kind of Romeo—that would garner too much attention. This was London, after all.

He tried the front door. Locked, of course. Same went for the windows. He went around to the mews, where he tried the back door and windows as well. All locked.

He could pound on the door. Someone would eventually answer.

But he couldn't very well take on all of Cherrington's servants as well as Cherrington himself. He had no doubt they'd throw him out on his arse. Probably call the watch, as well.

He needed to get to Frances without raising an alarm.

He needed to pick the lock, scale the wall, provide a distraction.

How could he do all that?

And then, realization struck.

He needed his brothers.

...

Twenty minutes later, he was upstairs in the nursery of his own townhouse helping the boys hurriedly dress.

He'd been worried about rousing them—especially Bobby, who slept like the dead. But they'd all popped up, ready to go. Only Mark appeared a little drowsy, rubbing his eyes every few moments as Evan told them what he needed.

Evan had awakened one of the coachmen, and by the time he and the boys came downstairs and Jasper had collected a few hairpins from Miss Renshaw, the carriage was ready. Evan told the man to park the carriage a block away from Frances's house and wait for them.

They walked from there. Evan held Mark's hand as he quietly pointed out the features at the back of the house. "I think her room might be one of those." He gestured toward the second floor, which boasted a row of four windows. Two of them were open to let in the cool evening air. "But if they're not, her room might be facing the street instead."

Bobby shrugged. "I'll check 'em."

"Good. If the window's open, go on in and wake her—but gently, do you hear? We don't want you scaring her and making her scream and rouse the house. If her window is one of the closed ones, tap lightly and see if you can wake her. Warn her that we'll be coming from the door." Evan turned to Jasper. "There's a lock on the back door, and I believe her bedchamber door is also locked."

"I'll manage," Jasper said.

Evan squeezed Mark's hand. "You have the most important job, Mark."

Mark looked up at him, wide-eyed. "I do?"

"Yes." Evan breathed in carefully. "You'll need to distract the footman so that Jasper can get to the door."

"What does *distract* mean?"

"You got to get him away from the door," Bobby explained.

"How do I do that?" Mark asked.

"Tell him you're looking for your brother," Evan said. "Tell him he's downstairs but you don't know where he went, and ask him to help you find him."

"And if I do that, then can I see Miss Cherrington?" Mark asked.

"Absolutely."

"All right," Mark said easily. Evan squeezed his hand. The whole plan hinged on whether his littlest brother would be able to convince the guard to move away from Frances's door. If not—God, Evan hoped he wouldn't have to revert to stronger tactics.

"Can I go now?" Bobby asked, gazing up at the wall looming over them.

"Yes. Be careful," Evan said. The back side of the townhouse was bare brick, with no convenient branches or footholds to help Bobby's ascent.

Bobby rolled his eyes. "It ain't nothin'."

He shoved off his shoes, grabbed onto the wall, and scurried up it like a spider, finding footholds in what seemed like impossible places. Evan could hardly breathe. He heard Jasper starting to work on the back door, but his eyes were riveted to Bobby.

He reached the first window of the second story, a shadowy figure in the London night. Evan thought he saw him push his arm through the opening and a rippling movement as if he'd moved a drape aside. Then he dropped it and jerked back.

Not Frances's room, then.

He tried a second window, then moved on. Same for the third, which was closed tight. The fourth was open, though, and Bobby peered inside before swinging his skinny body over the threshold and disappearing inside.

Evan blew out a breath. "He found her."

"Door's open," Jasper said, looking up at the window where Bobby had disappeared. "Let's go."

Evan looked down at Mark. "Are you ready, lad?"

Mark nodded.

The three of them tiptoed inside the scullery. They walked through a kitchen, then out into the small, tiled entryway, where they found the stairs. Before they mounted them, Jasper unlocked the front door to make their escape easier, and Evan told Mark to bring the guard downstairs and into the scullery if he could. "We'll collect you from there," Evan whispered. "On our way out."

They ascended the first flight of stairs quickly but took the second more slowly, Evan in the lead motioning the boys to stay back.

He reached the landing, and, knowing Frances's room was to the left, pressed his back flat against the wall and looked around the corner.

The guard sat in front of her door. A young footman, leaning with his head back against the wall, eyes closed.

Evan jerked back and descended the stairs. "Ready?" he mouthed to Mark.

Mark nodded. Evan drew him into a quick hug and then let him go.

Mark looked very small as he climbed the stairs and turned the corner. Then, Evan heard the soft, sweet sounds of his little voice. "Will you help me find my brother?"

...

Frances couldn't sleep. Her stomach roiling, she'd lain awake for hours, staring at the ceiling. It was brighter than usual tonight, and she could make out each crack in the plaster. She'd lived in this room since she was seventeen, but she had never been as well acquainted with it as she had in the last few weeks. She wondered if she'd ever see it again after tomorrow.

"Miss Cherrington?"

Frances sat bolt upright, looking wildly around. A figure stood at the foot of her bed, an apparition, and she scrambled backward before reality struck her—and his voice.

"It's me," he whispered. "Bobby."

"Bobby…Dickens?" she said.

"Shh." He hurried around the side of the bed. "We don't want the Salt man to hear."

"The Salt…what?"

"We've come to rescue you from him," Bobby explained, leaning close to her.

"We?"

Bobby nodded. "Me, Mark, and Jasper."

Frances closed her eyes.

"And Evan, too," he added.

Her eyes popped open. "Evan is here?"

"That's right," Bobby said. "Mark's going to trick the guard and Jasper's going to pick the lock, and Evan's going to bring you home."

"Home?"

"Yes," Bobby said, growing exasperated. "With us. So he can marry you."

Something squeezed in Frances's chest. So hard, she could barely wheeze in a breath.

"I..." She blinked. "You said Evan is here?"

He nodded.

"Are you certain?"

Another nod.

"And...you want to take me home with you?"

He scowled. "That's what I said, didn't I?"

"Yes, but..." She shook her head. "I'm to be married tomorrow."

"Right. You can marry Evan now, and not the Salt man."

"But—"

"You don't want to marry the Salt man, do you?"

"I... Well, no. I don't."

"And you *do* want to marry Evan, right?"

She stared at the little boy and drew in a shaky breath. "Yes," she whispered.

"Good. Where's your coat?" He turned away, and she slid off the bed, hurrying toward her clothes trunk.

"Here." She opened the trunk and pulled out the light summer pelisse that lay on top, but then she froze as she heard muffled voices outside her door.

She looked wide-eyed at Bobby. He nodded at her, fists clenched at his sides.

They waited.

She heard...was that sniffling? Crying?

Was Tom—the footman on duty tonight—scaring Mark?

But then, she heard the guard say, quite clearly, "Where did you come from, lad?"

Mark sniffed. "Down there, where the buckets are."

Tom sounded utterly confounded. "Was the back door unlocked? Did you come in alone? Is your brother outside? Where do you live?"

"I...I don't know."

"Well, let's go downstairs and see."

Miraculously, she heard the sounds of retreating footsteps. There was a moment of silence before odd scratching noises sounded at her door. "That's Jasper," Bobby whispered. "He's a good lockpick."

It seemed to take forever, and as Frances buttoned up her pelisse, she heard Jasper mumbling to himself on the other side of the door.

Finally, the knob turned, and the door swung open. Jasper stepped back to reveal Evan.

Lord, he looked like an avenging angel tonight. Perfect, handsome, his eyes bright and angry, every muscle in his body strung taut.

They stared at each other for a suspended moment. Then, with a sob, she launched herself into his arms. "Oh, God, Evan. It's you," she breathed. "It's really you."

His arms around her felt like protective bands of steel. Tight and secure. Then, he pulled slightly back, looking down at her. "Come with us, Frances. Will you come?"

There was so much to say. So much to worry about. She was supposed to get married tomorrow. She *had* to get married. She'd committed herself to this course.

But when she opened her mouth, she could only say one word.

"Yes."

Chapter Thirty-Six

After hurrying downstairs, they separated at the entryway, Evan and Bobby taking Frances out the front while Jasper went to fetch Mark from the guard.

"I'll meet you at the carriage," Jasper told them.

"Are you sure?" Evan asked.

Jasper nodded and disappeared into the kitchen. Evan hadn't been sure how Jasper and Bobby would handle another brother thrown into their mix, but they'd accepted Mark immediately, brought him into their fold, and protected him in a way that made Evan proud. He knew Jasper wouldn't return without Mark. But if they didn't show up within two minutes after the rest of them arrived at the carriage, he'd go back and get them himself.

They'd closed Frances's door, so if the young footman didn't check it, there was a possibility that no one would notice she was missing until morning.

That gave him a few hours, which was good, because this

was by no means over. She was still getting married tomorrow, and he still hadn't told her his secret.

They hurried down the block, Frances holding both their hands, and when they reached the carriage, Evan helped Frances and Bobby into it, then waited outside, watching.

"They'll come," Frances said softly.

And they did. Thirty seconds later, he saw them jogging round the bend and released a breath of relief. He held the door open for them, and they piled in.

There were five of them in a carriage meant to hold four. Squeezed together, but comfortable. Just like a family, he couldn't help thinking.

The carriage jerked, and they were off. Frances turned to Mark, who already had his little arms wrapped around her waist. She tucked him closer to her. "Mark, what did you say to that man at my door?"

"I asked him to help me find my brother," Mark said.

"But that didn't budge him," Jasper said.

"What did?"

"He started blubbering!" Jasper exclaimed. "It was brilliant!"

"How did you do that?"

"I thought that if he didn't go with me, then I'd never see you again, and that made me sad, so I started to cry." Mark grinned up at her. "It worked. And now I don't have to be sad anymore."

"I don't want you to ever be sad," Frances told him.

"I won't. Not if you're here," Mark said.

Frances blinked hard, then met Evan's eyes over the boy's head. She quickly looked away.

A few minutes later, the carriage dropped them off at

the front door of Evan's house. Mark was already asleep, and Evan carried him up to the nursery, Jasper, Bobby, and Frances trailing behind him.

"Time for bed, you two," Evan said as he tugged the blanket up over Mark.

"Right," Jasper said. "Because you need to talk. About *adult* things."

"Exactly."

Bobby crawled into bed without changing into his nightclothes and seemed deep asleep before his head even hit the pillow.

Evan smiled at Jasper. "We'll talk more tomorrow, all right?"

Jasper nodded, giving Evan a look as if to say, *"For God's sake, don't ruin it!"*

"Good night, Jasper," Frances said, coming up beside Evan. "Thank you for picking the locks to spring me out of that place."

Jasper tipped an invisible cap. "Anything for you, Miss Cherrington," he said, then grinned. "As long as you'll play cricket with me tomorrow."

Frances glanced at Evan and then looked back to Jasper. "I'll do what I can. I promise. There's nothing in this world I'd like better than to play at cricket with you tomorrow, Jasper."

They slipped out of the room, and Evan closed the door quietly behind them. Then, he took Frances's hand and led her downstairs into the drawing room. "Come."

He drew her inside, then helped her out of her coat and shrugged out of his own before having her sit on his favorite sofa while he lit the lamps and fetched them a drink. "I'm not sure about your brandy," she told him, her hands folded primly in her lap. "It's always rather...strong."

"Whisky, then? Or"—he held up a bottle—"a nip of the blue ruin?"

She snorted. "Brandy it is."

Smiling even as nerves pounded in his chest, he poured her drink and took it over to her. Then, licking his parched lips, he knelt before her.

Her eyes widened.

"Frances," he said, gathering her free hand in his own. "I would have asked you to marry me long ago if I thought that was what you wanted and if I knew that was what I wanted."

She closed her eyes, and somehow that made it easier for him to speak.

"But I didn't know my own mind, and I was worried..." He broke off and took a fortifying breath. "I was worried you wouldn't want me. And you still might not want me."

She frowned. "I—"

But he shook his head, cutting her off. "Please. Let me get this out." He squeezed her hand tightly. "I love you, Frances. I know for certain that I fell in love with you when I first saw you with Bobby, but I think it happened even before then. I didn't understand why I always sought you out whenever we were at an event together, but I was drawn to you. To the light hiding inside you that I wanted to coax out. To your intelligence and loyalty and forthrightness. To your beauty. And to your sweetness, which you try so very hard to conceal from me and everyone else."

She blinked at him, her eyes shining. She was holding onto his hand like a lifeline.

"Nothing would make me happier than for you to become my wife," he said, his voice growing hoarse. "Than for us to spend every day together wrangling these three boys whom I love as if they were my own sons, and who love you, too."

She opened her mouth, but he stopped her. "Please don't give me an answer. Not yet." Finally, he looked away from her, his grasp on her hand loosening. "Because there is something I have been keeping from you. Something I have kept from everyone."

He hesitated, the terror that had been thrumming inside him stealing his breath. He was quiet for so long that she prompted him softly. "What is it?"

He drew in a deep, long breath, and then he said the words he'd never said aloud. "I am not the true Earl of Winthrop."

It took a moment for that to sink in, but he saw it when it did. A deep divot formed between her brows. "What do you mean?"

He stood, letting go of her hand even though she was clinging to him. He took a few steps away to catch his breath and steel his determination, then moved closer again. Finally, he sat down beside her, keeping space between them.

All he could do now was tell her the truth.

"I went to the dowager countess when I learned about Bobby to ask her for information. She thought I was there for a different reason. She thought I'd learned about *my* true parentage and was confronting her with it. She told me everything."

She cocked her head. "And…what was 'everything?'"

"My father was the Earl of Winthrop. My mother, however, was not his wife. My father got a young woman with child, and the countess and the earl schemed to take me from her and pretend I was *their* child instead. That way, the earl could have his heir and it wouldn't be known that the countess was barren."

Frances sucked in a breath. "Oh, Evan. Where is she now? Your real mother?"

"She died when I was still a child."

"Oh God." Frances closed her eyes. "I'm so sorry." Then she gasped. "When you were in the corridor…that afternoon when we went to the British Museum—"

"Yes." He nodded. "That was the day I learned that she was gone."

Frances blinked over the sheen in her eyes. She reached out to him, covering the fists he'd clenched in his lap with her hands and squeezing gently.

They sat in silence in the flickering lamplight, both of their breaths tremulous.

Evan knew he had to go on. To tell her everything. So he gathered his courage and continued. "I am a bastard, Frances. I'm living a lie, and I will do so for the rest of my life." He gave a humorless laugh. "Well, that is, unless you reveal my secret. There are only three people left in the world who know the truth. The dowager, myself, and now you." He shuddered. "I hate deceit."

"Then why not give up the title?" she asked, frowning. "You certainly have enough to sustain you beyond the entail."

"I have decided to hold on to the title for my brothers, who deserve every privilege and opportunity being the brother of an earl can afford them. They have been through too much, too unfairly. I will never subject them to more. If I gave up the title now, they would have few of the opportunities in this world that they would otherwise be granted if they had my backing as the Earl of Winthrop."

He leveled his gaze on her, the frown on her face making

his cracked heart feel like it was going to shatter once and for all. "I understand if you do not agree with my motivation," he said. "If you think my deception undermines my integrity. Because you'd be right—it *does* undermine my integrity." He shrugged. "But I plan to continue it nevertheless."

The divot between her brows deepened, and his heart, which had already felt like it was hammering against his chest, surged into his throat.

"This is why I believed I couldn't marry you," he pushed out. "Because I couldn't lie to you, and I thought I could never tell you the truth. And then, even if I did find the courage to tell you the truth, you'd think me a devious liar. Finally, even if I did tell you and you accepted it and agreed to marry me, the line needs to stop with me. I will not continue the deception with my own sons."

She shook her head. "I don't think you are a devious liar."

"I am, though."

"No. It must have hurt so much to hear the woman you thought was your mother telling you that you weren't who you've been raised to think you were. And I don't blame you for holding onto the title. Even if the boys hadn't come into your life, I wouldn't blame you."

She leaned forward, taking his face between her palms. "Because you *are* the Earl of Winthrop, Evan. You have been since birth. Because there's some silly law out there that tries to control how our society manages inheritance and relates it to legitimacy and marriage means nothing. You *are* the earl."

He closed his eyes and rested his forehead against hers.

"And I love you," she said.

A great shuddering breath emerged from his lungs.

"I understand if you don't want any more children. I

already have three children I love," she whispered. "Their names are Jasper, Bobby, and Mark."

God. He loved this woman. He ached all over with it. His body trembled with it.

"But if, someday, you decided you did want a son, he'd be the true earl, too. Just like you are."

"Frances," he choked out. "Are you sure? This is so much to take in. It took me days...*weeks*."

"I've never been more sure of anything in my life," she said, giving him that candid stare he'd come to adore.

"Will you marry me?" he whispered.

She gazed steadily at him, then abruptly looked away. "You're not... Are you certain marriage is the course you want to take? I need to know if you're making me this offer simply to save me from marrying 'the Salt man.'"

"I planned to propose back when we were in Pleasant Hill and Mark was sick and the four of us were missing you so much." His lips quirked upward. "Saving you from the Salt man is merely a side benefit."

A smile reached her eyes a few seconds before breaking out across her face. She kissed him hard, then pulled back. "Yes, Evan. Of course I will marry you."

Shaking all over, he pushed his hands into her soft brown hair and drew her lips to his. She was warm and soft. She tasted like heaven and love and sunshine. All the happiness that he'd felt up at the lake came rushing back, but it was more than that—it was *completion*. She *knew* him. Everything about him. For the first time since he'd heard the truth about his mother from the dowager, he settled back into his own skin. The skin he thought he'd known his whole life but that had been stripped from him. The skin of the Earl of

Winthrop.

Still kissing her, he laid her on her back on the sofa and ran his hands over her glorious body. Her nipples were already in tight peaks, and he skimmed his fingers over them before muttering, "I need a taste." He kissed her over the thin fabric of her nightgown, first one breast and then the other until she arched into him, making those soft moans he loved.

Resting on his elbow, he pressed his lips down her stomach, hip, and down her leg as he unbuttoned the falls of his trousers.

When he reached her ankles, he kissed them above the edge of her little silk slippers, then grabbed the hem of her nightgown with his teeth, pulling it up and up, her wiggling to help him along and her other hand rucking up the fabric until the pale skin of her breasts was exposed, topped by the pink of her taut nipples. He licked one, then sucked it into his mouth, lightly grazing the sensitive skin with his teeth.

"Oh Evan," she whispered. "Oh God. I love you so much."

He rose up, kissed her on the mouth, then whispered, "Say that again."

"I love you," she said, her hands diving under the linen of his shirt and running over his chest. "So much."

"Vixen," he whispered, smiling.

"*Your* vixen," she responded. "Always."

As they gazed into each other's eyes, he nudged her knees apart and slid his cock over her entrance, up and down. She was hot and slick, the sensation making him gasp.

Slowly, he pushed inside her, watching her as she took him, her expression glazed with lust, her lips parted, her breath whooshing from her lungs.

He started a slow rhythm, keeping that soul-deep contact between them as he glided in and out of her.

The clasp of her body over his was perfect. Possessive. Almost greedy.

"*Yes*," she moaned. And then, as he settled deep inside her, "*Ooh*."

He did it again and again, slowly speeding his strokes until his cock swelled within her, and she arched up before crying out softly, her body reaching its peak, squeezing him tight in rhythmic pulses. He closed his eyes, letting go now, his strokes fast and hard, the hot rush of her release coating him.

One stroke more. Two, three, and he yanked out, working himself as his release landed over her stomach. When he was finished, every drop wrung out of him, he sank down, half on her, half on the sofa, and muttered in her hair, still gasping for breath. "I'll clean you…up. Just…give me a moment."

She turned to face him, and they stared at each other. They'd just come together, half-dressed, on his drawing room sofa. She grinned. He grinned back and touched her nose with his fingertip. "There's never been anyone like you, Frances. You are so, so damned perfect for me."

Tears glistened in her eyes, and her chin wobbled.

"What? Don't cry," he murmured, wrapping his arm tighter around her.

"It's just that…I never thought I'd hear anyone say something like that to me."

"That you're perfect?"

"Y-yes."

"Everyone should be saying that to you. Every day." She gave a hiccupping laugh, and he tilted her chin so she faced him. "I'm serious. And, since you haven't been reminded of it enough, I'm going to make it my personal goal to tell you how perfect you are. Every day. For the rest of my life."

"Really?" she asked.

"Yes. Really."

She blinked hard. "I love you, Evan."

"And that, right there, is the true miracle of the evening."

She shook her head, smiling, and he tucked her under his chin, holding her close against him and never wanting to let her go.

And there, on his drawing room sofa, half naked and completely in love, they fell asleep.

Chapter Thirty-Seven

Frances awoke a couple of hours later to a lock of her hair being gently tucked behind her ear. Her eyes fluttered open to see Evan smiling down at her. "Wake up," he murmured. "We have a wedding to stop."

That pulled her straight into wakefulness. "What time is it?"

"A little after seven."

Her wedding was in three hours. By now, Charles would know that she was gone, and the Cherrington household would be in complete chaos.

She sat up. "Martha will be beside herself."

"We'll leave straightaway," Evan said.

Fifteen minutes later, they were in the carriage. Frances had put up her hair as best she could, borrowing some hairpins from the housekeeper, and she'd buttoned up her pelisse, but it was obvious that beneath it she was wearing only her nightgown and slippers. Her entire family was going to be in a state.

But it didn't matter, because Evan was at her side. And there was no way he'd leave it. Not now, and not ever. So it was with renewed strength that she took Evan's hand as he helped her from the carriage at her brother's front door and held it tightly as he knocked.

The door swung open to reveal Rutherford, more flustered than she'd ever seen him. His jaw dropped when he saw Lord Winthrop and the tight grip of their hands.

"Miss Cherrington. My lord." He glanced back into the house. "Er...Mr. Cherrington is—"

"It is all right, Rutherford," Frances interrupted. "We need to speak to him."

Rutherford led them into the drawing room and went to fetch Charles. When he was gone, she turned to Evan. Every bit of him was hard and tight—his jaw like stone, his shoulders squared, his eyes narrow and sharply focused.

She took both his hands in her own. "I am glad you're here," she said quietly. "But please, let me do this."

He gazed down at her, his expression softening a tiny bit. "Are you sure?"

"Yes. I can handle my brother. Just you being at my side gives me all the strength I'll ever need." She smiled at him. "Thank you."

"I'll always be at your side, Frances."

"I know." She pressed a kiss to his lips. "And that is the most amazing thing of all: *I know.*"

He gazed at her for a moment, then nodded. "I will intercede only if you wish it."

She couldn't answer him, because at that moment, the door swung open and Charles strode in. She dropped Evan's hands and turned to face her brother.

He stopped in front of them, looking from Evan to Frances, back and forth. Finally, he shook his head. "What the *hell* is going on here?" he asked in a low voice, but before Frances could answer, he addressed Evan. "Lord Winthrop, I have no idea what your role is in this drama, but this is a family matter. I wish to speak to my sister alone."

He had no idea? Even with Evan standing right beside her, Charles didn't realize that he was the one Frances had fallen in love with. Was it so unfathomable that he hadn't considered it?

"He will stay," Frances said, her voice gentle but confident.

"Frances—" Charles said in warning, but she didn't wait to hear what he had to say.

"Charles, I will not be marrying Herbert Salt today. I will not be marrying him at all."

"Of course you will," he said instantly.

"No. I won't." She gazed at him calmly. "I am marrying someone else."

"For God's sake, Frances, I thought we already established that that fellow already took what he wanted from you."

Evan bristled beside her. He wasn't touching her, and she wasn't looking at him, but she could feel it. "Careful, Cherrington," he said in a low voice.

"Charles," she said, gesturing to Evan. "Meet Evan Locke, the Earl of Winthrop. The man I was going to see that day you decided to lock me in my bedchamber. My fiancé."

"You?" Charles blinked at Evan. "You want to marry…"

"I know it is utterly shocking, Charles," Frances said drily. "Take a breath, if you please. You're turning quite purple."

Evan took her hand in his own. "Yes. I would very much like to marry your sister. I can only hope that I will be a good enough husband to her, as there is no more deserving or beautiful or alluring woman in all of England. I count myself fortunate that she will deign to agree to marry one such as I. And that I wasn't too late in asking her."

"No thanks to you, brother," Frances put in lightly.

"But…but," Charles sputtered. "She's—" He gestured at her. "She's *ruined*."

"Again," Evan said, raising a sardonic brow. "No thanks to you."

Charles stepped back. "I fear you don't know what you're saying, my lord. You don't know what has happened. You—"

"Are you implying that I don't know my own mind?" Evan asked mildly, but there was an edge of warning in his voice.

The door burst open, and they all turned to it as Martha rushed in. "Frances…oh Frances! I was so worried." She pulled Frances into a tight hug, then pushed her back, looking her over. "You escaped." She looked at Evan. "And you found him! Oh, thank God. Thank God, thank God, thank God." Her shoulders rose and her chest heaved as she burst into tears.

Frances took Martha into her arms. "Shh," she said, rubbing her sister's back. "Everything's all right now, Martha. I promise."

Martha shot a tear-streaked glare Evan's way. "Are you going to marry my sister?" she demanded.

"Yes."

"Good," she grumbled. "It's about bloody time." She took Evan's proffered handkerchief and dabbed at her eyes.

Frances blinked. She'd never heard Martha swear before.

"When?" Martha asked.

"As soon as possible," Evan replied. "I thought I'd go apply for a special license this afternoon."

"Please hurry up about it," Martha said. "The only way my image-obsessed family will be mollified is if you marry as soon as you possibly can. My sister becoming the countess of the most eligible earl in England will rectify the scandal of her refusal to marry Mr. Salt, not to mention her scandalous behavior at the masquerade. You will be happy, my family will be happy, and London society will finally leave us alone." She smiled through her tears. "That way, everyone wins."

"While I do like the idea of everyone winning," Evan said, "I won't be leaving you alone here, Frances. I will take you home, and then I will go pursue our marriage license."

"She cannot stay at your house!" Martha exclaimed. "She and I will stay with one of our sisters until your wedding. Esther's house, I think." She glanced at Charles, who had stepped back, his cheeks still bright red. Frances thought the color might be more a result of shame than anger now, though. "We will not remain *here*."

Charles bowed his head but didn't say a word.

Evan smiled at Frances. "Well then. Would you like me to take you to your sister's house?"

"Yes," she said.

"Yes, please," Martha said. "But Frances will need to be at least somewhat presentable before she leaves the house again." She grabbed Frances's hand and drew her out of the room, looking back over her shoulder at Evan. "We'll be back in a trice."

...

When the women slipped out of the drawing room, Evan turned to Charles Cherrington. "I will await the ladies at my carriage outside," he told him.

Charles nodded, and Evan took a step toward him. "The only reason I am not beating you to a pulp for locking my fiancée up like an animal is for her sake, and for your wife's. But if you ever threaten, hurt, or demean Frances again, you will have me to answer to."

Cherrington gulped.

Leaving the man standing there, Evan walked out of the drawing room and went downstairs to where his carriage was waiting at the front of the house.

The women emerged several minutes later, Frances dressed in a pretty summer frock. Hardly able to take his eyes off his fiancée, Evan handed Martha into the carriage. But Frances hesitated as Evan held his hand out to her.

"What is it?" he asked.

She took his hand, but instead of stepping up into the carriage, she squeezed it. "I know you were going to take us to Esther's house, but I was thinking we might take Jasper to the cricket fields. I know it's a busy day, but I promised him I'd try."

"Of course," Evan said. "It's a perfect day for cricket." He glanced into the carriage where Martha was seated. "Would you like to join us, Mrs. de Havilland?"

Martha snorted. "I think not, my lord. Cricket has always been Frances's game, not mine."

"Very well. We'll deposit you at your sister's house and

then Frances and I will fetch my brothers for an outing of cricket." He shook his head. "Though I fear I won't be able to participate in the match. I have another task, and that one might take the better part of the afternoon." A smile pulled at his lips.

"Right," Frances said, smiling back. "The special license. But before all that, there's one more thing I must do."

"What's that?"

She sighed. "It's just…Mr. Salt. I need to tell him the wedding's off. It would be embarrassing for him to show up at St. George's and for me to never appear."

Evan bit back a groan. "He's not going to like this," he said grimly. Neither would Evan himself. But she was right. It had to be done.

"No," she agreed. "But we don't love each other, and we wouldn't have been happy together. It's for the best. He'll realize that sooner or later."

...

Twenty minutes later, Frances, Evan, and Martha knocked on the door of Herbert Salt's hotel room. Salt's manservant opened it and greeted Martha, then bowed to Frances and Evan before leading them into a small receiving area.

A moment later, Salt entered, wearing the smart coat that Frances knew he intended to wear to the wedding.

She rose. Evan and Martha followed suit. Salt looked at them warily. "Miss Cherrington. Mrs. de Havilland." He frowned at Evan.

"Lord Winthrop, this is Mr. Salt," Frances said. "Mr. Salt, this is the Earl of Winthrop."

"A pleasure," Salt said to Evan. Frances held back her flinch. "What's this about?" he asked them. "I was just preparing to head over to the church."

It was time. She just needed to be out with it. *Forthright Frances.*

"Forgive me," she said. "You have been caught in the middle of this drama. It is my fault, and I am so sorry about that. You didn't deserve it."

He looked at her, then his eyes flicked to Evan at her side.

"There will be no wedding today," Frances said. "I cannot marry you."

A furrow dug between his brows. "What's that?"

"I cannot marry you. Furthermore, I don't think you want to marry me. Not really."

He straightened. "That's—"

She cut him off. "I hope someday you will find a woman you truly love, Herbert. It wasn't me and wouldn't ever be. You are a good man, but a marriage between us could never have been a happy one."

"This is…" He hesitated, looking a shade paler than usual. "Most unexpected."

"I am so very sorry," she said again. "I believed my actions would have no impact on anyone else, but I was horribly wrong. I truly never meant for you to suffer any repercussions from this."

Salt's jaw worked, his fists flexed at his sides, and a flush crept up his neck. To his credit, he remained calm.

"I see," he said quietly. Then, he straightened and inclined his head genially. "I wish you nothing but happiness for your future, Miss Cherrington." He glanced at Evan standing beside her. It must have been something in Evan's expression that made the understanding dawn on Salt's face. "It appears you might have already found it."

"I hope that you find yours as well," she said, meaning it.

He straightened. "Oh, I believe I already have." When they all gazed at him, not comprehending, he clarified, "In my passion for antiquities."

Frances nodded. "Yes. Of course."

They all stood in awkward silence for a moment. Then Salt said, "Please, excuse me. I need to pack. I'm going on an expedition to Egypt tomorrow." He looked at Martha. "Mrs. de Havilland. Shall I fetch you at nine o'clock so we can ride to Southampton together?"

Martha shook her head. "I'm sorry, Mr. Salt. But I won't be going to Egypt with you tomorrow, either."

Salt opened his mouth, then closed it again.

"I intend to remain at my sister's side for the time being. But I'm certain I'll see you again sometime in the future. Perhaps in Cairo."

Martha took her hand, and Frances squeezed it tight. With her beloved standing on one side of her and her twin on the other, she had never felt more whole.

Chapter Thirty-Eight

As he'd promised, Evan was expedient in obtaining the special license, while Frances and the boys, along with Miss Renshaw, enjoyed an afternoon of cricket. The following day, the rector at St. George's Hanover Square managed to fit them into his hectic schedule of weddings.

There was no way he would have rescheduled Frances and Salt's wedding so easily. Frances was truly beginning to understand the privilege that Evan's title bestowed on him...and now, on her. The boys were certainly going to benefit greatly from it.

Since Charles was too embarrassed to show his face at the church, it was Mary's husband, Reverend Robinson, who gave her away. Beaming, he set her hand in Evan's and then squeezed their hands lovingly together before sitting down beside Mary.

As Reverend Hodgson recited the service, Frances glanced out at the pews. Her twin and the rest of her sisters and their husbands sat in the rows, along with Evan's friends, who'd brought Lilly with them. In the front row, Miss Renshaw sat with Jasper, Bobby, and Mark, who were sitting still for once in their lives as they watched Evan and Frances become husband and wife.

Everyone looked so happy. It made her own happiness unfurl inside her.

Evan began to speak, drawing her attention back to him. He was smiling at her, his amber eyes glowing with joy.

"With this ring," he said, "I thee wed. With my body, I thee worship."

She sucked in a breath at that. He had already worshiped her with his body, and she knew now that he would continue to do so. Again and again. Her own body felt lit with an inner glow.

"And with all my worldly goods, I thee endow," he continued, "in the name of the Father, and of the Son, and of the Holy Ghost. Amen."

He took Frances's hand in his own and pushed the shiny gold band over it. It was a new ring, he'd told her. He'd had it made while he was at Pleasant Hill and was dreaming that she might one day agree to marry him. He hadn't wanted to use a ring that belonged to the dowager, or to the earldom. He'd wanted something that meant something to him and could mean something to her. Something new, because that was what they were creating with their marriage. Something brand new.

"Please kneel," said Reverend Hodgson.

They turned to the altar and knelt. Bowing her head, Frances saw movement in her peripheral vision as Mark sidled up to her. He knelt next to her, and Bobby and Jasper followed him, completing their little family. The rector opened his mouth to object, but Evan said in a low voice, "Please continue, Reverend," and he snapped his mouth shut, cleared his throat, and then began, "Let us pray…"

Twenty minutes later, they signed the register, along with Martha and the Duke of Crestmont as their witnesses. It was done.

Frances Cherrington, covetous of eternal spinsterhood, was now a wife.

And she couldn't have been happier.

...

After the small wedding breakfast—Esther had made certain there was one, now that Charles wasn't in the way—Frances and Evan gave Miss Renshaw the rest of the day off. They took the boys to the park, where they sailed newspaper boats and fed the ducks on the Serpentine River.

They went home and for the first time ate dinner together as a family. Afterward, Jasper read aloud from his latest book, *Ivanhoe*, and then Evan and Frances tucked the boys into bed.

Finally, Frances was alone with her husband.

With her husband.

For a woman who'd never wanted to be married, it seemed so strange to say those words, even in her mind. Even stranger was the sense of delight she got when she thought them.

"What are you thinking?" Evan murmured, sitting beside her and drawing her into his arms.

"How strange it is to be a wife. Your wife."

"It is a good strange, I hope."

"The best strange ever." She grinned at him, and he touched the corner of her lips.

"I don't think I've ever seen you smile as big as you've smiled today. I love it."

"That's a good thing because I anticipate having many more of these big smiles in my future."

"I certainly hope so...starting right now," he said. "I have a gift for you that might make you smile even wider."

Her eyes widened. "A gift? But I didn't get one for you!"

"I could want for nothing more than for you sitting right there," he said. "But during those long days at Pleasant Hill when Mark was sick, I was thinking of all the ways I could prove to you that I would never hold you back, never cage you."

She laughed softly. "I think you've already proven that, Evan."

"I'm about to prove it doubly. And triply."

As he stood from the sofa, she sat up straighter. What was he on about? He crossed the room and collected a pile of papers from a side table. "These are for you," he said.

"Mmm," she said, teasing. "I know how dear paper is. Thank you, my love."

"Oh, it's more than just paper." He sat beside her, setting the sheets of paper on his lap. He pulled off the top one and handed it to her. "I know how much you love it at the lake. I could see it in your eyes, in the way you came to life when we were there. I wanted you to have the freedom to go there whenever you desired, and I thought you should have a place to stay when you were there. So—"

She clapped her hand over her mouth. "Evan. You didn't."

"—I bought you a house."

She gasped. "No!"

"Yes. This is the deed to Windermere Cottage. I bought it back from the man your brother sold it to."

Her eyes went hot with sudden tears. Setting aside the papers, he gathered her into his arms. "Hush, sweet Frances. Don't cry. I thought you'd like it."

"I d-do," she said. "I love it. I…more than love it. B-b-but, you didn't… You didn't need to do that."

"I wanted to show you—"

"You already showed me, Evan. A hundred times over."

He kissed the top of her head. "I love you. I wanted you to understand how much."

She nodded, sniffing. Evan saw her, *inside* her, like no one else ever had. She'd never felt so understood. So *seen*.

"Thank you." She sighed, and her eyes filled with renewed tears when she thought about Windermere Cottage, the inside of which she'd never thought she'd lay eyes upon again.

"We will go to the Lake District for the remainder of summer," Evan said. "But only if you wish it. And I'm not sure you will."

"Of course I wish it!" she said.

"I wouldn't be so rash if I were you," he said, his lips tilting up. "Because I have one more gift for you that might make you want to stay in London, at least for a little while longer."

"I'm not sure I can bear any more," she said shakily. "I feel overwhelmed by this. By everything that's happened over the last two days."

"I fear you will have to endure one more thing, sweet."

She took a deep breath. He shuffled through the papers, finally pulling one out and showing it to her.

"This is another deed," he said. "I bought a small space that I think might be ideal for a bookshop."

Her jaw dropped.

"I couldn't get the space right beside the Duchess of Crestmont's matchmaking business, but it is on the same street."

She couldn't speak.

He looked a little worried. "It's only three doors down. It's quite close, actually. And it's an excellent space. But…if you don't like it, we could sell it and buy another—"

"Stop," she said hoarsely.

He stopped.

Slowly, she shook her head. "I…I don't know what to say." In truth, she believed she'd given up a part of herself by marrying Evan, but she knew being his wife would be well worth the loss.

Now, he was telling her she didn't have to give up anything at all. In fact, she could have everything she'd ever dreamed of.

She swallowed hard and took the deed from him, setting it carefully aside before touching her finger lightly to his cheek. Awe filled her voice. "I am so lucky to have found you. You have given me a new family who loves me for who I am. You have given me my home back, and you have given me freedom. You have given me yourself." She gazed into his eyes. "And that is a gift I shall always treasure. *Always.*"

She kissed him, wrapping her arms tightly around him, wanting to show him with her kiss, with her body, how deeply she loved him. His arm went around her, pulling her even closer.

Shoving up his shirt, she moved her hands over the taut skin of his muscular body. He rucked her dress up over her knees and ran his fingers along the sensitive part of her thigh above the tops of her stockings.

Finally, he pulled back, his cheeks flushed. "I've already ravished you once in this drawing room, wife. Do you realize we've never joined together in a proper bed?"

She laughed softly. "You're right. We never have."

"I'd say it's about time, wouldn't you?"

"I would, indeed."

"Come with me, then. I'd like to introduce you to my bedchamber. I did say earlier today that I would endow you with all my worldly goods—of which my bedchamber is one. I also vowed to worship you with my body." He raked his gaze over her, his intent clear. Anticipation shuddered through her, heating the very core of her. "I intend to make good on both those promises." He gave her a wicked smile. "Right now."

"Lead the way," she murmured.

He led her upstairs to his bedchamber, where, using his mouth and hands and body, he did, in fact, make good on *all* his promises.

Epilogue

Six Months Later

The weather had grown too cold for pastimes like rowing on the Thames and playing cricket. So, in the afternoons, after his schoolwork was done, Jasper had begun to leave the younger boys to their play to help Frances in her bookshop. She'd named her shop Lockes and Key—and she thought it suited.

It was a busy, tidy little shop that smelled of new paper and ink. There was a tinkling bell above her door that chimed constantly throughout the day, and every time it did, a little bubble of happiness traveled through her chest and put a smile on her face.

What was even better was helping her customers find the perfect book. It turned out that Frances had a knack for asking a few questions that left the patrons of the shop certain they couldn't leave without the book she'd steered them to.

Honestly, she'd never really expected she'd be good at anything. She'd begun to think her sisters had hoarded all the talent in the family.

Esther's impressive social skills had led to her seriously being considered to take on the role of the newest—and youngest ever—patroness at Almack's Assembly Rooms. It seemed Esther's destiny to one day hold a role as one of the gatekeepers of London society.

Mary and her husband had partnered with Evan to take over the ownership of Harlowe's Home for Boys. The place had been cleaned up, painted, and a dozen windows had been added. It also possessed a real play yard and a schoolroom, and—Mary had made certain—a robust religious component had been added to the boys' daily lessons. They were also given clean clothes and healthy food, and they were treated with kindness and compassion.

Martha had decided to remain in London for the winter, and she had joined Evan, Frances, and the boys at Windermere Cottage over the holidays. Martha's husband was due back in London any day now, and she planned to go to Egypt again next year, but only for a short expedition. A temporary time away. For now, she was going to remain near her twin.

And then there was Harriet, of course. Dear Harriet, who was so large with child now, people were wondering if she might be having her own twins, and who, even with such an enormous belly, managed to excel at every pastime at which a lady could hope to be skilled.

Now Frances knew she was good at something, after all. She was good at selling books. And not only that, she had an aptitude for business. Her bookstore was thriving. She'd even hired a handful of employees and had trained them to manage the place in her absence, including Peggy, who far preferred her new role as a shopgirl over being a lady's maid.

Frances was happier than she'd ever been. Today, though, she was a little worried. She and Evan needed to have a serious talk tonight, and anxiety thrummed under her skin.

"There you are, Jasper!" Looking past a man who was perusing the gentlemen's magazines, she smiled at her brother-in-law. "I've received a new delivery of novels. Would you like to help me shelve them?"

Jasper's eyes lit up—eyes that reminded her of his brother's. "Of course!"

They worked companionably, the task slowed by the constant influx of customers. An hour later, she was taking payment from one such customer when the bell jingled. She looked up to greet the newcomer and froze.

Charles.

She turned back to the customer in front of her and handed her the wrapped set of books. "*Pride and Prejudice* is one of my favorites," she said to the young woman. "I am certain you will enjoy it."

"I am truly looking forward to it. Thank you so much for the recommendation!" the woman exclaimed. Tucking the books beneath her arm, she turned to leave, passing Charles as he walked in, looking around the place.

He'd never been here. In fact, Frances hadn't laid eyes on him since the day before her wedding. No one had. According to Lilly, he had remained in London, but even Lilly hadn't encountered him face-to-face.

Seeing him here, in her store, brought the past rushing back. Frances's frustration and anger and absolute certainty that no one would ever understand her. She clenched her hands into fists behind the counter.

He nodded at her. "Good afternoon," he told her. "This is a lovely store."

"Good afternoon," she pushed out.

He smiled at her, a little sheepishly. "I am looking for a book."

Her eyes narrowed. "What kind of a book?"

"One that will teach a man how to regain the love of a sister he treated badly."

"Ah." She looked down at the smooth gloss of the counter before squaring her shoulders and looking back up at him. "I fear there is no such book."

Charles gazed at her, sadness in the depths of his brown eyes—eyes so much like her own. "I am sorry, Frances."

She thought of those days she'd been locked in her room. She didn't know if a simple sorry was enough.

"I have searched my soul over the past few months," Charles continued. "My actions toward you last summer were unacceptable. I behaved solely out of fear and selfishness. If I could perform any penance to compensate for my failure to you as a brother, I would gladly do so. I know I have disappointed you—disappointed all my sisters—and lost your respect, which I valued more than I knew. I am…" He looked away, the shine of his eyes catching in the light. "I am wretched, Frances."

Charles's wife and child had left him. His sisters had abandoned him. She wasn't surprised he was wretched. But he'd brought it on himself.

Frances glanced over at Jasper, who was looking into the crate of new books, pretending not to listen. She was certain

Jasper knew more about what had happened last summer than he let on. He was an intelligent lad.

The door chimed as someone entered the store. She glanced at Jasper, who stood, straightened his coat in the same way his older brother did, and stepped toward the couple. "Good afternoon, ma'am. Sir. May I help you find something?" he inquired politely. He sounded more like a proper gentleman every day.

"I want to make amends," Charles said in a low voice. "I want to show you that I am a different man now. A better one."

She frowned at him. Could people really change?

Then she thought of the Charles she'd known as a child. That boy had been completely different from the stiff, unyielding, and demanding man who'd ordered her and her sisters to come to live in London when their father died.

He'd changed once. Perhaps he could change again.

Lilly thought he might be changing. She was still living with the Duke and Duchess of Crestmont, but she received letters from Charles every day. She'd told Frances she'd recently begun to write him back.

"I feel like I might be starting to forgive him, Frances," Lilly had told her, looking dismayed. "I feel so disloyal to you for saying that. I should never forgive him, should I?"

"Please don't stay angry at him on account of me, Lilly." Frances had been so blissfully happy over the past few months, it hurt to see Lilly in such pain. She just wanted her sweet sister-in-law to be happy. And if Charles made her happy…well, Frances would never deny her that.

Charles blew out a slow breath. "I should never have done what I did. You are my sister. My best playmate when we were younger. My *friend*. You were my closest sibling, and even though you were younger than me, you were the one I could talk to about anything.

"But when Father died, I believed I needed to be someone else. I could not be my sisters' playmate anymore. I needed to be the head of the family. The person who ensured everyone did what they were supposed to, behaved how they were supposed to. And I focused all that discipline on you when you were still that girl who loved to play cricket and race me to the island."

Charles looked down, his shoulders slumping. "It was unfair of me to expect you to want to be the diamond of the first water, the belle of every Season, try to catch the eye of every titled nob that perused the marriage mart. That wasn't you, and it never should have been. So…I am sorry. I drove you to rebellion. It was me, not you." He shook his head. "Now that I think back on it, I am proud that you rebelled. You showed your strength, your spirit, when you did so."

Frances stared at him, speechless.

Knowing the innate Cherrington pridefulness, she had never thought she'd hear her brother utter a single apology, much less all this.

"I understand if you want nothing to do with me. If I were you, I'd feel the same way."

A part of her softened—just a little—toward him. Still, it wasn't easy to forget what he had done. "I don't know if I can forgive you, but…I would like to begin to try."

He drew in a shaky breath.

"Would you like to have dinner at our house on Friday, Charles? I warn you—it will not be anything like the society dinners you are accustomed to. The boys eat at the table with us every night. It is inevitably a rather raucous affair." And a wonderful one, in her opinion—always full of banter and laughter and lively discussion.

Charles dashed his hand over his shiny eyes. "Yes," he said. "I would love to have dinner with you and your family on Friday, Frances."

...

Late that night, after the boys were in bed, Evan led Frances to their bedroom as he had every night since they married. As he had every night, he undressed her. Tonight, he stood her in front of the fire so she'd stay warm, and plucked each tape and tie and button slowly, pushing each garment off until her clothes pooled at her feet, running his hands over her body, making her tremble under his touch.

In turn, she unbuttoned his falls and pushed his trousers down his narrow hips, running her hands over the hard length of him again and again, until he said in a rough voice, "Enough of that," and tugged her into the bed, dousing the lanterns and the wall sconces on the way, leaving one candle flickering at their bedside.

Earlier, the servants had set hot bricks beneath the counterpane, so it was warm and cozy under their covers. As they lay facing each other, he kissed her, long and leisurely.

His allure was so strong, she almost let him draw her under. It would be so easy to give in to the pleasure of all her husband's body could offer her and put off the conversation she needed to have with him.

He swiped his tongue into her mouth.

She could wait until tomorrow, certainly.

No. She'd already put it off long enough.

Slowly, painfully, she pulled back, ignoring her body's cry to press tighter to him, to arch into him, to guide him inside.

"Wait," she whispered. "There's something I need to tell you."

He gazed at her, the candlelight flickering over the slight smile tilting his perfect, wicked lips. Lips that had stroked over every inch of her and would, he'd promised, do so again and again.

"Finally," he murmured.

She frowned, and he reached up to cup her cheek in his hand.

"I know, sweet. I was waiting for you to gather the courage to tell me."

Her breath caught. "What is it you think you know, exactly?"

"Hmm..." He ran his thumb over her lip, then dragged his fingers down her chin and neck, over her collarbones, and down over her nipple. She shuddered—hard.

"Your breasts are full. And so sensitive lately."

His finger moved down the underside of her breast to her still-flat belly. He briefly pressed his palm there, hesitating a second before dragging his fingers downward again until he slid through the folds of her sex. "Mmm," he whispered. "So wet already... You're ready for me. Do you know how much I love that? But there's a subtle difference here lately. How soft you are. How you taste. How you feel around me when I'm inside you."

"Evan," she breathed.

"I know you are with child," he said.

She blinked hard. "Are you...angry?"

Months ago, he'd told her he never wanted a son to carry on his "false" title, to live a lie as he was, but they hadn't talked about it since then. He had never spilled his seed inside her, though, always pulling out at the last second, so she'd assumed his thoughts on the matter hadn't changed, even if it had finally been proved that the technique they used to prevent conception hadn't worked, after all.

"You were right," he said.

"About what?"

"When you said legitimacy shouldn't matter. If my parents were married, it wouldn't have changed me intrinsically. The truth is, I *am* the Earl of Winthrop, no matter the route I took to become that man. And our child"—he kissed her gently on the lips—"will be *our* child, first and foremost. He or she will be born and raised in a home that prioritizes family and believes in love. Our child will be *wanted*. So, no. I am not angry."

"Are you sure?"

"Completely sure." His expression softened. "You and the boys are my life, do you know that? The four of you have brought love into this house. You have filled that lonely, dark hollow inside me with light and joy. And now, you will bear my child, and I cannot think of anything better."

Frances's lids sank shut. There was relief, but it was more than that. She had been so broken and lonely throughout her adult life, even though she'd always been surrounded by family. Jasper, Bobby, and Mark had helped her mend all those broken pieces, and Martha returning to her side had helped fill in the final gaping hole. But it was Evan who had bonded all the fragments back together, made her strong and whole and complete.

"I love you," she whispered.

"I love you, too," he murmured. Then his wicked smile returned. "Have I told you today that you're perfect?"

"Not yet," she said, giving him her own saucy smile. "I think you've grown lax, husband. I believe it has been approximately two-and-thirty hours since you last commented on my perfection."

"Ohh," he said. "Then I'll have to say it twice tonight to make up for it. You're perfect, sweet Frances."

She expected him to repeat it immediately, but he didn't. Instead, he turned her onto her back and settled between her legs, looking down at her, the candlelight casting a golden flicker over the taut lines of his body.

"I'm going to come inside you tonight," he said gruffly. "I've never done that before. I'm glad the first time will be with you."

She reached up to cup his cheek with her hand. "I'm glad, too."

He pushed inside her, and she arched to meet him until he was seated to the hilt. She let out a soft groan.

"I love the sounds you make," he said. "I'm going to make you make more of them."

And he proceeded to do exactly that, lifting one of her knees over his shoulder and holding his weight on one arm while he pressed his hand between them above the spot where they joined. Working the most sensitive places on her, he slid in and out of her in deep thrusts until her moans filled the room and she came with a sharp cry, ecstasy flooding her body.

He wrung out every drop of pleasure from her before lowering her knee and planting his elbows on either side of her head as he bent down to kiss her, moving with heavy, deep thrusts. When he pulled away slightly, his eyes glazed as he stared down at her, his body strung taut, his cock growing inside her, she wrapped her arms around him and met his every stroke.

And then, as she held him tight to her, he came, his body shuddering as he gasped her name, and for the first time, she felt his waves of pleasure deep inside her body as if they were her own.

Finally, he seemed to melt over her, managing to move them so they were on their sides facing each other. He was still inside her as if he didn't want to leave, not quite yet.

"Have I ever mentioned," he rasped in her ear, "that you're perfect?"

Her body shuddered with laughter. "Once or twice, perhaps."

He pressed a kiss into her hair. "I have a feeling you're going to hear it once or twice…or ten thousand times more, Frances. Because you are. My sweet, perfect love."

She held him close, burrowing deeper against his skin, breathing in the clean, woodsy smell of him and basking in their closeness.

She had found her perfect love. And the best part about it was that love wasn't a cage at all, but a wild, limitless, untamed, and beautiful thing.

Frances Locke, the Countess of Winthrop, had finally been set free.

About the Author

USA Today bestselling author Jennifer Haymore is the author of over a dozen award-winning historical romances. When she's not dreaming up scandal in Regency England, you'll likely find her avidly listening to an audiobook while sailing, walking her spoiled husky, or on an airplane heading off to visit the exciting locale of her next novel. Jennifer loves reading romance and writing happily ever afters, and she's grateful to all her readers for giving her an opportunity to share her stories with the world.

Bridgerton *meets* Trading Places *in this captivating and lighthearted masquerade romance.*

THE Heiress SWAP

RUBY® AWARD-WINNING AUTHOR
MADDISON MICHAELS

Evie Jenkins didn't know what she was thinking by agreeing to switch places with her American heiress cousin. After all, she's naught but a poor—and usually quite *sensible*—companion. All she has to do is spend six weeks among London society, pretending to be an heiress...and ensure that absolutely under no circumstances does she accept *any* proposals of marriage.

When his cousin declares himself in love with a new woman visiting from the States, Alexander Trenton—the sixth Duke of Hargrave—is determined to prove that the young lady in question is just another American "Dollar Princess" desperate for an English title. She seems innocent enough, but Alex is determined to expose her...by thoroughly seducing the lovely and fiercely intelligent heiress *himself.*

What he assumed would be just one simple kiss erupts into something wild, uncontrollable, and *much* too public. Now the duke must save her reputation with a betrothal...little knowing that his charming Princess harbors a secret that would certainly ruin them both.

A Lady's Rules for Ruin is a fun jaunt through Regency England in which a woman eager for freedom and an earl with responsibilities that seem to multiply by the day are thrust together by fate. However, the story includes elements that might not be suitable for all readers. Poor orphanage conditions, allusions to child abuse, philandering fathers, death of a parent, and emotional abuse are mentioned or shown in the novel, though the story itself is heartwarming and positive. Readers who may be sensitive to these elements, please take note.

*Don't miss the exciting new books
Entangled has to offer.*

Follow us!

 @EntangledPublishing

 @Entangled_Publishing

 @EntangledPub

AMARA
an imprint of Entangled Publishing LLC

Printed in Great Britain
by Amazon